D1557425

WATCHER from the SHORE

WATCHER from the SHORE

A Novel by
Ayako Sono

Translated by
Edward Putzar

KODANSHA INTERNATIONAL
Tokyo and New York

Publisher's Note: This book was adapted and translated from the novel *Kami No Yogoreta Te*, by Ayako Sono, originally published by Asahi Shinbunsha. Abridgements and revisions have been made with the cooperation and authorization of the author. The publisher wishes to express its gratitude to Stephen Y. Cheng, M.D., for his examination of medical terminology in the text.

The excerpts from *The Epic of Gilgamesh* in Chapter Eleven are from the translation by John Gardner and John Maier, copyright © 1984 by the Estate of John Gardner and John Maier. Reprinted by permission of Alfred A. Knopf, Inc.

Permission to reprint lyrics from the songs "Known Only to Him" and "Who Am I?" in Chapter Eighteen is gratefully acknowledged to the following:

"Known Only to Him": Words and music by Stuart Hamblen, copyright © 1952 by Hamblen Music Co. Copyright renewed, rights controlled by Unichappel Music, Inc. (Rightsong Music, Publisher). International Copyright Secured; all rights reserved.

"Who Am I?": written by Rusty Goodman, copyright © 1965 by First Monday Music (a division of WORD, Inc.). International Copyright Secured; all rights reserved. (Rights for Japan assigned to SONG-RISE.)

Distributed in the United States by Kodansha International/USA Ltd., 114 Fifth Avenue, New York, New York 10011. Published by Kodansha International Ltd., 17-14, Otowa 1-chome, Bunkyo-ku, Tokyo 112, and Kodansha International/USA. Printed in Japan.
ISBN 4-7700-1438-4 (in Japan)
First edition, 1990

Library of Congress Cataloging-in-Publication Data

Sono, Ayako 1931—
[Kami no yogoreta te. English]
The watcher from the shore/Ayako Sono; translated by Edward Putzar.
p. cm.
Translation of: Kami no yogoreta te.
ISBN 0-87011-938-9 (U.S.)
I. Title.
PL861.048K2513 1989
895.6'35—dc20

CONTENTS

WATCHER FROM THE SHORE

Chapter One

Wind and Light

Ten years had passed since Sadaharu Nobeji had found a bit of land where he could build his obstetrics and gynecology clinic. The place was as close as he could get to the ocean. He'd been born where the scent of the Pacific Ocean was always in the wind, even though one could not actually see the water. As though he had the instincts of some amphibious creature, when it came time to build his own home he sought a place where he could hear the sound of the sea.

But there was a problem. Most people did not live quite so close to the ocean, and the place he wanted was not convenient for his patients. Eventually, for the sake of his profession, he sacrificed his personal taste and settled on a spot along the west side of the Miura Peninsula, a cabbage field where watermelons grew in summer and long *daikon* radishes in winter. Standing there, on high ground, he could just glimpse the ocean from his two thousand square meters of land. As it was, when it came to actually buying the land, the most important point was that it was cheap. Even so, he had to sell property that he'd inherited from his long-deceased father, and some securities besides. Further, to make up the balance through a bank loan, he mortgaged the house and land occupied by his mother.

He was newly married then. The opening of the clinic and the birth of his daughter, Kaori, occurred within a month of each other. The residence part of the building was merely painted siding, the interior of the rooms painted plywood—inexpensive construction that barely deceived the eye. But since the clinic itself would be in use for a long time, Sadaharu allowed himself more extravagance there. A round hall served as a waiting room, and from the second and third floors there was a fine view of the ocean. This was partly based on his feeling that for a place like a clinic there could be no such thing as too much light.

Each morning at 8:45 Sadaharu appeared in his examination room to meet with the nursing staff, including the nurse on duty the previous night, the cook, and the maintenance staff, but on this particular morning, as soon as he appeared, a woman entered at the same time from the waiting room. About fifty years of age, she wore her hair up in a nylon scarf, her slacks baggy at the knees. She wore no makeup and began speaking immediately.

"Doctor, excuse me, but I must ask you something. It's true, isn't it, that all the babies born here are male?"

Sadaharu stared at the woman. At first, he thought she was a stranger, but then he wondered whether she might not know him. His eyesight was excellent. Had he been born at another time he might have become a fighter pilot instead of a physician. And he had an eye for remembering faces. But when it came to his patients—especially the farmers' wives with their faces covered by their straw hats—he had given up trying to keep track of them all. The enemy, so to speak, could see him clearly, while he could see little or nothing of the women's faces.

"Who told you all the children born here were boys?"

"No one in particular," she replied. "But the Tanaka family and the Hara family too had their children here, and they were all boys."

In a semi-rural place like this, there were Tanakas and Haras everywhere; Sadaharu had to ask which Tanaka and which Hara.

"Ah, the old Tanaka family, you know, and the Hara family with the variety store had a son about six months ago."

In an informal tone Sadaharu said to her, "Come, now. Think

about what you're saying! It makes no sense, and besides, what would happen to Japan if only boys were born here?"

"But so far in our family there have been two, both of them girls, and if she doesn't have a boy this time, well . . . She's been going over to the city hospital until now, but I want her to come here."

What a reputation to have! Sadaharu thought. If only they believed I was good at surgery, or could cure sterility, something like that. But these folks are coming for quite another reason.

"She's your daughter?"

"She's my daughter-in-law."

Not that the old lady cared if Japan became all male. She was only thinking about her family getting a male heir.

"Now, please, don't worry about whether the child is a boy or a girl; its sex has already been determined."

Sadaharu spoke without the slightest attempt to humor the woman, then strode into his examination room. He employed thirteen women at the clinic, all under the supervision of head nurse Shigeko Okubo. With one or two usually absent, the morning staff meetings included about ten people.

Five patients had come in the previous night. Three women were staying for postpartum care, and one farm girl was there for emergency treatment of a threatened miscarriage. Another patient was being treated for severe anemia after miscarrying. The woman who gave birth last night could not sleep because of severe cramps; otherwise, her condition was stable. Of the three newborns, two were boys. For the little girl with jaundice, they had begun phototherapy.

"Two appointments today."

Sadaharu looked at the memo on his desk. The appointments were with patients coming in for abortions.

Already a patient had arrived, but Sadaharu could not see her immediately. His desk telephone was ringing. He answered and heard the voice of his daytime housekeeper, Motoko Inoue.

"Is that Mr. or Mrs. Higuchi?" he inquired after a moment. The reply came and he asked Motoko to send Mr. Higuchi to the clinic.

During the few moments it took for Higuchi to walk over from the house, Sadaharu waited without seeing a patient. When he was younger, Sadaharu would have been impatient at this sort of interruption, but now, having passed forty years of age himself, to his own amazement he had become more tolerant. In medical school, all his classmates wanted to open an office in Tokyo, but Sadaharu had preferred a place even more remote than his rural home town. He had no taste for the fast track.

When it came down to financial matters, Sadaharu was still heavily in debt. He liked money and wanted to acquire it, but he didn't think earning money was everything in life. On rare occasions, his waiting room might look like a congested train station, but Sadaharu would never hurry. And he knew his patients were not really in a rush no matter what they said to the contrary.

Higuchi, a white-haired man in his late fifties with a vaguely perplexed manner, made his way through the waiting room, now filled with patients, and entered the examination room.

Sadaharu greeted him, and Higuchi opened the bundle he was carrying, removed the contents, and explained that he had intended to come earlier.

"This is just a small gift for your daughter," he said.

Sadaharu thanked him and asked where he had spent the night.

"I stayed further out on the peninsula last night, with a guest, a Swedish man who owns a villa there."

"On a yacht?" Sadaharu asked.

"Yes. We went up to Enoshima," Higuchi said. "How is your wife?"

"Well, she said she would be back by the fifteenth, but she hasn't appeared yet."

"Where did she go this time?"

"To Hawaii. She was at home during our daughter's winter vacation, but she left again, on the ninth."

Sadaharu had no idea how many times he had recited this account of his wife's activities. A doctor's wife might well enjoy traveling. There was enough money, after all, so it was understandable. But someone listening to Sadaharu might expect some change in his expression, might even wonder that he was not worn down by such a wife. The listener, however, was usually just perplexed when Sadaharu was neither disturbed nor showed anything but complacency with his wife's ways. It was nice of him to put on such a calm face, they said, and if he felt like going along with her behavior—well, it was no one else's business. And Sadaharu never indicated that anything was amiss in his married life. Mayumi was always on the move, but perhaps that was nothing more than a quirk in her personality. In any case, Sadaharu didn't think it was possible for her to change the way she was through any special training or reeducation.

But today he was discussing all this with Higuchi, a man who had a special place in Sadaharu's feelings. Mayumi had become acquainted with Higuchi's wife, Takako, after meeting her at a concert, and through Takako she became absorbed in astrology and fortune telling.

"Is your wife also out today?" Sadaharu asked cheerfully.

"No. She's at home."

"Hmm. It seems that even the closest friends don't always travel in the same direction," Sadaharu said lightly.

"She is not supposed to leave the house until after February 4. It's been going on since the end of last year. She doesn't even go out shopping."

Sadaharu smiled. "And my wife had to stay in Hawaii until then."

Sadaharu's nurse, Keiko Iwanami, yawned conspicuously. Nurse Iwanami was full-figured, but like other young women, she probably would have preferred to be thin. She had no idea how useful she was. With her sturdy body, she was the strongest of Sadaharu's nurses.

"My wife has really been a nuisance to you . . ." Higuchi began, frankly and pathetically acknowledging that it was his wife's fault that Mayumi had turned into a fanatic about fortune telling.

Sadaharu, on the contrary, did not imagine that Mayumi's attachment to fortune telling was due only to Mrs. Higuchi. She was the type of person who was easily influenced. Mayumi had once informed Sadaharu that these days fortune telling was terribly popular among upper-class wives.

Sadaharu had been reading his newspaper and without looking up said, "Really. And that makes you upper class?"

"Intellectual people are quite interested," she replied. "For instance, Mr. Shimokawaji's wife and Mr. Sudo's wife both go to our fortune teller."

Shimokawaji was an ex–foreign minister, while Sudo was currently minister of Trade, or maybe it was Finance, Sadaharu recalled.

"Then you must be an intellectual," he said.

"Don't tease me!" Mayumi was indignant.

"What are you going to ask this fortune teller?"

"About directions and about fixing dates. There is a right time for entering a hospital, or for travel. Did you know that?"

Mayumi had continued with a recitation of names of half a dozen wives of men well known in the financial world, all of whom followed the instructions of her fortune teller "so as not to endanger themselves." And none of their husbands, she insisted, ever objected. She gave the impression that the political and economic world of Japan was guided by fortune tellers.

Sadaharu felt that really might not be such a bad thing. In the world of politics, if it were not fortune telling, then people would cling to some other kind of fraud, just as individuals will fasten upon some kind of weakness in themselves as an excuse for the way they live.

The Higuchi couple was childless, but Mr. Higuchi often came to Sadaharu with gifts of cake or sweets by way of apology for his wife's throwing Sadaharu's home life into confusion. He thought that within the family the one potentially the most at risk was Sadaharu's daughter. But Kaori, a growing girl, nine years old, was healthy and suntanned, and her mother's nearly perpetual absence did not seem to have harmed her development. The path she took to school was a mere three hundred yards from home, and she loved to linger along the way. In fact, she was spared the kind of damage commonly inflicted on children by mothers overly concerned with their child's education.

Sadaharu talked with Higuchi for a few minutes before the man left. Nurse Iwanami, with her innocent yawn, was once again the catalyst for action.

"So. Let's get started," Sadaharu said.

He looked at the record cards lined up on his desk and spoke to his head nurse, Masako Ono. She announced the name of the first patient into a microphone.

Sadaharu often received questions from people about his work. Most had to do with his reasons for becoming a gynecologist, suggesting that the motive might be erotic interests.

Sadaharu's standard reply was that a person would only have to spend a day with him in the examination room to understand. To himself, he often compared his work to that of an automobile repair shop. As far as the work being interesting, Sadaharu had read somewhere about a writer remarking that for the most part writing was like laying bricks and another time that a tailor, seeing a concrete worker preparing a wooden form for his job, had observed that it was just like cutting a paper pattern.

The first patient called was the young woman whose mother-in-law had just asked Sadaharu about only boys being born at his clinic. The woman had been examined at the city hospital, but since her first two children were girls, she now wanted a boy and so had changed hospitals on her relatives' advice.

In examining her, Sadaharu found that the lower part of her uterus was already protruding between the navel and the pubic bone. Even the sound of the fetus's heart could be heard as a regular beat through a tiny microphone. She was in her fourth month.

After the examination, the woman said, "I'm so grateful to you, doctor. It makes me very happy to think that my next child will be a boy."

From time to time, the thought crossed Sadaharu's mind that some people in this world were truly experts at living. Others might detect a cynical tone in such an observation, but Sadaharu, on the contrary, frankly admired the ability of some people to master their own lives.

To put it simply, the sex of the fetus is determined at the moment of conception, and only God knows how. But some people ignored such facts. An extreme case was the woman now in front of Sadaharu, so utterly self-centered that if her child turned out to be a boy it would be through her own merit—and if a girl, it would be Sadaharu's fault.

Intellectual types took an even more deterministic attitude than Sadaharu himself. For a while, he was persistently badgered by a patient about AIH, artificial insemination between spouses, because the couple wanted a male child so much that they insisted on centrifugal separation treatment of the semen. The sperm determines the sex of a child, not the mother's egg, and the small Y chromosome produces a male, while the X chromosome produces a female. When the semen is treated in a centrifuge for five minutes or so, the heavy X chromosome and the light Y chromosome can be separated. The lighter part, the clear top of the liquid, is removed and used to impregnate the egg. For this couple the impregnation was successful, but every time the husband of the patient told Sadaharu how delighted he was with the treatment, Sadaharu felt like a miserable fraud. The doctor had nowhere near the faith in this method that the husband had. Sadaharu had preserved his reputation when the boy was born. But the chances were just fifty-fifty, and Sadaharu still believed the outcome had been only a matter of chance.

When the four-months-pregnant woman and her mother-in-law left, Sadaharu told Nurse Ono, "Call in the woman for the abortion."

A thin young woman entered wearing a pink blouse and a gray pleated skirt.

"Ms. Murata?" Sadaharu asked.

"Yes, that's right,"

Toshiko Murata, twenty-seven years old, an office worker, unmarried. The man whose name appeared on the consent form for the operation and who was not married to Murata had a different surname. But in confirming the patient's identity, Sadaharu was simply avoiding the kind of mistake made by a colleague who had performed an unrequested operation of this kind, hard as that was to believe.

Toshiko Murata was still in her tenth week of pregnancy. Yesterday, Sadaharu had inserted Laminaria, a material made of the dried root of a seaweed, into her cervix in order to expand the opening. While his nurse took the woman's blood pressure and otherwise attended to her, Sadaharu saw his next patient, a woman with a vaginal infection. At every gynecological clinic, about one-third of the patients were there for this sort of complaint.

"I was so surprised, doctor, by the sudden discharge. I thought I'd picked up a really serious illness somewhere." The woman's name was Tsugi Ueda, and she'd given birth to three children at the clinic.

"Why? Did you do something bad?" Sadaharu was amused, even charmed, by Tsugi's wholesomeness. She and her husband ran a grocery store in town.

"Really. I'm not kidding," she said. "Last month, my husband went over to Korea, you know, with a tour group. There's no telling what men will do at times like that."

"If you don't know, then you should ask your husband."

"Oh, I did. All he said was that a friend of his was cheated by a pimp who took his money and disappeared. He was afraid, so he just forgot about doing anything like that."

Sadaharu said, "That's enough to make anyone careful. Have you taken any medicines lately?"

"I had a terrible cold about four days ago and I took some antibiotics."

"Well, that may be the trouble."

Nurse Ono raised her eyes from the microscope and said, "*Candida* positive."

"It's a fungus called candida albicans," Sadaharu said to Tsugi.

"It is? How did I pick that up?" she demanded.

"That fungus is everywhere," he assured her. "When the natural resistance of your body is low, the fungus multiplies. A friend of mine thought he had athlete's foot between his toes and was worried enough to see a skin specialist about it. He found out it was candida albicans! Sometimes the infection is like that."

Tsugi said, "It's dreadful what can happen to you when you take an antibiotic."

"Do you have a bathtub at home?"

"Yes," Tsugi answered. "But last week it sprang a leak and we went next door to use the bath."

"You may have picked it up there, away from home."

"You mean fungus can live in hot water?"

"Oh, sure. Fungi get along quite well in any water you can get into."

Human beings live with bacteria all their lives; the large body of a human is attacked by bacteria that can only be seen with the aid of a microscope. Sadaharu had learned in medical school that the inflammation caused by *Trichomonas* was not called "infection" but rather "infestation." Infestation—in the sense of a swarm of locusts or the like—expresses the condition in which protozoans multiply and attack the human body. Through the microscope the nurse could see clearly the remains of dead white corpuscules and the whiplike protozoans.

The fungus called *Candida* multiplies rapidly when the acid level and blood sugar increase in the vagina. The immediate trigger for the infestation may be a condition like pregnancy or diabetes, or treatment with some antibiotics, or even oral contraceptives.

Tsugi brushed a few strands of hair from her face and said, "Doctor, this is the first time this has happened to me. Is there some medicine to cure it?"

"Yes, of course. Is the itching severe?"

"Yes, rather. You know," Tsugi said, "I thought I had some kind of venereal disease."

"I'll give you some medicine I think will take care of it, but if it doesn't go away immediately, have your husband take some too," Sadaharu said.

As he was finishing with Tsugi Ueda, Sadaharu received a telephone call transferred by his receptionist.

"Sadaharu? This is Yoko." It was the crisp voice of a woman past her youth.

"Oh, sorry not to have called you before this," Sadaharu said.

Yoko Kakei had been a close friend of Sadaharu's late older sister from their high school days.

"As a matter of fact, I have a favor to ask of you. May I see you this evening?"

Yoko was ordinarily a bit direct in her speech, but Sadaharu felt she was inclined to be somewhat formal with him, although they knew each other well.

"If it's easier for you, I'll stop by your house," he said, "That might be best for you."

"You'll come then?"

"Of course. A call from you is like a command."

"What about Kaori? Since Mayumi is still away . . ."

"I'll ask our housekeeper to stay over this evening. She is willing to spend the night when we go out."

"Oh? Then I'll expect you about seven-thirty."

As Sadaharu hung up the phone, he heard his nurse speaking in the examination room.

"You didn't have any breakfast this morning, did you, Ms. Murata? Not even water?"

"Nothing at all," the woman replied in a weak voice. Among the items written on the file card was the information that this was her first abortion. If that was true, she was probably quite tense.

"If you drink any water, you may vomit," the nurse said. "Under anesthesia, that would be dangerous if the vomit entered your windpipe, you understand. We'll finish the operation while you are asleep. You won't feel a thing, there's no need to be concerned."

Nurse Ono had earlier given emphatic directions to Murata not to eat or drink anything. Nonetheless, some patients ignored such warnings, and so she always exercised caution before the operation.

A music box inside the instrument sterilizer indicated that the machine was in working order with a tune called "The Maiden's Prayer."

Without especially intending to do so, Sadaharu noticed the address Toshiko Murata had entered on the file card; it was a pleasant residential area in Kamakura near the ocean. There were certainly plenty of gynecologists in Kamakura, and Sadaharu guessed that she had come all this way so as not to meet anyone she knew. On the other hand, the information on the card—her name, address, age—might not even be genuine.

So many unmarried women came to the clinic to have abortions; Sadaharu could hardly remember their faces or voices, so little impression did they make on him. For one thing, Sadaharu had little occasion to notice the faces of these women, and on their part the women often appeared at the clinic without makeup, without dressing carefully, and speaking in hushed tones. To some degree, every patient coming to a hospital has something the matter with her body and so does not come dressed stylishly and in a lively mood. Usually, she comes because she is ill and wants to obtain a cure. That is to say, when she is "cured" she is at least somewhat better than when she entered the hospital. But the women coming for an abortion were quite another matter, since they were not particularly ill to begin with. Medically speaking, they received an unnecessary injury. Some instinctive awareness of this may account for the dejected expression Sadaharu often saw on the faces he did happen to notice.

Never had Sadaharu been in the least curious about the men involved or the kind of relationships the women had with them. Insofar as the women were patients in a gynecologist's examination room, sexual matters were simply medical phenomena. For Sadaharu, the individuality of his patients was limited to the condition of their illness.

Sadaharu got up from his desk while Nurse Ono went on with her questions.

"Did you remove your lipstick?"

"Yes," the patient replied.

"Please remove your wristwatch, rings, and other jewelry." The patient complied in silence.

"Do you wear contact lenses or false teeth?"

"No, neither."

"Do you chew gum or have anything in your mouth?"

"Chewing gum?"

"Yes. When we begin the operation, there is some danger if you have anything in your mouth."

"Do people do such things?" Murata asked.

The atmosphere in the examination room had become a bit more relaxed. No one at this clinic could recall a patient who had undergone an operation with chewing gum still in her mouth, but it was possible that such a thing had happened at the clinic where

Nurse Ono had previously worked, and she was simply adding a bit to the procedure for abortions as it was written up in the nurses' manual.

The day was exceptionally bright, the lights and shadows of the world outside clearly transmitted through the frosted glass of the window. Next to the sterilizing cabinet hung a calendar showing the day to be the twenty-fifth of January. Sadaharu suddenly remembered this was his birthday. He had seen the calendar many times that morning, but only now did he recall the fact that today he was forty-two.

The patient's blood pressure was 114 over 58.

"No phlegm?" the nurse asked.

"Nothing at all," the patient replied.

"Please cough," the nurse directed. Then, "How's your tolerance for alcohol, pretty good?"

"Yes, I think so," Murata said.

"People wake up early from the anesthetic if they have a high tolerance for alcohol."

Sadaharu put on a rubber apron in preparation for the operation and stood at the patient's feet. A pale blue curtain was drawn so that he could not see the woman's face.

"Now, please count from one, slowly, in a loud voice," the nurse said.

From behind Sadaharu came the sound of a bird shrieking. Here, near the ocean, there were many kites, and at that moment the sound of the bird came through the window. The patient counted to twelve and stopped.

"Six point five cc," said Nurse Ono, opening the curtain between Sadaharu and herself. "Shall I go to fifteen?"

"Yes, please do. But slowly," Sadaharu directed.

The patient frowned and shook her head, but Nurse Iwanami gently settled her into position. Sadaharu often said that he liked novelty, but regarding surgical technique he was always conservative. The early method of artificially induced abortion generally had been replaced by the new "super suction" method, which worked on the same principle as a vacuum cleaner. However, Sadaharu continued to use the placenta extraction technique he'd always used. He felt that for Japanese physicians, the simpler the tools, the better for the patient, even though plenty of less skilled foreign doctors liked using the suction curette, or so it seemed.

Sadaharu had his reasons. Using the suction curette, material in the uterus passed through a tube into a bottle, and remained there. Only after the operation could it be examined. As far as Sadaharu was concerned, that was too late. He wanted to examine the tissue bit by bit with his own eyes. That was the operating procedure he was used to, and so far he had done several thousand such operations. He would not have admitted it, but he was the kind of perfectionist found all over the world. Since this was only the tenth week of pregnancy, he could not judge the fragments of the fetus, but spongelike chorion and bits of placenta could be identified.

When the procedure was completed, Sadaharu glanced at the time. There was a clock over the patient's head, so he could see it whether he wanted to or not. He noticed that from beginning to end the operation had taken just three minutes and ten seconds. His speed record for this operation was two minutes and thirty seconds. Some slowpokes—incompetent doctors—might claw around for many minutes, making the operation unbearable for the patient.

Nurse Ono said, "Ms. Murata. Ms. Murata. It's all over. Can you understand me?"

The patient replied sleepily with a murmur, but she had not really regained consciousness.

Now it was time for Nurse Iwanami to take the still-groggy patient to the recovery room next door, helping her to put her clothes in order. Not that Nurses Ono or Junko Kurata, the youngest and newest at the clinic, couldn't have done the task alone, but the two of them preferred to work together. By herself, Nurse Iwanami lifted the limp, 130-pound body without effort.

The next patient was beginning her third month of pregnancy, but she was having abdominal pain and a small amount of bleeding. Distressed, she had come to the clinic.

Sadaharu turned over her file card. "You have older children, don't you?"

"Two children. A boy five and a boy two," the woman said.

"And where are they now?"

"I asked the woman next door to look after them."

The woman was not wearing makeup and her body seemed bloated. Her back was hunched against the cold as she wore only a light quilted jacket over her dress.

Sadaharu spoke carefully: "Listen, now. If you really want to have this child, you must get some rest immediately. Is it possible for you to go home now and rest?"

The woman was silent.

"You simply must not do the usual shopping and washing and cleaning if you are going to avoid a miscarriage. You have to take it easy for a week, stay in bed. You can do that, can't you?"

"It's hard to do, with the two children at home," she said.

"Of course. Then the best thing would be for you to go into the clinic right away. Can you ask someone to look after the children? Can you get your husband to bring you a nightgown and your things?"

"He's not at home today," she said.

"Hmm. Can you contact him when he's away?"

Again she made no reply, so he repeated his question.

"No, I can't do that."

"What kind of work does your husband do?"

"He drives a truck. Long distance."

"I see. Still, this won't do. How about your neighbors? Especially at a time like this . . ."

The woman hesitated. "I . . . I'll go myself." And, still hesitating, she added, "I set out the bedding to air before I came, and the weather report for tonight says rain, so . . ."

The woman's expression, vague until then, suddenly became clear, as though she felt it was more important to save the bedding from getting wet than to avoid a miscarriage.

"I'll give you some medicine, just in case," Sadaharu said. "Take it for a week or so, don't overdo things, and rest as much as you can."

How many times each week such empty words passed his lips, Sadaharu thought. With two boys aged five and two it was impossible for this women to rest. Sadaharu had to say the words, but he had no idea what this woman might think of him. He could not even guess from the expression on her face whether or not she really wanted the next child. And on top of all that, there was her truck driver husband. Did he really like children enough to have three of them? Sadaharu could not know the answer.

As the woman left, Sadaharu said to her in a hesitant voice, "Ah, where's your house?"

"On the bus route, just left beyond the farmers' co-op," she replied.

"Did you come on the bus?"

"No, by bicycle," she replied.

"Bicycle? That's not so good." Sadaharu spoke in a half sigh. "You should leave your bicycle here at the clinic and take the bus home."

On foot it would take her about twenty minutes.

When he called in the second patient of the day for an abortion, Sadaharu felt he was getting into the rhythm of his work, but he hardly noticed her when she came in, odd as that might seem. In fact, Sadaharu saw little of his patients' faces or any of the rest of them. He examined them precisely from the point of view of their medical needs. A person with exceptionally red cheeks, however that feature might be understood by a layman, was a sign to the doctor that she could be suffering severe anemia.

That Sadaharu did not especially remember the faces of his patients, was not because of any deficiency in his powers of observation. His eyes were excellent. Some gynecologists were blessed with a certain charm that could bring forth such details of family matters as "In fact, this is not my husband's child"—all quite unsolicited. Sadaharu did not want to give the impression of being first and foremost a doctor, without any concern for extraneous details. He perfectly understood as well that the symptoms of some patients improved without any special treatment when he simply listened to their complaints about their husband's unfaithfulness or their mother-in-law's attitude. But although he couldn't help running into his patients among the shopkeepers and farmers in the neighborhood of his clinic, he didn't want to recognize any of his patients on the streets of a nearby town. Very likely, his patients also preferred it that way.

The name on the chart was Kumiko Shinjo. She was twenty-eight years old, and this was her second abortion. Counting from her last menstruation, she was in her sixth week. She had thought her period was merely late until she began to feel something like morning sickness, she said, and then she came in for an examination. Unlike most patients, she began to hiccup violently, perhaps due to the anesthetic. There was no need for concern. Noticing her determined jaw, well-fleshed cheekbones, and the calm of her rather wide forehead, Sadaharu found nothing memorable about her.

As it was still early in her pregnancy, the chorion could not be clearly confirmed. Her hiccups subsided quickly, and five minutes later Nurse Iwanami brought the patient into the recovery room to sleep. Toshiko Murata was awake now, after her operation, her eyes open but still in a daze, the room brightening for her. She did not yet feel like getting up and going home.

For Sadaharu, the morning's work was done, and he was about to leave for lunch when Nurse Ono called to him in a formal tone.

"Yes, what is it?" he answered.

"Happy birthday!"

She made a signal with her eyes to Nurse Iwanami, and immediately she brought in a huge bouquet of narcissus tied with a red ribbon and presented it to Sadaharu.

"We wanted to give this to you in the morning, but we'd asked Nurse Iwanami's mother to cut the fresh narcissus and bring them in, and she was a bit late."

That evening when Sadaharu went to Yoko Kakei's house, he would take half the flowers with him. He would not have mentioned it to the nurses, of course, but he felt as if the flowers they had presented to him for his birthday, a large bundle with prominent stems and small blossoms, looked like a bunch of green onions sold at the vegetable store. One did not often see this kind of half-wild narcissus in the city, and Sadaharu did not know whether these had been grown in Nurse Iwanami's family field or been brought from somewhere else. No matter. On the warm Sagami coast of Japan, along the south-facing slopes and in protected places, these flowers appeared at the beginning of January.

The flowers themselves were short and small, shaped rather like the spring orchid. Unlike the narcissus raised and sold by flower shops, these were marvelously pungent.

"How nice! What a magnificent fragrance," Sadaharu offered.

Nurse Iwanami said, "Really! And we used to think of cooking onions when we found narcissus like these."

From that moment, Sadaharu liked narcissus. Very possibly, Nurse Iwanami, who had been on duty at the clinic the night before, had asked her mother to bring the flowers because she herself had not been able to go home.

While Sadaharu was having supper later with his daughter Kaori, he had his housekeeper divide the bunch of flowers. He was not in the habit of bringing flowers to women, but the scent of these was not at all bad, he thought.

He thought it something of his duty to have conversation with his daughter during meals, and, if duty was not precisely the word for what he felt, there was indeed a sense of pity that his daughter, only in the third grade, should have to take her meals alone with the housekeeper. Most of what Sadaharu felt was surely his own sentimentality, for Kaori did not seem to mind in the least the absence of her mother. The day before on the way home from school, she had mislaid her knapsack somewhere, and when she went to look for it she had found it on top of the sea wall by the shore.

"It was out there for three hours and no one picked up my knapsack!" Kaori exclaimed.

"Why would anyone want to steal your knapsack?" Sadaharu said.

The knapsack was wet with spray. And the thought crossed Sadaharu's mind that knapsacks and narcissus did quite well by themselves around there.

Chapter Two

Horseback Hill

Yoko Kakei's house stood on a bluff overlooking the sea, seven or eight minutes by car from Sadaharu's clinic. One could take the bus but would still have to walk more than a half mile from the highway along a deserted road.

Whenever Sadaharu visited Yoko, he drove in his own car, and when he drank too much, as he often did there, he would take a taxi back home. Sometimes Yoko would bring his car to the clinic the next day and he would return her to her house. It was something of a farce, all that back and forth, and if Yoko herself did not drink she might have taken Sadaharu home in her own car, but she did like liquor and on nights like that, things weren't so simple.

Yoko Kakei was now a widow. She had married a young American lawyer who had come to Japan after the war, but five years ago he had died in the crash of a private plane. Until his death, the couple had lived in Washington, D.C., but for Yoko's sake the husband had long ago purchased this land on the coast and built a house. They had used the residence only about one month during the year, but both had loved to gaze out on the splendid view of Sagami Bay, a place famous for its west wind and evening sun.

Sadaharu got out of his car, leaned into the strong wind, and walked to the entrance of Yoko's house. The famous west wind had been blowing steadily, though it had not seemed nearly this strong at his place. As he rang the doorbell, Sadaharu noticed another car, a small one, parked by the house. It was not only small but also dirty, and certainly was not the car that Yoko drove.

Yoko herself came to answer the doorbell. She was wearing a thick gray sweater on top of a black pleated skirt.

"Sorry I'm late," Sadaharu said, presenting a bouquet of narcissus. It was fifteen minutes past the time of their appointment.

"I have another visitor today," Yoko said, "someone I want you to meet."

The other visitor stood behind Yoko, a man in his late thirties, wearing glasses and looking slightly shabby in pants that were baggy at the knees and a heavy, old-fashioned sweater.

"This is Father Munechika," Yoko said, adding, in response to Sadaharu's implicit question, "He is a Catholic priest."

Sadaharu introduced himself.

"He is here as pastor of the Kurihama Catholic Church. His sister was a classmate of mine in college," Yoko continued.

Sadaharu said, "We both seem to have disreputable sisters."

"How's that?"

Yoko pretended not to have heard.

In a clear voice that did not reflect his physical appearance, Father Munechika said to Sadaharu, "Mrs. Kakei has often spoken about you, and I thought I would like to meet you myself."

Sadaharu joked, "Ah, then you have certainly heard nothing but the worst." Then using a word he faintly recalled,. he continued, "You must be her confessor. Mrs. Kakei is a Catholic, after all, and so she has to confess her sins, doesn't she?"

"Quite so," Yoko said. "It comes down to that, but of course I wouldn't think of going to him, Sadaharu. When I go to confession, I go to another priest in Tokyo."

"It was my *oldest* sister," the priest said with emphasis, "who was Yoko's classmate."

Yoko said, "He's been like this since childhood. I never dreamt that he'd ever become a priest."

"Somehow I just don't trust people who seem like what they are.

It makes me uneasy if a judge is judicial or if a government official behaves like a government official," Sadaharu observed.

Father Munechika addressed Sadaharu: "You're a gynecologist, aren't you?"

"Oh, yes, and so I have to listen to Mrs. Kakei criticize me all the time. About abortions, too. I just did two today."

"Abortions! Oh, my. I wonder how many abortions have been done in Japan up to now?" The priest spoke in his normally smooth, clear voice. Meanwhile, Yoko poured whiskey for the two men. She knew what they liked, adding water to the priest's glass and some soda for Sadaharu.

"I've no idea, but I could guess," Sadaharu said. "The Eugenic Protection Law was enacted in 1949, or thereabouts. How long ago was that?"

"Thirty years?"

"Then assuming there are about one million abortions a year," Sadaharu calculated, "that would be about thirty million. Some years were probably below that estimate, but there is a black market to consider too. Then, supposing that children born about 1951 had reached reproductive age, we might estimate forty, no, say, thirty-five million."

"And so on those assumptions," the priest said, "the total comes to about the whole population of a country like Korea being simply obliterated."

"Quite a number."

"You know, someone remarked that performing abortions is really the biggest postwar industry, that Japan's present prosperity is entirely due to doctors of gynecology."

"Oh! Who says that?" Yoko queried.

"Merely a rumor," Sadaharu continued, "but I understand something to that effect was mentioned at a meeting of the Japan Association for the Protection of Mothers, by a prominent gynecologist."

Yoko replied, "I've often told Sadaharu that he should stop doing abortions."

He chuckled. "I'm grateful for your concern, but I'd be out of business if I stopped doing abortions."

She responded, "But you don't really need the money that badly. Didn't you say you'd repaid the money you borrowed to build the clinic? I suppose now you only need money for your family."

Sitting cross-legged on the sofa, Sadaharu said, "That's true, but . . . Let's suppose I become a Christian. I borrow a cross from the church, without paying, Father, and set it up on the roof of my clinic in place of the lightning rod. My patients arrive, and when they see the cross I will say: 'Look there! I'm so afraid of God I certainly will not perform abortions.' Now, Father, I ask you; What will that solve?"

Sadaharu's spirits were lubricated by his first drink, and he continued.

"I'll tell you what would happen. They would skip the sermon and go to another clinic for their abortions. That's all. And though I say it myself, if you will pardon me, I'm clever with my hands and my operations are good. Frankly, it's better for the patients that I do their operations instead of some other doctor."

"Well, of course I can understand someone going into medicine," the priest said, "but as a gynecologist you must have known ahead of time you would be doing that kind of operation as a matter of routine."

Sadaharu frowned. "You must be wondering why I went into obstetrics and gynecology. The point is, I thought I was good at it. I have skillful hands and good intuition. You know, the usual type of surgery is performed with the eyes to guide you, but abortion is sometimes done just by feeling around in the uterus. To do it, you must have a sense for it—delicate fingers, motor skills . . . something special. And so I thought it was the right thing for me."

Sadaharu's conversation style was always like this; for better or worse, he spoke bluntly, to Yoko or to anyone else. Most people believed only half of what he said—and this was Sadaharu's intention.

"Think of this, too, Father. Assuming that abortion is really such a terrible thing, let's say that as a matter of routine I suggest to the patient that she give birth to the child if she possibly can. In spite of my saying that, almost all of the women choose to terminate their pregnancies. At that point, there is nothing to do but perform the abortion. I could keep my own hands clean, of course, by asking the patient to go to some other doctor, but that would be despicable, don't you think? I really prefer to take the responsibility myself."

"Still, Sadaharu," Yoko said, "if you decline to do the operation, some people will reconsider, won't they?"

"No, that's just a layman's sentimental notion. Patients aren't that naive. Most patients look around until they find a doctor who will give them the diagnosis and treatment that they want."

Yoko was seated on a large, square stool in front of her two guests. The stool had been purchased by Yoko's husband when they built the house, and Yoko explained to Sadaharu that her husband always bought things that were of high quality and expensive because they were a good investment.

"There is something I would like to ask, Sadaharu," Yoko continued. "When does a human life begin, in your opinion?"

He shook his head. "It's been a long time since I left college and I think I've forgotten, I wonder what the textbook says."

Sadaharu's expression showed that he would have preferred to avoid the subject, but he continued to speak.

"I know you have always been amazed that I felt it was all right to perform an abortion, and you have been critical of that. But I really have no sense of terminating a life, not in the least."

Sadaharu was now quite relaxed, thanks to the alcohol.

"Tell me why you feel that way," Yoko asked.

"I don't know why, only that is what I feel. Of course, I'm speaking of the first trimester. I would have to ask God about why we gynecologists feel that way. If God exists."

"But I really wonder. . . . You're not an insensitive person. What do you think of during the operation?"

"I think just how neatly and cleanly I can remove the fetus."

"And what do your patients think of?" Father Munechika asked.

"Oh, some of them have an idea of sin about what they are doing, I'm sure. But we—I, that is—have none of that feeling. I must lack the philosophical outlook, or the imagination, that most people have."

"You mean you've gotten used to it?"

"No. Right from the start it meant nothing at all to me. I simply don't have any feeling that I'm taking a life when the fetus is not a living thing outside the womb."

"But if you left it alone, it would eventually grow up and live, wouldn't it?"

"You're probably right. I don't think about those details. But if I believed life was really there, right from the beginning, I really would be concerned about terminating it. It is legal to abort a six-month fetus, you know, but I really feel that is too much."

"Do you really perform abortions that late?"

"Hmm, these days it's rare, but it happens. Let's say the mother intends to give birth, but the father runs out on her. There are plenty of troubles like that in the world. Then she comes crying to me. There was a case like that just yesterday. Not even the woman herself but the grandmother."

"A grandmother!"

"Correct. That is, the one who was pregnant was a senior high school girl."

The previous afternoon, during his rest period, Sadaharu had had a visitor, a friend of his mother's whom Sadaharu remembered meeting long ago at his mother's house.

His afternoon rest was precious to him. In summer, he occasionally went for a swim, and in winter the time was just right for reading or listening to music. Sadaharu felt irritated when this special time was interrupted by a visitor without an appointment, even though he was used to being awakened or called out at odd hours. On this occasion, he appeared in the entrance hall like some fierce temple guardian to meet the unexpected guest.

The old lady, after politely explaining her connection with Sadaharu's mother, said there was a matter about which she wished to consult him. Sadaharu complied with her request, but he did not conduct the woman to his sitting room. Clearly, this was less than courteous, but he felt that any conversation having to do with his medical specialty should take place during his formal examination hours at the clinic.

According to the old woman, one of her married daughters had a teenaged daughter who for some time had not wanted to go to school. The girl had no particular symptoms of illness, and her appetite was good. There had been some problem between the girl and one of her female teachers, and the mother supposed this was behind the girl's wanting to miss school. However, one day the mother caught a glimpse of the daughter's standing profile, and, while the girl was naturally plump, the mother saw that her daughter's belly was noticeably enlarged.

Naturally, the mother did not contact a doctor in that area, because if a rumor got started it would make things even more difficult, and so she brought the girl to Kyoto to a physician. She learned that the girl was nearing the end of her sixth month of pregnancy. The summer before, she'd had a relationship with an older high school student she was in love with. The horrified mother wanted an abortion for her daughter immediately, she said, but the doctor in Kyoto refused. The old lady wanted Sadaharu to perform the operation.

"I turned her down too. Even if I'd intended to kill the fetus, there are plenty of live births in the seventh month. That's why we keep an incubator handy, in case there is a cry out of the child after it emerges. Things like this do not always end neatly. It's more traumatic for the teenaged mother to produce a child that way than simply by normal childbirth, and if the child is alive at seven months, it must be raised. Either way, it is a problem. I told her that as a warning and sent her home."

"Do you put the child in an incubator right after the operation?"

"Yes, exactly. In the old days, in winter, they would expose the infant in some nearby cold place and let matters take their course. Or if it came to that, the midwife would put the child upside down in a bucket of water. Anyway, there are stories. But nowadays, hardly anyone has the stomach for such methods.

"I suggested to the old woman that she take better care of the baby; after all, it was her great-grandchild. So I proposed that the girl go through with the pregnancy, give birth, and have the grandmother raise the child with outside help. Well, as it turned out—and contrary to what they thought—they ended up really wanting the child.

"There was another couple in the area who had only one son and a daughter, and after the daughter had an abortion, she found she could not have another child. Before the son could get married, he was killed in a car crash. If instead of insisting on an abortion they had adopted the daughter's child, their family line would have been preserved. I guess it was fate."

Sadaharu went on, "Yoko, I don't suppose you've been bothered by problems like the family line dying out." He was not at all reluctant to bring up a subject here that most people would avoid.

"On the contrary," Yoko said in a low voice.

"Really? I'm surprised you are concerned about something so ordinary."

"My husband often talked about it, even though he was an American. He had two daughters by his first wife and felt badly about our not having any children."

"Was it a matter of passing on his wealth to his own children?"

Yoko replied, "We didn't give much thought to such things. As a matter of fact, I don't trouble myself with thoughts like that at all lately."

"What do you mean?"

"It's all relative, in a way. Somehow I don't feel that today's world is a good place for children." She paused. "I was very close to my husband. He was so good to talk with. He used to sit in that chair where Sadaharu is sitting now, and I here, and we would talk for hours—it made this house such a pleasant place to be. We felt as though we could talk forever, endlessly, like the sea. Understand, it wasn't a lonely place, this house; it was two people's world."

"How nice for you," Sadaharu said, a slight edge in his voice.

Yoko went on. "And then my soul mate died. And the sea became empty. Strange, isn't it? That land over there is the Izu Peninsula, Toru. There is nothing between here and there now, but once it was filled with pleasure.

"A man and a wife being that close is really something to think about. If a couple does not get along too well and one of them dies, it can be a matter for celebration. I knew a man who was all smiles at his wife's funeral. But for a close couple, death is a terrible thing, a total sense of loss. When you come to think of it, whatever happens in your life, it all comes down to the same thing."

"You mean, whether your spouse is good or bad, the end is tragic?"

"Oh, no, not like that. I really had the opposite in mind. Hardly anyone goes through life without something good happening, some compensation. If life begins badly, then it ends well. If it begins well, then it ends badly."

Father Munechika said, "I had no idea you were so isolated, even though I knew you lived here by yourself. Is it that you can't sell the house because of all the memories it holds?"

"Yes, that's so. I'm not happy here now, but I remember vividly the time when I was happy."

"You were happy, you say?" Sadaharu asked. He murmured and closed his eyes, his whiskey glass in his hand.

"Oh, I know, those are women's words. Men don't often say

words like 'joy' or 'happiness.'"

"I wonder why men don't use them?"

"It may be because it's unusual for people to be happy in the present, so the word happiness is used about memories, or the past, or about dreams for the future. I think that men generally like to talk about the present."

Sadaharu nodded agreement with the priest's observation, saying, "My! Our priest turns out to be a genius after all. And until now I only suspected it."

"I'd heard that Mrs. Kakei lived in this house on a cliff by the sea, with no neighbors," Father Munechika said. "Japanese usually don't build their houses in such places, so far from other people."

"But the sea is so beautiful! Whenever I look at the beauty and wildness of the sea, I could give up everything else in life—in spite of the loneliness and the inconvenience and the strong winds."

"Isn't that always the way? When you think of gaining something, you have to be prepared for some sacrifice," Sadaharu said, intoxicated now. He closed his eyes and laughed.

Yoko went on reminiscing.

"That hill behind the garden gets a strong wind all year long, and so the grass and trees don't grow much. This is the prettiest time now, with the grass up to a person's hips, dry and pale and bending in the wind. It looks like the back of a horse. My husband used to call it Horseback Hill."

"Still, you feel lonely living here by yourself," the priest said. His pity for Yoko was unmixed with curiosity.

"Yes, I am very lonely," she said.

"She says that so calmly," Sadaharu remarked, "that we can't feel any pity for her."

"I've always felt that life involved putting up with a certain amount of loneliness. Besides, when I do go somewhere, or meet someone, I am quite pleased and grateful. If a burglar broke into the house and spent the night talking with me, I'd bring out the best cognac for him."

"Horrors! What a thing to say! It's as though you are talking about us. Please don't refer to us as burglars, right, Father?"

Yoko took this opportunity to step into the kitchen.

"Oh, my! The food is ready," she said.

Steam was coming out of the electric rice cooker.

"You two may have eaten supper, but I'm going to have a snack."

Sadaharu called to her, "I thought you might say that, so I only ate half a meal before coming."

"All I can offer you is miso soup and pickles with the rice."

"What's in the miso soup?"

"Seaweed and fried tofu," came the distant reply.

"That's not so bad."

Father Munechika asked Sadaharu, "How many patients do you see in a day?"

"Twenty, maybe thirty," he answered. "Two or three abortions, two or three births or miscarriages, and the same number of consultations about infertility. They don't go very well together."

"Do you provide artificial insemination at your clinic?"

"Of course. But I cannot do AID—artificial insemination with a donor—at my clinic because I can't find any donors of semen. Sometimes patients ask me to provide the semen myself."

Sadaharu said "sometimes," but in fact only once had a not-too-intelligent patient come in seeking such help, and when he told her she would need a donor, she said, "Oh, you would do fine, doctor. Can't I get it here?"

Sadaharu remembered the sudden inviting look he'd received from that patient at that moment, but the woman herself had left little impression on him. Of course, since she had come for artificial insemination, her husband had been with her. He operated a small plumber's business.

The husband was infertile because of alcohol poisoning. Sadaharu remembered telling her that the husband's sperm count was low and that he was intoxicated, something he could tell from his examination. He had told the woman it would be difficult for her to become pregnant by her husband. Someone else would be better, in fact, but since that would be a problem, she thought, perhaps the doctor . . . that was the gist of it.

"The food is finally ready," Yoko announced. "Please come and eat."

In spite of having already had dinner, the two men ate heartily. Sadaharu complained when Father Munechika took all the pickled radish, and Father Munechika replied that he would have to watch out for himself. Yoko went to the kitchen and brought in more.

At some point during the dinner, Sadaharu realized he felt the priest was a good fellow after all. He praised the cooking, saying that every time he came there Yoko cooked very well, especially the rice.

"Yes, the rice is fine and so are the vegetables," the priest said.

"Yoko, that was just flattery, I'm warning you. But since Father Munechika said it, it must be true, you see. And not only the vegetables—the soup was marvelous, too. I'm a true believer in fried tofu, you know. No matter what else you have, if you include that the meal will be delicious. Just the way Westerners serve bread and butter with every meal. That's what I think."

"You're right, but it never occurred to me before."

"There's no need for you two to be so polite. It's a pleasure to cook something nice for you."

"Ah, Yoko," Sadaharu said, "how like you to say that. Confused and drunk as I am, I thought you said to come early because you had something to ask me."

"Yes, that's what I said."

"Well, if you don't tell me pretty soon, I won't be able to understand it even if I try."

"It's not so urgent a matter," Yoko began, "but my friend Eiko Nakanishi has been unable to conceive, and she has just about given up. When I told her about you, she asked me to ask you if you would examine her. They have a place not far from here, so it wouldn't be any trouble for them to stop by sometime."

"Fine. I'll do an examination anytime. But how old are they?"

"Both are forty-six. Her husband has had a bad leg since he was a child, he said. His family owns a well-known fishing tackle store in Tokyo, and since he has a disability, and he doesn't have the responsibility of being the eldest son, they pay him to act as a kind of manager so he doesn't have to work very hard."

Sadaharu interrupted Yoko's explanation. "Now, I'm going to say the kind of thing that makes people laugh and say I don't act like a doctor. There must be something peculiar about this fellow."

"Oh? Why do you say that?"

"Well, in my experience, a man without much money lives by the sweat of his brow and at night works just as hard to make children. So as a rule, an honest, hardworking man has lots of children."

Still, Sadaharu was curious and listened to Yoko's narration without further comment.

The couple had been classmates in college and the woman had married the man partly out of sympathy for his crippled leg, or so rumor had it. Yoko had not known them long, but recently, at the yacht harbor, she had been introduced to the Nakanishis, and afterwards the two of them had come to visit her house at Horseback Hill.

"What's the matter?" Sadaharu asked. "Haven't they been to see a doctor until now?"

"They said that they had, more or less," Yoko replied.

"More or less?"

"After they were married for two or three years, they went for examinations separately. Neither appeared to have anything the matter."

"Then they weren't trying," Sadaharu said.

"It's not that. They said they had normal relations."

"Now, Yoko," Sadaharu began, "unless they were getting together only once a year like the lovers in the old legend, they were certain to have children. They're both healthy and they didn't produce a child? My guess is that they shouldn't have any great expectations."

"Why do you say that? You just said that if they were healthy they could have a child, didn't you?"

"And in spite of that, they haven't had one. So there must be something else wrong. I can't tell without an examination. It can happen that a person has an allergy to semen, rare as that is."

"The husband?"

"Either the man or the woman," Sadaharu said.

"Isn't that strange?"

"Still, if they were told there was nothing wrong with the man, then probably the wife has some problem. What happens is that when the husband's semen enters the body, an allergic reaction is set up that kills the sperm."

"Really! And is there any psychological connection?" Yoko asked.

"I don't know much about that," Sadaharu answered.

"Then nothing can be done for them?"

"It's not that exactly, but first the allergy would have to be cured. She would have to stop having relations with her husband for a time."

"For how long?"

"Well, the case I'm familiar with was for one year without intercourse. During that time, the woman's system evidently changed, and she was able to become pregnant."

"This woman is already forty-six years old, you know," Yoko said.

"I've been wondering about that. This is probably a last resort for her, but it's questionable whether it will be effective."

"Just a moment, please," Yoko interrupted. "I'll make a phone call. When can you see them?"

"Thanks for the compliment, but I'm not a celebrity specialist.

They can see me any time the shop is open," Sadaharu replied sardonically.

Yoko left the room to make her call. In an unpriestly tone, Father Munechika said, "The high point of my day was being able to meet you, doctor."

"Really? What are you interested in?" Sadaharu asked. "If it's my personal life, I'd be happy to reveal that to you anytime, Father. But according to what I've heard from Yoko, your business—oh, I shouldn't say business . . . Since you listen to the confessions of your parishioners, I assume that you understand the secret side of people."

"Secret side? Well, there aren't so many secrets, I assure you," Father Munechika replied. "Whatever people try to hide simply becomes more apparent. Frankly, there is not much difference between what people seem to be and what they are. But compared with my work, doctor, your work deals more directly with the reality of human life and death."

In his usual slightly sarcastic tone, Sadaharu asked, "You mean I deal with the body, not the soul?"

"At first, I thought you were only concerned with physical matters, but on closer examination there is a considerable spiritual side to your work," the priest answered.

Laughing into his whiskey glass, Sadaharu said, "Now that you mention it, I remember a time not more than a month after my clinic opened when the police came to call on me. An infant had died in the village and there was some question about the cause of death, so they asked me to come and take a look. We are not so far from Tokyo, you know, and I imagined this place would be reasonably civilized. But I was mistaken about some things.

"It was about nine o'clock in the evening and I had just had a drink, but of course I said I would come as soon as I could. I put on my rubber boots, took up my umbrella, and went out on foot with the police. We walked for about twenty minutes.

"There in a darkened farm house was an infant dead in its bed. The mother was about twenty years old, and she was just sitting in a corner, not even crying. The police didn't know what to make of it and asked me about the cause of death. I could tell immediately, but I hesitated a bit in replying. You see, there were strangulation marks on the neck of the baby. Then they asked if the child had been ill. I said no—I really had no choice—I thought the child had been strangled.

"In fact, I really wanted to avoid telling them the truth. I was so sorry for those involved that I felt like lying to protect the guilty parties, to cover up for them. If I hadn't been so worried that others might find out and criticize me, I never would have told.

"At that time, I knew nothing of the details, of course, but I had a premonition. The household consisted of the twenty-year-old girl, the one who gave birth, and her seventeen-year-old brother—the two of them did the farming—plus the old deaf grandmother, seventy-five, who was senile and knew nothing."

"And the father of the baby was someone in the village?" Father Munechika asked.

"No. It was the seventeen-year-old brother. If it had been some other man, there wouldn't have been a problem, but since it was the brother, they hadn't even had a doctor's examination. The two of them continued to go out to the fields to work and managed to hide her condition. You see, because it was the child of a brother and sister they had felt it was unnatural right from the start. She had intended to give birth and then kill the child, but she had difficulty with the delivery; she had screamed, or the child had cried. At any rate, neighbors in the village heard and came to see what was happening. When they arrived, the child had been born, but it was dead, the girl said. They thought something was strange about it all and called the police."

"What would you have told those two if they had come to you first?" Father Munechika asked.

"I would have told them there was nothing wrong with a child being born between brother and sister. It was perfectly acceptable, after all, for brother and sister and other close relatives to marry in societies like the royalty of ancient Egypt. I don't mean that it's a good thing, but once it happens there isn't much that can be done about it. I would have told them to keep the child and raise it."

"Is that a medical opinion?" the priest asked.

"I don't know about that. The medical reasoning in such a case would probably be to perform an abortion, at least in most cases, whether the pregnancy was in midterm or whatever—I'm not really certain. But if my personal ethical opinion became known publicly, I'd be ostracized by my colleagues and disqualified from performing abortions. And if that happened, I wouldn't be able to pay back what I borrowed to build my clinic. I keep a proper physician's face on the surface and work according to the world's common sense, but it's not really good sense. In your world, Father, how do you deal with such cases? The church feels abortion is murder, but what if a child is born between sister and brother?"

"Really, I can't be sure either, since I'm not a specialist in church law, but we couldn't marry brother and sister. Perhaps it would be best to raise the child without people knowing who the father was. Or, even better than that, have the child adopted and raised somewhere away from the eyes of the village people."

"Yes, that's what I thought, too, at least at the time. The child would be better off raised in some other household. But if I say something like that, there will always be objections. Some such children might feel themselves deprived of parents and background, but at least they would be alive.

"By the way, Father, I'm very pleased to have met you this evening. I feel quite free to discuss these things with you. It's refreshing to feel that no legal code or cheap set of moralistic views has a place in this setting."

"And I feel the same way," the priest replied. "This has been an educational opportunity for me."

Outside the west wind was howling.

Chapter Three

Thin Snow on the Mountain

Before noon the next day, Yoko's friends the Nakanishis appeared in the examination room. During the introductions, Sadaharu sympathized with them and remarked on how quickly they had come, that doubtless they had been urged by Yoko.

"No, we wanted an examination as soon as possible ourselves," said Satsuki Nakanishi.

On his business card was written TAIYO, INC., EXECUTIVE DIRECTOR OF MANAGEMENT. Nakanishi's large eyes rather emphasized his baby face, and when he walked his right leg was stiff, thrust out like a stick.

Eiko, his wife, wore her hair down to her shoulders and had attractive features. When she laughed, her eyes narrowed and her eyebrows turned down at the corners. As is usual, although they were the same age, the husband's youthful face made his wife seem older.

Sadaharu had once blundered in another situation like this. A man had come in with a woman in her seventies who suspected that she had cancer. Sadaharu imagined the man to be her son and addressed him accordingly, but it turned out he really was her husband, just two years younger than the woman. Since then, Sadaharu had been extremely cautious regarding the family connections of his patients, making no judgments until the other party had informed him of the specifics.

"I understand you have been examined before?" Sadaharu said to Mrs. Nakanishi.

"Yes, about fifteen years ago, but we've had nothing done since then. Instead of trying to discover which of us was to blame, my husband said we should think of it as fate, or as our mutual responsibility. I thought that was the best way, too."

"What kind of examination did you receive?"

Sadaharu really didn't care whether or not it was a question of fate; he had to pursue the issue from a professional standpoint.

"They told me it was a tissue analysis, but it was a long time ago and I don't remember clearly."

"Did they do an X-ray?"

"They were going to do it on my next visit, but I never went back."

Sadaharu knew how common that was. To examine a woman for sterility required keeping track of her physiological cycle, so two or three days were not enough to do it properly. But that kind of examination, unless it showed some medical condition like tuberculous peritonitis, was not covered by national health insurance, and such procedures now cost the equivalent of several hundred dollars. That was not a huge amount for people with a comfortable income, but a gynecological examination was a different kind of psychological burden from that of an eye test, for example.

"Now, about this physical examination: which of you suggested it? Was it your husband's idea?" Sadaharu asked.

"No, I wanted it," Mrs. Nakanishi said.

The husband with the childish face spoke: "I guess it's really my fault my wife is so unhappy. I had said we shared responsibility for our failure to have children, and perhaps she felt she couldn't raise the subject again. But there is so little time left for her to have a child, and suddenly she began to get irritated. If she told her friends, they'd be surprised and think she's being unreasonable. But she's forty-six years old, and if we miss this chance, I guess she feels that will be the end for us."

Sadaharu nodded. "Well, we can't brood over it." He looked at the faces of the two people, who seemed like brother and sister.

"I'm a lazy person, and when I brood about things nothing ever seems to get accomplished. As your doctor, I must demonstrate my commitment to your case, but since we must deal with the realities of nature, let's not worry about being called unreasonable."

That same day, Sadaharu began the basic examination, first taking a blood sample to calculate sedimentation rate, then explaining to Mrs. Nakanishi how to record her basic body temperature, giving her a chart for that purpose. He asked about her menstrual cycle and found her ovulation time was approaching, so he would now be able to study the cervical mucus. With the onset of a woman's monthly period, the cervical mucus shows particular changes under the microscope, becoming water thin and clear in color. The discharge is sampled with a pipette and when dried on a glass slide and examined, it shows what the priest might have called an "ineffable human drama." If an egg is released, then in the liquid appear crystals of cruciform or fernlike shape. These crystals are composed of salt, glucose, and other material.

"Mr. Nakanishi," Sadaharu said, "would you like to have a look?"

As Sadaharu turned to Mr. Nakanishi, the nurse said, "Plus three."

"This is what a specimen of the mucus looks like," he continued, peering into the microscope and then vacating the chair to permit Mr. Nakanishi to look into the microscope.

"Ahhh, isn't that pretty," he murmured, his posture suggesting he was captivated by what he saw through the lens.

And, truly, the fernlike crystals displayed a severely beautiful pattern. Could this be part of the structure of a confused, fumbling, deceitful, weary, sleeping humanity, this thing with its shining silver color, layered patterns reminiscent of pointed leaves? Human life was here revealed as neither chance nor some casual thought but as having a splendor only conceivable as a structure moving within an orderly plan.

"Is that what it should be? Is it all right?" Mr. Nakanishi asked.

Few men who gaze at photographs of their prospective brides

have had the same chance to see the structure of the cervical mucus. Yet it is difficult enough to judge a woman on the basis of her outward appearance, considering the likelihood of being distracted by such things as whether she is thin or fat; some men may prefer women with short legs. But when it comes to her health and vigor, or her potential fertility, it is more informative to examine the crystals of the cervical discharge than her outward appearance. If there are no fernlike crystals, then there is no egg. If there is no egg, there can be no pregnancy. This is the essential point.

"Her condition is quite normal as far as the egg is concerned," Sadaharu replied.

"Hmm, then the problem is all the more likely to be with me," Mr. Nakanishi said.

"Don't be so sure. We have a long way to go. We still have to do a semen test on you."

Sadaharu outlined the technique to Mr. Nakanishi, whose face showed his confusion. After four or five days of abstinence, he was to masturbate and bring in a semen sample in a specimen bottle. The test result would not be conclusive if the specimen was collected by a condom.

"Are you returning to Tokyo today?" Sadaharu asked, terminating this initial examination as soon as he could. No matter who they are, infertile patients are uneasy at revealing the details of their sexual lives at their first visit.

When they began to feel that child-making had became an ordinary daily procedure, just like carpentry or sewing, people would be able to discuss the most personal parts of their lives easily with Sadaharu. He would have to wait patiently for that change.

"We spend half of our days in Tokyo and half at the shore. I do some amateur painting, and my wife spends time with friends who work in ceramics."

Sadaharu said, "That's nice. I once was interested in fishing, but I didn't do very well—actually, I didn't become much of an expert.

It just feels so good to carry a fishing pole, you know what I mean?"

"Do you do any sailing?"

"None at all. I can't make a sailing date, in case an emergency patient turns up. If I got a call for an emergency delivery while I was on a boat, how would I be able to get back?"

"Well, I hope you will visit us."

Sadaharu thanked him.

"Now we have some hope of having a child. If we do, we will have to name it after you, won't we, Eiko?"

Mrs. Nakanishi smiled and said they would, her eyes disappearing beneath her arched brows.

After the Nakanishis left, Sadaharu telephoned Yoko during his afternoon break to report that he had begun the examination, so that she'd thank him. The truth was, though, that he did not feel she owed him any gratitude; rather, he felt like thanking her for the introduction to his new patients.

"Yes, and I had a call from them just an hour ago to thank me. They are very happy with the first tests and they feel you really helped them."

"I didn't guarantee them anything, really," Sadaharu said.

"Don't worry about that. Eiko is a rather intense person, you know, and once when she heard about a woman who stole a baby from a hospital nursery she called me to say what a pity it was that the woman was arrested by the police and so forth."

"She said that!"

Yoko replied, "Sadaharu, can you believe it? She was completely in sympathy with the kidnapper and only thought she should have carried out the abduction better."

"Yes, I get your point," Sadaharu said.

"And that's not all. She was riding on the Tokyo—Yokohama express train one day and there was a young mother sitting just in front of her holding her new baby. It was summer and the window was open in the train. Well, Eiko said she wouldn't mind if the baby was just sucked out the window, she was that overcome with jealousy."

Sadaharu said, "So it would seem. Still, no harm done." He was not at all upset. Sadaharu thought that only a person who has thought about killing someone can know the real meaning of giving life.

On Friday afternoon the weather changed for the worse, clouds sailed in low, and, just as he feared, one after another three women came to the clinic to give birth. In recent years women have been admitted to hospitals about the time they were scheduled to give birth, and even for a first child, the popular technique is to induce birth at about nine o'clock in the morning, and have the baby born at around 8 or 9 o'clock in the evening. It had been observed that this was convenient for hospital administration in determining how many nurses should be kept on for night duty or for insuring that the doctor does not have to get up during the night. Sadaharu did not regard this practice as being either good or bad, since not all labor could wait for a natural beginning. There are times when the baby's head does not come down, even though it is two weeks past the expected delivery date. Furthermore, if there are clear signs of toxemia, then the child must be born as soon as possible.

In the human world, there are two aspects to birth: controlled, scheduled procedures and births that hardly seem to have diverged from those of primitive wild animals. With a change of weather, for instance, births may suddenly follow one another regardless of when the babies are due; women who still have two weeks to go until their due date as well as women who are ten days overdue come into the clinic at the same time.

As it happened, the three births were all quite normal. Only in medical school had Sadaharu seen an example of dramatic hemorrhaging during a birth, and he had experienced nothing like that since. All three babies were girls. Sadaharu fervently wished he could have shown them to the old woman who believed that only boys were born at his clinic.

Chapter Four

Escape

Early the following week, a telegram from Mayumi informed Sadaharu of her imminent arrival, but he was not planning to meet her at Narita airport. She would land at one o'clock in the afternoon, she had said, but since her arrival was on a work day Sadaharu would not be able to get away.

Even groups of farmers from around the district frequently went on such trips these days, but Sadaharu himself had never been abroad.

And Mayumi might be waiting at the airport for Sadaharu to meet her. She understood perfectly well that he could not do that sort of thing, but she was the kind of woman who expected such treatment. Sadaharu did not go. Instead, at about four o'clock in the afternoon, Sadaharu found himself in his examination room confronting a serious-faced mother and her daughter. He spoke first to the mother.

"What seems to be the trouble?"

According to the information card, the patient seemed to be the thin younger woman, who was about twenty years of age, but since she looked so distressed, Sadaharu considered it best to address the mother.

"The trouble is that my daughter stopped having her period six months ago."

The mother was in her mid-forties. She was tastefully dressed in a dark brown pleated skirt, a silk blouse in brown, white, and purple, and a brown and black cardigan.

Sadaharu looked at the address on the card, and at the daughter's name, Chisa Asano.

"When was your last period?" he asked.

Her reply came in a faint voice, "July of last year."

"Are you a student?"

"Yes."

"Before it stopped, had your period ever been late, or did did it skip a few months?"

"Sometimes it changed."

"How much did it change?"

"It's been three or four days late. Sometimes it did not come at all for about two months."

"But in the past the delay hasn't gone on this long, has it?"

"No, it hasn't."

"Have you experienced any illness or discomfort, besides this?"

"I feel dizzy sometimes."

"I wonder if you might have low blood pressure," Sadaharu said.

The girl's health insurance was under her father's name, registered with a famous Tokyo trading company.

"We'll do a regular examination," Sadaharu said, "beginning with a urine test. After you are done, please come back in here."

When the problem was a missed period, Sadaharu knew that the first thing he had to suspect was pregnancy. And when mother came along, there was always trouble. A year earlier, a mother had started screaming at Sadaharu when he told her that her student-daughter was pregnant. "Nothing of the sort could happen to my child!" she insisted. Finally, the girl had the somewhat delicate operation of an abortion in mid-term, but Sadaharu had to show the mother the five-month-old fetus before she would acknowledge the pregnancy.

"And even then," Sadaharu had complained to his occasional relief physician, Dr. Hiroshige, "she looked at me as though I might have brought in the fetus from somewhere else just to shock her."

"There are times," Hiroshige had advised, "when you should make the mothers come in and witness the operation themselves. There's no other way."

Mother and daughter left the examination room, and Sadaharu called in the next patient. The office was crowded; he was trying to deal with the patients quickly. Without looking up at the face of the patient seated before him, Sadaharu verified that her surname was Yamamoto.

"I had a slight discharge," the woman began, "so I had an examination and the doctor said it might be cancer, so . . ."

Sadaharu looked up. Before him was Hiromi Yamamoto, age twenty-nine, two children, wearing a black skirt and dark green and red sweater.

"When was that?"

"About two months ago."

"Who examined you?"

Sadaharu disliked asking that question, to say the least. When a doctor gives such a diagnosis, it should be correct. But Sadaharu did indeed have some interest in learning the name of the physician in this case. We like to know about people who are more talented than ourselves, but there is also some satisfaction in knowing about people who are our inferiors. It gives a bit of confidence, perhaps, but there may not be really so great a difference between the two feelings, or not as much as the people involved might think.

"It was Dr. Sono," she replied.

Sadaharu was not surprised to find himself thinking that the man had done it again. Ryosuke Sono was much older than Sadaharu, and in this district he enjoyed considerable popularity as a doctor. Admired blindly, he was enormously arrogant. He was known as a martinet, yet when it came to dealing with patients introduced to him by cabinet officials, the governor, or members of parliament, the rumor was he would personally see them to the entrance of his clinic and bow them into their cars.

All such stories aside, when one went to his clinic, one saw displayed along the hallway from the waiting room photographs of the head of the Sono Clinic: seated with a cabinet minister on a sofa; yachting with a famous actress, jauntily wearing his captain's hat; playing Go with a renowned Go master at an inn in Hakone; having his palm read by a prominent fencing master–author; out drinking at a bar with an orchestra conductor who also appeared in commercial advertisements; and apparently learning a dance, with his rear thrust out beyond his suit jacket, posturing next to a beautiful female dancer of folk ballads whom Sadaharu himself greatly admired, albeit in secret.

"Patients come all the way from India to have cancer treated by Dr. Sono," someone had told him, "and there was a letter of thanks hung there in the corridor. Indian is certainly written in funny letters!"

Sadaharu had felt like saying that he wouldn't really know whether it was a thank you letter or not; it might be a complaint about something. He questioned Mrs. Yamamoto further.

"Did Dr. Sono tell you that it was cancer, exactly?"

"Well, he said that he would have a look again after a month, and if it got any worse he would operate."

"I see. Then at least we should have a look," he told her.

The patient prepared, Sadaharu went to the examination table. The condition was about what he expected. There was a blood red inflammation plainly visible in the cervix and uterus, and of course it would be necessary for him to take a tissue specimen for examination, but Sadaharu thought the diagnosis would be what is called follicular erosion. This was an extremely common condition, affecting up to fifty percent of women who had given birth, and was thought to be connected with an excess of the hormone estrogen. It also appeared in newborn children who had been exposed to placental estrogen and was especially widespread among pregnant women. Among postmenopausal women, the condition seldom existed.

Sadaharu removed a tiny specimen of the inflamed tissue with excision forceps, placed it in a saline solution, and told the patient that he was finished.

The cervix is less sensitive to pain than other parts of the body. It is possible to fasten sharp clamp forceps to part of the organ and pull hard enough to tear a bit away without the patient showing any reaction. Whether through God's design or through nature, this construction of the human body was precisely functional, since if the area were normally sensitive women could hardly survive childbirth.

Sadaharu returned to his desk, waited an appropriate interval, and called the patient.

"We'll do the tests immediately, and while I can't say for certain until I see the results, in all likelihood you do not have cancer. That's what I think."

"Oh, do you really think so?" she said. Sadaharu saw the expression of relief on her face.

"We should know within a week with this simple test, and then three days later we'll have the results of the other test."

"Then should I come back in ten days for your diagnosis?"

"Yes, that would be fine," he said, but he was disappointed by her less than enthusiastic response.

Nonetheless, after sending Hiromi Yamamoto home, Sadaharu remained in a pensive, unhappy mood. He had no wish to view a colleague in a bad light, but he had also been forced to see the kind of work Ryosuke Sono was doing. Cervical cancer often develops in the same area as cervical or vaginal inflammation. But for cancer, there must be abnormal cell growth. Cervical cancer is usually described as originating in the reserve cells of the outer surface of the cervix, or as abnormal growth in the basal cells. The change is known as a dysplasia and it can be mild or moderate, in which abnormal cells occupy less than half the thickness of the outer surface, or severe, in which the growth extends through half the surface or more. However, the difference is not always that clear cut.

Such ambiguities leave an opening for a doctor like Sono to make a diagnosis of something like "precancerous abnormality." If one supposes the condition will turn into cancer, then it will first begin on the surface, later developing into a deeper growth. No matter how one views the condition, it is possible to say "There is danger of cancer, you should have an operation," and no one can accuse one of lying. Cancer of the outer layer is defined as "a condition confined in its spread over the surface with strong appearances that are difficult to distinguish from cancer." But it has been well established that many years pass before cancer of the outer layer turns into invasive cancer, with ample time for warning signs during that interval.

Changes in the outer layer of the cervix can of course disappear without turning into cancer. Still, it is possible to argue that it is better to remove the tissue before it becomes invasive cancer. Even if no cancer is visible, there is some danger of cancer in such eroding tissue. Would it be too much to say this? Or would it be a kind of fraud?

The fact remained that people in the district considered Dr. Sono quite skilled at treating cancer of the uterus. People said things like, "Dr. Sono is a marvel at finding cancer. He found it in my wife's aunt, but they got it before it spread and she was completely cured."

To put the case plainly, if Dr. Sono operated for something, he called it cancer, even though it could not possibly really be cancer. In that way, he first of all received his fee for the operation, and, from the patient's point of view, the operation was a great success. If one gets Dr. Sono to perform the operation, chances are the cancer will not appear again. Naturally, he was famous in the district, a kind of god to his patients.

But even if Dr. Sono was the way he was, there was no practical way to denounce someone like him. Patients could never recall the exact words he had used so there was no proof of what was actually said. If a patient said, "The doctor said it was cancer," all the physician had to say in his own defense was, "No, I said nothing of the sort. I only said that there was danger of it becoming cancer." And that would be the end of it.

Meanwhile, Head Nurse Ono did the urine pregnancy test for Chisa Asano. She siphoned the liquid from the paper cup, strained it, and placed two drops on a glass slide. The test chemicals came in two vials in a kit and were added to the urine, first the red, then the white liquid, like ink eradicator. The mixture was stirred with a toothpick. If milky globules appeared, the result was positive.

When Chisa Asano and her mother returned to the examination room, Nurse Ono told Sadaharu that Chisa's test was negative.

It was no different from what he had expected, but if he had just said, "No, she does not seem to be pregnant," the mother would be certain to complain to him. And no matter how often he said, "I told you so" trying to defend himself, the message never got across.

"Have you been ill recently?" Sadaharu asked.

"No, not at all."

Sadaharu detected an angry edge to her voice.

"Still, she started getting thin a year ago, and she hardly eats anything at all. We've all told her that if she goes on like that she will hurt herself . . . ," the mother said.

The girl spoke fiercely to her mother. "That has nothing to do with it, and there is nothing the matter with me."

"How much weight have you lost?" Sadaharu asked.

"About eighteen pounds."

"And that was over how many months?"

"About a month and a half, I suppose."

"And before that, how much did you weigh?"

"One hundred and six pounds."

"So you are down to eighty-eight. How tall are you?"

"Five feet three inches."

"And right now are you still at eighty-eight pounds?"

"No. About eighty-five."

Sadaharu thought for a moment. "Do you know why you've lost weight? At your height, one hundred and six pounds is not at all fat."

The mother broke in. "I told her exactly the same thing, but she says she just does not want to eat."

"Do you really not want to eat, or is it that you want to lose weight?" Sadaharu continued.

"I just don't want to eat."

"That's not true," the mother countered. "You said that being fat is ugly, didn't you?"

The girl looked tense and made no reply. Sadaharu thought that Chisa's mother was quite right, even though most mothers supposed they understood their own children better than anyone else in the world, while they really understood nothing at all.

He spoke to Chisa: "At the moment, you are in good health even though you're thin, so there is no great concern. However, as your mother said, there can be serious consequences to this. It is only a general rule, but menstruation usually ceases when a woman loses ten percent of her body weight in one month." Chisa lowered her eyes. "This is not just in your case, you understand. These days, girls want to look stylish, and they try to become unreasonably thin. The result is that their menstruation stops completely. Now, if that were just temporary, it would be all right, but for some people it does not return without special treatment." Sadaharu was presenting her with a vague threat. "Today I want you to start establishing your basic body temperature, and then we'll do a blood test. I think the origin may be psychological—anorexia nervosa, as it is called."

The hypothalamus is affected by the environment and the nervous system in addition to physical factors, and this can result in loss of the hormone secreting function. Sadaharu explained these functions to Chisa. If there was insufficient secretion of gonadotropin as seen from the urine and blood tests, then along with medication it might also be appropriate to consult a psychologist. They might understand the consequences of her thinness, but the real problem was why she had gotten that way.

Observing mother and daughter, Sadaharu saw that the mother had pleasantly ample flesh by comparison, and in spite of the mother being older, Sadaharu felt she was the more attractive of the two.

He took a call in the examination room from Motoko Inoue, his housekeeper. She announced that his wife had returned. The time was just past five o'clock in the afternoon. The plane had been due at about one o'clock, and it seemed to Sadaharu that she had arrived early. He thanked the housekeeper.

Sadaharu returned to his patients. There were many women waiting, and he had not even noticed the sound of the car coming to the house because of the crowd. Kaori probably had come back from school, and so he thought it wouldn't be a problem if he did not go to greet his wife immediately.

It was past six o'clock when he finished with the last patient and returned to his house. He was told that Mayumi was upstairs in the bedroom, and Sadaharu climbed the stairs, slippers flopping on his feet.

"Welcome home!" he called.

He stepped over the open suitcase and sat down on a sofa near the window. Still dressed in her tweed suit while hanging her things in the closet, Mayumi turned to him and greeted him with only a laugh.

"You're early too. Did you take a cab all the way from Narita?" Sadaharu asked. It was incredibly expensive.

"That's right."

"Did you have a good time in Hawaii?"

"Actually, I came back by way of Los Angeles, nonstop from LA to Narita."

"Oh. I had the impression you were stopping in Hawaii again, after leaving Los Angeles."

Sadaharu, never having been abroad, knew less about air travel than the farmers in the neighborhood.

"Why do you think I went all the way to Los Angeles?" Mayumi asked him.

"I suppose the signs told you it was a favorable direction," Sadaharu replied.

"Yes, that too. But I met someone in Hawaii who asked me to go on to Los Angeles."

"Yes, I see. Well, that was nice, wasn't it?"

"Aren't you suspicious that I was seduced by someone?"

"Even if I objected, I doubt that would stop you."

Sadaharu was not trying to be sarcastic.

Mayumi said, "You're just not interested in anything I do, are you?"

"Because I didn't come to meet you at Narita? I can't stop working whenever I feel like it, you know. I have to be here for the patients' convenience."

"I'm not talking about that in particular. As far as you're concerned, I suppose you prefer it when I'm not here."

"No, not at all," Sadaharu said, but he also recognized that to a degree his wife's observation was true.

"Well. The trip was quite pleasant, nonetheless."

Sadaharu felt that at any cost he wanted to avoid confrontation with his wife.

"Yes, indeed," she continued. "And the reason was that everyone there needed me, and that's the truth."

"Oh, I need you too. And Kaori was waiting for you to return."

"Really? I suppose that's why she hasn't come home from school yet."

"That is a bit strange. She knew when you were coming home. I guess she's just wasting time on her way home from school, as usual."

Unlike the other girls in the district, Kaori was not forced to take piano lessons or some special training like traditional dancing. Although she knew her mother was coming home, if she had been tempted by some interesting diversion along the way, she might forget about her supper and dally until after sunset, as she had often done in the past.

"If I'd imagined it made so little difference whether I was here or not, I wouldn't have bothered to come back!"

Sadaharu knew how this script went. He had no idea of what to say in the face of this kind of attitude.

"You know, when you're not here we are really quite busy. The door to the storeroom wouldn't open any more, so we had Ohashi the carpenter come over. And then the pump broke down. They said it would cost so much to repair it, we had it replaced instead. But the man at Sagami Industrial is sneaky, and I wouldn't be surprised if he said that just to sell us a new pump."

As he was speaking, Sadaharu had the feeling he was offending his wife, and he realized that soon she would accuse him of wanting her around as a housekeeper or a manager.

"Kaori will be taking examinations at school before long," Mayumi said. "Even so, isn't this late for her to be coming home?"

"Hmm, I haven't heard anything about her test schedule from her yet. I think the tests start around the end of February, at the earliest."

"And since that's the case she's just been relaxing and playing all the time." After a pause, she went on, "I considered not coming back at all this time."

"What? You mean the signs told you to stay in the United States all year?"

"Not exactly. Away from this house there's someone who really needs me, that's all."

"Don't you think we need you here? I know that Kaori needs a mother very much, no matter what."

"I don't mean that."

When Mayumi went on a trip, she always had some romantic fling. Very likely, the man involved would find it amusing that he'd ensnared another man's respectable wife, but Mayumi always took it too seriously. She would think that the man needed her, and so she believed there was no reason for her to return home.

"You know," Sadaharu said, "that kind of talk about being needed or not being needed sounds like something from some modern foreign novel. There never even used to be that kind of expression in the Japanese language. What I mean is that in the old days, the mother was an important person in any household. And I think it is still the same with us."

He did not say this merely to put Mayumi off, but as soon as he finished speaking she fell silent, as though she had forgotten whatever reply she had prepared.

"Aren't you hungry?" Sadaharu asked.

"Yes, I am. I planned not to eat too much today, because I thought we might all have dinner together as a family. I brought some steak from Los Angeles."

"Oh? Is meat really so inexpensive over there?"

"It's not only cheap, it's good too. Marbled meat is fine for sukiyaki, I suppose, but for steak it's not firm enough."

"Thanks. I'm really grateful. Mrs. Inoue's cooking isn't bad, but it just never occurs to us to have anything but fish and vegetables. I don't think we had steak once while you were away."

Sadaharu had no intention of stretching the truth to accommodate his wife; he was in a good mood. Still, his concerned friends worried about his attitude toward his wife and felt that he shouldn't humor her so much. But even from the beginning of his relationship with Mayumi, Sadaharu never felt he had to pretend to outsiders about his life with her. He had long ago decided to treat the world with equal parts of sincerity and insincerity. And toward his own wife he had adopted the same attitude, no more and no less. In human relations, he seemed to feel that nothing more was expected, because real sincerity was not likely to satisfy other people. Some of his relatives were critical of this attitude, as they understood it, while others felt upset with Mayumi. Sadaharu himself made no particular point of the matter and felt it was no one else's business to interfere. Yoko Kakei saw the situation clearly and said nothing about how Sadaharu's wife conducted her life.

Kaori returned a little before seven o'clock. With a laugh she said, "I haven't seen mother in a long time!"

"And mother brought some steak from America. We'll have it for supper this evening," Mayumi said.

"I don't want any. I don't like meat much," Kaori replied.

Listening to this dialogue between mother and daughter, Sadaharu recalled this peculiar quality in Mayumi: how little she tried to understand her own daughter's preference in food.

"But this is steak. You certainly must want some."

"No, I don't want any. Isn't there some dried fish?"

"What a selfish child! And after mother brought this especially for you."

"Oh, mother, don't you understand? If you'd asked me what I wanted, I would have told you I prefer fish!"

The tone of the conversation had become quite unpleasant, reaching the point where Mayumi was accustomed to begin crying and complaining, "No one needs me in this house."

Sadaharu grew distressed listening to the conversation; the two females were at the same psychological level.

It was not so much that Kaori disliked steak, but that she preferred fish. And this was something her mother knew. In spite of the obvious, Mayumi stuck to the idea that any child must be fond of meat. When Kaori became a bit older and developed adult tastes, she would be able to pretend to like steak, even though she had no particular desire for it. It was Mayumi's nature to remain frozen in one psychological set, and so if she ever cooked something and a person praised it, she would continue with the same thing until the other person had to hint that the compliment was really mostly politeness.

Every time Sadaharu heard the word "sincerity" he associated it with this quality in his wife. He thought also how it was not really difficult to learn to enjoy something one at first did not like to eat, if that was what it took to please someone else. This was what Sadaharu wished for his daughter, in spite of Mayumi: that she should grow up to have the subtlety of mind and patience of heart this embodied.

"If father and I could share the steak, it would be easier to cook it all at once."

Mayumi said this with a childish kind of pout, and she began to fry two steaks on top of a thick iron griddle. The telephone rang just as she brought the meat to the table. It was Nurse Ono.

"A patient has come in with an emergency, doctor."

"What are the symptoms?"

"It seems that she was just passing through the neighborhood, and about thirty minutes ago she began bleeding and having abdominal pain. She arrived here about two minutes ago."

The tension in Nurse Ono's voice conveyed more than her words.

"I see. I'll be there in a moment," Sadaharu said.

He replaced the phone, slipped into a white tunic, and said to Mayumi, "I'll just see what this is all about."

In a conscious move that he often used, Sadaharu spoke without looking at the other person's face, never having to notice their expression.

The receptionist already had gone home, and the activity in the round reception room had subsided. In the examination room, a middle-aged woman sat uneasily on the bed. Nurse Ono seemed to have dismissed the younger nurses by this time and herself had already changed into street clothes.

"I came here to visit a relative this afternoon," the woman said, "and after staying for about two hours my belly began to hurt. Just before that, I went to the toilet and noticed some blood, so I thought I should go home as soon as possible. I tried to walk to the bus stop then, but I felt queasy. Then I saw the sign outside your clinic, and so . . . I'm sorry to put you to all this trouble."

Sadaharu asked her to undress and to lie down. Nurse Ono pulled the curtain hanging from the ceiling around the bed, and while the patient was disrobing, Sadaharu asked her name and address, writing the information on the examination card. From inside the curtains, she said her name was Yoshie Ninomiya, that she lived in Kurihama, that she was forty-three years of age.

Sadaharu began his examination by asking her in a conversational tone, "Mrs. Ninomiya, is your abdomen always this large?"

"Yes, I'm usually this heavy, that's true. My stomach has gotten big, and they say I should lose weight, but I love to eat, you know. Since I've gotten heavy, my period has gone crazy, really."

"Your period is irregular?"

"Yes, for a long time. Maybe I've started menopause; I haven't had a period for a long time."

"When was the last time? Since it stopped . . ."

"Since last year . . . about a year, I guess."

"Mrs. Ninomiya, are you married?"

"My husband died nearly ten years ago. Our daughter is a freshman in senior high school."

"And you say your abdomen has started to hurt?" At that moment, he felt the uterus contract.

"Yes, a little."

"Mrs. Ninomiya, you say you have a daughter already, so I'm a little surprised you haven't noticed the changes in your body." She looked concerned, but she made no reply.

"You don't just have a pain in your stomach," Sadaharu said. "I think that you've started to go into labor."

He felt the area of the uterus with his hand. Afterward, he would have to write up a report, surely, so he quickly measured the width of her belly and the uterine fundus.

He moved the patient to the internal examination room and found that the cervix opening was already large enough to accommodate three fingers. Through the chorion membrane he could feel the baby's head.

"Well, Mrs. Ninomiya, if this goes along on schedule, you will give birth in two or three hours."

From the other side of the curtain, there was only silence.

"Mrs. Ninomiya, do you hear me?"

"Yes."

"All right. You can get up now."

Nurse Ono helped her to get down from the examination table. More than simply assisting a pregnant woman in her awkward movements, Nurse Ono tried to support her spirit, as Ninomiya seemed to have lost her sense of self through the suddenness of the sentence Sadaharu had handed her. She dressed herself, and, with an empty expression on her face, sat in the chair before Sadaharu.

"You didn't know you were pregnant until now?"

"No. I'm so surprised."

"If the irregularities in your period had a long history, then that would be no indication, but the child must have moved inside you."

"I'm usually constipated," Ninomiya said."I imagined it was just my intestines moving."

"Well, that's difficult to believe from a person who has already had one child, but you are in good condition, and the position of the baby is fine. It will be born in just a little while."

"I'm so surprised. . . ," Ninomiya said.

"So am I," Sadaharu answered.

Years ago, when he was in medical school, he had learned in gynecology class that the first assumption on seeing a patient was that she was pregnant. Sadaharu thought this patient was a classic example of that rule. In those days before the simple urine test that produced results in a minute, it was a complicated matter involving the use of a male toad, or a domestic rabbit, to determine pregnancy. After graduating from medical school, Sadaharu's first job was to raise thirty or so toads just for the purpose of injecting them with the urine of women being tested for pregnancy. Then one had to wait a couple of hours to examine the toad's urine to complete the test. Sadaharu's colleagues used to call it "watching for frog pee." The test itself was a nuisance; there were other cases, however, of physicians misdiagnosing an enlarged uterus and trying to operate on a pregnant woman to remove a fibroid tumor.

Perhaps in the case of some women it was because of their apparent youthful innocence; for others like Yoshie Ninomiya perhaps it was because of the possibility they had been through menopause. Cessation of menstruation seldom gives rise to the idea of pregnancy. Yet although usually no egg is discharged with the irregular menses that occur during the onset of menopause, occasional ovulation may occur, and that might possibly lead to pregnancy.

"I don't think you will have time to return home," Sadaharu said rather vaguely. "Is anyone there besides your daughter?"

"No, no one else."

"Since you didn't anticipate being pregnant, I suppose you've made no preparations for a baby."

"That's so. Even if I go home, there is nothing ready." Ninomiya's mind seemed to be elsewhere.

"Then after you return home there will be time enough to take care of the baby's things. While you are here in the clinic, we will supply clothing. And we can have your personal things brought here by your daughter, later on. After all, Kurihama is not all that far away."

Sadaharu spoke as casually as he could, but he felt the matter was not really as simple as all that. It was his nature to try to put as good a face on things as possible, insofar as he was able. And if he did not dwell on matters too much, he found he could generally settle complicated situations easily enough. If he could, he preferred to treat such situations lightly.

"I can't phone her," she murmured.

"But you need to get in touch with her, don't you? If you're used to staying out late without telling your daughter in advance, that's all right, but otherwise you should call her. She might worry that you had an accident or were kidnapped, and call the police," Sadaharu said.

"I can never tell her that I've had a baby."

"I'm not one for getting involved in other people's lives," he told Ninomiya. "But wouldn't the father of the child offer some help at a time like this?"

"He's not here," she replied.

Sadaharu wanted to say, "He must be somewhere, dear. This is not the Immaculate Conception." He controlled the urge. "Is he dead?"

"I don't know where he is. He's just someone who stayed a few days on business at the dormitory where I worked. And then he left."

"Yes, well, that's all right. The matter of who the father is is not really important, anyway. But you should at least telephone your daughter. She will be worried. After that, the nurse will show you to a room upstairs and provide you with a nightgown and other things."

As Sadaharu started back to his residence, he heard the voice of Nurse Ono saying, "Mrs. Ninomiya, shall we go?"

How fortunate it was that Nurse Ono had remained. He thought that since Shigeko Okubo, his other head nurse, was coming in for night duty later, no matter how the delivery went, some assistance would be available.

He went into his dining room where Kaori was watching television; Mayumi was seated alone at the table.

"A woman came in for delivery," he said, but other than that Sadaharu did not feel like offering further explanation to Mayumi.

"And the steak I bought especially for you has gotten cold," she complained.

"Yes. Just heat it up again. I like it well done."

"You used to like it raw."

"Hmm, but nowadays I like it well done," he said.

He was talking at random. Patching up his relationship with Mayumi was one thing, but when it came to how he liked his steak cooked, he did not care if he seemed to change his mind every day.

"You know, our kitchen is just terrible," Mayumi said.

"I suppose it is. But, Mayumi, do you think we are especially poor?" he asked.

"Of course not. But we still ought to be able to eat together as a family."

"Sometimes we eat meals together."

"It's just that abroad, even among ordinary people, they take pleasure in a meal."

"I wonder. Certainly Americans are not always like that. They eat sandwiches on the run sometimes, don't they?"

"I'm just saying, it's terrible you're so busy. No matter what you say, the truth is that you like your work better than you like us."

Here it comes, Sadaharu thought. In spite of her foolishness about so many things, she seemed to be able to see through people. He laughed.

"I suppose that's true, but it's hard to believe."

Really, though, that was no more than a bold lie on Sadaharu's part. Were his wife just a little more mature psychologically, Sadaharu might have calmly said, "Most people like their jobs better than their homes."

He had been coming to the inescapable conclusion that while people might protest about how disagreeable their jobs were, in fact they did not really mind doing things they said they considered distasteful. That is, for something so contrary to their liking, they could still put up with it. And so men liked their work.

"We just had a call from Mrs. Kakei. It seems she is going to

Brazil with some friends."

"When is that?"

"I didn't ask."

Sadaharu just finished eating the warmed over steak when the telephone rang again. It was Nurse Okubo.

"Doctor, Mrs. Ninomiya, the patient we just admitted—I put her in the birthing room, but she says that she really wants to talk with you."

The nurse spoke in an urgent voice.

"Has her water broken yet?"

"Not yet."

"I'll come right over."

As he walked the few meters to the clinic, he tasted the smell of the night sea air before going inside. As he entered the delivery room, two ward nurses were preparing instruments and garb for the baby.

"Well, Mrs. Ninomiya, it happened quite quickly." Sadaharu spoke to her as she lay on the delivery table, her eyes averted, as he put on his rubber gown and washed his hands.

"Doctor, there is something I'd like to ask."

"What's that?"

"When the nurses are out of the room . . . please." Sadaharu considered this a moment, then asked the nurses to leave. As a rule, doctors in obstetrics-gynecology never create a situation for themselves to be alone with a patient, but under the circumstances, feeling the urgent weight in Ninomiya's tone, Sadaharu overlooked the rule.

"You said that I might call home, so I called just a while ago on the public phone to my daughter."

"That's fine. I'm sure she's relieved."

"But that's not it. You see, I just couldn't say where I am. I told her I'd be home in the morning, that I couldn't make it home today." Tears flowed from Ninomiya's eyes. "My daughter is taking her examinations now, so she was angry with me because I couldn't get home. I told her to cook something herself and that in the morning she would have to fix her own lunch."

"Since she's a senior high student, I don't think you need worry about her." As far as possible, Sadaharu spoke as though he was talking of everyday things.

"But still she was suspicious. She was going to call a relative, and I told her if she did I was probably going to kill myself."

Sadaharu said, "But even so, somehow she will understand. If you call your daughter, I'll talk with her myself."

"Doctor, I have to ask this. When the baby is born, could you please kill it? You're a doctor; you can do it with just an injection. . . ."

In the old days, one could put a wet piece of paper over the mouth of the newborn child, or hold it upside down in the bathtub. Or so the stories went. Only the midwife would know, so it would be all right. Or in a house where there was no midwife, the pregnant woman's sister or mother could do it.

"Mrs. Ninomiya," Sadaharu said, "I can't do that. If I did, think what would happen; I'd be taken by the police."

The woman was silent.

"The present law lets us terminate a pregnancy up to the end of the sixth month. It used to be allowed right up to the end of the seventh month. The sixth month itself is unreasonably late, but in the case of a seven-month term baby, some of them cry weakly. You see, in the past I used to do such abortions, but if the child was born alive, we'd try to help. That's our obligation in doing an abortion. You know about the incubator, I suppose. We keep it warmed up for that."

Ninomiya made no response.

"Excuse me for saying this, but when you have the child, can't you take care of it? If you are a dormitory matron you can explain to the company and get help, and . . ."

"About six months ago, I became manager of the food section in a store."

"And what about today?"

"The market is redecorating for a couple of weeks. I'm on vacation."

"Can't you raise the child somehow? Take the child to the market. You could put it somewhere, in a corner. You could take care of it that way."

"No, I couldn't do that."

Sadaharu was silent.

"Everyone would talk about me, my reputation . . ."

"Then you should put the child up for adoption. There are lots of people these days who want children. There are ten parents waiting for every available child!"

"Are there people right here at your clinic who want a child, doctor?"

"I haven't particularly made a list, but I'll look around for you."

"Then can I leave the child here with you? I'll pretend I didn't give birth and someone else can pretend to have had the child, and she could take it over, couldn't she?"

"No, a doctor in a northern district tried that. They said it was a violation of the law and dealt severely with him." Sadaharu was still seeking some way to calm the woman. "I think you're distressed about the child because you don't have a husband, isn't that it? Well, times have changed. Young unwed mothers raise their children with dignity, so a grown-up like you who has a child by someone she likes shouldn't have any trouble."

"But that's not it at all," Ninomiya said. "If people know that I've had a baby, they will treat us with contempt. And even if I have the baby quietly adopted, it would still be put on our family register—what a disgrace!"

"All right, then. After the baby is born, we'll talk this over carefully," Sadaharu said.

During labor there are moments when the pain subsides, and these intervals of relief are called "when the gods take over." But during those intervals, Ninomiya probably got no rest at all, with thoughts floating through her mind about how she would manage her unforeseen disaster.

"Stay right with it, now. You told your daughter you would be home tomorrow, so you have to stick with it."

"Go home tomorrow? So soon?" The young ward nurse, knowing nothing of the situation, reacted with surprise.

"That's what she intends to do. I haven't actually given permission yet for her to leave the hospital tomorrow, of course. But people like farm wives with lots of children give birth at home, and the next day they are up and working and they are quite all right."

Even as pregnant as she was, Ninomiya probably had been away from home late at night in the past. Very likely, she'd told her daughter something to the effect that she would be away just for this one night, using the kind of excuse she had in the past. She would put on an innocent face, give birth, and try to return home alone tomorrow.

She might well be criticized for her selfishness. But from the viewpoint of a country doctor like Sadaharu, there were so many things that needed to be put in order before preaching to her; and before anything else, including what the mother would do with the child, it was necessary that the baby be brought into this world.

Giving birth also has psychological factors. If a relationship of trust is established between the pregnant woman and her doctor, then except in the case of some severe physical problem, the baby will be born easily, whether by God's design or something else. As a general rule, Sadaharu did not ordinarily use laughing gas as an anesthetic during birth, or an episiotomy to hasten delivery. His skill was evident in the fact that most babies were born at his clinic without any complications. Nurse Okubo had worked with Sadaharu for a long time, and Sadaharu felt that she was quite satisfied with his approach. She was an old-fashioned nurse with the skill to assist at a birth without causing any perineal tears on the mother—a matter of professional pride. Generally, these days when the perineal tissue did tear it was because of careless treatment, including the tendency to use an episiotomy to speed up the birth, but because healing took so long, Sadaharu was reluctant to perform episiotomies even with drawn out deliveries.

Ninomiya was not mentally prepared to give birth, and so she was not an ordinary patient at the clinic. When her labor pains began, she did not listen to the nurse's directions; instead, she seemed to be trying to escape from the pain, twisting her body on top of the delivery table.

"Mrs. Ninomiya! The pain can't be helped. Do you want to sleep?"

She replied, "Yes. I want to sleep!"

If her pains became too severe, Sadaharu thought, he would put her under.

Laughing gas was not really an anesthetic. According to a physician who had come back from practicing in the United States, what causes a woman giving birth to be in pain was the effacement of the cervix rather than the actual moment of birth, so at that time the procedure used in the States was a saddle block anesthesia in the lumbar region. Anesthetics like laughing gas were merely palliatives, virtual placebos.

The degree of pain felt during childbirth was confirmation of the large psychological elements at work, and with this woman, for whom giving birth could only be considered as an unleashing of a flood of disasters, there was a considerable chance of her feeling strong pain, much more than for a mother who wanted her child.

However, after the third round of contractions, the baby was born smoothly, covered with a glistening yellow substance. The time was five minutes before nine.

"Mrs. Ninomiya! It's a boy. You have to take good care of him. And you can rest now."

Sadaharu spoke casually, familiarly. He knew it would be best to find some positive meaning, anything at all, in Ninomiya's raising the child. Nonetheless, her eyes remained shut; she neither looked at the baby nor thanked Sadaharu or the nurses.

The nurses were busy with such tasks as rubbing the baby with oil, cleaning the delivery room, recording the weight of the placenta, and transporting the new mother to her room, but Sadaharu did not wait for any of this to get done.

"Nurse Okubo," he said, "when you're done, would you mind coming over to my house?" Then he left for his residence.

Happily, his wife and daughter were chatting in the dining room. Sadaharu called to Mayumi, "When Nurse Okubo comes, I'll be in the study," and withdrew to his place of refuge. When his wife was away on a trip, Sadaharu rarely went in there. He read books in his bedroom. But when Mayumi returned, he felt that his study was the only place his soul could be at peace. It was not that Sadaharu hated his wife, but somehow he needed somewhere he could be alone.

Of course, there was a desk in the study, but he also placed there a most expensive reclining chair. Guests were seated in cheaper chairs, while he himself sat in that most expensive chair. For Sadaharu, sitting in this chair was a symbolic act.

Nurse Okubo arrived some thirty minutes after Sadaharu.

"Welcome home, madam," Okubo called in greeting to Mayumi, and Mayumi in return said, "Oh, Nurse Okubo, I have a present for you. Now please don't tell the other girls, all right? I didn't get anything for them."

Sadaharu overheard this. There were thirteen employees at the clinic, at most, and since almost any trivial present would have sufficed—even thirteen of the exact same thing would have been all right—Mayumi's concern struck him as being somewhat childish. But he did not wish to find fault.

As she entered the study, Okubo said by way of greeting, "I received a gift from madam."

"Oh, that's nice," Sadaharu said, smiling only with his eyes. "Please sit down. The woman who just gave birth—is she resting comfortably?"

"Yes. There is no bleeding. I don't know whether she is sleeping or not, but she is quiet, with her eyes closed."

"Did you hear about her situation from Nurse Ono?"

"Yes, a little."

"You know, she wasn't aware that she was going to have a child until just a short while ago. I don't know to what extent, but she is clearly frightened."

Nurse Okubo acknowledged this.

"And so there seem to be two possibilities. One is that she will say nothing and return home," Sadaharu said, while his nurse listened in silence. "When she gave us her address, she was not aware of her pregnancy, so at least there isn't much concern about that. It's just . . . well, would you keep the door to the nursery room tightly locked for a few days? Even during night duty. The nurses may doze accidentally, so tell them to be certain that the door is securely locked.

"It's probably just my imagination, but Mrs. Ninomiya just might make off with the child. No, that in itself would not be a problem, but if she grabbed a child that was not her own, then there would be hell to pay."

In fact, Sadaharu felt like adding, to be quite clear about it, "If she were to grab the wrong child and kill it, then I'd really be in a mess."

Sadaharu spoke. "You know, she has a teen-age daughter. She didn't want to tell her directly that her mother was about to give birth. She was terribly worried about that. Please keep that in mind."

"Hmm, I heard as much from Nurse Ono, and the patient is currently working at a supermarket near her house. She knows her by sight."

In most cases, though, no problems result from such circumstances. So, when next morning Ninomiya seemed in fine shape, Sadaharu decided to put his mind at ease about the rest of the situation. The phrase "at ease" was one that he liked.

Because Mayumi had returned, that night Yoko Kakei came to the house to visit, and even when she talked about a subject related to Ninomiya, Sadaharu was unaware at first, for he did not put the two sets of circumstances together.

"Do you ever arrange for adoptions through your clinic, Sadaharu?"

"I'm a gynecologist, remember? I haven't gotten into that line of work."

Someone unfriendly to Sadaharu might easily have misunderstood his flippant tone.

"What's this about? Are you finally going to adopt a child?"

"No, no. A couple who were friends of my late husband are coming to Japan in April or May, and they say they'd like to adopt a Japanese child. They sent a letter asking if I would introduce them to someone."

"Really? Very kind of them indeed."

"You seem to have some reservations."

"Perhaps I do, yes. I'm forty years old, you know. I just can't swallow lovely stories any more."

"This couple—their name is Laurie—have already adopted an Italian child and a black child."

"What? Black, yellow—are they putting together a rainbow?"

Sadaharu was running on unthinkingly. He had gone beyond the relaxed stage and didn't care what he said.

"Ah, if only I believed in God! Yoko, your bringing up that matter just now . . . In fact, there is just such a child who probably was guided here by God himself."

"Oh? When was it born?"

"Yesterday. It's a boy, however."

"It makes no difference whether it's a boy or a girl."

"I could have a talk with her. The child's mother is a widow, you see."

"A widow and she has a child? That's marvelous, isn't it."

"Ah, Yoko, believe me! Even if you came here to my clinic to have a child, there would be no problem. Because I never, ever ask who the father is."

Yoko simply frowned at Sadaharu's bit of humor and did not encourage him.

"Did she say she wanted to put the child up for adoption?"

"Yes, I think she did. At any rate, she said she couldn't take care of it."

"It does seem like an act of God, doesn't it?"

"Just a coincidence, really," Sadaharu said, drawing toward him a squat bottle of whiskey.

A few minutes later, Sadaharu was again called to the phone by Nurse Ono, who was on night duty.

"Doctor, Mrs. Ninomiya says that she wants to leave the clinic immediately."

"Now? But it's almost ten o'clock at night!"

"Yes. She asked me to call her daughter, and I did. She got here a while ago, and they apparently talked for a while. Then she said she really had to go home."

"All right. I'll come right over," Sadaharu said, and with his face still red from the whiskey, he walked over to the clinic.

Mother and daughter were together in the room. Usually, there were two patients to a room, but circumstances being what they were, and because there were few patients then at the clinic, Sadaharu had instructed Nurse Okubo to put Ninomiya in a room by herself.

"How do you feel?" he asked.

"Oh, very well, thanks to you. I think I'd like to return home," she said with an ingratiating smile.

"Go home? Well, if you insist, there is nothing I can do about it. But what about the baby? It hasn't even lost its umbilical cord yet."

"I'd like to leave the baby with you, just for a while. If I take it home, people will talk," she said.

"Well, we can't do that. We aren't running a nursery," Sadaharu told her.

"But I can go home and talk with my relatives, and then, of

course, I'll come back to get the baby."

"You mean your mother, or who?"

"My mother is with my younger brother, but I'm not on good terms with him these days, and I don't see much of my mother, either. She is old and senile; I think she's forgotten me."

"Then who are you going to talk with?"

"My dead husband's younger sister. I thought I'd talk with her. Anyway, my daughter refuses to let me take the baby home with me."

Ninomiya's daughter, dressed in her school uniform, was sitting on the empty bed all this time, her eyes downcast. She seemed to be crying and held a crumpled handkerchief in her hand.

Sadaharu, sitting on the bed next to her, asked her name.

In a tiny voice, the daughter replied, "Kozue."

"That's a fine name," Sadaharu said. "What high school do you attend?"

"Nobi High," she said.

"I see. I've been waiting to meet you."

Kozue did not raise her face.

"You have a younger brother now."

The girl looked up, surprised, but then lowered her face, her eyes full of tears, as though she did not want to meet Sadaharu's gaze.

"You saw the baby, I suppose?" he asked. The girl nodded her head, saying nothing.

"He's a fine baby. Pretty soon he will be calling you big sister and be looking up to you. When he goes to school and is having trouble with his homework, you will have to teach him. And when he grows up . . . What did your father do for a living?"

Ninomiya replied for her daughter, "He worked in a shipyard."

"There. He may take to the same kind of work as your father. Building great ships is important work. Japan is a small country and has to import food, oil, wood, and all the rest from abroad, you know. We Japanese can now eat what we like, wear what we like—and all those things come to us on ships that someone has to build. And though he is still a baby now, your younger brother may grow up to do such work."

At that moment, Sadaharu was not deliberately erasing the image of the child's father; rather, he was thinking of the girl's father and the baby's father as one and the same person.

"Your mother asked me whether she couldn't send the child away, out of consideration for you. But you love your mother, don't you?"

The girl again looked down.

"This is quite an event, your mother having a baby. You can't have all her attention now. She is mother to the baby too. Do you understand?"

The girl made no reply but fiercely kneaded her handkerchief, as though her life depended on it.

"Did you bring your mother's nightgown for her, and her toilet articles?"

The girl nodded, and her mother said, "Yes, she did. I asked the nurse to phone her and tell her that I was in the hospital. Kozue knew enough to bring them."

"Did you tell her about the baby on the phone?"

"No, I told her here."

"Hmm, so it was a bit of shock for her, of course. Still, she seems to be all right. And you too. You are a grown-up now, Kozue. It's not as though your father were here and your mother had been unfaithful. She is single, and it's not at all strange that she would really like someone and that she would want to have a child with him. Women all think that way. You will, too."

Kozue made no reply, and Sadaharu asked the mother, "If your daughter understands the circumstances, won't you feel better about it?"

"Yes, of course, but I can't go through with it. There are my dead husband's relatives. . . . And the work I do now, I can't keep a baby around."

She let out her breath, a raspy exhalation.

"We can't take the child in here," Sadaharu said. "But if you wish, I'll look for a chance of adoption for him. You can take care of the child until then, surely."

Sadaharu thought sarcastically to himself how quick he was to offer this help after his conversation with Yoko.

"Can't you care for him until then?" he repeated. She remained silent. "You gave birth to the child, didn't you? Not to take any care of him is quite irresponsible."

She replied, "I'll pay for care, but if the people in my neighborhood learn of this, it will be hard on me."

"All right, then. You look for someone to care for the child, some foster parent just for a little while. I'll find someone to adopt him, but that will take time. This is not just a puppy; we need to find a good place for him."

Ninomiya asked, "Would that person register the baby as her own?"

"No, no. We can't do that. It's against the law. The child is usually registered with the mother's family and then properly adopted."

Ninomiya persisted. "Doctor, would you give me the address of that Dr. Kikuda you mentioned? Perhaps if I went there, he might accept it as someone else's child."

"That's impossible now. Then he would be in a bind with the law."

"I should have given birth at home," Ninomiya said very clearly.

"Would you have killed the baby if you had given birth at home?"

"If I'd known, I would have," she said.

Kozue began to weep violently.

"Well, how about raising him for two or three months until adoption? I'll find a family that's perfect. The child will be quite happy. It is ironic, of course, but eventually he will be happier than with you, even. So please arrange for a legal adoption. If it is too much of a problem for you during that time, then get someone to take care of him."

"But the family registration is a big problem," she said. "If there is any irregularity, then my daughter will have trouble getting married. And my dead husband's relatives, they are sure to criticize me. Registering the child is just like raising him. I can't register him without giving the father's name."

"You'll all have to give that matter some thought," Sadaharu said, in a way that indicated he was through with the matter. "Just remember: killing is no way out. I know. Don't even think of it."

Sadaharu left mother and daughter alone in the room, slowly closing the door behind him.

Chapter Five

Ocean Roar

A week later, when Yoshie Ninomiya left the clinic, Sadaharu felt as though a storm had blown past. There was truth in the saying that those who complain the most live longest. When Sadaharu tactfully inquired of the nurses, he learned that a somewhat older woman had appeared—they didn't know whether she was a relative or a friend—and quite nonchalantly wrapped up the baby and took it away.

Ninomiya had said, "It's cold today, so it's best to wrap him in an extra blanket under his jacket."

The child thus left the hospital without having a name recorded, but a young nurse who had casually asked Ninomiya if she had thought of a name recalled that Ninomiya had said, "Oh, his older sister is calling him Nozomu, which means Hope, so that's what it will probably be."

To a casual observer, the mother and daughter, older sister and younger brother seemed quite reconciled. The sister giving him a name was probably the mother's doing.

Spring arrived early and in a rush that year. And every day, it seemed, Mayumi went off somewhere, as though she was afraid of staying in the house. Sadaharu had no idea of where she went so often, but when he asked there was always a simple explanation: there was a sale on some delicious free range chicken; she was having a spring dress made by a Tokyo designer; she was visiting a sick friend in the hospital.

One day in early April, when they were alone in the examination room, Nurse Ono said to Sadaharu, "Doctor, wasn't there a woman named Ninomiya who gave birth to a son here at the clinic?"

Sadaharu grunted acknowledgment.

"Well, quite by accident, I met her near the station the other day."

Ninomiya on that occasion had seemed to recognize Nurse Ono and for a moment seemed somewhat confused, but when the nurse said, "Mrs. Ninomiya, has the baby been well?" she replied, "Yes, thanks. The baby is doing very well, thanks to all of you." But still she had an exhausted look about her.

"Are you ill?" Nurse Ono asked.

"No, I'm quite all right. But my daughter . . . tried to kill herself with gas," Yoshie replied.

Astonished, Nurse Ono had asked about the girl's condition. She hadn't remembered seeing any such news on television or in the newspaper.

"She said she was a high school student," Sadaharu remarked.

"Yes, that was what she said. Apparently, after Mrs. Ninomiya left the clinic she didn't go home but to the house of a friend in Osaka. She phoned her daughter at home any number of times, but the girl kept saying she hated the baby. Then, finally, when she was about to return home with the child, the daughter seemed to relent. But, in fact, the night before Mrs. Ninomiya and her baby were to return home from Osaka, her daughter attempted suicide, and is now in a hospital in Tokyo."

"Where did she do it?" Sadaharu asked. "There's no gas in the houses around here."

"One of her favorite teachers from junior high school had married and moved to Tokyo, and apparently she went to visit her. She told the teacher about the problem and when she reassured her she seemed to brighten up. But it got late, and the teacher's mother-in-law was concerned about her going home alone on the last train to an empty house, so she urged her to stay over night. Well, that night she opened the gas valve in her room. . . ."

"Was it really a determined effort at suicide?"

"Well, it seems there was a farewell note addressed to the teacher. She said she was sorry for going back on her word. The teacher got up during the night to go to the toilet, noticed the gas and turned off the valve. That's what Mrs. Ninomiya said."

Sadaharu sighed. "And what happens next will be worse. It would probably have been better if she had died."

Nurse Ono did not know any more about Yoshie Ninomiya. Only Sadaharu knew that Ninomiya had asked him to kill the child as soon as it was born.

"But you know," she added, "she is realistic, in spite of everything."

"What do you mean?"

"Mrs. Ninomiya must realize that if something happens to her daughter or she turns out to be a disappointment to her, then it will be a good thing she had another child."

That night it rained. When he went over to his house, Sadaharu immediately telephoned Yoko Kakei.

"Will you be at home after dinner this evening?"

"Yes, I will," she answered.

"May I stop by?"

"Yes, of course."

Later, when he set out, the rain drops were so large they looked like silver rods. And the cabbages looked like flowers on the shiny dark earth. Arriving at Yoko's house, he recognized the shabby automobile already parked there.

"I invited Father Munechika, since this is a good opportunity for him to see you," Yoko said as she opened the door. Behind her Sadaharu saw the slightly rosy forehead of the priest, who had already had a drink.

"Good guess," Sadaharu replied.

"What do you mean?"

"You must have guessed that I have something on my mind that I want to confess," he said, laughing.

"No, I had no idea. If that were the case, I would have to call the priest everyday."

"Very likely. Anyway, may I have a drink?"

"What about Mayumi?"

"She's spending the night in Tokyo. And I sent her off with pleasure. What a good husband, eh?"

Sadaharu had his drink and his mood improved.

"So. While I'm still sober, let me get down to business. Your American friends who want a baby . . ."

"The Lauries?"

"I've been keeping in mind the fact that they want to adopt a baby," Sadaharu said, "but the plan I had in mind fell through, and I currently don't have a baby available. That's what I came to tell you about."

"I expected to see the Lauries this coming summer, but they have postponed their trip. I suppose that by the time they arrive another baby whose parents don't want it will turn up."

"It's not as simple as that. I'm not suited for this kind of work."

"What's the matter? I've always assumed that if a child is not put up for adoption, that's a good thing."

"It wasn't so good in this case. It would have been better if this child had been taken in by the Lauries. Now he will have to grow up to take care of not only his mother but also his crazy older sister who tried to kill herself because her mother gave birth to an unwanted baby. Adding insult to injury."

The alcohol was strong enough to induce Sadaharu to give a detailed account of Ninomiya's story, but to preserve the patient's privacy, he did not mention her name, simply speaking of Ninomiya as the "mother."

"Father Munechika, what do you think of this case? As a physician, I performed my duties as best I could, but the result of my actions was terrible. If I had done as the mother asked at the time, if I had given the baby an injection, none of this would have happened. I really mean that."

"But if you'd done that," Father Munechika said, "you would have committed murder, and I think the crime would have stayed on the mother's conscience forever."

In spite of his being a man of the cloth, Father Munechika's words showed Sadaharu that he had missed the point completely.

"What are you saying? I don't think that would happen at all. Suppose the girl dies. The baby would be responsible for her death, even though it has no awareness of what's going on. It's a good thing he doesn't know because unless he is abnormal or insensitive it would warp his life. If I were in such a situation, I think it would do that to me.

"On the other hand, if the girl does not die, then he will be forced to care for his mother and his crazy sister for the rest of his life. Whichever way it turns out, it's not a good way to live. It would be better if he was adopted by the Lauries. If he is formally adopted, then his natural mother would have no idea where he has gone. He wouldn't know his natural mother and he could just get on with his life quite nicely."

Yoko replied, "I am surprised to hear that his natural mother doesn't want to raise him for reasons besides economic ones. She's worried that people will find out that she has had a child. If not that, then she'll worry about having trouble later because it's listed on the family register. You know, in English-speaking countries there is no such thing as shaming your family name."

"Hmm, really, what a bourgeois attitude!"

Sadaharu spoke with his eyes half closed when he was drunk.

"And if the politicians in Japan don't start realizing the problems the family register system causes for women with unwanted babies, there will be no end to killing or abandoning children. Right? How could officials or intellectuals accept the kind of society where people can produce children so irresponsibly? They insist that if society goes in that direction, irresponsible mothers will increase, so women must take responsibility for getting pregnant. And when a woman cannot take responsibility, she is the loser. And that leads her to kill her child or abandon it. Actually, getting rid of it is not such a bad idea. If I were a priest, Father Munechika, I would put a sign up outside of the church: Kill Not the Children But Leave Them Here."

Just then the telephone rang. Yoko answered and called to Sadaharu, "It's a call from Nurse Ono at the clinic."

Sadaharu, anticipating the call, went to the phone.

"Hello. I'm sorry to disturb you so late."

"Not at all. It's just a social visit," Sadaharu assured her.

"I called your house first and your housekeeper said you'd gone to have a drink, so I took a chance on calling."

"Right. What's going on? I'm rather drunk and can't be very helpful."

"It's . . . I heard that Mrs. Ninomiya's daughter died today, this morning."

Sadaharu said, "Oh. I see."

"I was on my way home and did some shopping at the market where Mrs. Ninomiya works. There is a fish store right in front of the market, and since I needed something there I stopped. The fishmonger mentioned that he thought I knew the woman who worked at the market across the street. . . . And he told me about her death. I pretended that was the first I knew about it."

"I see."

"I knew you were concerned, doctor, so I thought it would be best to let you know as soon as possible."

"Yes, thanks. You did the right thing."

"I hope so. I hope it was right."

"Yes, yes it was. Thanks for calling, really."

Sadaharu hung up and turned to the others. He was chuckling to himself. "The baby we were just talking about has just been promoted to murderer. His older sister died."

"Oh! Could she really have resented the birth of a younger brother so much?" the priest said.

"I have no idea. But that's the mind of a girl for you." Sadaharu spoke in an unconcerned tone.

"Well, I'm a woman, and I think I understand. She was probably at the age when she thought that anything sexual was dirty. So if her mother produced a baby under such circumstances—that would be unforgivable."

"Yes, I see your point."

"After all, she didn't kill her little brother. She just hated the idea that both of them were living, so she decided that she should be the one to die. At least she made an effort to deal with the situation as it was."

"Yes, and because the mother understood her daughter's feelings about her younger brother, she went off to Osaka. But wherever she went, eventually it would all have to come out, that's obvious, so she should have come home. And the baby—if the girl had seen it, she might have had some feeling for it, even approved of its existence. She killed herself the night before the baby was due to come home, didn't she?"

"You're right. If she had seen its face, she might have come to love it. But she might not; she might have resented it."

After a pause, the priest said, "The rain seems to have let up. Shall we go out to the terrace?"

Yoko agreed.

"A good idea. There is an overhanging roof from the sun room, so even if it drizzles a bit we will be all right."

The night was warm and humid, clouds beginning to part, while from below came the beating sound of the sea.

Sadaharu spoke. "I had an interesting experience recently. Nothing terrible, really. Our friend the priest will like it. The husband of a couple that wanted a child suffered from a lack of sperm, and while I didn't have much hope for him I began hormone treatment. I cautioned him that he should not get his hopes up too high and so forth. I'm casual, you know, but I'm also a conscientious doctor. But contrary to expectations, she got pregnant."

"How nice to hear," Yoko said. "Please tell that to Eiko Nakanishi."

"Yes, I will. Well, I had expected some improvement in the husband's condition, but when I examined his semen I was surprised to find that there was absolutely no sperm."

"How could that be?"

"Precisely. At first, I thought there had been some catastrophic coincidence, as anyone would have."

"You mean that she was unfaithful?"

"That would be the first thing to expect. And, of course, I had to ask her about that. But she smiled quite calmly and said nothing like that had happened."

"Then . . . what happened?"

"The only possibility is that for a day, two days, a week maybe, the husband produced sperm. And during that time, she got pregnant. Then sperm production stopped just as suddenly. That's the only explanation."

"But is that possible?" the priest asked.

"It doesn't happen all the time, but I would not say it can't happen at all. You know, Father Munechika, at times like that I'm really sorry I don't have faith. If I were a believer, I could see the hand of God in this. Something as unbelievable as this can hardly be the work of human beings."

"But if the wife is content, then all is well, isn't it?"

"Hmm. When the child is born we will quietly do a blood test, however. Even though that is usually routine," Sadaharu laughed through the sound of the ocean. "It will only be an ABO test, but it would be grand if it all matches up."

"Well, if the blood types match, then the parents and child do too."

Yoko spoke obliquely, but Sadaharu thought she probably meant that the child could still be by another man if the father were by chance a man with the same blood type as the husband, and he offered no denial.

"I was at a high school reunion once," Sadaharu said, recalling a long forgotten incident, "and met a fellow who had become a lawyer. When he went to France, he was invited to a party by a colleague, and at the party he said something about determining parentage by blood type. Well, a sudden chill descended over the party. In the first place, most of the people there did not know their own blood type or their family's, he said. And after the party was over, his friend scolded him, saying that this kind of subject shouldn't be mentioned in public. If French families knew their blood types, there is no telling what kind of tragedies might arise. In France, if a child who was thought to be of a certain family turned out not to be, the family would completely fall apart."

"Oh, I'm sure your story is exaggerated. But I suppose such families do exist."

"Yes. I laughed along with everyone else, but I thought about it afterward. The reason is that your own child and heir is one thing, but if it is not your child, then automatically it isn't so loveable, which seems rather sad. If it is a child your wife has borne, then you think 'That's my child,' and that thought is quite attractive to human beings, isn't it?"

"At such times, a priest has nothing to say," Father Munechika said, "and since I don't have a wife I can only add that I've never been in that position, so it's sometimes difficult for me to admonish other people to be trusting."

"Father Munechika, I don't think that is a problem. No matter what other people do, a priest preaches. I think that's perfectly all right, and you are free to tell others that they are sinners," Sadaharu said.

That night it was past eleven o'clock when Sadaharu took a taxi home, and as he entered the house he enjoyed the refreshing taste of his wife's absence.

Not that there was anything he was particularly ashamed of, but when Mayumi was present he would have to offer some kind of excuse about returning this late. Mayumi did not harbor any suspicions about Sadaharu and Yoko, but she was not completely insensitive and would have felt uneasy with the knowledge that Sadaharu had some secret pleasure from which she herself was excluded. Yoko did not shun Mayumi, and when Sadaharu went to Yoko's house he had never once consciously prevented Mayumi from accompanying him. But, in fact, had Mayumi gone there she surely would have made the other guests feel uneasy—or she would have been bored—and so she made no effort to be included.

Today, Mayumi was supposed to be staying in Tokyo at the home of a friend from high school days. Nonetheless, Sadaharu doubted half of that story, thinking that while she might be staying there, she might also be somewhere else. He did not consider using the telephone to try to determine exactly where she actually was. Confusing as that surely was to Mayumi, to Sadaharu it was even more so.

For more than a year, Sadaharu and Mayumi had not lived together as husband and wife. On that point, Sadaharu was prepared with an explanation that might be taken as serious or in jest. There were, after all, various ways of dealing with sexual desire, and he could say that even without a partner one could be comfortable alone. Of course, if he did not have a physical relationship with his wife and she got pregnant, that rather precisely fixed the blame. In fact, there would be an element of punishment in assigning blame, no doubt about that. But even should that kind of situation arise, Sadaharu thought, and Mayumi took him into her confidence, Sadaharu would revert to his role of physician, and, after the fact, so to speak, reliably minister to her. That would be the safest thing by far, rather than entrusting the matter to another physician.

Nor were they preserving the appearance of being a married couple simply because they had a child. From time to time, Sadaharu thought that no one loved Mayumi as much as he did—but not, he thought, as a wife.

In Sadaharu's mind, Mayumi had gradually become his blood relative, rather like a younger sister. In that role, she was hardly a sex object. And simply because of that, no matter how foolishly she might behave, Sadaharu could not abandon her now.

A clear morning dawned. When Sadaharu left for the clinic, Mayumi, of course, had not yet returned.

That morning the first patient to arrive was Eiko Nakanishi, who was putting her last hopes on infertility treatments.

"Doctor, I'm sorry for the trouble. My period this month was right on time."

What had seemed to be a good start in Sadaharu's examination of Mrs. Nakanishi had not made satisfactory progress. Mr. Nakanishi's mother had broken a bone and gone into a Tokyo hospital, and Mrs. Nakanishi had accompanied her to help with her care. Sadaharu had found nothing wrong with the husband, so he wanted to do an examination of the wife's oviducts, but such an examination could only be done between the end of menstruation and the next ovulation.

After care of her mother-in-law was entrusted to her husband's sisters, Mrs. Nakanishi hoped to be examined that month, but unfortunately she had caught cold and developed a fever. If it was just a cold that would probably still have been all right, but when she telephoned Sadaharu he had preferred to wait another month.

The oviducts carry the eggs down from the ovaries; if there is an obstruction in the tubes, the eggs cannot join with the sperm, and to determine just how clear the way is an iodine preparation is injected through the uterus and an X-ray is made of the pelvic area. Sadaharu did not intend to do an X-ray of Mrs. Nakanishi today. Before this test, he would have to examine her sedimentation rate and the condition of the vagina, clean the vagina, and give her an antibiotic. Should any harmful bacteria from the vagina be carelessly injected into the oviducts, that might in itself produce an infection that could cause sterility.

"That's all for today. Come back tomorrow, and if the sedimentation rate is normal, we can do the examination then," he said, after completing the preliminary work.

Mrs. Nakanishi thanked him and left with a happy smile on her face. In a few moments, Nurse Ono called for a patient on the clinic public address system.

"Ms. Serizawa. Ms. Serizawa."

The girl who came in was dressed in a brown skirt and a navy blue sweater and had her hair styled in a bouffant with bangs. She was tall and slender, with long eyelashes.

"Mayuko Serizawa, isn't it?" Sadaharu asked. "What seems to be the matter?"

According to the patient's record card, she was twenty years of age and worked at the Yokosuka office of a large car company. The girl madc no rcply, and Sadaharu looked up from the card.

"What is your trouble? Where are you feeling bad?" he said to the girl with bangs. "Are you employed?" He asked this even though he had the information on the card.

"Yes."

"You must have come here because you have an ailment somewhere, I suppose."

"I'm not sure. You see, I went to a motel with a man."

"Yes, all right."

"And he said that my body was strange, somehow."

"Was that your first time? I don't suppose you are married," Sadaharu said.

"I'm not."

"Well, that makes no difference, but have you had a relationship with a man before?"

"Some men I've liked."

"And have you gone to a motel?"

"This was the first time."

"And you went there for that purpose?"

"Yes."

"And things didn't go well."

"That's what he said, and he was really in a bad mood."

It might have been a problem with the hymen, or perhaps a double vagina, or perhaps a septum had developed. The problem of a congenitally tough hymen was discussed these days in articles in the weekly magazines, so the information was widely known, and women came to consult doctors directly from motels as well as from their honeymoon.

"Is your period regular?" Sadaharu asked.

"I've never had one."

"Not once?"

"That's right."

"Aren't you concerned? At your age, you should be menstruating, of course."

"My mother began late, and so . . ."

"Yes, but even though you don't menstruate, don't you experience a painful swelling of your stomach each month, a feeling that your stomach is swollen and enlarged?"

Sadaharu's question was directed toward the possibility of an imperforate hymen. In such cases, even with the onset of menstruation at adolescence, there is no way for the blood to discharge. The first symptom is swelling due to blood in the vagina and uterus, then closure of the oviducts at the distal end. The blood cannot flow into the abdominal cavity and consequently produces a swelling of the oviducts. If this condition goes on very long, there is pain in the lower stomach. After that, as the swelling from the entrapped blood enlarges, the bottom of the uterus is shoved up, and the woman appears to be pregnant.

"No, I've never had that," Serizawa replied.

The girl's tight skirt suggested a rather slender torso. Sadaharu evaluated her general physical condition. When he inquired about her period, he was first of all looking at her chest. Even a girl who had not yet produced a child might have a rare ailment that caused her to produce milk. This condition that accompanied lack of menstruation was called the Argonz-Del Castillo syndrome, or Forbes-Albright syndrome. To the lay person, Sadaharu explained that after she had a child and was nursing, she would probably not menstruate, that the logic was the same. But it was thought that the symptom appeared when there was enlargement of the part of the anatomy called the Sella turcica, or Turkish slipper, because of its shape, and was accompanied by a pituitary tumor.

Mayuko Serizawa's chest could not be called especially abundant, but she had a swelling about appropriate to a girl of slender figure. She said she had had no lactation, but her nipples were small and the color of the areolae was light. Her underarm hair was sparse.

"All right, then, let's do a pelvic examination. The gentleman said something was strange, I know, but I am sure whatever it is can be corrected without too much trouble," Sadaharu said.

The young woman appeared to agree. Her facial expression was clouded by the slight darkness of her complexion, a coloration not unusual with many handsome men and women from the Miura Peninsula, suggesting a Polynesian kind of beauty.

As always, Sadaharu had his nurse prepare the patient. He waited until she was ready and then seated himself on a round stool. And yet somehow he found it difficult to begin his examination. Even aside from Serizawa's evident lack of pubic hair development, Sadaharu felt instinctively that he should not simply use the instrument he had taken in hand. He was not concerned about irregularities of the hymen, but the vagina was barely one centimeter long and seemed to come to a dead end. Sadaharu slipped on a rubber glove, lubricated the fingers, and did a rectal examination, but he could not feel any sign of the uterus. He next did a palpation examination of the girl's groin. When he had confirmed his impression through feeling with his fingers, he inquired of her in as controlled a tone as he could manage:

"Ms. Serizawa, when you've had medical examinations in the past did the doctor say anything about a hernia?"

She replied, "Oh, I'm in good health; I've never been ill before."

"I see," he said. Sadaharu gently confirmed the anomaly he had discovered and then added, "Fine. You may get dressed now, Ms. Serizawa."

He then returned to his desk and began writing in his own style of clinical description: Nipples small. No body hair. External sex parts female. Insufficient development of the labia. Vagina depth 1.5 cm. Small clitoris. Feeling of undescended testicles inside a groin hernia.

Even with her dark coloration, Serizawa, when she came out of the examination room, showed an expression of relief on her face, a peaceful look.

"Please come over here, Ms. Serizawa," Sadaharu said from his desk. "I can't be absolutely certain about this, of course, but I think that we should do a further examination. Not that there is anything lifethreatening. It's only that in your case the vagina is clearly much shallower than with other people. And that's why your friend said that something was strange."

"I see," she said.

"But we still have to find out why at your age you have not begun to menstruate. So an examination is in order, but at a large hospital, and for this you will probably have to remain as an in-patient for a while."

"Will it take a long time?"

"It will take about three weeks. The hospital is at my old medical school, Meirin University. You may have heard of it. I'll introduce you so they will accept you there for the tests."

"Can't you do the examination here?" she asked with an anxious look.

"The problem is that a hormone test and the other things necessary are quite complicated, and proper equipment is needed; it's a delicate procedure."

"But if I go to the hospital, will you be coming to examine me?"

Sadaharu had only spoken with Serizawa for a few minutes and it was hardly likely that she was infatuated with him, or so completely trusting of him. But patients of gynecologists, after they had been examined, usually did not wish to change doctors.

"Well, I do appreciate your trust, but we have to allow others to do the examination. I'll introduce you to a classmate of mine who is a fine doctor."

He had no further patients to see immediately, so he spoke in an informal tone that suggested he would like to go on chatting.

"Do you have any siblings, Ms. Serizawa?"

"An older brother and a younger brother."

"I see. Have you lived all along in Yokosuka? I mean, were you born in Yokosuka?"

"No. When I was born, my mother and father were living in Iwate, in the country."

"I'd like to ask you a little about that, about your birth. Did your mother tell you any details? How much you weighed, or whether you had any sickness just after you were born, or anything like that? Were you born in a hospital?"

"No. I think a midwife came from nearby. I weighed about six pounds."

Sadaharu tried to continue his reassuring tone to his patient, and said, "Well, that's about normal. So, are you commuting from your parent's house, at present?"

"No. I'm living at a boarding house."

"Alone?"

"No. With a girl I know. We're renting the rooms."

"Are your parents living in Iwate?"

"They're in Shizuoka. My father works for an engineering company, so he has to move around from place to place. When we were all in Yokosuka, I found a job and decided to stay there."

"That was a good chance for you," Sadaharu said. "And what about meeting your young man friend?"

"Last autumn I went to see a soccer match, and someone I know introduced us."

"Is he employed?"

"He is still a student. He was out of school for two years, and now he is in his second year at college."

"He isn't your first boyfriend, is he?"

"No, but I'm rather old fashioned."

"And you really like him?"

"Well, the truth is that he talked about marriage right from the start. Until I met him, I hadn't had any serious relationships, but he seemed serious and I liked him, so I didn't feel I should refuse when he suggested we go to a hotel. I'd never been to a place like that, but there is a hotel called The Strand near here, you know."

"Oh, yes," Sadaharu said, "the place with the pointed roof painted red, isn't that it?"

"That's where we went."

"You know, I've always wanted to see what that place looks like."

"Inside it was cleaner than I'd imagined. When we went there, we passed right in front of your clinic. Since it was on the way to the hotel, I thought that if I had a baby I'd come to your clinic to give birth."

"A little premature, but thanks for noticing us," Sadaharu said.

"It seemed to really shock him—my body being strange," she said.

"Well, we still have to see about that," Sadaharu said to her.

"Even so, after we left and I went home, he called me on the phone. He was very considerate, the way he spoke. He said he really didn't know, but he thought there was something wrong with me and that I should go to see a doctor for an examination."

"And you've done what he suggested. You did the right thing. Now then, I'm going to write a letter of introduction for you. You take the letter and go the university hospital at Ofuna. The doctor is my classmate, Dr. Kotaro Yagihara."

Sadaharu took some paper from his desk drawer and began to write.

Without seeing the results of the tests he could not be absolutely certain of his judgment, but it seemed to him likely that Mayuko Serizawa was biologically male. He was sure that what he had felt in Serizawa's groin was undescended testicles. When they did a chromosome study, they would find out clearly which she was, but it depressed Sadaharu to think about the enormous psychological shock coming to Serizawa when she found out.

Once at the home of a physician friend, he had met a certain woman, a critic. It was so long ago that he did not even remember her name, and all he could recall was that she was a large woman—round-shouldered, nearsighted, bowlegged—and that for a woman she was oddly rough mannered. There was some talk at that time about hermaphrodites. Sadaharu was drunk on that occasion, but he recalled her offhandedly remarking, "I think it might be fun, being hermaphrodite. I'd know how a woman feels, and at the same time I'd be able to enjoy the pleasures of a man. That could be a real kick."

Sadaharu thought to himself how she spoke without really understanding what was involved, but he also remembered that on that occasion he had heard about the hermaphrodite statue in the Borghese Gallery in Rome.

"When I was there, the statue was displayed backward, pushed up against the wall," said his friend.

The physician had made a trip abroad, which was something Sadaharu had never done, so he had to accept the idea without comment. The marble statue in question was neither a man nor a woman, but rather something only describable as a seated, naked human figure, half crouched in sleep. And when one went around to the other side, what was there presumably was a male figure with prominent breasts. But the museum seemed not to appreciate that side.

What is called sexuality in humans is generally thought to be determined at the moment of conception, and this is what Sadaharu told his patients. But to put it a bit more precisely, during an early stage of human development in the womb there is a period of non-differentiation in the sex of the fetus. Textbooks state that under the influence of the Y chromosome, in most cases a male embryo develops internal sexual organs, which in turn produce the male hormone testosterone after about the fifth month of pregnancy. But when testosterone production is not adequate, the fetus that was originally male displays female characteristics after birth. Consequently, while we cannot say that the basic sex of all animals is female, we can say that whether a female changes into a male is determined at the moment the sperm joins the egg.

The individual has no role in this, of course. In a way, the fate of human beings is irrational, and Mayuko Serizawa's condition was the result of a very tiny disorder.

Sadaharu had no religious faith. Yet when he faced such realities, he felt overwhelmed by the absurdity of any human belief in self-control or free will. Fun to be both sexes? That was hardly the point. The question of which sex a human being is endowed with must be fundamentally a matter of supreme grace, and a hermaphrodite like Mayuko Serizawa was a person without a firm foundation on which to exist. Properly, the true hermaphrodite is rare, yet men are often false sex hermaphrodites, with the male-female biological characteristics being clearly differentiated. Except that the sex organs are not developed, and the as-yet-unsuppressed characteristics of the opposite sex remain in evidence.

Sadaharu had asked Serizawa about her birth because he wanted to know who had said "It's a girl." But in the case of a birth attended only by a country midwife, naturally the midwife would assume the child was a girl, since it lacked a penis.

For twenty years, Mayuko was raised as a girl, and now she loved a man. Without her noticing, Sadaharu had seen attached to her purse a little charm in the form of a tennis player, a natural thing for a girl to have, he felt. But what would happen when all that changed?

Twice before leaving, Serizawa asked Sadaharu, "Whatever they tell me at the hospital, is it all right if I come to see you again, doctor?"

Sadaharu felt an indefinable heaviness in his reply. "Yes, of course, come any time." But in truth he did not want her to come again. His classmate Kotaro Yagihara would surely take good care of her. Sadaharu's real inclination was to try to forget about troublesome patients.

When he went home that evening, Mayumi had already returned. His housekeeper said, "Madam said she felt that she was coming down with a cold. She has gone upstairs to rest."

Sadaharu went up to see how his wife was doing.

"So, did you catch a cold?" he said in greeting.

Mayumi's face was turned away from him. She seemed to have been crying, and Sadaharu caught a glimpse of red-rimmed eyes, but since the room was darkened he pretended not to notice.

"I caught cold yesterday in the rain," she said.

Sadaharu wondered whether she might not have gone walking in the rain. "I thought the fortune teller said Tokyo is in a favorable direction," he said. "Isn't that why you went?" But he regretted having spoken. That was that, he thought, and what a mess.

Chapter Six

A Home for Unwed Mothers

Two weeks later, just before the Golden Week holidays at the end of April, Yoko Kakei stopped by the clinic with a bottle of cognac for Sadaharu. She was about to leave for Brazil and Argentina, but besides that, Sadaharu felt, she came to offer him some comfort and support.

"Eh? This expensive kind," he said, holding it, "even feels different from what I usually drink."

He was pleased with her gift. But, in fact, he was not fussy about the kind of alcohol he drank. Whether it was imported or made in Japan, he got the same glorious feeling when drunk. Sadaharu thought that Dr. Hiroshige, who substituted for him on occasion, was snobbish for saying that he drank imported Scotch when in fact he also drank domestic brands, just as Sadaharu did.

"You must excuse me for imposing the Nakanishis on you," Yoko said.

So that's her motive today, Sadaharu thought, but he merely brushed the matter off with a laugh. He had taken X-rays of Mrs. Nakanishi's oviducts earlier that month on schedule, but the result did not seem favorable. The pictures were made after he injected a liquid opaqueing material, but in the first image he could not see the oviducts, only a shadow from the uterus, and shortly afterward the second picture showed nothing more. The indication was that the entrances to the oviducts were closed on both sides.

"It looks hopeless, it really does," Sadaharu said in a clear voice, and Mrs. Nakanishi, who in her heart must surely have felt as though she had been handed a death sentence, smiled, her eyebrows arched, and said, "Thank you very much. I will have to resign myself to this." She then departed.

"Eiko was satisfied, nonetheless," Yoko said. "She told me that, psychologically, for her the matter was settled."

"Oh, perhaps, but personally I thought the examination was a total loss for her."

"No, not completely. That's what life is all about, isn't it?"

Sadaharu replied, "What are you going to do in Brazil? Attend the Carnival?"

"This isn't the season for Carnival. No, I'm just going to accompany the Lauries and to meet some other people, old friends of mine."

"Hmm, that's nice. I would really like to travel and at least see the United States."

"Then why don't you go?"

"Because my patients come in all year round. And besides, everyone else is going, so I might as well stay home."

"I get a kind of empty feeling when I travel," Yoko said. "But when I stay home too much, I'm afraid I become a little odd."

"Why don't you look for a suitable man? There are a lot of men alone in the world, and it would be good for you to live with someone."

"In theory, yes." Yoko nodded docilely but with an expression that said she did not in the least agree with Sadaharu.

That afternoon, Sadaharu, assisted by his sometime associate Dr. Hiroshige, performed an operation for an ovarian cyst. This was one of the biggest tumors he had removed since beginning practice.

The patient was a woman thirty years old, owner of a coffee shop, whose abdomen had swollen greatly within a few months. To her acquaintances, it seemed apparent that she was pregnant, which was not unusual in itself, except that the woman herself could find no explanation for her condition. At least her abdomen grew as large as in the final stages of pregnancy.

Even with her abdomen opened up, the tumor was so large that Sadaharu could not remove it all at once. The patient could hear what was happening, since she had only been given a spinal block anesthetic.

"This is really filled up!" he said, then with a syringe he drew out more than a liter of water mixed with blood. When he slid out the resisting tumor, it was nearly the volume of the receiving pan.

"This one could be put on exhibit. It's the biggest I've seen since graduation. How do you feel?"

Sadaharu spoke to his patient as he was suturing the incision, and with her eyes shut, face white and plump, she replied, "I'm hungry."

The nurses burst out laughing.

"I can well imagine. Taking out something this big must leave your stomach empty," he replied cheerfully.

After the operation was concluded, and just before he was about to leave his office for the day, Chisa Asano and her mother appeared. Chisa had stopped having her period because she had suddenly quit eating.

"And how have things been going?" Sadaharu asked.

The girl's mother replied, as always. "Well, she has not had her period yet, but we've stopped her getting any thinner."

"Stopped getting thinner . . . But she hasn't gained any weight?"

"Not yet," her mother responded.

As instructed by Sadaharu, Chisa had brought the chart on which she had written her daily body temperature. A look at the chart showed Sadaharu what he had expected to find. The usual pattern was a period of low temperature prior to ovulation and then a higher temperature afterward, but her body temperature chart did not show any variation.

"I was going to make her keep recording her temperature, but she had a bad cold and a sore throat, with a slight fever, so I didn't have her record it for two weeks. I thought it would be useless to take her temperature then."

"Yes, yes that's fine." Turning to Chisa, Sadaharu spoke casually. "I had an idea that the temperature pattern would look like this. Beginning today, I want you to take some medicine. Take this, and, very likely, in a little while, your period will begin. Now remember, your menstruation will be the result of medication, not a natural occurrence. The treatment will have to be gradual, and to make it work you will have to eat and put on a bit of weight. And after that you will get well."

"Chisa!" the mother said. "Do you understand? The doctor is speaking to you."

Instead of answering, the girl looked down.

"You know," the mother went on, "my husband—her father—normally works in Tokyo, but when we spoke the other day I learned that he met your wife in Los Angeles by chance."

"Oh, really, is that so? My wife travels quite a bit, unlike me. I just stay at home. I'm sure he was very kind to her."

"I told him I was taking our daughter to the clinic, but I didn't say which one, and so two or three days ago he asked and was quite surprised and said to give his greetings to you."

"And please send my compliments to him, too. Does he often work away from Tokyo?"

"Yes. He is in automobile exporting."

"Really? To think that in the old days automobiles were something we imported, and these days Japan supplies the world. Amazing, isn't it? That kind of work must be quite challenging."

"My husband likes it quite well."

After they left, Sadaharu thought for a while about what Mrs. Asano had said about her husband liking his work. Considering his own principle of not doing what he did not like, what she had said was very likely true. But he had the feeling that while the husband might work enthusiastically for his company because he took pleasure in it, she possibly felt some resentment at being excluded.

Sadaharu returned home and bathed. Still in his terry cloth robe, he asked Mayumi, "Do you happen to know someone named Asano?"

"I certainly do. Why?" she replied, not turning toward him as she readied dinner in the kitchen.

"Nothing in particular. Mrs. Asano said that her husband had met you, that's all. She and her daughter came in today."

"The wife is quite a piece of work, I understand."

"Hmm. I wouldn't know about that. I would call her pleasingly plump."

"I met Mr. Asano in Hawaii, and he really opened up about his wife. On the surface, she seems to be the perfect wife and mother, but while Mr. Asano is away from Tokyo, she fools around, he said."

"I thought you met him in Los Angeles."

"No, I met him in Hawaii. I was introduced to him at Yamamoto's house, and he suggested that if I went to Los Angeles we could get together again. So we had dinner a few times and so forth."

Yamamoto was the husband of Mayumi's cousin, and a banker. He was presently in Hawaii as a liaison with an American bank, and Sadaharu was supposed to believe that his wife's going to Yamamoto's for a visit was perfectly natural. He imagined that Asano was the real reason for her trip to Los Angeles.

Mayumi's story was not too specific, but ordinarily, until a relationship has deteriorated to a certain point, a man does not speak of his own wife's infidelity.

Of course, it would be impossible to know which happened first. Because he had no way of knowing what his wife was doing while he was away on business, Asano may have approached Mayumi; or perhaps because Asano was a man who naturally enjoyed being away from home on business, Mrs. Asano, in retaliation, did whatever she felt like doing.

"In any case, the daughter thoroughly despises her mother's lifestyle, Mr. Asano said. She can't trust her at all and even watches her when she goes to the bank," Mayumi continued.

Even if there were other reasons for her condition, Sadaharu felt that behind Chisa Asano's unnatural denial of food was surely her wish not to become like her mother.

He was not happy when he thought of his own wife together with the man called Asano. On her return to Japan, Mayumi had said that she went to Los Angeles because someone had urged her to go. Mayumi had asked him if he wouldn't mind if there was someone accompanying her. It now seemed clear that person was Asano. Mayumi said that she had only shared a meal with him, but it was not likely that they had simply had dinner together and just spent the time talking about themselves, a man and a woman abroad. Along with displeasure, Sadaharu felt a degree of pity and annoyance with a busy man like Asano who, for whatever flimsy reason, might approach a simpleminded soul like Mayumi. He thought, too, that he might be trying to protect his own feelings, concealing them from himself; he went to the refrigerator, opened a bottle of beer, poured, and drank it straight down while gazing out the window. Glancing up to the shelf beside him, he noticed some mail that must have come in the afternoon delivery and been placed there by someone.

Among the letters were two he could tell from the outside were of little interest and which he set aside. But there was an air mail letter from Yoko Kakei, and that he took to the special chair in his study.

"From the other side of the earth to you by Japan Air Lines," she'd written.

What a funny woman, he thought. Although she had long been married to an American, she was totally Japanese in outlook, and when she traveled she invariably went on Japan Air Lines. This was so even though she understood that JAL stewardesses, more than those of any other airline, were like women police officers, trained to be totally inflexible.

"On the way, leaving New York, we landed in Puerto Rico for fuel and to change crew. We were crowded into a waiting room where the toilet did not work. I have no idea how the U.S.-Japan negotiations about air travel are getting on, but I hope the Japanese side makes its points strongly enough."

Sadaharu was amused by Yoko mentioning that she could not use the toilet in Puerto Rico—only because it was broken—in connection with U.S.-Japan air travel negotiations.

"Since you probably have no interest in talk about sightseeing, I thought I would tell you about things of a different sort.

"I am with Mr. and Mrs. Laurie, and yesterday we went to look at two homes for unwed mothers. One is operated by the Salvation Army, the other is managed by the Catholics. As you know, there are many Catholics in this country, and therefore abortion is not legal; when a girl gets pregnant, she has to give birth.

"The Salvation Army establishment is small and can take in about fifty people. It was raining, and the view from the courtyard was dismal. Donations from church supporters provided the necessities of life, simple as they are.

"One fourteen-year-old girl, with a still timid look in her eyes and a big belly, is entrusted with giving milk to the newborn infants, changing diapers, and so forth. That's really fine, isn't it? In a little while when she becomes a mother, she will know what to do without hesitation.

"In the food storage room, there is an excess stock of oranges, watermelons, and limes. There is a well-equipped laundry room, and in another room women who are clever with their hands gather to knit and use the sewing machines. The bedrooms are plain but clean and are decorated with cute toys. At any rate, pregnant girls who are thought of as disgraced and who can't be taken in by their families or community can at least find a place to have their babies in peace here. There is even a nursery school, and mothers who have no place to go after delivery can live here for a time with their children and prepare for the future.

"Like the rest of Brazil, this is a pastiche of humanity, the children here being white, black, yellow, and every color of skin and combination of blood. While I was visiting, there was one particular boy who seemed to be dozing against the wall and couldn't overcome his drowsiness. Finally, he seemed about to fall over. I suppose he was about two years of age, but even though he was young he was very responsible, and when the other children were getting up he had to wake up too, and he seemed to be telling himself that.

"If these had been Japanese children, they would have been taking their naps in bed, with grownups looking out for them nearby. But this lad, young as he was, took responsibility for himself, and he touched our hearts with his gentle self-reliance. I know that in raising children it is best for the parents to be always at hand and material things to be provided, but children who grow up in other circumstances quickly acquire a persevering attitude toward life that is quite natural to human beings.

"When my traveling companions asked what kind of girls become unwed mothers, we were told that many had worked away from home as maids. Possibly, they are used by the master of the house, or perhaps they meet a man somewhere.

"Even if they have sexual relations, it is interesting to see that any children born from such unions are not affected by those relationships. Such children—individualistic and pure—may be the highest rebuke adults receive from God—supposing, that is, that God hands out punishment to us in this world."

Reading Yoko's letter, Sadaharu began to pick his nose. Terribly impolite, but he felt this allowed the letter to better penetrate his mind.

"And so yesterday we visited one other place, the home for unwed mothers managed by the Catholics.

"A Catholic priest, a Brazilian, accompanied our group and although he has been at his parish in Hiroshima for only three years, his Japanese is unbelievably good.

"The facility is large and takes care of three hundred women. The head of the hospital—a nun—is a quiet and impressive woman who acts as though she is beyond race or nationality. She told us that there were two special problems with the women there: the first was finding the father of the child. Even when found, and even if parenthood is acknowledged, most of the fathers are usually without any financial capacity. For instance, one of the girls—quite unsophisticated—had her baby by a lad of fifteen, and he could do nothing at all for her.

"The second problem is when the mother is retarded or mentally ill. In Japan nowadays, they say that we must not use the word 'retarded' because it is a discriminatory term, but I prefer to use it, and I think you will understand why when you read all of this letter.

"However, to get back to my story, when such girls become mothers they must not, after all, raise their children. This problem is not dealt with by the state welfare offices, so there is nothing left but for the church to do it.

"As a matter of fact, it seems this society does not permit operations that would keep women from getting pregnant. But in reality, some women have the operation done secretly. If they are found out, there is big trouble. And it is a reflection of the social and religious atmosphere of Brazil that of the three hundred beds here, sixty are used to treat infections started by illegal abortions.

"The great majority who are taken into homes for unwed mothers are just little girls with big bellies; they are not sick or anything. One girl, whose very pregnant form was hidden under a maternity dress, was walking the hall arm-in-arm with another girl swollen to about the same size—they looked like schoolgirls going to class. The priest knows them by sight and stopped to chat with them. I asked one when she would give birth, and the priest translated for me and touched the girl's stomach. I was afraid that he was getting a little too physical, but in fact the girl herself replied while running her hand over her stomach, not in a suggestive way but openly stroking herself with both hands. Really, it was a healthy scene and a bit humorous, as though the priest and the girl were talking about how ripe the melon was. Then, turning to me, the girl said the baby would be born in about three weeks.

"However, in the the sick ward were women who had gotten illegal abortions, and they were miserable. All the women were pale, and of course some were suffering from venereal disease, malnutrition, tuberculosis, miscarriage, cancer . . . and other things too. I was told that they took in women who could not get social welfare assistance, for whatever reason. It seems that the São Paulo government supplies money for food, medicine, blood for transfusions, and surgery. The women could live there without cost to themselves, so in a sense they were supported, but we might also say that their ignorance had brought about their difficulties.

"In trying to get rid of the fetus, some women had forced soda straws into themselves. (Is there any basis for the notion that this works?) Others made a hole in the uterus with a needle. One of the things that impressed me: there was a baby with syphilis in an incubator, probably going through treatment, illuminated by a red light. It was scarcely born, and already it had to bear such problems. And when I think of how most Japanese just go through life so easily!"

The way her handwriting had gotten all scrambled made Sadaharu guess that Yoko was excited as she wrote this.

"The priest and the rest of us were shown around by the remarkably strong-willed Catholic sister who was head of the hospital. We came into a certain large room where about thirty women were gathered, women who had given birth and would soon be discharged from the hospital. Near the entrance was an older woman with a squarish face and grimy skin; she seemed out of place in the crowd of younger women.

"We Japanese, of course, are jaded with living, Sadaharu, but truly I have never seen such a weary, wasted look as on this woman's face. I suppose that she was not more than thirty-five, but she was so thin that her collar bone stuck out, and her hair was a rat's nest. She seemed to lack even the spirit to repair the button that had come off of her dress, which was open at her chest.

"I asked the priest to ask her if she was an unmarried mother, too, and the woman answered him in a broken voice. It seems that she was married. Her last child was her sixth, a boy. Her husband was a plumber, but he drank to excess. When he drank, he forced her to have sex. What with their poverty, and too many children, her health had been broken. She was not yet twenty-seven years old.

"So once again her husband had overwhelmed her, got her pregnant. She had no money for the birth, and so she came to this home for unwed mothers, even though this was a disgrace in Brazilian society. Yet there was no other way. She'd come from a town almost forty miles from São Paulo to have her child.

"Before she came here, the people around her had advised her, it seems. She could not take care of any more children than she had; they told her to leave the child with someone.

She had intended to do so, but after giving birth and nursing the baby, she found she could not part with it. As she spoke, a stream of tears ran down her cheeks. I nodded in sympathy. She was so poor, she had no education, but she had deep feelings; she had nourished life, and she was unmistakably a mother."

Sadaharu put Yoko's letter aside and went to pour himself another beer. It was his braking system, to help him take lightly what other people took so seriously. He resumed reading.

"There was another person in that large room who drew my attention. I'm not sure I can explain it very well. Her bed was at a distance, and she was dressed in pitiful pajamas. Her actions were somehow different from the other women, and I knew that she was a retarded mother with a problem.

"Our going into that room was probably not so special (though our group consisted of the head of the hospital, a priest the women knew well, and a foreign woman), but we received a bit of attention, and everyone smiled at the priest, noticed us, and responded somehow. But there was this one woman, completely disconnected from the rest of the activity, facing the other way.

"All of a sudden, this woman who seemed not to notice us took her child in her arms, wrapped in a blanket worn thin with too much washing, and came directly over to us. Well, there were other young women who wished to talk with the priest, but they had hesitated, I imagine because he had come in with the head sister and me. This woman was totally lacking in subtlety. She was stoop-shouldered, and acted totally without thinking, I felt.

"She was of mixed blood, with predominantly Negro features. Short hair, crinkly—and her old pajamas must have been someone's hand-me-downs, with the upper and lower parts in different patterns. Her stooped shoulders were really ugly, and her movements were sluggish. She paid no attention at all to the looks or presence of people around her.

"I know I'm putting this badly, but when she came over to us she thrust the baby—it looked like a monkey—toward the priest. The priest didn't change his expression a bit and continued smiling. He nodded and touched the baby's cheek lightly with his finger, then asked the woman something. She replied with a word or two, and I asked the priest what they were talking about.

"'I asked her whether it was a sweet child,' he said in a slightly awkward tone, 'and she answered that her child was beautiful like love.'

"Sadaharu, the moment I heard of that retarded young mother saying of her child that it was as beautiful as love, something broke inside me and I just couldn't control my feelings.

"I suppose she had become some fellow's sexual object and then been discarded. Girls like that are convenient targets for callous men. And they aren't capable of being careful of men who approach them, nor do they have the ability, even if they are raped, to know which man it was, to extract a promise, to inquire, or even to remember. Regardless of the circumstances, because of their mental condition the world will disregard their testimony, and that sort of attitude works in favor of men.

"But never in my life until now have I heard even once such an eloquent expression—and from the mouth of a retarded unwed mother. For a few seconds, I was stunned, as though knocked unconscious, and I thought I might not recover my composure. I wondered what we Japanese have come to.

"Japanese are clever and well educated. But I've never heard, either from religious people or from university professors, such a clear, concise expression of the essence of motherhood. (And surely Japanese mothers never speak this way.)

"As I write this, I can almost see your cynical face. 'A retarded girl is not capable of saying anything so direct and profound; she's probably just repeating something she's heard,' you're saying. Well, that's what I thought at first.

"But remember: the Holy Mother Mary was herself just thirteen or fourteen when she was pregnant with Jesus, they say. When the angel Gabriel announced to her that she would be a mother, Mary was astonished and said, 'I will serve you and give my body as you wish.'

"Now, cynical people like you, Sadaharu, have read that passage in the Bible and said, 'That's a bit much to expect from a child of thirteen!' But the interesting thing is that the first part of Mary's answer appears earlier in Samuel, and it's been assumed that she learned it from there. In Samuel, when King David requests Abigail's hand in marriage, she says that she is no more than a serving girl fit to wash the feet of the King's servants. And Mary, having heard that anecdote from an early age, remembered it at a crucial moment and reacted with a phrase that resembled what she had heard, I suppose.

"Still, when I think of all that, I wonder about the words of that retarded girl all the more. Even for a girl who can't think too much for herself and has been taught such a phrase by adults around her, love is a beautiful thing. The sincerity in those words, for her or for any adult, exactly conveys her true feelings. And I wonder if anything like the natural elegance of those words really exists in Japanese society today.

"Sadaharu, I suppose that if someone is retarded he or she can't teach a subject like mathematics or a foreign language. But in her attitude toward life, that girl shows a profound sense of truth—at least she impressed me. And she alone said what a hundred million smart Japanese could not say, even in her simplemindedness, you see.

"I was exhausted and felt I wanted to return, but the priest said that there was one more baby that we had to go and see. Somewhat at a loss, we went to a room occupied by children who needed adoption—abandoned children. It was explained that more than half of the children were already spoken for. This child would go to the States, another would go to Venezuela—it was all arranged.

"Then the priest found one child and said that this was the one he wanted us to meet, and truly she was a very cute little girl. I was just thinking that after all the priest was a man and would be attracted to a cute girl, when the head of the hospital said, 'She is a thalidomide baby.' And when she opened the child's robe, instead of arms and legs there were only stubs attached, like wings of angels.

"Sadaharu, I just don't know what to say. The child laughed quite happily, and they said she was not yet six months old. Anyone, not only a priest, would have traveled any distance just to see that smile. And in spite of her tender age, I learned from her. If we could only smile as she does, we should all be unconditionally forgiven our sins. Truly, I feel that I am one of those many in the world who fails to carry out the most basic obligations of being human, as she does so naturally.

"No one as yet has asked to take her in. In spite of that, the mother has surrendered all legal rights to her child. The head of the hospital said that now they were responsible for her. I asked an almost shameless question: if no one takes responsibility for this child, what will you do? When she heard the priest's translation of my query, a suspicious look passed over her face. And then she answered that someone will certainly want her for the very reason that she is a thalidomide baby.

"Regrettably, that would very likely not be a Japanese. (Maybe Mrs. Laurie will be the one!) At any rate, the experienced head of the hospital was convinced. This earth is

> not such a disappointing place as we suppose. People who know the beauty of love really do exist—and to a degree that would not occur to us Japanese, who have lost our souls in a sea of prosperity."

Sadaharu was moved by Yoko's letter, but he still had reservations. Ordinarily, and, indeed, almost instinctively, he would take an opposing position to any story he heard, deliberately producing another interpretation. Otherwise he wouldn't feel right.

The retarded mother, for instance. No matter how he tried to think of her child as lovable and cute, there remained the clear possibility that the mother would not be able to provide for the child adequately. She would not offer it proper nourishment, and if some charming fellow came along, she might just go off with him and leave the child in spite of its being "beautiful like love." Then how shining would be her words that now strike people with amazement?

And because he foresaw such a future comedy, he had no intention of challenging Yoko's statement. It was a matter of not mixing soup and slop, and even if the woman herself could not be held to her words, the words themselves had an independent life of their own.

Not that Yoko dealt with such matters, but in Japan when a mother killed a child and shoved the body into a closet or a locker, the mass media immediately wrote about the "demon mother." But in writing like that they were only reassuring themselves that they were not such demons—a childish kind of thought. Behind the "demon mother" was a social reality that had created her, and every member of society shared some responsibility for her.

The Brazilian outlook, social or religious, did not recognize abortion at all, which was why the retarded mother could feel that her child was beautiful like love. But common social sense in Japan had made abortion legal, and even though a mother might kill her child and hide the body, this was not considered so strange.

Once, long ago, Sadaharu had said to a senior high school girl who came to him toward the end of her pregnancy that if she had an abortion at this point it would simply be murdering the child. The uncomprehending girl then tilted her head and said, "If it is all right to do it at the sixth month, isn't it the same when the baby is just a little bigger?" Yet if that logic were pursued a bit further, then you might ask: "How is killing a newborn child different from aborting a six-month fetus?" Of course, Sadaharu did not lack for a response. On one occasion, he said to Yoko that he felt there was a great difference between a creature that could live outside its mother's body and one that could not.

But to his friend Yoko this response was not a refutation. During pregnancy, the spontaneous abortion rate was from eight to fifteen percent, and a four-month fetus, if carried to term, would have an eighty-five percent chance of being born. Even aborting a very young fetus of four or five weeks was terminating a life.

The problem was that the consciousness of the average Japanese—and that included Sadaharu—was quite fixed on the idea that abortion was an ordinary, daily sort of "medical treatment." And to that extent, it is hardly strange that young people come along who say that in following their own conscience, they find nothing wrong even with killing their own newborn child. Everyone upholds the importance of human life and voices concern for the welfare of small children. Yet people can get abortions by simply filling out a form, and everything else is forgotten. All this passed through a corner of Sadaharu's mind, and somehow he never resolved the matter of abortion.

Chapter Seven

The Carpenter of Nazareth

It was only when a call came from Sadaharu's former classmate Dr. Yagihara that Sadaharu recalled that he had referred Mayuko Serizawa to him.

"After I wrote the letter to you I forgot all about it. Sorry."

He was flustered. These days, Sadaharu did not consider himself to be as conscientious as he ought to be, which had provoked his atypical apology.

"Don't mention it. Anyway, I really haven't done anything at all," Dr. Yagihara answered.

"Thanks. What's the story?"

"She came in to the hospital, finally. We did the examinations, and she left immediately. Then she sent us a letter saying she would go to you to get the results."

"I see. Then that's that. She hasn't come in. And the result of course was . . ."

"Right. She is male."

"I thought as much."

"The test showed a negative sex chromatin, chromosome 46 XY; urine 17 KS was 2.7 mg, gonadotropin 26 mu; estrogen 27 mg."

"Did you tell her anything?"

"No, she left before the results were in."

"She probably has undescended testicles. I told her that it might be a kind of hernia."

"And that probably should be removed; it could turn cancerous. If it comes to an operation for an artificial vagina, Dr. Abe here is a specialist, but she would have to be told very clearly what that would involve."

Sadaharu did not necessarily agree with Dr. Yagihara's opinion, but he quite understood the implications of what he was trying to say. After all, if they made an artificial vagina, sexual intercourse would be possible, and then a moral question would arise. She would have to understand that even if she acted like a woman she would not really be a woman. Furthermore, she would be free to deceive men, and the hospital could not be a party to the consequences of deceit. This was the sense of Yagihara's idea, and it was also simply common sense.

But Sadaharu was not convinced that was the only course available. The real problem was whether the person herself thought of herself as a woman or as a man. He was not sure what the answer would be with Serizawa, but if she thought of herself as a woman, then she should become one. There was enough talk about men who went to Morocco to get a sex change operation, but Japan was really the best place for that kind of surgery. And as far as making Serizawa into a woman, except for the function of having children, to a reasonable degree the change could be accomplished.

For a while, Sadaharu talked with Dr. Yagihara about matters unrelated to their work, then he hung up.

Again, that afternoon, Sadaharu was made keenly aware of his carelessness about social amenities when Eiko Nakanishi came into the examination room. She had not been there in a long while.

"Please excuse me for not thanking you for your gift," Sadaharu had to say in embarrassment.

After his previous examination of Mrs. Nakanishi's oviducts Sadaharu had received a cardigan sweater as a gift from Mr. and Mrs. Nakanishi. He had never traveled and was not at all accustomed to dressing himself well, so he thought it was simply a nice sweater the color of red bean paste, but his wife informed him that the sweater was wine-colored and that even in France the manufacturer was famous. This was no item from a department store sale, his usual source of attire, but a luxurious article costing quite a lot of money.

Sadaharu merely remarked on how extravagant it was. "Put it away in moth balls," he'd said, "I'll wear it next year." And he even neglected to write a thank you note.

With his receipt of the present, both Sadaharu and the Nakanishis had assumed their dealings were ended, so Sadaharu was surprised to see Mrs. Nakanishi's face in the examination room. At first, he was sure that she had come with some complaint about his treatment. Not a few doctors these days felt threatened by the legal power of their patients. Given correct diagnosis and identical treatment, it was still obvious that a few cases would not turn out well. In the past, such situations were attributed to bad luck or failure to respond to treatment or something similar, but nowadays patients were apt to claim that even death was the sole responsibility of the doctor. Even a doctor with as arrogant an attitude as Sadaharu in particular would automatically react defensively to the slightest suggestion of blame.

Sadaharu asked Mrs. Nakanishi how she was getting along.

"Well, as a matter of fact," she responded, "since that test my condition has gotten a little worse. My period has stopped completely, and that's very unusual for me. . . ."

The problem was leukorrhea, white vaginal discharge. After drinking a barium solution for examination of her intestinal tract, the color of her stool had changed, so she had thought there might be some kind of infection remaining. But eventually, her body felt heavy, and she had fevers, and, finally, there were days when she simply could not get out of bed.

"My husband said that because I am approaching menopause such changes should be expected. And since I didn't want to make any fuss . . ."

Her color was bad, but for the first time her eyebrows tilted, indicating her laughter.

"Well, it's no trouble. We'll do an examination and find out," Sadaharu reassured her.

"Also, doctor, I wonder if you know that Mrs. Kakei returned yesterday?"

"No, I didn't know that."

"I'm a rather indecisive person, and I thought a long while about whether I should come to see you. But yesterday, finally, I called Mrs. Kakei to discuss it with her. I thought that she might have returned. She said that she'd been back just two hours and urged me to see you without hesitation."

"That's fine. Quite right. Now, let's have a look at you," Sadaharu said.

Mrs. Nakanishi broke off her story. While she was away for her urine test, Sadaharu telephoned Yoko.

"Welcome home," he said. "Mrs. Nakanishi just came in to see me and told me that you were back. How have you been?"

"Just fine, thanks. I didn't feel any jet lag this morning, so I've been up since seven o'clock taking care of things."

"Strong as a horse, aren't you? Thanks for your letter from São Paulo. It gave me a lot to think about."

"And the trip was a marvelous experience for me. If not for the kind of things I wrote you about, if it were just a sightseeing trip, I don't think it would have been worth going."

"Hmm. Well, they say there are a lot of beautiful women there. Since you are a woman, though, I don't suppose you have any interest in that sort of thing."

"Ah, but there are also beautiful men," Yoko replied. "Compared with Japanese men, they are much more gallant, you know."

"So, anything to report on your experiences?"

"In Brazil, people enjoy an active sex life as long as they live, I gather. As for me, I don't find anything attractive in that sort of thing."

"Really, is that so? How very Japanese you are."

"We can talk about all that at our leisure. Please come over for a visit."

"Yes, sure. I'd like to hear about your travels. But you should rest for a while."

When Sadaharu hung up the phone, Nurse Ono called to him.

"Mrs. Nakanishi is a positive." She was referring to the pregnancy test.

"What!?" Sadaharu cried out in shock. Then, "Are you sure there is no mistake?"

"No mistake. No other patients are here now."

The drop of urine on the specimen glass slide had turned white, showing a positive pregnancy reaction.

"Of course. Our batting average is surprisingly good for springtime," he said, as though to cover his embarrassment.

Eiko Nakanishi returned. Sadaharu smiled broadly and laughed. "Well, something unexpected has turned up!"

"Is it cancer?"

"Not at all. A blessed event."

"Oh! That can't be!"

"I'm just as baffled," Sadaharu said. "Last time we spoke, I told you to forget about becoming pregnant. And now, when you thought there was no chance . . . I'm terribly embarrassed about my prediction. If I'd just stretched things out a bit and been less certain, I'd seem like a great doctor."

"Yes, but are you really sure it's true?"

"Really. This kind of thing often happens after that kind of examination, you know."

Sadaharu was full of explanations, but there were two possibilities about this kind of pregnancy. One was that the test itself had opened up the tubes. Another possibility was that Mrs. Nakanishi's oviducts had been functional from the beginning but that the contrast media used in the test failed to enter the area. That was not necessarily due to any failure in Sadaharu's technique. With people who are tense, when the contrast media is injected, tubal spasms occur. To overcome this, an antispasmodic is given, but such functional obstacles as lack of response in the autonomic nervous system might still occur, and it was not unusual for the contrast media not to enter. In such a case, the tubes will appear blocked.

Suddenly, Sadaharu became aware that Mrs. Nakanishi was crying profusely, and he felt perplexed.

"You probably want to call your husband; please use the phone here," he said to her, as though to blunt the force of her outpouring.

"Oh, no. I'll use the public telephone."

"No need to be so formal; use this."

"But my husband is in Tokyo."

"Fine. Call him in Tokyo," Sadaharu said, laughing and handing the receiver to Mrs. Nakanishi.

She thanked him. On the telephone, she began with the word *o-ne-e-san*, and Sadaharu supposed that she had reached either her husband's elder sister or the wife of an elder brother.

"Has my husband gone out? I see. No. There is just something I wished to tell him. . . . No . . . Well, I seem to be pregnant."

In spite of speaking in as calm and controlled a tone as she could, there was an unconcealed agitation in her voice that swept over her in waves.

Sadaharu's attention shifted when he saw the receptionist bring in Mayuko Serizawa's chart, and he was able to ignore Mrs. Nakanishi's conversation on the phone. When she hung up, Sadaharu set the time for her next examination, gave her various instructions, took a deep breath, and had Serizawa shown in.

"Well, it's been quite a while," he greeted her. She did not reply. He continued to watch her dark, silently laughing face. "When did you leave the hospital?"

"About two weeks ago."

"I see. And what was Dr. Yagihara's diagnosis?" he asked, tapping the blunt end of a ball point pen on a card. Whenever he did this, the nurses knew he was either worried or uncertain.

"I haven't yet gone to the hospital to hear," she said. "I thought he might have sent the results to you."

"I haven't heard in any detail. But, in fact, you should consult Dr. Yagihara directly. He isn't a fussy sort, so he won't be offended, but it is a little inappropriate for you to consult me about his examination."

Serizawa was silent, and Sadaharu tried to make conversation.

"You need to ask Dr. Yagihara formally for the results. But that aside, how have you been getting on with your boyfriend?"

"Oh, I didn't have any problem with him."

"I didn't think you did."

"The fifth of May was his birthday. I sent him a present and he telephoned to thank me and ask how I was doing."

"What did you send?"

"A sweater. Last year, I bought a knitting machine, so now if I make a pattern I can knit any design at all very easily. I decided right away that I would knit him a sweater, so I was five days late entering the hospital because I wanted to finish it first."

"Hmm, you're keeping up a good friendly relationship."

"Yes, that's true."

"And Dr. Yagihara told you nothing at all about the test results?"

"He said the same thing you said."

"What was that?"

"He said there was something like a hernia in my belly. If left alone, it might get larger, so he thought it might be better to have it removed surgically."

"Yes, I see."

"And because my vagina was so shallow, there might be something the matter with my uterus, he said."

Sadaharu acknowledged her words.

"When I asked him whether I could have a child, he said very likely I could not. I was depressed that night and couldn't sleep. It's all right if I don't marry my boyfriend, but I did want to bear his child."

"Of course, I understand, but there are more people than you might imagine who can't bear children. It's not only you."

It occurred to Sadaharu to ask what kind of work her roommate did.

"She used to have an office job. She wants to become a dietitian; she's studying for that now."

"Do you get along? She's your roommate, after all."

"Well, we're not really close. . . . I mean, on our days off we walk around Kamakura together, or we go to bargain sales, things like that."

"Where do you go?"

"Oh, there are lots of places in Yokosuka. Last time, we went to a shopping mall near Yokohama Station. There are department stores and specialty shops in the mall, you know, and we stayed from opening until closing time."

"What energy you have!" Sadaharu said. "What did you buy in all that time?"

"Some jeans, a blouse, a negligee. They were selling a lot of winter things terrifically cheap."

"Winter things? Now? You really are prepared."

"We always do that—buy things for next year. That way they are really cheap."

"And who prepares the meals?"

"We take turns every other day, but she ducks out a lot. In the afternoons if she's studying we just have some instant noodles, so at times like that I make the meal."

"Good for you. And do you like housework?"

"Well, I like cooking and sewing well enough. I still don't care much for cleaning house."

Sadaharu smiled. "I'm the same way. Maybe because it's a negative kind of work, putting things in order. Cooking is more positive work. You know, this may seem like an odd question, but which did you like better, your mother or your father?" Sadaharu asked this in a casual tone.

"My mother. But my father was a good person too."

"And was there anything the matter with your father?"

"He was easily seduced by women; he often had affairs. He and my mother would get into terrific arguments."

"Yes, all men are like that."

"I know."

Sadaharu hid behind a hearty laugh.

"But you understand, of course."

"No, I don't understand at all."

"Oh? But all men are promiscuous," he replied. "Can't you forgive him?"

"Yes, but it is hard on my mother."

"I suppose that women are hard to seduce."

"Not really," she said. "When women fall in love they think of nothing but their lovers. I think that is hard on them."

"Men are different. Even if they love someone, when a beautiful woman comes along they always look her over," Sadaharu said.

"Oh, that's terrible," Serizawa exclaimed.

"Then there are different types. They like pretty women, and they also like pretty men."

"You mean gay?"

"Yes. Well, bisexual."

"That gives me the creeps."

"But sometimes a man dressed up like a woman is even prettier than a real one."

Serizawa said, "That seems unhealthy!"

"Well, that's what one hears, but I don't know. I like women myself. A real woman would be better than loving a man who is like a woman."

"The husband of the owner of the bathhouse we use is weird. He is always looking into the women's side of the bath."

"Oh, that's not really so bad. I do the same thing," Sadaharu replied.

"Well, someone said that his wife is always peeking into the men's side."

"Well, that's perfect. It cancels out."

"Honestly, doctor, you talk just like my father."

"Hmm, really?" Sadaharu laughed.

It was Sunday afternoon of the first week in June. Sadaharu met with Yoko, who gave him as a present from South America a small silver picture frame.

"Ah, this is pretty. Not factory made, I suppose. It looks handcrafted."

"Yes, it's silver work from Peru. It will tarnish, but I was captivated by the handmade feeling."

"Why, it's just fine, and I won't notice even if it gets tarnished. It's natural for things to tarnish when you live near the ocean and get a lot of humidity. Even when it turns black, silver retains a silvery quality. So, you also went to Peru?"

"No, I bought it at the airport when the plane landed there. The truth is I had a larger one for you, but when I heard that Mrs. Nakanishi was going to have a baby, I decided to give that one to her."

"Well, all that is my fault."

"Fault? Let me tell you: as far as the Nakanishis are concerned, you are something like a god, so don't be so modest."

"Perhaps, but it was quite unplanned. I feel as bad as though someone had complained. When someone thanks me after I've done nothing, I'm embarrassed. It's unlucky, too."

"Oh, that's nothing to worry about. When we pray and ask forgiveness for our sins, we pray both for the sins we know we've committed and for the evil we've done unintentionally. You see, if we turn that upside down, even things that happen by chance are to your credit."

"Really?" Sadaharu replied.

"The whole Nakanishi family is delighted, you know. Mr. Nakanishi has a crippled leg, and even at his age he is still the darling of the family. This expected child has the whole family going crazy with excitement. Last week or this week, I'm not sure which, they had a family dinner, and everyone is tremendously happy."

"Hmm. That's fine. Just fine."

Sadaharu allowed himself a soft smile, but there was something else on his mind.

In recent years, Sadaharu had put on some weight around his middle and so felt the need for exercise. He had no time for golf, and he did not feel attracted to jogging, which was so popular, or to foot racing. Whenever Sadaharu mentioned to people that being a physician involved physical labor, they would make some comment to the effect that that was no reason for him to develop a paunch. He really could not devote himself to a complete exercise program, but in the summer he often went swimming in the ocean. Outside of that, walking was his only physical exercise. Once every two months or so, he would go as far as Yokosuka, or to Zushi to browse in book shops. Still, the simplest thing for him was to walk about the harbor town of Miura Misaki, near where his clinic was located. And so on the day he saw Yoko off on her trip, he had gone there by bus.

Misaki was the headquarters of the local fishing industry, processing tuna caught in distant oceans. Directly in front of the bus terminal was the harbor inlet with its slick of diesel oil; along the stone wall was the refrigeration plant. The breeze carried an odor of ocean and fishing tackle. Nearby were stand-up bars, cafés, and a ships' supply store called Yaoya. There were plenty of sake shops. A hat shop sold caps worn by the crews of fishing vessels, and in the ship chandler's were displayed colored bands of nylon along with durable clothing.

Sadaharu's walking route was more or less established. From the end of the bus line, he would pass the police station and then stroll along the quay where the fishing vessels were moored on his right. Presently, he would arrive at Jogashima Bridge and from there meander through the winding streets of the residential area. He might stop at a shop specializing in live fish. Because Sadaharu lived in the area, he did not buy the more expensive fish or shellfish as someone from Tokyo might do. His favorite was clam soup. He would buy clams, shrimp, and perhaps white-fleshed fish and later make a sort of bouillabaisse. Like a primitive gatherer, when he saw certain kinds of crab in the shop window he thought of the phases of the moon. The crab at full moon is thin and bad tasting, so they say. He thought about crab, but it was expensive and he rarely bought any.

This was the season when bonito was cheap. One fish with a belly the color of steel had its head thrust into a bucket of ice. Even in the live fish shops he'd never seen live bonito. He was wondering why that was when he heard a woman's voice call "Sensei!"

These days, all kinds of people were called *sensei*—teachers, doctors, barbers—and Sadaharu had a psychological brake associated with the word. He did not turn around. Besides, on his walks he had no desire to meet an acquaintance. But the voice called again: "Nobeji-sensei."

Hearing this, Sadaharu submitted and turned in the direction of the voice.

The woman was about thirty years old, not large, with a healthy, relaxed look about her. She wore dark blue slacks and a red blouse, her ample black hair tied at the nape of her neck.

"Excuse me," Sadaharu said, "but who . . ."

"I'm Kumiko Shinjo, but I don't think you remember me."

Not from around here, he thought. Her complexion is too light.

"At the end of January, I came to your office," she said, her voice dropping a bit.

"Oh? Really?"

She held a plain leather purse. She gave the impression that she lived nearby and had just stepped out to buy some fish.

"May I walk with you for a bit? If you're busy buying fish, I'll wait."

Her tone of voice was not in the least pressuring.

"No, this is fine. I didn't come to buy. I'm just strolling about to see the sights."

As they spoke, he walked with her toward the quay where the ships were moored.

"I'm sorry, but I tend not to remember patients' faces. If I had your record card in front of me, I could remember immediately, but I don't recall what you came to see me about," Sadaharu said frankly.

"That's all right. I came for an abortion."

"Ah, yes, I see," he said, but still Sadaharu didn't see at all. Abortion patients, after disposition, were all told that they must return in a week for at least one postoperative examination, and for another one, especially, if menstruation did not resume within a month afterward. Of course, some patients deliberately failed to appear, and there were some cases Sadaharu still wondered about. As far as this woman before him was concerned, though, he had absolutely no recollection of either the operation or the follow-up.

"And how did you get along afterward? It's possible you did not return for an examination. I usually tell patients to come in after a week, but I may not have told you."

"No, you told me, but I didn't go."

"Why not?"

"When I went to you, I had severe morning sickness. I'm not married, and I didn't want to go to the child's father. I wanted to manage it myself. So I went to your office and had the operation, but my morning sickness didn't get better, even a little bit, and I didn't feel well."

"Eh? That's strange. Morning sickness is a toxic condition of early pregnancy, so when the placenta disappears you should recover immediately."

He thought suddenly that this might be a case of stomach cancer, but one glance at her healthy looking face convinced him otherwise.

"I'm not complaining, doctor. It's just that I don't think the baby came out."

"Did you go to another doctor after that?" Sadaharu asked, feeling uneasy.

"Yes. I went to the municipal hospital at the end of February, and I was still pregnant after all."

Sadaharu muttered to himself and said, "Well, I'm not saying it's your fault in the least, but why didn't you come back to my office? If I failed, I would have corrected it; it's possible for an abortion to fail, of course. Still, I suppose it was natural for you not to come again if you thought I wasn't competent."

"My mother thought that, you see, and she complained and said that I should ask you to refund the fee for the operation."

"Would you mind going over this in more detail somewhere?" Sadaharu asked.

"Sure, that's fine with me. How about going to a coffee shop around here?"

At first, it occurred to Sadaharu that this might be a new kind of fraud. But that sort of thing, if examined scientifically, would be obvious at once. Furthermore, the woman's expression was not in the least threatening. On the contrary, she seemed pleased to have met Sadaharu.

He could not remember having failed at such an operation in the past, and his uneasiness arose from quite another source. Since in a year he performed some two hundred such operations, in the decade since he had begun his practice he must have experienced two thousand of them. He was not at all concerned that he did not remember this particular one.

By her expression the woman walking with him seemed to be enjoying the breeze, and at last they entered a coffee shop called Wild Pinks, a shop that faced toward the sea. It seemed to have just recently opened. In this part of town, Sadaharu had imagined he knew every tiny back street, but the place was new to him.

"Will coffee be all right for you, doctor?" she asked, then told the waitress she would have black tea. "When I got pregnant, I stopped drinking coffee."

"What did they tell you at the municipal hospital?"

"I went there in my third month. They told me there was nothing at all the matter with me, that everything was in order."

"Didn't you tell them you'd had an abortion?"

"Yes, I told them. But I didn't tell them where I'd had it, and they didn't ask. But a doctor at the municipal hospital said I should go back to you and get another examination. The doctor also suggested that I have another abortion, but I decided not to, and I told them that."

Sadaharu said to Shinjo, "No apology for what happened would be sufficient. What they told you at the hospital must have been correct, I think. Why didn't you come to me sooner?"

"Well, I'm sorry about that, but I run a beauty shop close to here and what with being busy—and when the morning sickness got better, I felt much better—and then the baby began to move inside of me. . . . And so I put it off from day to day."

Sadaharu said, "You know, I had a case the other day—a woman who had not seen a doctor until the day the child was due to be born. She had a splendid baby, but she acted unreasonably by not seeing a doctor. She should have had a blood test and had the position of the baby checked. So please come to see me tomorrow."

"Yes, would the day after tomorrow be all right? Tuesdays the beauty shop is closed," Shinjo said.

Sadaharu was silent. He felt an obscure weight in his chest, a slight unhappiness that the operation had not accomplished its objective.

"I don't want to pry into your private life, but when did you decide to go ahead and have the child? Usually when someone learns the operation was unsuccessful, their first thought is to have it done again."

"Yes. Only, this was my second abortion," Shinjo said. "The first was when I thought I was going to have a very proper wedding. The father was the son of a lumber dealer from my home town. We went together for a long time, so we had a physical relationship even before the wedding. I was pregnant—I thought that was all right—and we calculated the time of the wedding ceremony for seven months or so ahead. His mother thought it was indecent, and she asked me to get an abortion.

"I wanted to have the baby, but because he and I were both young, we were optimistic. We thought that we could have a child any time, and how nice I would look in my wedding dress, and that I should do what his mother asked. So I had the abortion. But then two months later, he was struck in the head by some falling lumber, and after living for about three months like a vegetable, he died."

Sadaharu shook his head. "Do such accidents really happen?"

"It must be very rare, but what happened to me was that I became a widow without ever having been married."

"And did you begin training to be a beautician after that?"

"Yes, after that. His mother wept and said how much she wished I'd had the child, and they gave me a lump sum of money. They told me to make a fresh start. After I finished training, I went into the beauty shop business here in town when someone told me there was an excellent place available. It was hard for me to stay where I was because of the memories."

"And is this place really so good—for business?"

"Yes. People in the fishing business tend to be rather flashy, you know. I have one assistant, and I'm independent."

Shinjo told Sadaharu the rest of her story. After the death of her fiancé, she half felt as though she were a widow, but last year, in December, she had become acquainted with a Tokyo man who worked for a trading company. One Sunday evening when Shinjo had just closed her shop and stepped outside, a man of about thirty got out of a car that was stopped right in front of her shop. The fan belt had broken and the car was overheating. All the big repair shops were closed, but he asked if there might be some small place in the neighborhood where he could get the belt changed even on a Sunday.

Happily, Shinjo knew a man who ran an auto repair shop just a couple of blocks away. The man's wife was one of her customers. So Shinjo lent the young man a bicycle and on another bicycle rode along with him to show him the way. By good luck, the husband was at home and agreed to change the belt. Meanwhile, the young man invited Shinjo to have something to eat, and the two of them went to a nearby pizzeria and ordered the largest pizza they had.

He was charming. He produced his name card, according to which he was a businessman named Mizutani. There was a celebrated fishing spot nearby called Bishamon, and he had been there to stay and play mah-jongg at a friend's country house. He was now on his way back to Tokyo. He spoke openly to Shinjo, saying she was a good-natured and open-hearted person, that he intended to return next week, and that he hoped she would give him the pleasure of her company next Sunday evening. Shinjo had long dreamed of having an elegant date like this. Usually she associated with women connected with her work. Her mind was already made up, she wanted to talk with a man, and so she agreed without a second thought to meet him the following week.

Mizutani told her that he was expecting to get married early the next year. Shinjo asked why he wasn't seeing his fiancée the next week, and Mizutani said that the girl had gone on a trip to Europe with her mother before getting married, so even though he wanted to be with her, he couldn't.

The next week, Mizutani came by as he had promised. And he invited Shinjo to a nearby motel. He was a man full of vitality, and when adult men and women become acquainted, this kind of thing happens naturally—or so both of them agreed. The relationship between them continued until close to the end of the year, when Mizutani's fiancée returned from abroad.

For Shinjo, her affair with Mizutani had been a complete pleasure. But even more, it was a refreshing "until we part" kind of association.

"Both of us were independent and free, so an affair like that was of no particular consequence."

Finally, Mizutani wished her the best for herself and her business, and Shinjo told him what great fun he had been and that she was sure he would be successful at his company. She wished him happiness with his new wife, and they parted.

The New Year arrived, and even though she knew she was pregnant she felt there was nothing she could do about it. If she went to the man and asked for money for the operation, that would spoil her feelings for him. Of course, she had absolutely no intention of continuing with the pregnancy. To her mother, who lived with her, her severe morning sickness was quite apparent, but Kumiko said nothing about the man she had been with.

"Of course, I was sure that if I went to you, doctor, there was no chance the operation would fail," Kumiko added, in a tone that Sadaharu found distasteful.

She was angry at first that her physical condition did not improve. Customers came to the shop, and she continued to deceive herself and attend to business, but, finally, at her mother's urging, she went to the municipal hospital instead of back to Sadaharu. Of course, she harbored a feeling of mistrust about him, yet when she was told that she was still pregnant, she was overcome by a strange feeling. A child that could survive all that and still remain alive must be blessed with a remarkable life force, she began to think. And though it was only her imagination, she thought perhaps the child would excel in sports—sailing, swimming, soccer. But it did not occur to her that it might resemble Mizutani, who was so confident of his own strength.

For herself, for her hopes for a real marriage, however, she had taken a false and fatal step. Soon she would be thirty years old and would have a child. Despite everything, she wanted to keep to herself the memory of Mizutani as the father of her child. If ever Shinjo at last succeeded in marrying, having failed in two attempts, she did not feel it would be impossible to find someone who could understand her feelings in this regard. In any case, she did not intend to reveal the father's name, acting as she believed an independent woman should. She thought the worst thing women could do was to push their way into a man's house threatening a paternity suit.

Thinking that she would then try to keep the child, she was glad that the operation had failed. For the child, she thought, it was a major test, winning a battle with fate. That thought became Shinjo's pride. If the child was that strongly destined to survive, Shinjo came to feel, then it would certainly lead a life worth living.

Sadaharu detected not the slightest ill will in Shinjo, but he could not help but feel a certain irony about the precariousness of his own skill, considering how much more grateful Shinjo was for the baby she was carrying as a consequence.

"Come without fail the day after tomorrow," Sadaharu instructed Shinjo, and when they parted she expressed her concern about his finding his way home, telling him the way to the bus stop. Sadaharu did not feel like going home directly.

"I think I'll walk a little more," he told her, going on with no particular destination in mind. But then, after he had walked for only ten minutes, along came an empty taxi, and Sadaharu raised his hand to stop it. "Do you know the Catholic church in Kurihama?" he asked, intending not to take the cab if the driver did not know.

"Sure, I know it," the driver replied, opening the door. Sadaharu felt torn about getting in. Should he arrive at this strange hour, Father Munechika would assume upon seeing him that he was about to receive another convert. He might even start smirking a bit inside. But in this world things are not quite so easy, and Sadaharu thought how he would never become a believer. He thought of Yoko and Father Munechika as people to whom he could reveal his weaknesses, and that, in fact, is an extreme form of respect for another person.

The Kurihama church was built away from the highway and halfway up a hill. Being relatively new, the front garden caught the sun from the west and was wide and bright. Sadaharu thought that if the priest was absent, he would be happy to return home, but when he inquired at the rectory he was told that the Father was there. He appeared in a moment wearing pants bagging at the knees and a sports shirt.

Sadaharu told a believable lie: "I happened to be passing by and saw the spire and thought I'd see what kind of a place this was. But I'm afraid I've caught you at a bad time."

"No, no. I've just finished. In the morning, I was with the Cub Scouts, and after that, from one o'clock, the children's Catholic instruction. There was a meeting of the youth group at half past two, but I'm all finished now and I was just thinking of having a sabbatical bottle of beer. You're just in time; please join me."

Sadaharu accepted the invitation. He removed his shoes, entered, and passed through to the priest's reception room and study on the second floor where there was a view of a bit of the ocean.

"Have you seen Mrs. Kakei?" the priest asked Sadaharu.

"Just a short while ago," he replied.

"She visited with a present for me and seemed quite well."

From a refrigerator in a corner of the room, the priest promptly brought a beer. He got two glasses from a cabinet, filling them immediately.

"Well, you don't live badly," Sadaharu remarked as he gazed about.

"Do you think so?" Father Munechika seemed pleased with Sadaharu's observation.

"I don't suppose you will believe this, Father, but in my experience a house stays in order when there is no wife around. That's what I find," Sadaharu said.

"My housekeeper, Mrs. Ogata, is really a demon for keeping things in order. I'm not very well organized myself."

"But being a housekeeper is a good position. A wife is like a bird making a nest. She brings in all sorts of foolish things."

The moment Sadaharu drank his beer, his spirits relaxed; he began to think that he was becoming an alcoholic.

"True. Birds are a marvel. When we left the rain shutters closed for a week, a grey starling made a nest in the shutter box."

"Living alone all your life must be difficult, really. I don't mean that in a banal way, because Mrs. Kakei said that you chose that path for yourself. Still, it isn't a completely happy life, wouldn't you say?"

"Well, that's true," Father Munechika said in a cheery tone. "If you say it is difficult, then it is, but when you have faith you experience a transformation in your values. For instance, not having children, not perpetuating oneself after death in a form that you can see—faith is a response to that."

Sadaharu asked how that happens.

"What we call life is not simply an organic thing. One can take a more abstract view of life. After all, it is something that is given and passed on."

"Exactly," Sadaharu said. "In that sense, sex, or the act of reproduction, is a truly simple principle. As a device, it is a magnificent thing, but as was once said, it does not matter how it turns out."

"Do you understand it?" Father Munechika asked.

"Well, we think sex is so important because it involves the child to be born, or one's own partner. If not for that, then sex is not much of anything at all. But for the life of the priest, what is painful, I suppose, is that no other involvement produces such an effect in people."

While Sadaharu was going on with this inconsequential matter, in the back of his mind was the affair of Kumiko Shinjo. He was not involved with her in any significant way, and yet he was aware of being involved with the process of sending a human being into the world. Such had not been his intention, and it had happened as the result of a blunder.

When Sadaharu and Shinjo parted, she'd said that if she gave birth she would eventually tell the child everything except the name of the father. Her mother had said doing that would warp the child, but Shinjo did not think so. There was a man in his fifties, she recalled, who had been the eighth child in his family, and if he had been conceived during the hard times after the war, he would never have been born. And another man said that his mother once had been at the point of drowning both him and herself. In each case, the parent would have been in the position of a murderer, but neither man showed any resentment toward his parent. It would be the same thing if one told a child that it had been saved from abortion; the child would not feel any shock, Shinjo believed.

In this situation, Sadaharu was only a hired physician who performed a single function, and thirty years or so later Sadaharu in his seventies could hardly expect to hear from a man or woman: "I heard from my mother that I owe my existence to you—or rather to your mistake in technique." Sadaharu was not afraid of that. But he was very ill at ease with the magnitude of his error.

"This church isn't so old, is it?" Sadaharu said, the liquor affecting him as he tried to push the matter of Shinjo out his mind.

"That's right, only about thirteen or fourteen years old. I've heard that Mrs. Kakei's husband was a major force in collecting money for the building. He contributed the picture at the entrance to the church. It seems that he received it as a gift from an Italian gentleman for whom he successfully settled some legal matter, but he had no place large enough to hang it. He always wanted to donate it to a church, so he arranged for a mural space in the church just for the picture."

"Is it by some famous artist?" Sadaharu inquired.

"It is the work of a nineteenth-century Italian artist. He wasn't so famous, but it's a fine portrayal of Jesus of Nazareth."

"I've heard of the word *Nazareth*, but I'm ashamed to say I've never read the Bible. Of course, I know what it's about in general, but that's about it. So what's the connection between Jesus and Nazareth?"

"He worked as a carpenter there during his youth. It's what we would call his hometown."

"I suppose I shouldn't discuss this with you, but I've encountered something strange," Sadaharu said, unable to avoid what was on his mind. "A friend of Mrs. Kakei's is pregnant, a Mrs. Nakanishi."

"So I heard," Father Munechika said.

"We did an examination, and right after I gave her my opinion that her fallopian tubes were obstructed, she got pregnant. I don't know whether it was the medicine I gave her to make the X-ray images that made the tubes open or something else."

"But isn't that a happy event? Mrs. Kakei says that at the Nakanishi house they talk as though you're some kind of god."

"Hmm. I'd be proud of that if it had been something I'd planned, but it really wasn't my doing. To put it in your terms, it was really an act of God. Still, at least I collected the fee," Sadaharu chuckled.

"But that's all right, isn't it? Generally speaking, God does not need money," the priest said.

"Yes, and I decided to accept that it was my doing with a straight face. But as a matter of fact, the same kind of thing happened again not long ago."

Sadaharu disliked leaving himself completely open, so he was less than precise about whether this event happened the same day or only a moment ago or whenever.

"I did an abortion at the end of January," he went on, "for a certain patient, you see. I don't recall the case exactly, but she was probably in her fifth or sixth week, very early on I think it was. So what I removed from her was not clear evidence, given the length of her pregnancy. I had no idea at all then that I'd failed. It would make Mrs. Kakei angry to hear this, but by my calculations I've done two or three thousand such operations, including those before I began the clinic."

"Indeed," the priest said.

"The patient didn't even come back for a checkup afterward, so I just forgot about her. But I happened to meet her, and she told me that the abortion was unsuccessful. She had an examination at the municipal hospital and was told that her pregnancy was progressing normally. So, suddenly, she felt like having the child, since it seemed to be blessed by fortune. Of course, the child is not the product of a formal marriage. It made me uneasy to hear about this, Father."

"What does it mean?" Father Munechika asked, ignoring Sadaharu's complaint. "Did the operation really fail?"

"I won't know about that until I do an examination. Technically though, I don't think I can properly examine the uterus before the baby is delivered."

"Then there are possibilities to consider."

"Exactly. There could be a variety of deformities, like uterine myoma, or uterus bicornis, or uterus didelphys. The uterus might even have divided into two parts inside, or at the cervix.

"What we call a malformed uterus differs according to its shape, but two identical chambers can form, or the uterus may have corners." Sadaharu was trying to put this all in terms suitable for a layman. "If the uterus is healthy, even a fumbling operation that reaches to some part of the uterus can be confirmed through touch, even though you don't see it with your eyes. On the other hand, if you make X-ray pictures in advance you can deal with malformations. But if you don't know about the malformation, then sometimes a part remains that you can't deal with.

"In extreme cases, when there is one entrance but two separate uteruses inside, the egg may remain affixed to one side while the other side swells up as well, and then there forms what is called deciduous membranes in the inner coating. When you operate, even though you dislodge the side where there is no embryo, there is a discharge of matter just as when there is a pregnancy. Strictly speaking, there is a slight difference, but in the fifth or sixth week the amount of material is so small that we can't tell the difference. The embryo on the opposite side simply remains completely unharmed and untouched."

Father Munechika nodded. "That's very interesting. But whatever the case, the result is your responsibility. You have caused a life to exist."

"That's a very depressing way to produce life, Father. Just what am I in that case? In your way of speaking, I'm an instrument of God. But I'm a rather dirty instrument, I'm afraid."

"Dirty? That's not so clear, I think. Neither the good nor evil of humanity, nor the process of becoming so, is at all simple until we know the results."

There was a knock on the door. The priest acknowledged it, and a woman of about sixty appeared.

"Ah, Mrs. Shoda, please come in," he said.

"Excuse me for disturbing you." The woman entered, but perhaps out of politeness for Sadaharu she did not move to sit on the sofa.

"And how is your granddaughter?"

"I've just returned from the hospital. Thanks to your help, she will be able to have the operation in a week or so."

"Your grandchild is five, isn't she?"

"She just turned six."

Speaking to both Sadaharu and Mrs. Shoda, Father Munechika said, "She has a congenital heart disease, and now at last the chance for an operation has come along. You may know the institution, doctor—it's the prefectural hospital."

"Yes, I know the prefectural children's hospital by name, but I haven't been there," Sadaharu said.

"They took her in thinking they could operate immediately, but she developed pneumonia and they had to postpone it."

"What kind of heart trouble does she have? Is it an atrial septal defect?" Sadaharu asked of both the woman and the priest.

The woman knitted her brow and said, "I've heard the name many times, but it is somehow so hard for me to remember it. Something like tetra . . ."

"Fallot's tetralogy?"

"Yes, that's it."

"Mrs. Shoda is a very devout Christian," Father Munechika said, "but her granddaughter's father, her son-in-law, is not a believer. So he would not allow the child to be baptized, and Mrs. Shoda is very worried. Especially since because of the heart trouble the child could die at any time. All the more reason for her to be baptized, isn't that right, Mrs. Shoda?"

"Yes, that's right."

"The son-in-law is reluctant, but because it is a girl it may be all right with him if she becomes a Catholic. He's agreed that especially before the operation it would be a good idea to call upon God."

Sadaharu said, "Indeed."

"Well, Mrs. Shoda," Father Munechika said, "when shall we perform the baptism?"

"Whenever it's convenient for you, Father. You can come to visit her."

"Fine. Until Friday I'll be directing a retreat for the Sisters at Hayama Monastery. Of course, if your granddaughter's condition is bad I can put that off."

"No, I think she will be all right. Her fever has subsided."

"Then I'll come Saturday afternoon. Three o'clock is too early, but I can arrive in Yokohama at four."

"That will be fine. Thank you very much. I feel much better about everything now."

"And where shall we meet at the hospital?"

"I'll be in the waiting room, near the entrance, at four o'clock," the woman said.

"If you have time, Dr. Nobeji, please come too. I really recommend that you visit the hospital if you haven't done so before," the priest said. "The assistant head of the hospital is Catholic and I know him well, so I'll call in advance."

"Yes, I can go with you," Sadaharu said. "Saturday afternoon my replacement will take over at the clinic."

"Well, at any rate, Mrs. Shoda, I'll be there next Saturday," Father Munechika said.

As the woman thanked him and went toward the door, Sadaharu too stood up.

"Oh, are you leaving?"

"If I stay too long, I won't be able to move," Sadaharu said to the priest.

"Then before you leave perhaps you might like to have a look at the picture I mentioned, Jesus of Nazareth?"

Father Munechika's church was a modest structure, neither dark nor impressive, and the stained glass window was a mere sheet of colored glass that formed a tall, narrow window with the cross upon it, but thanks to the western sun, its light filled every corner of the church.

The picture was hung on the rear wall; it was large, about thirteen feet high and ten feet wide. The artist's name was Vittorio Biancchi. Sadaharu had no eye for art, but he thought it was a nice image, easy to understand. The subject was the bearded Jesus repairing a broken cart. Looking on beside him was the Virgin Mary holding a water jar, and scattered around Jesus' feet were wood shavings and carpentry tools. Five or six children of the village were also looking on beside Jesus. In the garden behind them were doves and a tethered goat. In the distance, on a gentle hill, a vineyard could be seen, and an old shepherd walking along the road tending his sheep.

"A peaceful picture, isn't it?" Sadaharu remarked. He thought it might not be termed a particularly skillful work. Something was not quite right about it; it seemed to him as if it was taken from a child's picture book. But that was exactly why he liked it.

"I often use this picture in my sermons. Until Jesus was over thirty, he helped his father and mother in Nazareth, working as an ordinary carpenter. His daily life was not in the least unusual. He repaired whatever was asked of him, making the small things needed in life. The message of the picture is that people who are not concerned with the matters of their daily lives in the end are not qualified to deal with great things."

"I see. That's a fine idea," Sadaharu said.

"Little things are tied to big things, and big things sustained by little things. I suppose that is an invariable rule."

"In spite of that, Jesus' hands are dirty. It looks like he is doing agricultural work instead of carpentry." Sadaharu was pleased with his own discovery.

"Oh, yes. Mrs. Kakei has criticized the picture on that point, but she was being sarcastic. If, to be realistic, the hands were painted dirty, then the face should be just as dirty. For the face here to be so godlike and unsullied is peculiar, and the Virgin Mary should be clothed more suitably to a poor life, Mrs. Kakei said."

"Well, the material of the clothing does not seem to be particularly fine, but it would have been better to make it all a little older and dirtier," Sadaharu said.

"But even the hand of God is dirty when He is at work. If His hands are not dirty, then He is not actually working."

Sadaharu pretended not to have caught the priest's words. "But it is really quite a nice painting," he said politely. "For a long time, I wanted to see what kind of church you had here, but I didn't want to trouble you by making a special appointment.

"Well, until Saturday then. I'll call you beforehand."

Father Munechika saw his visitor off as far as the front garden filled with the slanting rays of the afternoon sun.

Chapter Eight

The Chosen One

The following Tuesday morning Kumiko Shinjo did not appear, and Sadaharu wondered whether she would keep her appointment for a checkup. He considered looking up her file to get her address and telephone number. He completed his morning tasks and was on his way to lunch when, as though to deprive him of his meal, a telephone call came from the mother of Chisa Asano.

The night before, Chisa had fainted, the mother said, the second time this had occurred. When she lost consciousness the first time, about two weeks earlier, they immediately went to the municipal hospital where X-rays, a blood sample, and even an electrocardiogram were taken. Chisa had shown slight anemia and low blood pressure but nothing else abnormal, she said. But the second time Chisa fainted, Mrs. Asano became quite concerned. As usual, the girl was not eating to the point where her mother wondered whether she could live on what she took in. When she suggested to Chisa that it might be necessary to hospitalize her to nourish her, Chisa answered that she would consent only if she could go to Dr. Nobeji's clinic.

"The truth is, it would be best to deal with the problem through an internist," Sadaharu said, "but it's all right with me. If it will make Chisa better, then by all means, come here. But what about her schooling?"

"I haven't given much thought to that yet," the mother said. "If she can't earn enough credits, then keeping her back a year would be better for both of us than this kind of mixed up life. It's better to cure her first."

"Then please bring her in. But I don't think that we can put her in a private room. There are a lot of patients here now—and even if we had a room open, it's better for her not to be alone."

"Yes, that kind of room arrangement would be fine."

Sadaharu hung up. He thought that the tone of Mrs. Asano's voice indicated how unbearable she found her relationship with her daughter. Where the psychological root of that lay, he could not imagine. But he knew there were many examples in this world of parents and children wounding each other. In such cases, only when the parent-child relationship ended could they get along well together. But if they tried to maintain their association in the same household, they risked coming to actively despise, or even destroy, each other. In such situations, if they can only forget the parent-child relationship, then the main part of the problem is solved. But if things got to the point of one hating the other, of a deterioration to the point of murder or suicide, then clearly the best thing to do was to leave the house. Perhaps even just temporarily living apart, or as in the present case, something not quite so serious, like entering a hospital, would help. Given all this, Sadaharu thought it best to provide an escape route for Chisa.

It was past three in the afternoon when Shinjo appeared, a time when the western sun was flowing into part of the examination room.

"Where have you been? I was worried about you," Sadaharu said.

"I'm really sorry. The girl at the grocer's next door wanted to buy some clothes for a meeting with her future in-laws, and so I went shopping with her during the morning," Shinjo said.

"Oh, yes, I see. So that was it." Sadaharu thought it was nice that she could be so casual.

While Shinjo was preparing behind the curtain, Sadaharu used an old curvature chart to calculate how far along her pregnancy was. Gauged from the time of her last menses, which was noted on her chart, she was now in her twenty-sixth week.

"Yes, indeed. You've gotten good and big."

Nonetheless, Sadaharu could not keep himself from entertaining the cynical idea that the first operation had been successful after all, and that something had happened and Shinjo had actually gotten pregnant again after that.

"What month am I in?" Kumiko asked.

"About the middle of the seventh month. I can let you hear the sound of the baby's heart," Sadaharu said.

He applied an electronic stethoscope that used ultrasonic waves, and the beating of the infant's heart could be heard like the sounds of waves against a roaring sea.

"Oh! It's really alive. How marvelous!" she said.

Sadaharu had decided not to indulge in self-blame, but when he heard those words he felt it natural for him to remain silent. He completed the examination and returned to his desk.

"Ms. Shinjo, I can't know for certain until we have the result of the blood test, but everything seems to be in perfect order. Do you have a pregnancy and birth notebook yet?"

"Yes. I was told I am due at the end of September."

"I didn't mention it, but it will probably be close to September 20."

"The twentieth? That's the anniversary of my father's death," Shinjo said.

"Then maybe you will have a boy as his replacement."

"That's a sad thought; but the twentieth, you say?"

"You mean the anniversary is no good?"

"No, not that, but it means I'll be very big through the hottest months of the year and there won't be any way to hide it."

"Do you intend to hide it?"

"Ah, no. That's really not possible."

She continued speaking in a low voice. "The fact is, the day before yesterday, after I left you, I met him. The baby's father.

Quite by chance." Her voice was rough with emotion. She had been on the street and someone tapped her on the shoulder. She turned to see the face of the man she thought she would never see again. He had come to town to play mah-jongg with a friend, and before returning to Tokyo he had stopped off to eat some of the town's famous mackerel sushi. As they were parking the car next to the fishermen's cooperative, he saw someone who looked to him like Shinjo, so he got out and went after her, he said.

"You look well."

Shinjo laughed. "Yes, thanks, I'm doing all right."

"Are you pregnant?"

Some men would think this but not say it. To say it outright was very much in this man's character.

"Yes. That's right," Shinjo said. She added, "You weren't my only boyfriend. That's the way it goes." She affected a laugh.

"Oh, I see," he said, smiling. Then, with a wink, he slapped her on the shoulder, Shinjo said.

"He said to take care. And then good-bye, and then thanks."

Sadaharu nodded and said he understood.

"I suppose it is just womanish of me to say this, and you may laugh at me, but he didn't say 'Thank you, good-bye.' After I got home, I thought a lot about the order of those words."

"Is there a great difference between 'good-bye, thanks' and 'thanks, good-bye'? I can't understand such things because I haven't got much of a literary imagination."

"I feel there is some difference, and I guess that he understood the real situation, so in the end he said 'thanks'—I'm sure of that."

"But it was irresponsible, wasn't it?"

"It was my decision not to tell him the truth. I'd made up my mind, and that was that. I'll never utter his name as long as I live, I've decided. Having that secret makes me happy."

"Whatever gives you pleasure. If you don't mind," Sadaharu said, "I'd like to stop by your house sometime."

He wanted to be sure he would have no problems with her later.

Shinjo agreed, and while Sadaharu thought no difficulties would arise, since she had accepted the consequences of continuing her pregnancy, there had been a case in England a while ago, a case like this, that had ended up in court. A woman, age twenty-nine, living in Surrey, had an abortion at a hospital in London, but the operation had failed and she gave birth to a male child seven months later. The child was six years old when the mother claimed that if the operation had succeeded this child would not exist. But because the operation had failed, she had lost her job and her dream of marriage as well. As a consequence of having established laws recognizing abortion, the court concluded that the nation accordingly should have laws protecting women who have been injured physically or mentally by failure of the operation. In that case, the court ordered the physician involved to pay over eighteen thousand pounds in damages to the unwed mother.

This was all the information Sadaharu had received, so there was little more he could say, but he did not imagine that the physician in the case had been silent. Malformations of the uterus are common, and full responsibility could hardly lie totally with the physician.

Sadaharu explained his procedures to his patients, but he did not ask their permission for each treatment. He thought of the unwed mother in England who, in front of her six-year-old son, had said, "If the operation had been successful, this child would not exist, and if he had not been born then my own fortunes would likely be much better." A bad joke. With such a foolish woman, Sadaharu thought, to give her money was like throwing it in front of a pig.

But it wouldn't do to criticize the English woman. Whenever something unfortunate happened to a person, no matter what reason, then the entire country—politicians, university professors, the mass media, or some other interested parties—immediately offer protection to the miserable soul trying to get some money under the pretext of receiving appropriate compensation. And in that sense, the entire country falls to the same moral level as that of the English woman.

"Then I'll stop by about half past one in the afternoon, next Tuesday," Sadaharu said to Shinjo.

"Oh, yes, anytime is fine," she replied, delighted but hardly aware of what was on Sadaharu's mind.

As Shinjo was leaving, Nurse Okubo entered the examination room. "Doctor, it's Chisa Asano. Where shall we put her?"

As a rule, the head nurse would not be concerned about such a thing, but with Chisa she understood some preparation was advisable.

"Well . . . How about with Mrs. Koyasu?" Sadaharu suggested.

Mitsuko Koyasu had given birth to a seven-pound, fifteen-ounce baby girl the previous evening, and being twenty-eight years old and large-framed, she'd had a very easy delivery and appeared to be in good shape.

"Mrs. Koyasu is still having a problem urinating and is very uncomfortable," Nurse Okubo said.

"Have you tried getting her on her feet?"

"She tried, but she said it was too painful, so we used a catheter." Mrs. Koyasu had had such an easy delivery with her first child that when she heard the child's cry she asked, "Oh! Is it born already?" But since that morning and all the next day, she had experienced a temporary obstruction of the urinary tract. Ordinarily, a woman in labor is not given water before delivery, so for some hours afterward no urine is discharged as a rule. Usually, any abnormal condition corrects itself within twenty-four hours, but Mrs. Koyasu was not making any progress.

Sadaharu had noticed Mrs. Asano and her daughter entering the reception area, but he left all the paperwork to his head nurse. When he finally went to the room Chisa Asano was now sharing with Mrs. Koyasu, it was ten past six in the evening and he had seen his last patient for the day.

Passing Nurse Ono in the hall, Sadaharu remarked that it had been a long day.

"When the days are long, it makes me feel as though I am saving a lot of money," he said.

"Saving money?" said Nurse Ono, perplexed. But Sadaharu walked on.

Sadaharu paused for a moment before opening the door of the room, waiting to see how things were going inside, but just then he heard a sound like teenagers laughing, so he knocked and entered.

"Mrs. Koyasu, how are you doing? Any urine yet?"

"No, not yet. What do you think the trouble is?"

"It will come soon."

"The nurse said the same thing, but I don't think that it ever will," she replied.

"Now, don't exaggerate. That has never yet happened to anyone," Sadaharu explained.

"Really?"

"And Chisa, how are you doing? Since you are not really ill, you shouldn't be in bed all the time, you know!"

Sadaharu had decided not to prescribe any special treatment for Chisa, at least partly because he knew if he were to urge her to eat at this point she almost certainly would refuse. Mothers distressed by children with no appetite would place a delicious-looking meal before the child and urge her or him to eat—and this was Sadaharu's impulse as well.

He had asked the head nurse about Chisa's appetite, and she had replied that she was not certain but it seemed to be about half what was normal. Once each day, he would summon Chisa to the examination room, but only to take her blood pressure; he never asked whether she liked the food or not.

"And what do you do all day?"

"Oh, I write up my school notes, read a book, or do needlework."

"Well, I won't order you to do so, but you may walk around if you like. Is your mother worried?" he asked.

"She comes every day. But I tell her that I'm not sick and not to worry about me."

"That's fine. It's good exercise for your mother, so make sure she keeps coming."

Sadaharu also did not insist that Chisa be weighed often. All the expressed concern about her weight was unnatural, and, in fact, it is normal for human beings to experience fluctuations in weight. But one afternoon when Sadaharu was returning from his walk, Chisa came up from behind and joined him.

"Hello. Where have you been?" he asked.

"A friend of mine said he would like some bird feathers, so I went to gather some."

In her hand she held a number of dark feathers.

"And what is he going to do with them? They aren't very pretty, are they?"

"He wants to use them to decorate the front of his straw hat."

"Oh, I see. They make a more striking impression than peacock feathers," Sadaharu remarked.

"Doctor, I think that I'd like to talk with you sometime," Chisa said, squinting her eyes against the fierce midsummer light. "Mrs. Koyasu has already taught me a lot."

"Mrs. Koyasu?" For a moment, Sadaharu failed to connect the name with the patient in the clinic.

"The lady who just had a baby who's in the same room with me. I talked over a lot of things with her. She looks like she's just big and fat and easygoing, but she is really a smart person."

"Oh. I didn't know that," Sadaharu replied, now remembering the woman who had had her first child.

"She said she was raised by her stepmother and that at first she felt a grudge against her. But now when she looks back on that time, she thinks her stepmother was probably treated badly by her and her sisters. She and her older and younger sisters ganged up to tease her stepmother a lot." Sadaharu acknowledged her observation. "And she said that one day she mentioned that to her stepmother, and then her stepmother began to weep terribly and thanked her so much for telling her that so honestly. And then the two of them became really close, more like older sister and younger sister than stepmother and stepdaughter."

Sadaharu said, "That's very good to hear. When a parent and child don't get along . . ."

"And after that, Mrs. Koyasu felt that if they let nature take its course everything would start going really well. And when she told me this story, she was still so uncomfortable because she couldn't urinate. That was strange too."

"Why strange?" Sadaharu asked.

"I think it was the day after I came to the clinic. The head nurse was taking Mrs. Koyasu to the toilet and I happened to be coming back from reading a magazine in the waiting room. I suddenly stopped in the toilet doorway, but Mrs. Koyasu had a serious look on her face and didn't seem to notice me or anything. When she went to the toilet, the head nurse asked her if she was all right, and I could hear her say 'Yes, I'm all right.' And then the nurse said, 'Just relax, now, and imagine a mountain valley where the pure water is flowing down naturally. If you try to stop it, it just won't stop, will it? The water flows down the mountain to a lower place. Now it has flowed, hasn't it?'—and she ran the water in the sink. 'Now the stream is getting stronger and stronger,' she said. And then just a few seconds later, I could hear the sound of water coming from inside the toilet. 'Here it comes, here it comes!' Mrs. Koyasu said. Really, Mrs. Koyasu is such a great person, isn't she?"

Sadaharu did not remember until just that moment that he'd gotten a report from Nurse Okubo that day. Nor did he recall until then the method of resolving a temporary cessation of urine by using the psychological technique of having the patient listen to the sound of running water, a method often referred to.

"Without thinking, I said congratulations to Mrs. Koyasu," Chisa said. "I've never thought much about how vital this sort of thing is, so when it finally got cleared up, I understood how important health can be."

"When we're healthy, it means before anything else that we can walk and see and hear and talk and eat—and eliminate without trouble," Sadaharu said.

"I really didn't mean to tell you all this about Mrs. Koyasu. Actually, there is something else I wanted to ask, doctor."

"And what is that?"

"Doctor, you know about your wife, I suppose, that she often goes to meet my father?"

"Yes, I know. I'm not totally in the dark."

"And do you intend to just leave it as it is?"

"I don't know what to do. You can't just lock up a grown person when she goes out walking."

"I don't want to be a grownup. I felt that way even way when I was small."

Sadaharu offered no comforting answer to that, saying only: "You don't want to grow up? But that's impossible; it's like being crippled."

"But my mother often used to say that it's a shame I had to grow up."

"Well, that's an absurdly dangerous idea, you know. You are simply not complete if you don't become an adult, and that's the way it is. Did you think that by not eating you would stop yourself from growing up?"

"What?" Chisa said, surprised. "No, nothing like that."

"But if you don't eat, you'll just be an adult without any energy, and you'll look old. But if you do eat, then you'll grow up to be a productive adult," Sadaharu said.

"I never thought of that until now, but I suppose it's true, isn't it?" she said in a low voice. "My mother is proud of her breasts. She's always been like that, but now she's proud that her figure hasn't gone to pieces. I think it's really disgusting to talk like that."

"You know, there is only one way for a woman not to get old and that is to have pride in herself and to work at it," Sadaharu said.

"You mean to exercise, right?"

"Exactly. For example, insomnia is cured one hundred percent of the time if you do farm work. Wives in farm families in this area don't work in fancy places like Tokyo office workers, but they enjoy the blessing of a natural life, and that's the truth."

Sadaharu considered himself a coward because of his frequent inability to refuse people, and he constantly hoped that somehow they would forget what they had asked.

Before the granddaughter of his parishioner was to have her heart operation, Father Munechika was to baptize the girl, and although Sadaharu surely should have declined, in the end he had said that he would accompany him. Secretly, he hoped that the priest would forget about it. For Sadaharu the agnostic, there was always a feeling of awe, of the unapproachable, about such things as Shinto, Buddhist, and Christian altars, a kind of primitive reverence for the deities of Shinto and Buddhism. He had read the autobiography of the great educator Yukichi Fukuzawa, and what impressed him most in that work was Fukuzawa's stepping on an amulet while in the toilet in an experiment to see whether he would be punished or not.

Sadaharu felt embarrassed to go to the baptism of someone's sick child with whom he had absolutely no connection. He was hoping that he would not hear from Father Munechika, but the day before their appointment the priest telephoned to say that he would pick up Sadaharu in his car.

"There's no escape, none at all," Sadaharu said to Hiroshige, his relief physician at the clinic. "Tomorrow I'll go to see the children's hospital."

Father Munechika appeared punctually at the promised time in the middle of a rainstorm and took the captive Sadaharu away in his rickety car.

It was Saturday, but the rain-drenched road was empty, and the priest drove through the gate of the greenery-shrouded children's hospital at the appointed time.

"Actually, Father," Sadaharu said, "since I have no connection with the girl's family, I'd rather not attend the religious ceremony. I'll just wait out here until it is over and then have a look around, if that's all right."

"That's fine. Whatever you wish. The baptism ceremony will take only ten minutes or so."

Sadaharu doubted the ceremony would be quite that brief and brought out the paperback detective novel he had in his back pocket. What a strange place to read a murder mystery, he thought. Besides that, it felt odd to be in the position of a visitor at a place of medical treatment. As it turned out, Sadaharu did not read but, rather, watched the people coming and going in the waiting room. Because it was Saturday, there were many visitors for the patients, most of them young mothers or fathers at an age appropriate to members of the kindergarten PTA.

Suddenly, he was overcome with the feeling that perhaps Mayumi's unhappiness stemmed from the fact that she did not have a child in this kind of hospital, or a husband in prison. Of course, if he ever said that, he would be violently criticized by parents of sick children, and mothers who dragged themselves to visit their imprisoned sons would be troubled.

In any case, Mayumi was completely incapable of appreciating what she had been given in life.

Young mothers coming to visit their children on a rainy day kept entering the reception area, drops like tears falling from the tips of their closed umbrellas as they passed into the waiting room where Sadaharu was seated. Some women wore lipstick while others appeared pale, their hair disordered. Most of them, thought Sadaharu, were in torment, even though they did not express it; for them, such concepts as "equality" and "human rights" must seem totally empty. No matter how much medical treatment the national government provided, for certain kinds of congenital deformities no help was possible. Children thus afflicted were condemned to a fate for which they could bear no responsibility.

The priest appeared sooner than Sadaharu expected, accompanied by a physician in a white coat.

"This is Dr. Inage, assistant director of the hospital," Father Munechika said.

Taken by surprise, Sadaharu hurriedly searched for his business card, but he discovered he had forgotten to bring any.

"Perfectly all right," Dr. Inage said.

"And your parishioners?" Sadaharu asked.

"Oh, that's all right. We can visit them later on."

Dr. Inage invited the visitors to his office, and the priest and Sadaharu followed him down the hallway. Tea was served in the office, and while the other two men talked Sadaharu paid close attention to eating a sweet cream cake. Sadaharu knew that there was a difference in attitude between specialists in pediatrics and obstetrics, a difference in philosophies that extended beyond individuals, yet he was annoyed when he encountered that aspect of medicine. He was not now involved in any kind of unpleasant discussion along those lines, however, and, presently, the three of them began walking to the wards. Soon they reached a veranda decorated with large red artificial flowers where they met a young woman who had been looking for Father Munechika. Sadaharu guessed she was the daughter of the parishioner, Mrs. Shoda, whom he had met a week earlier.

"Mother is waiting for you," she said to the priest.

Sadaharu sensed that since the family had called in the priest, her words meant that they were unwilling to allow the priest to spend time with anyone else. Father Munechika said he would follow her.

"Mother told me to find out where you had gone."

"Well, then, shall we go along to the room?" Sadaharu suggested.

The Shoda granddaughter, Yoshiko, was asleep in the farthest bed of the room at the end of the hallway. Fortunately, this also happened to be the most natural place for them to begin their inspection. Sadaharu went over to her and stroked the thin child's curly hair.

"That's good. Her fever is down, now she can be operated on," he said.

"Yes, we're so thankful. Other people around us here envy my granddaughter because she can have this operation. I feel ashamed when I come here and see children who can't be cured and go home like Yoshiko."

The grandmother Sadaharu had met at the rectory was speaking in a low voice. The grandmother, the child's mother, and another young woman had come for the baptism.

Meanwhile, Sadaharu, glancing about, turned to the bed next to Yoshiko's, where a baby whose illness he could not guess was pounding its legs against the mattress.

The child seemed to be seven or eight months of age and looked normal to Sadaharu. Over its diaper pants it wore a neat shirt, and like a little turtle placed on a rock the baby was pounding its legs earnestly without crying, just playing alone.

Sadaharu, his arms folded on his chest, asked Doctor Inage, "And this child—what is the matter with it?"

"We've not yet gotten a proper chromosome test, but the indications are Down's syndrome."

Dr. Inage turned the baby on its back to put it to sleep. As he did so, the baby showed the warm brightness of its eyes, spaced wide apart and gazing at the ceiling. Down's syndrome, a type of chromosome malformation, was named after a physician who identified the condition in 1866. The characteristics include: flatness of the skull; upward tilt of the corners of the eyes; narrow eyes, with an epicanthic fold; low nose bridge; large tongue; constantly open mouth; small, shell-shaped ears; short neck; loose muscles; weak stomach muscles; herniated navel; short, splayed hands; short fifth finger curved inward; monkey lines; fan-shaped very wide bottom on the feet; widely spaced feet.

In simple terms, the eyes of the afflicted child were widely separated and gave the impression that the inside corners of the eyes were not properly formed, that with a pair of scissors the eyes might be snipped free. Its mouth was open and a thick tongue protruded. The palms of the child's hands seemed to be shortened, and across the middle ran a single crease; Sadaharu had this line too. What most clearly set apart sufferers from Down's syndrome was the retarded development of both height and body weight. Many such children had intelligence quotients below fifty but had quite cheerful personalities.

A young doctor in charge of the ward appeared to greet the assistant head of the hospital, and Sadaharu and Father Munechika were introduced to Dr. Kodama.

"I don't understand this thing called Down's syndrome. Is it mental retardation?" Father Munechika asked.

"Yes. But more generally speaking, it is a consequence of chromosome abnormality."

"And so the child is still all right; it can do things like agricultural work?"

"Yes, but this child is an extreme case. To begin with, it has a closed anus."

"What?"

"A congenital problem. The anus was closed at birth. As an emergency measure, we created a temporary anus while making a lower opening," Dr. Kodama replied. He seemed to want to show his success and removed the child's diapers. Only vestiges of the temporary artificial anus on the left side of the stomach remained, and where the permanent artificial anus was installed they could see only a smear of healthy, glistening feces.

"Is this an artificial anus? It looks normal, as though it has a sphincter." Father Munechika admired what looked like the anus, yet he could not tell whether the sphincter actually functioned or not.

The closed anus abnormality occurs when the colon terminates somewhere along its length and does not connect with the sphincter, but the same condition may appear if the colon descends far enough but terminates higher up. In such cases, there is little chance of a functioning sphincter. Whichever the case, the trick in repairing the condition is to pull the colon down and to attach it without damage. Even if the operation goes well, one has to be aware of occasional incontinence in many cases. A complicating factor exists when children are of such low intelligence that they cannot consciously make up for their physical impediments.

Unlike the priest, Sadaharu did not go so far as to admire the artificial anus as a work of art. As though aware of Sadaharu's concern, Dr. Inage asked, "Dr. Kodama, is the child a boy or a girl?"

"Oh, a boy, as you see, but the there's a problem with the urethra—hypospadias—and that must be corrected by the time the child is of school age. Otherwise, the child will have to use the girls' toilet."

Having explained this, Dr. Kodama turned to Father Munechika and said, "When the hypospadias is as pronounced as this one is, even though it is repaired by surgery, it is quite possible that the patient will never be able to have sexual intercourse."

"Ah, really?" the priest answered. "His nose is twisted, isn't it?" he added, as though wishing to direct his eyes elsewhere.

"A harelip. It has been operated on, so it's not conspicuous."

The priest acknowledged the improvement.

"But it was not only a split lip; there is a cleft palate, right up the back of the mouth. It can't be operated on until the child is at least eighteen months old."

"And how old is the child now?"

"Just eighteen months. The time is about right, but as you can see his development is retarded. . . ."

"And what about his heart?" Dr. Inage asked.

"There is a ventricular septum defect. That will also require surgery."

"Surely that must be all!" said the priest, his words indicating his unwillingness to hear any more.

"No. In fact, this child is totally blind."

Father Munechika was silent.

"The parents considered their child a nuisance and hit him with something and broke some ribs. Sometime later, his head was injured, and I would guess that caused his blindness."

The priest turned his face away. Even after a year and a half of life, the child with no reaction to light offered an unimaginably clear and gentle expression. And as his face was turned up to Father Munechika, it seemed as though the priest could not endure his apparent gaze.

"Did the parents hit this child?" he murmured.

"Yes, it appears they did. I don't know the details of what transpired, but they have not come to see the child even once. I don't know what you would call it—an abandoned child, I suppose."

With a sigh Father Munechika said, "I come here often, but I've never seen a child as bad off as this one."

"Over there, in that room, there is a child with heart ailments, extra digits, and a cleft palate. Because of the grouping of symptoms, its deformity is particularly burdensome."

The priest said, "A child like Christ, carrying upon his shoulders the suffering of others."

And it seemed that the child, banging its arms and legs, looked on with blind devotion as Father Munechika stroked its head.

"This child over here suffers congenital closure of the bile duct, the Oddi's sphincter," Kodama said.

The child was a large-bodied female with a strangely dark earth color to her face.

"How old is she?" the priest asked.

"A year and three months," the doctor answered.

"Her physique seems fine. Is she asleep or in a coma?"

"She is sleeping now. But in a little while she will be as you said.

She has cirrhosis of the liver."

"Fifteen months old and she has liver cirrhosis? She seems so well developed."

"Yes. Right after she was born she took in a lot of milk, so she seemed to be well nourished. Jaundice—you often see that condition at birth, and it eventually disappears. But at her one-month examination we found the jaundice had not cleared up. The mother thought she was only dark complexioned. This coloration is a little different from the usual jaundice, somewhat cloudy."

"Can she be helped?"

"No, I don't think so."

A woman entered whom they realized was the child's mother, and so their conversation ended. Her hair was parted in the middle; she wore a dark blue skirt with a white blouse. Without glancing at the assistant director or at Sadaharu, she sat down beside the sleeping child.

"Kasumi, dear. Kasumi, dear." She spoke to the child, but the child neither opened its eyes nor responded.

The mother did not utter the sick girl's name again. Drawing a small wooden chair as close as she could to the little bed, she began stroking over and over again the head of her sleeping child.

Chapter Nine

A Visitor in the Summer Rainy Season

The rain gave no sign of letting up at all when Father Munechika and Sadaharu finally set out from the hospital.

"Father, would you like to stop for a drink?" Sadaharu asked. "I'd be glad to drive for you, if you'd like."

"No, not for me, but perhaps you would like one."

"Thanks, but I'm rather used to the sort of things we just saw. I've delivered hundreds of children, and even when everything goes well I still can't help feeling that some abnormality is bound to appear, statistically speaking."

"Are children like that found often?"

"Well, what we call a chromosome abnormality is not so rare. It's thought there may be some connection with the age of the mother. At the age of twenty, the rate of occurrence is about one in a thousand. By forty-five, the chance is one in forty. Even so, one in forty wouldn't be considered very good odds in roulette," Sadaharu said.

"Still, that child with the completely malformed body was truly Christlike. His face glowed," the priest said.

"Oh, certainly. Down's syndrome does give children a gentle and attractive personality. The sickness of angels, really. That kind of child will never steal, or set fires, or murder. That innocent look on their faces is full of love. The problem is that while they are cute when children, their intelligence is inadequate. When they grow up, a lot of them lose their parents' love. Really. There's a lot of that. People take in a puppy, but when it grows up they lose interest in caring for it, and they let it off the leash. Psychologically speaking, it's about the same with those children."

Sadaharu then spoke to the priest in a way that suggested his own psychological brake might have slipped: "But the parents of the child we just saw seem to have beaten him despite the fact that he was so small. A child as helpless as that. I doubt that they beat him because they hated him, though. But a moment ago, the thought crossed my mind that the opposite could be true."

"How is that?"

"Oh, that ordinarily they would expect the child to grow up to be self-supporting, and probably they could not face the reality of the situation. You know how a talented parent will sometimes bitterly criticize his son, call him a fool? But if the parent has no expectations, that kind of scene won't take place—at least that's what I think," Sadaharu said.

"But do you mean the talented father's concern about his son's education, and his scolding, can be considered the equivalent of the parent of the Down's syndrome child breaking the child's ribs?"

"Oh, I don't mean to say that," Sadaharu said. "But Father, when you see a child like that, do you really believe it's better for the child to live?"

"Well, life, what we call life, isn't something human beings can understand, nor can they decide about matters of life or death. That's true of life in general. Life is God's work," the priest answered.

"If that's true, it's a blessing and a comfort for all of us, I'm sure. But there is one point on which I can agree with you, Father. As far as that child is concerned, all it will ever know about life is what it knows now. I don't particularly sympathize with its condition, however. I'll give you an example of what I mean. That child with its artificial anus will very likely be incontinent in its bowel movements. With training, the child will gradually be able to dispense with diapers, but unlike a healthy person he will not be able to control diarrhea, so he will nonchalantly soil his pants. Then, once the pants are soiled, he will not have the intelligence to realize that the odor is repugnant to people, so he will not clean himself. And the parents must care for the child whether they want to or not, and the child can never train himself. Eventually, it all becomes a vicious circle.

"In such cases, it is not just the afflicted child who must carry the burden; so must parents, friends, anyone who comes near him. But the child himself has no idea of how miserable they all are.

"You know, it's bad enough when a person knows the feeling of good health and afterward declines, becomes incontinent, for instance. But that child, from the very beginning, has no anal sphincter and knows nothing about caring for itself or the agreeable sensation of clean elimination.

"Of course, all that is obvious. What's so terribly sad is that once he could at least see, but even that was taken from him. He had some early memory, but then his vision was destroyed. That makes him quite different from us; we've always taken the ability to see for granted."

To the extreme case that Sadaharu presented, the priest simply replied, "There will be some help for that, I suppose."

Sadaharu said he supposed there would.

"After all, it is better to live than not, I believe. Even knowing how bad the prognosis is, the mother of the child with cirrhosis of the liver still fervently stroked her child's brow. To me, it seemed that she was convincing herself, in her heart, of the child's existence. And she must wonder how long she will go on stroking its hair—a few days, even a few minutes? Yet although the child seems to be sleeping as in a coma, she still gives the mother some happiness. Yes, and sadness, too, I suppose. But my impression is that this child who will live for only a year or so will still give the mother a profound sense of having once been a mother."

"Yes," Sadaharu said, "and one explanation for that is that mammals recognize each other when they are young if they maintain skin contact. The concern about newborn babies being separated from their mothers and all is preposterous. What counts is being held, being given milk, being made comfortable, and so forth."

"Yes, I've heard that," Father Munechika said.

"It's even possible for a baby to survive getting its ribs broken by its parents, so long as someone else will hold it. Anyone will do. If you hold the child tight, then it will grow up trusting."

"You may have noticed," the priest added, "that in the room with the less severely ill children there was one who had been there a long time. The child has an incomplete esophagus, not connected to its stomach, and she has had an operation for a tracheal fistula. A child with Down's syndrome was put into the playpen with her, and instead of being held he enjoyed rubbing her cheek to cheek."

"At any rate, thanks to you, today was most enlightening for me," Sadaharu said with polite formality.

"That's kind of you, but it seemed rather like explaining sutras to Buddha," Father Munechika murmured, turning his eyes to the green trees that overhung the road.

"To live is to suffer, no matter what," Sadaharu said.

They reached Sadaharu's house and were met at the gate by Chisa Asano.

"Where have you been?" Sadaharu asked, thinking of the rain.

"I went to post a letter," she replied.

Chisa had made no rapid improvement, but she seemed to feel better and showed a good attitude as the days passed. No longer did she spend the day in her robe. First thing each morning, she dressed and helped the ward patients. Occasionally she would clean the hallways without any suggestion or help from anyone.

Sadaharu told Chisa about going to the prefectural children's hospital. "It was strange—no, pitiful. I saw a girl there who was born with an incomplete esophagus. Of course, with surgery the esophagus was more or less repaired, but for a long time she never ate through her mouth. Food was delivered directly to her stomach. From one point of view, eating is nothing more than an instinctive pleasure, but that girl had to be taught how to swallow. Isn't that strange?"

"Anyway, nowadays I enjoy eating too," Chisa said.

"That's fine. How unnatural to have to be taught how to eat!" Sadaharu laughed.

On Tuesday, before going to Kumiko Shinjo's house, Sadaharu thought of discussing the situation with Mayumi, but after thinking it over he decided against it. Not that he wanted to keep the matter secret from his wife, but whenever anything unusual came up Mayumi seemed to lose control of herself. She would either become inordinately fearful or else unbelievably dense.

Instead, Sadaharu told the facts to Nurse Ono. Then, consulting his ledger, he put an envelope with the appropriate sum in cash into his back pocket, separate from his wallet. With that he set out for the beauty shop, following the directions he'd received from Shinjo.

That day, too, it was raining, and Sadaharu, finding that he was gratified to be able to walk with an umbrella concealing his face, weighed in his mind whether his response to the Shinjo incident might not be influenced by a guilty conscience.

On the door of "Beauty Salon Kumi" was a sign indicating that the shop was ordinarily closed that day, but the door itself was not locked.

"Oh, I've been waiting for you, doctor," Shinjo said. She was wearing a dress in a checkered red-and-navy pattern, with a large white collar; it seemed to be a maternity dress. She came out hurriedly from the rear of the shop, and there was no sign of anyone else with her.

"Isn't your mother at home today?" Sadaharu asked as he entered the room at the rear.

"She went to see my aunt in Odawara. And in spite of the rain, the girl who works with me in the shop went off with a friend on a day trip to Nikko."

"Ah, youth! What energy!" Sadaharu said. "Well, I'd like to explain to you why your operation didn't succeed."

"That's all right," Shinjo interrupted. "In fact, I'm just as happy with things as they are."

"I wonder if you read in the newspaper about this case in England?" Sadaharu took the article he'd saved from his wallet and showed it to Shinjo, who read it slowly and sighed.

"And she is a mother. It's really an awful story to tell to a child, though."

"Do you think so?" said Sadaharu.

"At the beginning, I suppose I felt the way she did, but when I began to feel the child move inside me I really understood how wonderful it was. Now the child is my treasure."

"Well, that's fine. Really. Nonetheless, since we didn't achieve the desired result, I'd like to return the fee for the operation." Sadaharu took the brown envelope containing the money from his back pocket.

"Oh, please, doctor. I was the one who asked you, and I've caused you a lot of bother," Shinjo said, leaving the envelope between them on the table. "But I'm anxious about one thing: the degree of shock to the fetus at that early stage of pregnancy. I just hope it won't cause any abnormality."

Her concern was typical of the worry felt by many pregnant women. Since the thalidomide incidents, women during pregnancy had become more than necessarily cautious of medication, and some would not even take medicine for colds. As a consequence, at the clinic Sadaharu sometimes even prescribed traditional Chinese herbal remedies.

"Very likely, everything will be all right. Even in perfectly natural circumstances, there is an abnormality in only one of every six hundred cases. We can't be absolutely certain, but in general there is no cause for worry, I'm sure of that. If your embryo had been affected by the abortion operation, your pregnancy would have stopped."

Shinjo said she understood. "Then do you think it will be all right for me to go ahead as I had planned and take care of the child right here in this room while I work in the beauty shop?"

The area consisted of a medium-sized room equipped with three chairs and mirrors for hair styling and behind that a smaller room that seemed to be a rest area for employees.

"Oh, it's quite adequate, isn't it? I think a natural environment is best for raising a child," Sadaharu said.

"I don't much like the idea of leaving a child in a day care center," Kumiko said, "and I couldn't stand to be separated from my own child like that."

"That's a truly healthy outlook," Sadaharu remarked. "You have to hold them all the time and talk with children whether they understand you or not," he went on. "I once read a book by Shiro Nakagawa, the head of the Department of Animal Breeding at Ueno Park Zoo. And he said the chimpanzee's keeper talks to it a lot every day. He didn't think he communicated any meaning, but he thought the feeling got through. But you know all that already. I wonder whether being an unmarried mother in a town like this might not subject you to a lot of psychological pressure."

Shinjo's eyes twinkled merrily "I lie," she said. "Women have a weakness for romantic stories. So I say that the man I was married to died of cancer. He knew he was ill and asked me to have a child. The child inside me is a keepsake. I'm really quite a novelist, don't you think?"

"Really! But you ought to put on a sad face now and then. As it is, you look much too happy," Sadaharu told her.

"But you see, before he died he said that he would be angry with me if I cried. What a liar I am!"

Sadaharu laughed. "A marvelous liar!" adding, "But it's not really lying, I think. It's more like a true romance from your own heart."

The envelope containing the refund for her surgery fee remained untouched on the table, and when it came time for Sadaharu to leave he explained that Shinjo should take the money and use it for the child.

Suddenly, she agreed. "Thanks, I will. Shall I write a receipt?"

"That would be marvelous. It will make my accountant very happy," Sadaharu laughed.

"What shall I write? Just that this is a refund of the fee for surgery?"

"Yes, that will do quite well."

As she wrote, Sadaharu looked closely at Shinjo's profile. The worst that might be said of her was that she had rather simple features, but he felt that spending time with this woman would make everything in life somehow feel more natural. Sadaharu thought that kind of change might be fascinating.

At his desk in the clinic, Sadaharu saw at a glance that the patient before him had come with a person who seemed to be her mother, but he directed his attention elsewhere at first. The patient's history card, filled out and brought in by his receptionist, showed that the girl already had been diagnosed as being pregnant. A notation on the card indicated that she could no longer go to the other physician and that she wished to have an examination at the Nobeji Clinic.

"Sakiko Moji?" As was his custom, Sadaharu confirmed the patient's name without raising his eyes from the card.

"Yes, that's correct," came the reply.

"How are you feeling?"

For a moment, there was no reply. Then, just as he was looking up, the mother—or mother-in-law—accompanying the girl spoke.

"You see, doctor, my daughter-in-law is expecting, and she saw a doctor near her parents' home in Chiba, but that is quite a distance from where she lives now—and the doctor there frankly does not enjoy the best reputation. That's why we've come to you."

For the first time, Sadaharu looked at her face. She seemed to be in her early sixties, her white hair undyed, and while not beautiful she was well groomed and wore gold-rimmed glasses and a white summer kimono. He sensed a slight tension in her voice.

"Where do you live now?" Sadaharu asked.

"We are near Akidani. My son and his wife, however, live in Tokyo."

There was something wrong about this situation, Sadaharu felt. If the young woman's family and the clinic near it were far away in Chiba, wouldn't it be likely for a young couple living in Tokyo to find a physician on the Miura Peninsula to be rather far, too? But in such cases, he deliberately avoided showing curiosity outside of matters directly connected with his work. "Do you have a pregnancy and birth notebook?"

"No, not yet," was the reply, but again from the mother-in-law.

"And when was the last menstruation?" he asked, expecting the older woman to respond.

"March 26."

Sadaharu moved his eyes, looking directly at the face of the patient. It was typically Japanese, full in the upper eyelids, a layer of fat beneath the skin. "All right, then. Let's proceed with the examination." He indicated the bed enclosed by a curtain. While Nurse Ono prepared the patient, Sadaharu calculated the number of weeks of pregnancy and found that she would seem to be in her seventeenth week.

"And when was the couple married?" Sadaharu felt he might just as well ask this of the mother-in-law.

"The ceremony was March 17 of this year."

"I see."

Nurse Ono opened the curtain halfway, and Sadaharu went over to the patient. As he looked at the shape of Sakiko Moji there on the examining table he felt, out of his years of professionally honed intuition, that her pregnancy had not begun at the end of March. Perhaps it was the cotton dress that clearly showed Sakiko's figure, but more was indicated by the degree of swelling of the uterus from the navel area.

"Mrs. Moji, you can feel the baby moving, can't you?" Sadaharu asked.

"Yes, I can," she replied.

As usual, Sadaharu had the expectant mother listen to the sound of the child's heartbeat through the stethoscope, but Moji, with her eyes closed, seemed less happy than she was absorbed in her own thoughts. Sadaharu summoned her back to his desk.

"According to the date you mentioned, Mrs. Moji, your due date would be in December, about the thirty-first, but I think the child will be born a little earlier than that," he said.

Without the least expression of surprise, the mother-in-law said, "What exactly does that mean?"

"Just that the child is a bit larger. As you said, your last period was March 26, and this should be the end of the fourth month. But the fetus is already moving, you see. Fetal movement occurs at the end of the fifth month, not earlier."

The older woman was silent. Then, in a quiet tone, she asked, "According to your examination, doctor, how far along is the pregnancy?"

Sadaharu replied, "The lower uterus is close to the level of the navel, so it seems to me she is about at the end of the sixth month. Of course, there are differences, depending upon the particular person."

"Yes. Well, so small a discrepancy with young people is quite all right, doctor, but the fact is that Sakiko's elder sister passed away with stomach cancer about a month after Sakiko's wedding. She was only thirty-two, and we were all terribly shocked. At the time, Sakiko's mother had Sakiko get a stomach X-ray. Now, what we are concerned about is that she had an X-ray during early pregnancy and that there may be some cause for worry. There has been some talk about her not going through with this pregnancy. If she were to have an abortion, we are wondering about how late it can be done."

The white-haired lady's voice was a bit too composed, and Sadaharu wondered how much he could rely on what she said.

"Legally speaking, the operation can be done up to the end of the sixth month, but a midterm abortion is a serious matter. With a one-time X-ray, there is really not much to worry about."

The patient herself spoke. "I want to have the child."

"Oh, I understand how you feel," the mother-in-law said. "But you two are still young, and you can have lots of children. Isn't it best not to take any risks?"

Sadaharu felt that the two women were at odds.

"Well, then, no matter what we decide to do, today's meeting has been quite satisfactory and quite a relief for us."

The white-haired lady spoke very properly, while the younger woman remained silent, her face lowered. After they left, Sadaharu remained at his desk, tapping the record form with the blunt end of his ballpoint pen.

"Hmm, something's wrong there," he muttered to the nurse.

"Premarital intercourse?" Nurse Iwanami asked.

"I suppose so," Sadaharu replied.

"Well, that's the best way," said the young nurse.

"You approve of premarital intercourse?"

"It's not a matter of approval, but it's kind of unnatural to rule it out completely."

"Even the old lady wasn't against it."

"Then she should say so openly."

"Anyway, I really don't know what was going on with them."

But, thought Sadaharu, someday she will make her reasons perfectly clear. But he had no idea that she would do so quite so soon.

It was close to noon when the receptionist came into the examination room and said, "The lady who came with the patient

Mrs. Moji this morning would like to see you briefly, doctor."

"That's fine. Show her in after I finish with the next two patients."

A short time later, the lady in the smooth white summer kimono appeared in the doorway.

"Thank you so much for seeing us earlier," she said.

"Not at all," Sadaharu said. "Please come in. I've finished with the morning consultations, if there is anything you wish to discuss."

"I just saw my daughter-in-law off at the station and I was about to return home myself, but since I asked about an abortion earlier, and there is not much time, I decided to see you again."

"Please be seated."

She thanked him. "As a matter of fact, the physician we saw earlier, who was close to Sakiko's family, was not at all bad, but the date of the pregnancy was a somewhat difficult point, and I finally decided I needed a second opinion. The two were actually married April 17, you see, and if the baby had been conceived immediately afterward would she now be at the end of her fourth month? Do you think it's possible?" she asked in a low voice.

Given the number of months the younger woman had said she was pregnant there were few possibilities to explain the size of her abdomen. In the case of multiple fetuses or hydatiform mole, the bottom of the uterus may rise to the level of the navel in the third or fourth month, and in case of acute hydramnios (excess amniotic fluid) the abdomen becomes rapidly larger through an acute excess of amniotic fluid only in the fourth or fifth month of pregnancy.

Beyond that, it should have been impossible to feel the fetus from the upper abdominal wall, as Sadaharu's examination showed. To feel that, she would have to be into her fifth month, and to be able to distinguish the fetus itself would mean that she must be at the end of her sixth month.

"I cannot tell precisely, but my opinion is that she is probably in her sixth month. That's just my feeling. However, considering the time of the wedding ceremony, I really can't say this is a honeymoon baby."

"Yes, I quite understand that," the older woman said. "If that were the case, everything would be fine. But the girl was employed at my son's company, and in the past there was some gossip about her. Her father was head instructor at a middle school, or something like that, and since she came from an educated family we thought perhaps she would make a suitable daughter-in-law despite the rumors. But then it turned out that with a straight face she would leave the office in Marunouchi after work and visit one of the executives of a small real estate company in Kanda. When the male employees of that company went drinking, talk of this girl inevitably came up. Frankly, they were not remarking about what a fine young lady she was. She was the object of the most indecent interest, indeed. Now, our son, who is oblivious to such things, fell in love with that girl, and . . ."

Nurse Ono noticed that Sadaharu was tapping the patient's chart with the top of his ballpoint pen, so she immediately went out for lunch with the other two young nurses.

"Is he your only son?" Sadaharu asked.

"We have two; he is the older."

"I see."

"His friends and seniors in the company tried to warn him, but his feelings did not change. In the meantime, someone quite suitable for a properly arranged marriage appeared, but he wouldn't even consent to meet her."

Inside himself Sadaharu felt an emotion flaring up in resistance to all this. Among the sons and daughters of people in the financial world, a spouse was not chosen as an individual. The usual concern was to chose a mate according to family business connections. But this lady's son simply had the feelings of a normal man.

"My husband was angry and said that he would disown our son if he married this girl. But I calmed him down, and we had a traditional wedding ceremony for them, although my husband did not invite his long-standing business friends. People from our son's company came, but somehow they understood the situation, and it was more like an invitation to a wake."

"And the marriage ceremony was April 17, just after which her menstruation stopped, is that it?" Sadaharu asked the question with his eyes on the patient's record, while reaching for his memo pad.

"It wasn't simply that her menstruation ceased, not at all. It is obvious, looking back, that she began to have morning sickness about that time. The two of them went to Hawaii on their honeymoon, and while there—according to what our son said—Sakiko had had a weak stomach, she did not eat much, and in the morning was such a sleepyhead she never got up. Then, after a while, she told him that she had missed her period."

"If her last period began March 26, then her next menstruation would begin about April 24," Sadaharu said. "It would be quite something to have morning sickness just after the ceremony on April 17."

"I asked our son to tell the truth about that. He said that before the ceremony they had twice gone to a hotel. Apparently, she wanted to wait until the ceremony, but he insisted and so . . ."

"When did that happen?"

"April 5 and April 10. He remembered the precise dates because the fifth is his birthday, and on the tenth the section chief at his company died of cancer and he went to the funeral."

"All right," Sadaharu said. "And it was only those two times? Nothing before that?"

"It seems it was only those two times. At least that is what he said. Only twice. But of course, there is no way to tell if he is lying. Even if he said there were more, it wouldn't be relevant."

"That's quite true," Sadaharu answered.

"And so whichever of those days they say the child was conceived, I wonder if it corresponds to her present condition?"

Sadaharu had asked whether the two had had intercourse before marriage; he supposed that the elder Mrs. Moji thought that conception would have occurred on one of those days. But the problem was to calculate backward from the next menstruation to the twelfth or sixteenth day, the time when the egg would have been released and it would be possible for the younger Mrs. Moji to become pregnant. The calculation would be the same if he figured April 5, or even April 10. Still, under the psychological pressure of getting married, the menstrual cycle might be off. There was wide possibility for error in conceiving.

"I can't say for certain, but I have doubts about her last period beginning March 26," he said. "Perhaps there is some misunderstanding, but looked at objectively that is a pretty long interval. On the other hand, about one person in four will have what seems to be a slight menstrual discharge on the day anticipated for the menses, even after conception. When the person normally has only a slight discharge, then it can seem to be another period. Still, it would be a little implausible to assume that."

"And if," Mrs. Moji began, "as you say, we suppose she did not have her period at the end of March . . ." She left her thought incomplete.

"Then the question is whether she had it in February. Or when in February," Sadaharu said.

"Could she have had her last period so early? Suppose her last period was around the middle of February. Would that correspond to her present size?"

"Yes, it would. But we have to consider individual differences. And . . ."

"She says that she wants to have the child, but we've told her to have an abortion. I'm sure you think I'm a terribly cruel parent, but the truth is that I believe the child Sakiko is carrying is probably not my son's. I'll put it another way. I think that Sakiko is carrying someone else's child, someone she cares for, and that she consented to marry my son in order to keep the child."

Sadaharu said nothing, and Mrs. Moji continued.

"Be that as it may, since she is the girl my son has fallen in love with, we would like to receive her into the family unconditionally. But, no matter what, we simply can't recognize a child that is not our son's. Of course, this may be unfair to Sakiko, but we could let bygones be bygones and make a fresh start if she has the abortion. We shall have this untimely pregnancy terminated, and we will not refer any longer to Sakiko's past. If she has the operation now, then we can set matters right. Someone will be hurt unfairly, and everyone will experience some suffering, but if everyone accepts that, we can work together to correct matters."

It was Sadaharu's turn to speak. "Yes, that would be fine. But the only thing I can do is convey the medical facts. The rest you will have to decide yourselves, of course. But please come to a decision soon, because legally an abortion can only be performed up to the end of the sixth month."

Mrs. Moji thanked him. "This is difficult for us, but we can't escape reality. No matter how hard I think, I can't come up with any other solution."

Sadaharu thought how often in this world such things happen. And how in the end the solution lies not with the parents but rather with the young couple themselves. He took some consolation from this idea.

In the evening, quite unexpectedly, he received a call from his mother in Zushi.

"Sadaharu, are you all right?"

"Yes, quite all right. I'm sorry I haven't called you. Is that neuralgia still bothering you?"

Less than a month ago, she had mentioned some slight pain in her legs and that she was worried about how she might feel during the rainy season. The very next day, Sadaharu had sent some medicine to her by special delivery.

"That medicine you sent, I only took it three times and the ache went away, so I thought it was nothing serious. I suppose it's best to take as little medicine as possible."

"Yes, that's the right thing to do. The best thing is to let the body cure itself naturally," Sadaharu said.

"Some time ago, a person by the name of Komatsu called on you," his mother said.

"Komatsu? I don't recall," Sadaharu said.

"My tea ceremony friend. Her granddaughter, a senior in high school, was pregnant. She came to your office for consultation."

"Ah, yes, was that Mrs. Komatsu?"

It may have been evening, or perhaps it was during his midday rest, but in any case she had come at an odd hour. Sadaharu was slightly annoyed and so he had not invited her to his reception room, nor had he taken careful note of her name.

"Well, she telephoned me a while ago."

"How is the baby? Already born, I suppose."

"Yes, she said the child was born May 9. She said her great-grandchild was a girl."

"Yes, I don't recall the details of it all except that the girl was too far along to have an abortion."

"Well, I haven't heard the details myself," his mother said, "but even if I'd been told I would have gotten confused as ordinary people usually do about such things. However, she said that she would like to visit you again, so I imagine that she'll be coming around."

"But if the child has been born, it should go to a pediatrician. If it is about the high school girl, I'll see her, of course."

"Well, whatever you think best. Please do what you can within your specialty."

He made no particularly encouraging reply, but her last remark somehow stuck in his mind. The fact that Sadaharu was able to live in relatively good social circumstances was due to the support and assistance of the mother who had raised him. And when she asked him to do what he could, he felt the full weight of her words in his heart. If the child had some physical defect, he thought he might introduce the people concerned to a pediatric clinic he knew about. But as it happened, matters took quite another turn.

The first patient to come in the next morning was an older woman holding a baby in her arms, and since Sadaharu had completely forgotten about the telephone call from his mother, he had to think for a moment about which patient this was. The thought passed through his mind that perhaps the infant was the patient, that perhaps she'd been brought in about a vaginal discharge of blood, which in rare instances occurs a week or two after birth.

"My name is Komatsu," the elderly woman began. "I'm terribly sorry to bother you again, but I asked your mother to call you. . . ."

"Oh, yes, please sit down, won't you?"

Nurse Ono thoughtfully took the baby from Mrs. Komatsu's arms.

"So. What seems to be the difficulty?" he asked.

"It concerns my granddaughter, the girl I spoke to you about before."

The girl, still in high school, had given birth to a six-pound baby girl at a Kyoto hospital, far from the offensive gossip of their home to the west on the Japan Sea. But the entire matter had turned into a disaster. The family nearly went crazy when they learned of the girl's condition, behaving as though the baby was the leader of a conspiracy designed to disgrace them. If only the grandparents themselves had been a little more firm and protective, matters might not have gotten out of hand, Mrs. Komatsu thought, but the grandfather, a man in his early fifties, could only think of what people would say. And the young mother, of course, was completely confused. The father of the child was also a high school student and therefore in no position to take responsibility.

Considering all this, the child was put into the care of the wife of a Kyoto man whose family already had three children, for a monthly fee of one hundred thousand yen. The young mother's family felt they had rid themselves of their troubles and gave little further thought to the child. Only the great-grandmother remained concerned. Just two months after the child was born, and without forewarning, she went to visit the foster home. What she found, while not quite actual child abuse, was inadequate care giving, which involved the child not being fed properly and being left without proper attention.

"It was an old Kyoto house, very dark, and nothing could be done about that since it was built so that the sun never came in all year round. It seemed that the child had never been taken outside in the baby carriage, and I truly believe it hadn't ever been in the sun since it was born."

She was angry and scolded the foster mother, and then she brought her great-granddaughter with her to Zushi. She was told by her daughter and her son-in-law that she could never bring the child into their house. The foster mother seemed to have had a fixed schedule for changing the baby's diapers—only so many times a day even if they were soiled. The child's bottom was sore and red. It seemed that the baby had never been held, and the back of its head had become flattened. And the woman had done nothing to prepare the baby for solid food, such as giving it an occasional spoonful or two of fresh juice.

Perhaps it was anger over the family's selfish concern for appearances, or the heartless attitude of her daughter and son-in-law, or the result of her exhausting trip to Kyoto and caring for the baby, but the elderly Mrs. Komatsu had experienced a sharp rise in her blood pressure since the incident. Even now she was taking medicine to bring the pressure down, but what with the baby and all the rest she felt she might have a stroke at any time. And she still hadn't been able to find someone who could take care of the child.

"And so, I really have no one to turn to but you, doctor," she said in a weak voice.

Sadaharu asked, "Do you want to place the child in an orphanage?"

"Yes, that might be all right. But after that I won't be able to take responsibility for her. And at my daughter's place . . . well, they only want to keep anyone from finding out. They are pleased that there is now a law prohibiting easy access to the family register."

"And if someone would take over the child? Would you let it go?" Sadaharu asked.

"Yes, I would. I once thought that if my daughter and her husband saw the child, after it was born, they might change their minds. It is their grandchild, after all. But I was mistaken. They don't even visit the baby, and it is impossible for me to take care of everything."

"Yes, I see your point. There seems to be no other course than to have the child adopted," Sadaharu said.

"I can't sleep at night worrying about all this. I've come to think there is nothing to do but what you suggest. It may not be the best thing, but I feel sorry for her, I'm concerned for her, and I have no idea what else to do."

Sadaharu asked, "Would you wait just a moment more and let me take your blood pressure?"

He brought his gauge and tested Mrs. Komatsu. The reading was 215 over 105.

Sadaharu lied. "Well, now, it's not two hundred, but it is close."

"Oh, my, if that's all then it has gotten better. The day I returned from Kyoto with the baby was the worst. My head was pounding, and since I had the child with me I couldn't get any rest at all. That day was like a bad dream."

"Mrs. Komatsu," Sadaharu said, "I have a proposal. Now, without making any commitment about what we discussed, you might leave the baby here for a while. We have a nursery, and the nurses here will look after her. And in the meantime, you should take it easy and rest, get your blood pressure down. Matters can't be settled while you're upset. And you can think over what I suggested. I'm sure some good person will appear, someone who wants a child. And I know the child will be much happier than if she were being raised by natural parents who have no love for her."

Sadaharu spoke with feeling.

"I didn't think I could let her be adopted at first, but now I'm so tired I think it really might be best."

He undid the child's clothing and examined her. She was thin, her face an emaciated triangle. For that reason, her eyes seemed large. She had a high-bridged nose. The irritation on her bottom had not yet completely healed, but the old lady had taken care of her; he could see traces of the talcum powder she had applied.

"I'll do a blood test later. By the way, I don't know her name yet," he said.

"Miyako Sato. You see, she was born in *Miyako*, the old capital." And as she spoke, the old woman wiped her eyes with her handkerchief.

Chapter Ten

Line of Succession

The summer monsoon had passed and the people around him became more animated again, but Sadaharu felt the change was not simply due to the weather.

One day, when he was passing the operating room, Sadaharu heard the voices of some nurses preparing for a Caesarean section that afternoon. One phrase in particular came to his ears: "I just want to see Miko's face for a moment; I don't feel right when I can't see her every day."

Someone answered, "Oh, sure go ahead—run. You can't wait for anything, even going to the toilet."

The nurses laughed, and Sadaharu immediately walked on. He was surprised at how infatuated the nurses had become with baby Miyako, yet he felt that it was half intentional on their part.

Only rarely was an infant like Miyako taken into the clinic, but at times, when a mother was giving birth to her second or third child, she might come to the hospital with her older children. As often as not, it was after vainly hoping that at birthing time someone might come around to lend a hand. The mother-in-law could be on in years, or not even want to see her grandchildren, or there simply might not be anyone willing to go to the trouble of taking care of an older child. Such cases occasionally came along, and then even while the mother was beginning labor she was still involved with the older child. Only once she was actually in the birthing room would a nurse with some free time look after the older child. From the very next day, the mother could see to the older child while she herself took a meal, and if the child were to get bored and come out into the hallway, then one of the nurses would usually keep it company.

From a medical point of view, it was considered advisable that the other child not get too near the newborn infant, but when the family returned home the infant would have to coexist with germs, so Sadaharu thought that either way it came to the same thing. He considered it important for the nurses, too, that they see that all sorts of patients could live normally after treatment. If they didn't grasp this concept, then they couldn't perform effectively as nurses.

It was clear from the day she was brought in that Miyako Sato was an exceptional child. Sadaharu decided to take a blood sample from her just as though she was a newborn at the clinic, but even when he cut the bottom of her foot with a scalpel Miyako only made a face; she did not cry. A soiled diaper, thirst, hunger, being too warm—all the kinds of things that caused loud cries from other babies did not raise a sound from Miyako.

"It's really strange, doctor. I wonder if she is deaf," one nurse said. Meanwhile, all the nurses took turns holding her, one after another.

"Children cry whether they are deaf or mute."

"That's right, they do."

"I think you're prejudiced," Sadaharu joked. "All you do is hold her."

"Oh, but Miko is such a sweet little thing."

"You mean because she doesn't cry? Because she doesn't give you any trouble? Now, that's pretty calculating, really."

"Oh, doctor, that's not true."

Sadaharu was not about to open a home for infants, and he gave a good deal of thought to Miyako's situation. He felt chilled momentarily, not so much with concern for what might become of this child born to Mrs. Komatsu's granddaughter, but because of the possibility that the infant's family might be angry with the old great-grandmother for carrying off the infant from the foster mother who was being paid each month no matter what she did. With no concern for her age, she had boldly intervened and, uncaring for her rising blood pressure, assumed this responsibility.

"Look, doctor, Miko's bottom is completely healed."

Sadaharu let the elated young nurses show him the baby. Showing the results of recent regular bathing and care, Miyako's sore bottom seemed to be healing with new skin almost before their eyes. But still she did not cry. Sadaharu was no specialist in pediatrics, and he was not absolutely sure about what could be considered normal, but he knew he'd never seen a child that never cried. Even a child born a deaf mute would surely cry. But the fact was that Miyako did not produce any sound like a baby crying. If she were a year old or more, he supposed, there might be some reason to consider the possibility of a psychological element in her lack of crying. If each time she cried someone shouted "Stop that!" and struck her, then soon, out of fear, she would cease crying as a kind of conditioned reflex. But there was no reason why a child of just two months should have this kind of psychological reaction. Even so, not crying out evoked pity. Furthermore, no one at the clinic knew whether Miyako had ever cried. As though testifying to her capacity to feel, the infant sometimes produced huge tear drops, while not uttering a sound.

"Poor thing, Miko, dear. You must have been so mistreated. Were you punished for crying? Well, you're safe here. Cry if you like. Go ahead, try crying as loud as you can, try!"

Wishing to please her, the nurses would speak this way.

"There now. Instead of crying, you can try laughing. You're big enough now, you can laugh, Miko."

For an ordinary child, she was certainly old enough to laugh aloud.

Once, Sadaharu telephoned to the elderly Mrs. Komatsu's house.

"How have you been since you got home?" he asked.

"Oh, my blood pressure has gone down a bit, thank you, but I've felt physically run down since you've taken over care of the child. I'm afraid I've caught a cold." Her voice was indeed hoarse. "I thought I might stop by," she added.

"Oh, Miyako is doing quite well," Sadaharu told her. "Her bottom is healed, and the nurses are giving her lots of loving attention. Really, if you are going to let her be adopted, I do think it would be best if you didn't visit, Mrs. Komatsu."

Some nurses overheard Sadaharu's conversation with Mrs. Komatsu.

"Doctor, will Miko be adopted soon, if a good place is found?"

"No, not very soon. She's still too thin. Wait until she puts on a little more meat."

"If Miko leaves, we'll all be sad," Nurse Iwanami said to her friend Nurse Kurata.

"I don't want her to go anywhere."

"And shall we run a nursery here just for her, forever?" Sadaharu asked.

"I'd love it."

That night while Mayumi was once again away from home, Sadaharu went through an assortment of reading material until after midnight. Among the things he perused was a gossipy article that clarified the identity and character of the patient named Moji who had come to the clinic with her mother-in law.

Sadaharu often received promotional magazines from drug companies, but while he did not read all of them in detail, that night by chance he came across a familiar face in a magazine called *Health News,* published by Aoki Pharmaceutical Company.

The article was titled "Discovering Couples," and was a regular feature page that interviewed prominent couples of relatively advanced years and presented their formula for good health, their hobbies, and so forth. The photograph this time was of the elder

Mr. and Mrs. Moji in training suits, jogging along a road by the ocean.

Gennosuke Moji, age sixty-four, was vice-president of the Chubu Shipbuilding Company. His wife, Mieko, was fifty-six. It appeared that she was the younger sister of Mitsuo Kosugi, president of Kanto Natural Gas Company. Mitsuo Kosugi and Gennosuke Moji had been friends since high school, when they were members of the crew team, and Kosugi's sister had married Moji. Moji's sister was the wife of someone in the Japanese Foreign Office, and this man himself had been a younger classmate in the boat club at High School Number Three, as it was then known, in Kyoto. These three fraternal comrades were like sons of Neptune, and through sports each had been tempered in body, all boasting good health: one in Japanese swordmanship; another in the marathon; the third in horsemanship.

In response to the question, "Do you always accompany your husband in the marathon?" Mrs. Moji concluded the piece by saying, "No, our pace is different and on days when I'm busy with housework I'm tired enough without running. I just want to sleep."

So, thought Sadaharu, that's the kind of household it is. If he had been a person in the financial world, he would have immediately recognized the name Moji when he'd heard it, he suddenly realized. Now the situation began to make sense. A member of that kind of family, Sadaharu thought, would be concerned about problems with publicity, and that's why she deliberately sought out a country doctor like me. She was afraid that gossip would result if she went to a Tokyo clinic.

The next morning, as Sadaharu was beginning consultations with outpatients, he received an unexpected phone call from Mrs. Moji.

"Please excuse me for disturbing you when you are so busy. I'm afraid that I'm imposing on you, but we are still concerned about the problem with the X-ray, and after I spoke with her again,

Sakiko gave her consent to an abortion."

"I see."

"Since the decision has been made, we think the sooner it's done the better. How long do you anticipate she would have to remain in the clinic?"

"Oh, from five days to a week would be best," he answered.

"And would a room currently be available?"

"Of course. Anytime would be fine."

The sun on the shore of Sagami Bay announced the arrival of summer. Sadaharu was walking to the examination room when he heard a burst of laughter coming from the double doors of the nursery. Automatically he stopped and peered in.

"What's up?" he queried, some slight irritation in his voice, wondering what the commotion was all about. Of course, anyone would agree that newborn infants ought to be able to sleep in a quiet place, but no one could be sure that their healthy development did not require a daily dose of noisy laughter.

"Doctor, please come in!" came a voice more like a shriek than the usual call from the nurses.

He entered the nursery. In addition to the two young women on ward duty, Nurses Iwanami and Kurata were there.

"Well, what's going on?" Sadaharu asked, standing in the doorway.

"Doctor! Miko laughed!"

The young nurses did not merely announce the event, they shouted, wildly happy.

"Is it true?" Sadaharu did not disbelieve, but he went over to the edge of Miyako's tiny crib.

"Miko, it's the doctor. Show him you can laugh, will you?"

"What? Reiko, you're the one who's really trying to laugh, aren't you?"

"If she tries too hard, she won't be able to laugh."

The young nurses went on talking to each other. Sadaharu caught Miyako's eye, and the infant contorted her face in an expression that could be called neither crying nor laughing.

The next morning, Sakiko Moji was brought to the hospital, along with all her things, by her husband. Naokata Moji was a handsome man, tall and sensitive-looking. If his family was upper class, then he, at least in outward appearance, was surely a prime prospect as a son-in-law. It was also reasonable for his parents to look for a girl from a "good family" as their daughter-in-law. But, in fact, human feelings and mutual attractions do not follow rules, and Naokata could quite easily fall in love with a girl who was neither a great beauty nor possessed of any notable intellect.

Sadaharu took a look at Sakiko Moji's face. She was not there for pleasure, so there was no reason for her to have a joyful expression. Her downcast eyes, somewhat swollen, seemed directed neither at Sadaharu nor at her husband but rather closed within her own mind.

As calmly and casually as possible, Sadaharu spoke to her. "Mrs. Moji. First we need your signature and seals on the consent form."

He put the papers in front of the couple. The document was something all patients having an abortion had to sign; its gist was that they consented to performance of an induced abortion, a matter pertinent to the Eugenic Protection Law, Article 4, Paragraph 1, Item 4.

"You sign it, please. I don't want to lose the child."

Sadaharu had not been watching the couple, but he looked up on hearing Mrs. Moji's voice.

Timidly, the husband said, "We are supposed to sign individually."

Sadaharu spoke up. "It's all the same to me, but please decide one way or the other. It's really inconvenient if you change your mind in the middle of the operation."

At last, the husband put his name and seal in the spouse column, then Mrs. Moji, too, reluctantly signed in the main column, placing her seal where her husband indicated.

"Your case, Mrs. Moji," Sadaharu continued, "is different from the usual pregnancy. The entrance to the uterus is most difficult to open at this stage. It will take time, about three days, before it will gradually open. We will prepare you by inserting laminaria today and again tomorrow."

Sadaharu did not provide such technical details to the usual patient, but he felt he had to extend himself for Sakiko Moji, so dark was her expression.

"And then . . . until the child appears, how many days will it take?"

"Probably three days, I would guess. Since it's your wife's first, the uterus is difficult to open. We have to be careful not to cause any damage. On the third day, we can proceed to induce labor."

The husband asked, "Won't the procedure be painful for her?"

Sadaharu tapped the chart with the end of his pencil and said, "This is a kind of birth, you see. If it is completely painless, the child will not come out. But the amount of pain experienced varies quite a bit with the individual. To make it as comfortable as possible will take a few days."

"Thanks for explaining. Please do whatever is necessary."

First, Sadaharu told the couple to go the patient's room, where Mrs. Moji could change her clothes and leave any necessary items. He told them to proceed afterward to the outpatient's room.

The truth was that Sadaharu rather disliked performing midterm abortions. No matter what else you said about it, compared with an early-term operation, which was over in a few minutes, this was a major procedure. Simply put, this was more difficult than actual childbirth.

Ironically, that very day just a little past eleven o'clock in the morning a patient named Takako Ogura had come to the clinic with signs of early labor. She was in her twenty-ninth week of pregnancy, just into her eighth month. Ogura was the daughter-in-law of the owner of a rice shop not far from the clinic; her mother-in-law accompanied her to the clinic.

"Doctor," the older woman said worriedly, "isn't there some

way you can save the child?"

"You have already miscarried twice, isn't that right?" he asked the pregnant woman.

Her cervical canal was weak and could not be kept closed, a condition called incompetent cervix. Sadaharu had not been her physician at the time of her two previous miscarriages, but with this pregnancy he had examined her from the the beginning.

"Yes," she replied, "and this time I have been taking special care of myself. For the last month, I've been resting half of each day."

"The present situation is still a little dangerous," Sadaharu told her.

"What if the child were born now, wouldn't it be all right?"

"This is the twenty-ninth week, and a child that should be in the womb forty weeks is only three-quarters term. It's very hard on the baby. But it all depends on its weight. Things are probably all right if it is over three pounds four ounces, and that seems to be quite possible in your case."

A premature infant was born to Takako Ogura a little before three o'clock that afternoon. Sadaharu had not informed either the patient or her mother-in-law, but at the time she was brought in her bag of water was already protruding from her cervix.

The child was a boy and weighed three pounds six ounces.

"Three-six? Pretty close. Just two ounces to spare."

Receiving the weight report from the head nurse, Sadaharu spoke loud enough for the new mother to hear. The infant looked like a wrinkled monkey, but even so it made a faint cry. Outside the delivery room, as expected, the mother-in-law and her son—the husband—were waiting.

"Mrs. Ogura did very well," he told them. "The child is a boy, and we have him in the incubator now, but I think he will be all right."

The husband thanked him for his help, and so did the mother-in-law, but beyond this expression of appreciation her face did not reveal the slightest joy in the birth of her grandson.

Sadaharu finished his work with outpatients for the afternoon. When he went for his evening rounds, Sakiko Moji was lying on her bed looking at a movie magazine.

"How are you doing? Does your stomach hurt?" he asked.

"There is just a little feeling of swelling, hardly anything at all," she told him.

"And your husband has gone home?"

"Yes. With me like this, even if he stayed, I told him, there would be nothing for him to do."

Everyone passed the first two days like this. When it came to giving birth, the rest of the family had nothing to do. And this was even more true in Mrs. Moji's case. Even if the husband had stayed, there would be nothing to talk about. It seemed to Sadaharu that Mr. Moji was being very gentle with his wife. He felt her pain as his own. No matter what was in Mrs. Moji's past, if her husband acted as gently as possible with her, they would surely be able to make a fresh start. And that was the only saving grace in this sort of situation.

Next door to Mrs. Moji's room was Ogura's room. When Sadaharu entered, the father-in-law, the owner of the rice shop, was already there and Ogura was at ease talking with her family.

"Mrs. Ogura, how are you doing?"

"Very well, thank you," the mother-in-law replied, and her daughter-in-law smiled broadly.

"Do you hurt anywhere?"

"No, I'm fine," Ogura replied.

"The baby was a little small, you see. That's probably why. We can't say that everything is one hundred percent sure yet, but the baby seems healthy and we'll keep a careful watch on him."

"Thank you very much," Ogura said.

Sadaharu said a few more words and left the room, but the mother-in-law followed him into the corridor and, catching up with him, spoke in a low voice.

"Excuse me, doctor."

Seemingly afraid that she would be overheard if they remained just outside the room, she took Sadaharu's arm and walked him to the waiting room.

"I really wanted my husband to talk to you," she began, "but he said that he couldn't and that I would have to do it. I suppose I must. I've heard that if you put too much oxygen into the incubator the child will go blind. The idea of this worries us very much. And we thought that you could stop the oxygen."

"But we can't do that. He will breathe more easily this way," Sadaharu told her. But to have to explain even this much annoyed him, and he broke off abruptly. For an undeveloped infant of twenty-eight to thirty-six weeks—compared with a fetus of twenty-seven weeks—with the decline in the likelihood of a brain hemorrhage there arose a respiratory distress syndrome that in most cases required the use of oxygen.

"I see," the woman replied. "So without oxygen there is no way for the baby to live."

Sadaharu remained silent.

"Doctor, this is the first grandson in our family. While we want him very much, of course, if he were blind it would be a pity for the child and quite a burden for us all. So we would like you to know that if his eyes are not going to be bad, then we very much want him to live."

Which was to say that if his eyes *were* going to be bad, please be certain that he dies, Sadaharu thought. He wondered whether that kind of decision was really within a physician's control. If the child's eyes were bad, let it die naturally; if the child was all right, then it would have the necessary qualifications for being a grandson in the Ogura household. A blind child was not what they wanted to take home.

"But Mrs. Ogura, that isn't something we can guarantee. Please understand that."

Sadaharu realized that even at such moments he did not lose his temper even slightly.

"I see. You can't do anything? I thought that perhaps there were things doctors could do, you know, so that the baby wouldn't live."

The old lady of the rice shop was purposely belaboring the point, so Sadaharu replied rather harshly.

"Well, I can't do them, and I doubt that any other physician could either."

For people like this, such things as respect for life were merely convenient words, to be used only when a convenient reason existed. Probably there were those in society whom people would want to see live, but by the same measure there were those whom people would rather see die. In either case, judgment was related to profit and loss. His mind thus occupied, Sadaharu coldly walked away.

Chapter Eleven

One Who Has Seen It All

Sadaharu reached Yoko's home that night after supper, and Father Munechika arrived a short while later. Sadaharu went to the foyer to greet him, thanking him for having taken him to visit the hospital.

"But there was surely nothing new for you to see at a place like that."

"On the contrary. I was really grateful. There is a great difference between gynecology and pediatrics. It's always a shock when one encounters it," Sadaharu replied.

The priest turned to Yoko. "I brought the book I promised you," he said.

Sadaharu saw a bit of the cover; it seemed to be in English, and, while he tried to restrain himself, his curiosity got the better of him.

"What's the book?"

"It's called *Mount Ararat.*"

"Where Noah's ark is said to have landed."

"Is it a mythical mountain?" Sadaharu asked.

"Oh, no, it really exists."

"Ah, that's a surprise. Where is it?" Sadaharu did not try to conceal his ignorance.

"It belongs to Turkey, but in fact there is really no proof that it is the real Mount Ararat."

"So perhaps it is only a myth after all," Sadaharu murmured as he listened to the priest.

"Yes, to some extent that seems to be the case. Assuming that the mountain is near a place called the Arasu River—or a name like that—it would be in Turkish Armenia and be over 16,000 feet high. No matter how much it might have rained, it's doubtful that the flood water would have gotten that far. Still, it is said that fragments of the ark have been discovered. Ferdinand Navarre, a Frenchman, found pieces of shaped wood in a glacier in the valley below the mountain and had them examined at research facilities in universities in Madrid and Bordeaux. They determined that the wood was between three and five thousand years old."

Sadaharu remarked that that was interesting.

"The legend of the Flood belongs to an agricultural people. The Sumerians wrote in cuneiform and a pictographic script and left a narrative poem of Gilgamesh, their legendary king. In the eleventh book of that poem is a story very similar to that of the Flood in the Old Testament of the Bible."

Yoko interjected, "Be patient, Sadaharu; I'll lend you a copy of *The Epic of Gilgamesh.*"

"Thanks, but I don't read English," he replied.

"Oh, but this is a good Japanese translation."

He glanced at the book that Yoko handed him, riffling the pages.

"Noah's ark? It carried his family, I suppose. What happened to the rest of the people?" Sadaharu asked the priest.

"I assume they died. Because humanity had fallen, the purpose was to eradicate them for their sins."

"And the animals, too, had one pair each on the ark."

"That's right."

"I suppose there were other people who said they'd like to go along too. Pretty sly, Noah arranging for just his family. Imagine what a mess it would have been if everyone had tried to crowd into the ark, animals pushing in, too. Who would live, who would be left behind to die in the Flood? I suppose some of them were thinking about that kind of thing," Sadaharu said.

"I have never heard such a story," said the priest.

"By the way, I came over to confirm what I told you before," Sadaharu said, turning to Yoko.

Still, when it came to putting Miyako Sato up for adoption, although Sadaharu was ninety percent sure it would be all right, he continued to have reservations. The infant had once wrinkled its face and smiled, but it had not yet made a sound. The Lauries had said they would come to get it, and that was splendid, but Sadaharu thought that the child had better produce a cry by then, or he would have to warn them.

All of these considerations aside, and in spite of his slight intoxication, Sadaharu remained obsessed with another matter.

"When the Lauries and you went to South America," he began, "didn't they get a thalidomide baby at the home for unwed mothers? Doesn't that make one more for them?"

"No. They did not get the thalidomide child," Yoko replied.

"Oh, I see!" Sadaharu spoke with some vague malice in his tone, but Yoko let it pass without comment.

"They thought that they would be able to, but someone else took the child away just before they came. It was only a difference of half a day, but the child had been promised and they could not adopt it."

"That's quite something. I don't suppose there are as many chances to adopt pretty little girl babies."

Sadaharu was again speaking purposefully.

"You know," Yoko replied, "from the point of view of some superstitious people, it is considered quite lucky to get hold of such a child since it is supposed to bring good fortune. It's both more challenging and more rewarding, just as it's more interesting and demanding to manage a ten billion yen company than one with capital of one billion—and somehow more praiseworthy."

"Not for a lazy guy like me," Sadaharu said.

Yoko challenged him. "Anyone can raise a normal child, but a thalidomide baby requires great attention and labor. I'm sure that

God is pleased when people raise a child like that. I'm sure He rewards the parents."

"Really. But do people always make a profit that way?" Sadaharu said.

"Of course. Christians are always concerned with saving up things. They say you store your riches in heaven, so you shouldn't be content with riches of this world that grow dull or are destroyed. One always has to be concerned with fire or theft—there's no end to that. So if you save up, you have to save in a form that won't be lost or destroyed."

Sadaharu chuckled. "I don't know whether it is Jesus or the gods, but whoever is in charge is surprisingly parsimonious. Just like me, don't you think? I'm just like that. I fear loss by fire, and so we don't buy paintings. I don't buy jewels for my wife because she might lose them, and that would make me mad. And we don't save too much because I'm sure inflation will wipe out our savings."

Finally, Yoko laughed. "Oh, what fine talk!"

"Thank you. So, when will the Lauries come to Japan?" By that time, Sadaharu thought, it would be necessary to determine whether or not Miyako would ever be able to speak.

"I don't know exactly, but when the time approaches they will let me know, I'm sure."

"Please let me know when you hear," Sadaharu told Yoko.

Even as he said this, Sadaharu had the strange feeling that even if he were forewarned about when the Lauries would come, he would never be able to fatten up Miyako like a chicken, by doubling her rations.

"Father Munechika," Sadaharu said, "please excuse me. I seem to say something foolish every time we meet. This afternoon at the clinic we had a premature baby born. We took all kinds of special care because the mother had already miscarried twice before. And then, after all was said and done, the infant was born weighing about three and a half pounds."

"But will it grow at that weight?" the priest asked.

"That's not the problem. The smallest quintuplets weigh in at two pounds in this country. The problem is incomplete development of retinal membranes, or retrolental fibroplasia."

The priest asked the only question he could think of. "Can't you put the infant in an incubator?"

"No, not really. It's not as simple a matter as that. Since I'm not so conversant with that subject I've checked into the latest pediatric literature, and found that of babies weighing between three and a half pounds and three and three-quarters pounds—at least in the statistics of one university hospital—42 percent are normal, and retrolental fibroplasia is found in 58 percent of immature infants. But the extent of damage varies. Some of them develop normal vision despite the formation of scar tissue. There is some damage in vision, but not to the extent that it precludes normal life. Some children require special education for thc blind. With quints, even when they were around two pounds, according to the university report, they all developed without health problems despite anticipated damage."

Sadaharu thought he must be really drunk to have talked about his profession this much.

"That's enough about pediatrics," he said. "It's not my specialty anyway. But I was told by the infant's grandmother that I should let it live *if* its eyes were all right. I was really annoyed when I heard that, Father. Of course, the implication was that if the baby could not see I should not let it live."

"Of course, people can't say who should live and who should die," Father Munechika said.

"They can't, but when they try to it's terrible. What it comes to is no more than saying 'If the child is intelligent, let it live; if it is a fool, then eliminate it.'"

"Yes, and there is a connection with the quintuplets you just mentioned. Nowadays, when an infertile woman is given some medicine or hormone she often conceives more than two children.

There are lots of instances of that, I suppose," said the priest.

"Yes, that's due to an ovulation-stimulating medicine, but it's not definite that everyone will have three or four children," Sadaharu said.

"However, with such a medicine the probability of births of three or four is higher than without, isn't it?"

"Yes, I suppose it is."

"And with several children being born at once I suppose raising them could be a problem. Aside from that, if there are more than two, then the newborns are small. If they are small, then don't problems like underdeveloped retinas arise?"

"You are right, Father. You are too much of a priest." Sadaharu laughed. "And it's true. And against such abuse there is only one answer, from your point of view. What was it you said? Right. Neither planning nor control. It is all God's plan, or something to that effect, I believe."

"Do you mean Providence?"

"Yes, that's right. People usually don't have quads or quints, while multiple births commonly occur through artificial management. Then, inevitably, the body weight is small, the birth is early, and the infants are born with incomplete eye development. . . ."

"But still, we can understand the feelings of couples who want children."

"And that's the thing, Father. I understand both sides. I'm some sort of a genius to be able to see it both ways," Sadaharu laughed and continued his thought. "But what I'm talking about is this wanting—but without wanting the whole thing. It is unreasonable; indeed, it is a surrender of reason. It's no problem for human beings to desire, and to desire a lot. It is the nature of man that he be greedy. I'm not saying that there should be no scientific advances, but, oddly enough, it is when you go too far that one way or another things get irrational. Surely it's irrational to force a child to live when that child has been born too soon. A physician gives all his strength to relieving human weakness; but even so, some weakness is innate, part of us when we're born.

"I can only talk about this here, Father Munechika, but I feel there is some unrelenting intellectual resistance among Japanese people today to the concept of 'congenital' weakness. Some people feel that because human beings are equal, the idea that we all carry different inborn destinies is unacceptable. If someone said there are those who, for example, are innately unintelligent, he would be attacked on that assumption. So no one says anything.

"Father, I think it's simply untrue that there is freedom of speech in Japan today. Wherever one goes there is such violence that one cannot tell the truth. It really seems strange that one can only speak the truth at Yoko's house."

With this Sadaharu vigorously scratched his head. It was an odd habit, but when he was drunk his scalp itched. People near him might get the unhappy idea that he was unwashed, but the itch was probably caused by increased blood circulation, or so Sadaharu thought, and he felt quite unconcerned about it himself. He considered that insofar as his scalp itched, blood was circulating to his brain, but that was probably just wishful thinking. At the moment, he felt somewhat drunk, but not so much that he had lost his ability to reason.

The priest began to ask a question: "Suppose the possibility of three, four, five children born at once is increasing. The problems connected with birth increase also, and . . ."

Sadaharu raised his hand to agree with the priest's comment.

"In such cases, there are only two—no, three—problems. In the first place, the possibility of retrolental fibroplasia remains, to some extent. There is nothing that can change that, the goods are delivered half done, so to speak. But the second matter—and this is the really big problem—is the power that the patient has in blaming the hospital for the child's defective vision, quite without considering that the child was born with incompletely developed physiological equipment."

"Yes, I suppose that the situation at your clinic today was just like that. How do you handle the problem?" the priest asked.

Sadaharu almost smiled. "I'm clever about that and pretend to make the patient choose. For instance, I say 'My opinion is that if we don't administer oxygen to the baby its lungs won't function well, but since there is some danger of blindness resulting we'll have to take it out of the incubator, I suppose.' The truth is, there is no room for choice on my part. We doctors are here to support life. To put it plainly, Father, no matter what we have to do, we do it to support life. We support lives of academicians and politicians, of course, but we really support life for everyone, including those who might turn out to be thieves, mad killers, grafters, drug addicts, whores. No matter what their potential, we take them all.

"Even when I'm told just to save those who are good or useful, I can't do that. And I don't want to see doctors being forced to make that kind of judgment.

"What we call human society is really an odd lot, and that is the beauty of it, the beauty of the whole thing. It is an orchestra, you know, not a solo performance. And because it's an orchestra it is large and magnificent. The Nazis killed millions of Jews because they didn't want them on this earth, isn't that true? We condemn what Hitler did, but there are still lots of fellows like that around. There's one right here. When a patient tells me to abort a child she doesn't want and I take money for doing it, I'm one of those, you see. But if the child is malformed and someone even unconsciously wants it dead—and I think that's really not so unusual—such people are halfway to being Nazis."

"And what is the third thing?" the priest asked.

"Oh, God's something—I've forgotten what you said."

"Providence."

"Yes. And in connection with that, for instance, the matter of the quintuplet fetuses. As far as I'm concerned, the team that helped them live deserves nothing but praise. Infants of that weight have become healthy children, but that team had both skill and luck, in my opinion. And in the background there is a feeling of mission, like that of raising Japanese Olympic champions. But the parents of the five have no responsibility for that. The two parents are grateful for their luck and just want to raise healthy children. That's enough.

"However, there is a problem in all that. Suppose that in the future hundreds of groups of quintuplets and sextuplets are born. There's a question of whether the resources of the country can sustain the cost of raising them. The number of children born with retrolental fibroplasia would probably increase. People made a fuss over the first quintuplets. But after several hundred—no, even just the tenth set of quintuplets—I don't suppose they will receive that kind of treatment. No, Japan is now wealthy and would probably pay for the medical costs. But, really, the third thing I want to point out is that multiple births produce small babies, and as a consequence all kinds of functional defects are likely to appear in such underdeveloped infants. You really have to want children after taking all that into consideration. And if that's not the case, then we are all in trouble."

"Let us pray, then, that the child born this afternoon will have good eyes. At such times, there is nothing else to do but pray," the priest said.

"Thank you very much, Father," Sadaharu said, feeling the effects of his drinking and commendably bowing his head before continuing. "I hope you don't think my thanks are insincere. I myself do not pray, but I very well understand the feeling that there is nothing else one can do but pray. It shows a real spiritual impoverishment to condemn prayer as unscientific. It is human arrogance. We do what we can, and then there is nothing we can do but pray. But I wouldn't say that openly. People would say that Dr. Nobeji lacks confidence in himself and so he prays, and that would be bad for my reputation and business. I put on a front as though only I have the qualifications to give or withhold human life."

"Really, Sadaharu," Yoko said, "the liquor has gotten a real hold on you today."

"Drunk, but not out of control," he replied. "When I go home, I'll read the story of Mount Ararat all night long."

When he left, he completely forgot the socks he had taken off at Yoko's house and left under the table, but strangely enough he did take with him the book he planned to borrow.

He arrived home in the taxi Yoko had called, and as he emerged in front of his house Nurse Okubo, who apparently had just seen a patient's visitor, announced, "I gave Mrs. Moji some sleeping medicine and she is resting."

"I see. That's fine," Sadaharu said to her, as though the thought of the patient who had come in for an abortion that day had never left his mind.

Mayumi was at home, itself a rare event, and was talking with a friend on the telephone. When at home, she was either forever talking on the telephone, going out shopping, or out at night on a date, and at present it pleased her to think that she was in love. That was Mayumi's one great wish, and often Sadaharu felt that he would go along with anything she did if Mayumi could be satisfied with such a simple thing.

Instead of calling out his usual greeting on returning home Sadaharu good-humoredly waved his hand, and before going to his study went to the refrigerator for a cold glass of water, which he gulped down. He then retired to his special corner in his room, relaxed into his finely made easy chair and opened the book called *The Epic of Gilgamesh*. Sadaharu thought it interesting that a company would bring out a book like this, one that would hardly be expected to sell to many people, and he wondered at the erudition of the scholar who had translated from an Assyrian manuscript, a work said to be the world's oldest epic poem, the most complete literary work of the ancient world. The original, besides Assyrian, contained Hittite, Sumerian, and possibly dialects of Assyrian and Babylonian.

The preface to the book mentioned that *The Epic of Gilgamesh* had been confirmed as originating with the Sumerian people. The

Sumerians were an ancient tribe living in the region of the mouth of the Tigris and Euphrates rivers; they used a wedge-shaped script called cuneiform. Gilgamesh was the name of a Sumerian person and it seemed that in the distant past the work had taken on that name as its own, although the epic was also called "The Man Who Saw Everything," based on its first sentence. Sadaharu mused on that title, murmuring it to himself. He rather liked the sound of it.

If we imagine that he really had seen everything, what an unfortunate thing, Sadaharu thought. Human happiness does not lie in seeing "everything" but in seeing just a small bit. Rather than thinking one has seen everything, it is when one dies feeling there is yet some part one has not seen that one can feel satisfied and complete. But when Sadaharu opened *The Epic of Gilgamesh* he felt like extinguishing all such thoughts that it would be better not to see everything of the world by the time one died. The text contained parenthetical insertions and began:

> The one who saw the abyss I will make the land know;
> of him who knew all, let me tell the whole story
> (as) the lord of wisdom; he who knew everything,
> and carried back word of time before the Flood—he
> traveled the road, exhausted, in pain,
> and cut his works into a stone tablet.
> He ordered built the walls of Uruk of the Sheepfold,
> the walls of holy Eanna, stainless sanctuary.

Sadaharu thought this was a good beginning, striking a high, pure, philosophical tone. He thought that it was impossible to see everything, but he was sorry not to have learned about this book sooner.

> Gilgamesh rises, speaks to his mother to untie his dream.
> "Last night, Mother, I saw a dream.
> There was a star in the Heavens.
> Like a shooting star of Anu it fell on me."

Sadaharu murmured to himself, "Pretty good," rose to get himself a whiskey, and returned to his reading.

In the eleventh tablet was the story relating to the great Flood and Mount Ararat.

> Utnapishtim says to him, to Gilgamesh:
> "I will uncover for you, Gilgamesh, a hidden thing,
> tell you a secret of the gods.
> In Shuruppak—you know the city, I think—set on the bank of the Euphrates—the city was old and close to the gods.
> The great gods stirred their hearts to make the Flood."

According to the footnote, the place called Shuruppak was the old capital of Mesopotamia, one of the five castle towns recorded by the Sumerians as existing before the Flood. There were no maps in the book that Sadaharu was reading, and, while there were no old place names in the atlas, he thought that he would have a look at the shape of the Euphrates River and so went to his bookshelf. Just then Mayumi ended her long telephone conversation.

"Really, that Akiko amazes me!" Mayumi said in an angry voice as she came into Sadaharu's study.

Akiko had been Mayumi's classmate in senior high school; she often accompanied Mayumi shopping, to play golf, to concerts, and such things.

"Oh? What's the matter?" Sadaharu asked.

No matter how busy he was Sadaharu was always ready to talk to his young daughter, and he responded to Mayumi in the same spirit.

"Well, when my old teacher Ms. Taguchi came back from America she contacted me, remember? And so I told Akiko the news. But she told all our classmates and made arrangements on her own for a class reunion."

"And just as well—someone would have had to go to the trouble of doing it," Sadaharu said.

"Ms. Taguchi told me first, before anyone else, about her return to Japan. She even wrote in her letter to me that I was the first to know that she was returning. Also, she made a point of mentioning that she wanted to see me. How was I supposed to know that she wanted to see anyone else?"

Ms. Taguchi had been Mayumi's high school English teacher; she was now married and living in America. Perhaps out of all her students she had paid particular attention to Mayumi, and the two had corresponded for a long time. The thought had crossed Sadaharu's mind that perhaps the two were lovers.

"But as a school teacher she never showed you any favoritism. She wouldn't have been able to do her work if she behaved like that. Still, she surely she will be pleased if lots of people come to the class reunion."

"Even so, since she let me know first that she was coming back I think Akiko should have asked my permission before informing everyone!"

"Hmm, well, I suppose that actually either way would have been all right," Sadaharu suggested.

"Either way! Listen to you! I feel like Akiko is making a fool of me!"

"I don't think she is making a fool of you. Perhaps Akiko simply intended to take on some of the bother, that's all."

"But I'm the only one who really knows what Ms. Taguchi likes to eat. Akiko didn't even ask me about that but just decided herself on Chinese food. She's a perfect egotist, as far as I can see!"

Sadaharu returned to his book. He supposed the existence of this kind of foolish agitation on his wife's part was proof of the world's diversity, but at the moment he wanted to escape into the world of Gilgamesh.

> Reed-wall, reed-wall! Wall, wall!
> Reed-wall, listen! Wall, pay attention!

Man of Shuruppak, son of Ubaratutu,
Tear down the house. Build an ark.

The son of Ubaratutu was the Noah of the Old Testament, and boats of that time were made of reeds, the same material used in houses.

Abandon riches. Seek life.
Scorn possessions, hold onto life.
Load the seed of every living thing into your ark.

Sadaharu grunted his perception of this passage aloud. Noah, who was the son of Ubaratutu, had different names—Jiustoria in Sumerian and Utnapishtim in Assyrian—but the notes indicated that all those names meant "he who sees life."

"I may be a kind of Utnapishtim," Sadaharu murmured. Among physicians there are many who are intellectually curious. On the other hand, plenty of them lacked culture, so they would not know the origin of Utnapishtim. Perhaps he should display his learning with an essay in his alumni magazine on the subject of Utnapishtim.

I butchered bulls for the people
and killed sheep every day.
Drink, beer, oil, and wine
I gave the workmen to swill as if it were the waters
of a river,
so that they made festival as if it were the days
of New Year's.
I opened the bowl of ointment and applied it to my
hands.
On the seventh day the ark was completed.
The launching was not easy:
The hull had to be shifted, above and below,
until two-thirds of the structure had entered the
water.

All I had I loaded into the boat:
all I had of silver I loaded,
all I had of gold I loaded,
all I had of the seed of all living creatures I
loaded;
I made all my kin and family go onto the boat.
The animals of the fields, wild beasts of the fields,
the children of all the craftsmen I drove aboard.
Shamash had set the time for me:
"When he orders bread at night, he will rain down
wheat,
Enter the boat and close your gate."
The hour approached:
"When he orders bread at night, he will rain down
wheat."
I saw day coming on.
To look at that day filled me with terror.
I went into the ark and closed the gate.
For the caulking of the boat I gave to Puzur-Amuru,
the shipbuilder,
my palace with all its goods.

Having read this far, Sadaharu muttered to himself, "They left it out." He couldn't accept that there wasn't a fight with someone who wanted to get on the ark. And not just humans would have pushed in: dogs biting monkeys; crows plucking at the tails of parrots. He read on with this silly sort of expectation, but he found no passage like that. The passages describing the Flood were supposed to have been passed down virtually complete.

Six days and seven nights
the wind shrieked, the stormflood rolled through
the land.
On the seventh day of its coming the stormflood
broke from the battle,

which had labored like a woman giving birth.
The sea grew quiet, the storm was still; the Flood
stopped.

I looked out at the day. Stillness had settled in.
All of humanity was turned to clay.
The ground was like a great, flat roof.
I opened the window and light fell on my face.
I crouched, sitting, and wept.
My tears flowed over my cheeks.
I looked for a shore at the boundary of the sea,

He set down his whiskey glass.

"Terrific," Sadaharu muttered, imagining all of humanity returned to dust, houses buried in earth, land covered with grass roof high.

"What a magnificent scene."

He didn't mean that it was good that humanity had perished, but the vision of humanity dying so quickly before the overwhelming force of nature was a vision to shake the soul. The literary concept of humanity's "right to survival" was here totally annihilated. Before Sadaharu's intoxicated eyes appeared his own corpse, decaying and covered with mud. For some reason, in the scene his muddy hair floated like algae, a pollywog swimming in its midst. The creature tickled Sadaharu's hair, and his head became unbearably itchy. While he was vigorously scratching his scalp, he yawned widely. At that moment he seemed literally to taste the flavor of returning to mud.

Suddenly, he was aware of the sound of a kettle whistling in the kitchen and the brightness of sunlight. He thought that he must have had quite a long nap.

"Papa," Kaori was calling.

"All right," he replied.

"You slept in your chair all night. Isn't there a bed upstairs?"

It was indeed morning.

"Of course there is a bed upstairs, but this chair is more expensive, so I prefer to sleep here."

Sadaharu realized he had slept very well.

"I'm glad you weren't bitten by mosquitoes," Kaori said.

"Oh, I'm not too tasty," Sadaharu told her.

Mayumi poured coffee without any expression on her face. Sadaharu thought it tactful to leave matters as they were, without giving Mayumi anything to say. His wife had that good point at least, and he could hardly overlook it.

Sadaharu stretched his back and went into the bath. Not having showered the previous day, he felt as though he owed it to himself.

As scheduled, he went to see his outpatients and receive reports from the nurses who had been on duty the previous night. Happily, there seemed to have been no changes among the patients that night for which he might be blamed for his getting drunk and sleeping all night in his chair.

"How is Mrs. Moji doing?" he asked.

Nurse Yuasa had been on duty the night before and replied, "There's nothing special to report."

"Well, I'll have a look at her first anyway," Sadaharu said. "Please have her brought down to the examination room."

The day before, he had given her medication to dilate the cervix.

Mrs. Moji came in with a nurse before he attended to the other patients; her expression did not indicate any particular emotion.

Sadaharu asked her whether she had slept well while, as usual, not looking up from the patient's chart before him on the desk.

"I woke up several times," she replied.

"Yes, but you did sleep?"

She replied, "Yes."

The look on her face made it impossible to know what she was thinking.

Later that afternoon, when Sadaharu made his rounds, he found the older Mrs. Moji in her daughter-in-law's room.

"I see you've brought something for the patient to eat, haven't you?" Sadaharu said to the senior Mrs. Moji. He noticed a number of plastic containers on the table at the patient's pillow.

"Your clinic has really provided so many nice things already, doctor, but I made some of the roast pork that Sakiko loves, and I thought I would bring her just a bit of salad made from the tomatoes from our garden. . . ."

"Oh, my, how I envy her!" he said.

"Thanks to you, she has gotten along well. You've certainly relieved us all."

"Ah, yes. And today she can spend all day reading the weekly magazines."

"I brought a few for her since she seems to have read most of the ones at the hospital, you see."

"But perhaps she has not read *Weekly Marriages and Divorces,*" Sadaharu suggested.

"Is there such a magazine?"

"No, no, just a joke," Sadaharu laughed.

Next day, just before noon, Sadaharu made final preparations for Sakiko Moji.

Sadaharu had just begun his lunch when Nurse Okubo called on the phone.

"Doctor, I wish that you would have a look at Mrs. Moji," she said.

"I'll be right there."

"I think it would be all right for you to finish your lunch first," Nurse Okubo advised.

Sadaharu did as she suggested; Nurse Okubo never said anything lightly. In an emergency, she would summon him without hesitation, and if she said it was all right to take his time, that meant it was all right for him to take his time.

At any rate, he hurried through lunch. He could eat in haste or linger through meals, whichever was called for; he was very flexible that way.

When he entered the patient's room, he saw that a liquid meal had been brought to her, but it didn't seem that she had taken any.

"How do you feel?" he asked. "Have you had any pain?"

"Yes, I have," she answered, hiding her swollen red eyes with one hand. It seemed she had been crying. Nurse Okubo, having noticed Sadaharu's arrival, joined him.

"How are the labor pains going?" he asked Nurse Okubo.

"They are coming at ten-minute intervals, but she says she wants to go the bathroom frequently."

When the body receives a shock like the artificial dilation of the uterus, it is not just labor pains that the patient feels but a continuous painful pressure, feeling like a need to urinate or defecate. This was why Mrs. Moji asked to go to the toilet. From Nurse Okubo's casual and brief report, Sadaharu guessed that Mrs. Moji was the kind of patient who would make a fuss. Such behavior might be attributed to human nature and simply left at that, but in the case of a midterm abortion, one had to feel pity for the patient who endured labor pains without psychological preparation.

Only once had Sadaharu performed an abortion at the beginning of the seventh month—the operation then being legal because the patient had claimed she'd had no money to obtain the operation earlier. Even though he was skeptical, as Sadaharu perceived the patient there was something special, even noble about her. She was a widow; to support her three children she brought fish caught in local waters up to Tokyo to sell.

An outsider might wonder why she hadn't found a way to get an abortion prior to the seventh month. Still, she had not uttered a word about pain during the procedure. At that moment, she had wanted to achieve her goal quickly, because if she did not lighten her load, so to speak, she would not be able to go on taking care of her remaining three children. With the sole idea of freeing herself from pregnancy possessing her, she rang for the nurse only once. Without complaint or sentimentality, she dropped the fetus, a boy, which fortunately made no birth cry, so neither mother nor child experienced the mutuality of their existence.

In fact, for nearly all the patients who had a midterm abortion (including Sakiko Moji) there was no positive meaning whatever in being rid of the child. It was no more than an action taken as a consequence of some blunder, bad luck, perhaps, or unhappiness. Along with the pain of delivery in a usual birth, there was that shining sense of purpose present for a mother who had looked forward to having a child. Even a mother who had lost the chance for an abortion was somehow transformed, anticipating the child that was to be born.

For Mrs. Moji, the pain was met reluctantly, in expectation of a violence that would lead not to life but to death. Simply put, it was totally futile suffering. How could she bear it? All that she might endure for the sake of a goal was eventually suffused into unquenchable pain. The only course then was to somehow soothe the patient's mind. Sadaharu guessed that Nurse Okubo had called him because she saw the need for that solicitude.

"Did she come to help you eat, or bring you some juice or soft drink?"

Sadaharu asked this of Mrs. Moji after Nurse Okubo had left, leaving the door slightly ajar.

"Yes, but I didn't want what she brought," Sakiko replied.

"And did you eat yesterday?"

"Yes, a bit."

"I think it would help if you watched TV or listened to music," Sadaharu said.

"Oh, that's all right. I don't feel like it, really."

"It's hard for your husband to visit you, except on Saturday or Sunday, isn't it?"

"He came last night, but there's not much use to his coming now."

"Why is that?"

"I've been thinking about things. If I were allowed to have the child, I would stay with the Moji family, because I would be obligated to them. But because they made me have this abortion, I've decided that when I leave here I won't go back to him."

Sadaharu sat down on the chair beside the bed. "You know . . . I don't want to pry into your personal affairs," he said, "but about the size of your child . . . what you say doesn't agree with my observation. Just for my own sake I would like to confirm it." Mrs. Moji was silent.

"I'm not concerned with your personal life," Sadaharu added. "Won't you tell me when you had your last period?"

For a short while, she paused, gazing at the ceiling, then she said, "It was February 5."

From his pocket Sadaharu took out a small calculator.

"Hmm. Exactly right, after all."

This was the twenty-fourth week, exactly six months, as he had thought.

"It's not my husband's child, the child I'm carrying . . ."

"Then why didn't you marry him, the father? If you love him you should have refused Mr. Moji and gone to live with the other man. Wasn't that possible?"

"He's not the marrying kind. He said he was already living with someone. But getting married—he doesn't want to marry anyone. He said he likes my type, and I like him too."

"What does he do? I don't think there is any kind of work in the world that really precludes marriage."

"He's a bartender."

"Well, then, it's just a problem in his personality. The husband of one of my patients is a bartender in Yokosuka, but every Sunday he takes his family out and goes fishing. Really. He doesn't talk much, but he is a warm and steady fellow. But you know, having a child by someone who is not your husband and then making your husband think it is his, as you have done, and getting him to marry you, that's not good."

Sadaharu rather directly spoke his mind to Mrs. Moji.

"I thought that I would tell him, before."

"And if you tell him? I suppose that would be the end of your marriage."

"I think he would accept it. He really loves me."

"But the family would assume the child to be the child of their oldest son, the heir of the family. That's a kind of fraud."

"I didn't particularly want it to be the heir of the Moji family. Only, since I love the father, the bartender, so much, I wanted to have his child and raise it."

"In that case," Sadaharu replied, "wouldn't it be just as good to have the child and raise it yourself? One of my patients is doing that just now. For various reasons, she can't live with the person she loves. And yet she works and tries to make a life for that person's child. I suppose the world still thinks that is extraordinary, and certainly from the child's point of view it is better to have both parents together, but I don't think it's altogether wrong, believe me."

"I thought I'd try that at first, but he wanted me to marry him so much."

"Yes. Well, all of that is beside the point now. People have to make choices. You can't have things both ways, that's unreasonable."

From outside the room, the nurse called, "Doctor. Telephone."

Sadaharu left the room and took five or six steps when the nurse spoke to him in a low voice.

"I think it is from Mrs. Moji's mother-in-law."

Sadaharu went to the phone just next to the nursery for newborn babies.

"This is Sakiko's mother-in-law," the voice said.

"Oh, yes," Sadaharu answered.

"We were getting worried. How is she doing?"

"The contractions are progressing right on schedule. I think it will be over today," Sadaharu told her.

"I don't suppose you have any idea what time that will be?"

"It is the same as having a child. If you are concerned, I can call you when she goes into the delivery room."

"Thank you, yes. I wish you would."

"I'll have the nurse call you."

"Thank you so much. I'll be waiting at home. I'll leave as soon as you call."

Sadaharu took down her telephone number and hung up.

As he was on his way back to the house, a helicopter came swooping by. When the number of swimmers increased at this time of year, a small helicopter or plane patrolled the shoreline in case a rescue was necessary.

A little before five o'clock, as he was continuing his outpatient examinations, Sadaharu was called to the delivery room, where Mrs. Moji had been taken some time before. As he went up, he passed Nurse Okubo in the hallway.

"She's raising quite a fuss, complaining of pain," the nurse remarked.

Mrs. Moji was already on the delivery table. Sadaharu briefly examined her, then gave her nitrous oxide as an anesthetic. After Mrs. Moji had two or three contractions, Sadaharu used an extraction cup and a tiny baby boy was born, his fingers not larger than matchsticks.

"Did Mrs. Moji say anything in particular regarding the child?" Sadaharu asked.

Mrs. Moji was semiconscious from the gas, and Sadaharu addressed the nurse in a low voice. If no wishes had been expressed, the six-month-old fetus and placenta would be turned over to a removal company, which collected them as a kind of stillbirth. In fact, the fetus would be handled the same as garbage.

"No. She said nothing in particular. But just a while ago, the mother-in-law asked that the fetus be dressed in this," the nurse said.

Baby clothes made of gauze, sewn loosely, without knots, just like a shroud. Just as she would have done with a live birth, the nurse weighed the baby and applied baby oil, then wrapped the dead infant in the large, flimsy, threadbare cloth. In the delivery room, there was none of the usual conversation. Even when he had administered anesthetic, when the afterbirth was discharged Sadaharu usually spoke in a voice that was pitched to awaken the mother. "Mrs. So-and-so!" he would say. "It's all over! It's a baby girl, six and a half pounds," he would tell her, or something like that, and generally the new mother would say in a clear voice, "Thank you very much," or "Is the baby normal?" or "What a loud cry!" to express her feelings. But on this day no one said a thing. Sadaharu said merely, "Mrs. Moji. It's all over," and her only response was, "Yes."

There was no sense that she had completed her labor, only that the pregnancy had been terminated early. Sadaharu had long known how the atmosphere of the delivery room changed when there was no sound of a newborn's cry. Even Ogura's tiny infant had managed a weak voice. And weak though it might be, if the infant cried, Sadaharu felt he need offer no apology to the nurses for making them work. But when he had to ask them to perform a task like today's, he felt like asking for extra compensation from the patient, to divide among the nurses. He had only heard of the practice secondhand, but it seemed to him like the ration of sake received by the executioner on the day punishment was carried out. He could not help thinking this kind of duty had a detrimental effect on nurses trained to support life, when they had to work to destroy it instead.

The nurses placed Mrs. Moji on a gurney and wheeled her out, still under the influence of the anesthetic. Then Sadaharu was alone with the Nurse Okubo.

"Please excuse me for what happened before, doctor."

Perplexed, Sadaharu asked, "What do you mean?"

"When I called you from the house, Mrs. Moji was making a great fuss and was in a lot of pain. I thought that if you were to speak with her you could calm her down. . . ."

"I just talked with her for a few minutes and she seemed calm."

"She was probably reluctant to speak with you, I suppose. After you went away, she was very upset."

"Oh? What about?"

"She wanted to stop the procedure, she said."

"Because it hurt?"

"Yes, but besides that she said that she wanted to give birth to the child, she wanted to keep it."

"And what did you do?"

"I told her that it was impossible to interrupt the process. We couldn't stop an operation halfway through, and no one could stop labor once it has begun."

"I see. That's a good theory, indeed," Sadaharu mused.

"Well, I encountered someone like that once before. She was a rather self-centered young woman who said, 'If it hurts like this, I'll stop right now.' She was fretting and talking nonsense."

"Oh, I nearly forgot about that one."

"At the time, you were very amused by it. You laughed and said, 'I've seen many kinds of patients, but this is the first one I've met one who wanted to stop a delivery halfway through.' I remembered you saying that, and I thought it would be a simple explanation for Mrs. Moji."

"I would probably not have done as well as you," Sadaharu replied.

He approached the fetus as though it was an object on display. Because it had been removed with the aid of the suction cup the head was purple.

"She was so reluctant to have the abortion, I thought she would ask for its ashes."

When Sadaharu had a patient like that he simply told the woman: It's done, forget it. But the present patient was an exception. If she wished, the fetus could be cremated and a bit of the ashes sent to her.

"Well," Nurse Okubo said, "she didn't say anything like that, and I didn't offer any suggestions."

"Yes, that's just as well."

Sadaharu tried to look at what was in front of him merely as an object. Though less than ideal, perhaps, it was an attitude formed by his training and experience. If an explanation was needed, Sadaharu thought, perhaps the priest could supply that more easily than he could.

Next day, the elder Mrs. Moji called on the telephone, saying that she wished to meet with him. It seemed to Sadaharu that he must be feeling some degree of goodwill toward her—at least compared with his attitude up till then—because he suggested a time when he usually took his midday rest. He would have been angry if the person were someone he really disliked, or someone with whom he did not have some particular psychological connection.

Nonetheless, Sadaharu did not invite Mrs. Moji to his home. Instead, he met her in the outpatient examination room, where there was no nurse present.

"And have you visited your daughter-in-law?" he asked.

"Yes, thank you. Last night, she seemed to be asleep, and today she seemed much recovered. But she complained that her breasts were swollen."

"We stop the milk with an injection," Sadaharu said.

"I heard a new mother who gave birth just three days ago was complaining that she wasn't producing milk. Isn't that ironic?"

"Yes, that's the way it goes," Sadaharu said.

"Now, about the present situation . . . It was hardly a good thing for any of us, but thanks to you our family has resolved it."

Sadaharu remained silent.

"Just a little while ago, Sakiko herself told me that she wanted a divorce. When she leaves the hospital the day after tomorrow, she won't return to our house but to her family in Chiba, she said. And I told her if that was the case, we would send all of her things to her. She said she would not ask for any money and so forth, and I told her that we are the ones who should be receiving compensation, but we would not go into all that. Nonetheless, my husband wishes to give you some pocket money, I told her, and she had nothing more to say."

"And has your son consented to all this?" Sadaharu asked.

"He came here the night before last. After the two of them talked about various things, Sakiko told him that the child was not his—that gave him quite a shock, indeed. I suppose it's her selfish attitude or something, the style these days maybe, but because she told him the truth, she seems to have expected Naokata to forgive her."

"Really?"

"As a matter of fact, I thought from the beginning that it was all too peculiar, but when we asked her to have an abortion we thought that even if it came to divorce, she would not have an abortion if she really loved the father of the child. To tell you the truth, I would have preferred that she had the child, even if it meant getting divorced from Naokata. When a mother is forced to choose between her marriage and preserving the life of her child, there should be no alternative, don't you agree? And even if she did divorce Naokata, we would have been left with a very good impression of Sakiko's character."

"If she's gone this far," Sadaharu said, "I wonder why she didn't seek a divorce earlier? She would have had the child of the man she loves."

"No, not at all. I suppose she had no stomach for working while raising a child. I guess that she wanted to find a respectable husband if possible and raise the child of her former lover while living a life of luxury. Even her family in Chiba did not seem at all willing for her to have the baby. Her own mother told someone we know that if Sakiko had an abortion, we should pay for it because Sakiko's marrying Naokata delayed the abortion. Well, Sakiko herself seems to have taken this suggestion from her mother to heart."

"Even so, I imagine you're quite content to pay the expenses, under the circumstances."

"Exactly. That's right, doctor. In the end, it is better to suffer a loss than to inflict one, at least insofar as one's feelings afterward are concerned. Our son is such a fool. And as far as Sakiko is concerned, she was able to catch someone to help her out of her difficulty. If I were her, I would do the same. When all's said and done, however, I really feel sorry for her. But we have to pay for the lessons we learn in life."

Sadaharu said that was probably so. "Somehow, we all tend to push the responsibility for things onto other people, but in fact we all share responsibility equally for almost everything in the world."

"You're quite right, doctor," Mrs. Moji answered.

"Still, you seemed to get along quite well together."

"Sakiko and I?"

"Yes."

"That's only because I myself am a liar and rather deceitful. Overbearing, too."

Mrs. Moji laughed at herself and continued. "At first, I thought how awful it was, but after a while I began to feel that it would be cruel to be too hard on her. She's not very bright, you know. It would have been useless for me to expect more of her. I thought to place her in a position where she could be easily led, but it didn't turn out quite right. It turned out quite pitifully, really."

Mrs. Moji stopped speaking suddenly at that and then asked whether the child was a boy.

"Yes, it was," Sadaharu told her.

She sighed, "It was a pitiful thing to do to the child. It will haunt me the rest of my life."

"Now, there's no need for you to feel that way. Inevitably, at some point, every human life becomes damaged."

And this Sadaharu said from the bottom of his heart.

Chapter Twelve

Road into the Sunset

Kumiko Shinjo came for her periodic checkup, Sadaharu's last patient that day in August. At a glance, Sadaharu noticed that her glossy black hair was done up casually; Shinjo was quieter than usual that day.

"Not very lively today, are you?" Sadaharu said.

"Really? I don't feel ill any more."

Sadaharu spoke in a voice loud enough for Nurse Ono to hear and take notes: "Abdominal circumference, 37; fundal height, 32, 12.2; fetal presentation, vertex; heart tone, plus; edema minus." Then he had Shinjo herself listen to the thumping of the fetus's own heart.

"So, everything is normal, Ms. Shinjo," he informed her.

Shinjo thanked him, but her expression was still glum.

"Is there something the matter?" Sadaharu asked.

"I'd like to talk with you, if I may," she answered.

"Please do. You are my last patient for the day," Sadaharu said, looking down at her chart on the desk.

"May I talk about him—the father of my baby?"

Sadaharu looked at her with an expression that invited her to continue.

"Well, it was really a coincidence, but among the people who regularly come to my shop is a woman who once worked in the same office with him. This woman went to work there right after high school, but now she's married and has stopped working, and she's been living in our area ever since. But when she was at the company, she was in the same section as he, dealing with lumber, and her desk was diagonally behind his. This customer of mine and he knew each other well because they were on the same basketball team."

Sadaharu said he understood, thinking, as he listened to the story, what a horror it was when a woman sniffed out such a connection.

"How did you find out about her?"

"My customer likes to gossip, and when she comes to the shop she talks about the past. She said proudly that when she was at a certain company she was popular with the men in the office. And I asked her where she worked, and said how nice it was, and wouldn't I like to work at a first-class company in Tokyo—that sort of thing. And so naturally his name came out, and I pretended to be surprised and said, 'Oh, that man. I know him.' "

"I thought you were determined not to say anything?"

"But I didn't say anymore than that. I just explained that I had directed him to a repair shop when his car broke down in front of my shop, and he gave me his card and treated me to pizza. I certainly couldn't lie about it."

"Yes, you were right about that," Sadaharu agreed.

"Now whenever she comes to my shop my customer always talks to me about him, even though I don't say anything."

"And what does his former colleague say about him?"

Sadaharu did not particularly want to hear the answer, but he asked Shinjo anyway, feeling this was part of his professional service.

"She said that his wife had suddenly died."

"Eh? You mean he's not married anymore?"

"She didn't make that clear, but she said that his wife had had some illness of the pancreas."

"When did the wife die?"

"She said it happened July 16. But I didn't have a chance to see you until now."

Sadaharu felt that he understood, but he knew that fathoming a woman's heart was beyond him, and so he asked, "Why is that?"

"I heard the news on July 23 or 24, but that would have been just at the end of the first seven days of mourning. He was probably very saddened, I suppose. But even so, I thought he might have called me on the telephone anyway. And so I thought I wouldn't go out for a while."

"Yes, of course. And did he call?"

"No. I thought he might, but he didn't. I suppose he was tired from the funeral and couldn't get over the shock. I suppose he just doesn't have the energy to call me, but I couldn't help but think he might."

"And if he does call, will you tell him about the child?"

"I don't know. I think probably I won't."

"Well, then, it's about the same whether he calls or not, isn't it?"

"Oh, doctor, you're a man, and . . ."

"No one has yet mistaken me for a woman," Sadaharu laughed.

"But you see, yesterday that customer of mine came in to the beauty shop, and she said that she heard he was back at work and seemed all right."

"Well, after all, usually a man doesn't take much time off from work even if his wife dies," Sadaharu suggested.

"Yes, I can understand that, but still I can't help imagining all sorts of things—that he has to work late and can't call me. That he goes home late and suddenly thinks of me and hesitates, worried that it's too late at night to call. That's the kind of man he is, that's why he didn't call."

"Hmm, I see," was Sadaharu's response.

"It rained hard the day before yesterday, you know. I thought he would call then. Somehow I felt that he would, because rainy days make everyone sad. I waited until half past eleven. Once, about nine o'clock, when I was in the bath, the telephone rang and I jumped out all excited. Then I slipped and thought that wasn't acting right, so I calmed down a little and decided to wait until eleven-thirty. So then about midnight I cried myself to sleep."

"You say you slept?" Sadaharu was smiling as he asked this.

"I fell asleep while crying."

"You must have been sleepy. And have you given up on him?"

"Oh, I just don't know how I feel."

Shinjo sat quietly, her expression showing that she was deep in thought.

"But you've left home today to come here. Suppose he called while you were away. What do you think?"

He said this deliberately to tease her.

"No," Shinjo answered, "I left someone there at home, a friend of mine who is going to work in a big beauty parlor near the naval base in the fall—she's looking after the shop for me while I'm out. I asked her to let me know immediately if a call comes in from him."

"If you want to meet him that much, wouldn't it be best to call him yourself?"

"I don't want to do that. I suppose I'm old fashioned in some ways, but I want to be passive. Or cunning, I suppose. I'm afraid to decide for myself what to do, and I don't think it's at all attractive when a woman is too aggressive."

"Then do whatever you want to do," Sadaharu said with a smile. "At any rate, you're gaining weight properly, and the baby's development seems to be normal."

"Yes, no matter what the mother has on her mind the child remains healthy."

"Are you very depressed?"

"Yes, rather," she replied.

"Then let me take you someplace."

"Oh, that would be nice!" Shinjo said.

"But I'm not sure our days off match, and you may have to keep the shop open."

"Oh, that's all right. The person I mentioned will come to help me out anytime."

"Fine. Then next Sunday afternoon I'll come for you. I can't make it in the morning—I stay in bed pretending to doze and reading."

"The afternoon will be fine. I haven't gone out on Sunday for a long time. This will be lots of fun."

"But we're not going to any fancy place," Sadaharu warned.

"Anywhere will do. When I stay home, the only thing I notice is the telephone not ringing."

Sadaharu saw off a Shinjo who was suddenly much happier. He put his desk in order. As he walked to the house, he thought how long it had been since he'd been on a date with a woman. To put it bluntly, he had no idea where his companion might like to go. He was not the right age to go to a movie and stop at a coffee shop afterward. As he arrived at his house, an idea came to mind quite in keeping with his personality.

The following Sunday at two o'clock in the afternoon Sadaharu arrived at Beauty Parlor Kumi together with his daughter, Kaori, who was wearing a straw hat and carrying a rucksack.

"This is my daughter," he said to Shinjo. "She's bored with her summer vacation. May we take her along with us?"

"Oh, of course. That would be fun. What's your name?" Kumiko asked.

Somewhat bashfully Kaori gave her name.

"And in the car out front," Sadaharu said, "is a friend of mine, Yoko Kakei. I asked her to come because I thought we would need two cars today. You don't mind? You won't need slacks or anything, but please wear comfortable shoes for walking. We'll be walking a short way."

Shinjo said, "That's the only kind I wear these days."

She came out to the car and politely introduced herself to Yoko.

"Well, now, shall we be off? The four of us can just fit into this car."

"Sadaharu," Yoko asked, "where are we going?"

"Ah, in the summer the railroad companies run strange trains. Like "The Milky Way Special 999," destination unknown. We'll be like that—only not quite. Anyway, we'll take a hiking trail you two ladies know nothing about."

"Is it all right for Ms. Shinjo to walk?" Yoko asked.

"Oh, it's a distance even a child or a woman could easily walk."

"Then let's go."

Yoko was doing the driving. "And where are we going?" she asked.

"Toward Hikibashi, along the crematorium road."

Kaori said, "Papa likes the crematorium road."

"Indeed I do. The babies born at my clinic will all finally grow old and go to the crematorium, so we need both hospitals and crematoria. The main road is impossibly crowded on Sunday, so let's go by the road I've personally trailblazed."

Sadaharu was putting on a pompous air. Even so, at the congested spot called Hikibashi there were two lines of cars hundreds of meters long waiting to turn off either toward Yokosuka or Zushi.

"Yoko," Sadaharu said, "You can go straight here, and about two hundred meters ahead we can leave the car, so don't worry."

But Kaori was concerned. "Papa, what do we do when we get out of the car? Is there someplace to rest along the way?"

"Yes, there certainly is. There is even a refreshment stand, too."

"Really? You're not just fooling me?"

"Let's see. . . . If I were a murderer, I could take people out here and then kill them all."

Kaori was unimpressed. "My father! He wouldn't even kill a lobster even if he wanted to eat it. Once when mother was away and someone gave us some, he had to do the cooking and he made such a terrible face!"

"And is this the end of the Milky Way Railroad?" Yoko asked, as she parked and locked the car on a road between two fields.

"Perhaps it is—either the end or the beginning. But from here, we can walk at our own pace for about a mile and a quarter," Sadaharu said.

"Why did you choose this road?" Kaori asked her father.

"It's my secret hiking route. The scenery is like Kamakura, with trees like those in Shinshu, and there is a hill with a view of the sea. In fact, there are all kinds of scenery along this short path."

"Really?" Kaori was dubious.

"Oh, it's true. Let's get started, then. Everyone put on hats."

Kaori said, "My father is such a stingy person!" And everyone laughed.

"And why am I 'stingy'?" Sadaharu asked.

"Well, I think you don't like taking long trips because you think it's a waste to pay the train fare."

"I'm sure that's true, but there are all kinds of interesting things close by, so it's not necessary to go a long way to see something worth seeing."

The hillside path was a farm road built for agricultural machinery. It ran along the top of the hill, and on the way a variety of miniature landscapes could be seen. When the road came to an orchard of mandarin oranges, Sadaharu announced, "This is Izu."

"No, it's not," Kaori corrected. "It's the Miura Peninsula."

"Well, if you think it is Izu, then it is," Sadaharu retorted.

When they passed through a grove of various trees, they had no sense at all that the sea was close by. Sadaharu declared that this area was Shinshu.

"It really seems like it is," Shinjo said. "I went to Matsumoto once, a long time ago, and there is a place there that feels just like this."

Yoko said, "This really is an interesting path. The scenery changes every hundred meters. Sadaharu, how did you find this road?"

"Oh, I like to wander around, on foot or driving."

"It's an unbelievable place. The main road is congested with cars, but this back road is a quiet hiking trail."

"Exactly why I brought you here today. I'm also a bit selfish about sharing this place. I wouldn't have come here in a taxi.

Sometimes, when I'm in a taxi around here, the main road is crowded as it is today, but I never suggest going this way to save time. If one taxi driver learned about this road, all the taxi drivers would know about it and it would be ruined. I don't tell people about this place. Anyway, you should all keep this a secret place to walk along with your children or sweetheart."

"But father," Kaori complained, "you didn't really tell the truth. You said there was a coffee shop along the way, but there's no such place on this path, is there?"

"Oh, but there is," Sadaharu answered calmly.

"Where?"

"Just a bit further."

As they walked along, Kaori caught crickets and chased butterflies with her hat.

"Oh, oh. Here is the coffee shop," Sadaharu finally said.

"Oh! Where?" Kaori asked.

In the corner of a watermelon field, there stood an old shack covered with battered advertising posters proclaiming such products as "Okame Cotton," and "Daigaku Brand School Uniforms." Sadaharu reached the shack and stopped.

"Yes, this is the place," he said, responding to Kaori. "The owner of this field is the husband of one of my patients, and I called him yesterday and asked permission to eat one of the melons."

"Did you pay him?" Kaori asked.

"I said I would gladly pay, but he said not to worry and to take any one I wished. Only we mustn't step on the vines."

"Then you should go in by yourself and pick out a good one," Yoko said. "If we all go, we'll cause some damage walking around in the field."

Sadaharu agreed.

"Papa, I don't feel right about this. We'll look like melon thieves," Kaori called out.

"Just be patient. If we are in the right, we need not care about what other people think."

Sadaharu went into the field where the bamboo poles stood marking the location of the fruit, and, finally, after examining five or six melons that were shaded by their leaves, he cut off one especially large melon with his pocket knife.

"Luckily, there is a water pipe here. We'll just wash off the outside and eat it right away."

Kaori mentioned how surprised she was that her father had worked everything out to the last detail.

They washed the melon at the faucet next to the old shack, and Sadaharu broke the melon by dropping it on a rock from just the right height.

"Ah, perfect. You broke it into pieces just right for eating," Shinjo said admiringly.

"Be careful not to scatter the seeds around, everybody," Yoko said. "Sometimes the youngsters eat melons on my lawn and leave seeds all over. Then they sprout and make a mess."

"Ah, Yoko, that's terribly lazy of you not to weed your lawn," Sadaharu teased.

"But I'm just being logical. You, on the other hand, are primarily concerned with using your head so as not to make work in the first place."

The group walked on, enjoying the scenery as the narrow road dipped and climbed among the trees, then dropped into a tiny valley and finally rose again for a view of the ocean.

"When I walk along this path, I think how much like the course of a human life it is. There are lots of places one does not go to see in this world, lots of people one does not meet, and everyone has ups and downs in his own life. Then in the end one dies without accomplishing much at all. All one's life is a series of good and bad times, happy and sad ones, too. But that's really something to be grateful for. When I walk along this path, I'm intensely aware of that."

"Yes. And, Sadaharu, it's wonderful for me to walk this path once with other people. I'm grateful for that. No one would bring me here besides you."

"That's right," Kaori added. "If it weren't for my father, I wouldn't be walking on this dumb path either. And you told me there was a coffee shop, and I really believed I would get some ice cream."

"Ah, do you really want ice cream?" Sadaharu inquired.

"Of course!"

"All right, then. At the end of the path is a yacht harbor where you can have some."

"Wow! Hurry!" Kaori shouted.

Yoko laughed. "Well, that's the way little girls are. Ms. Shinjo, when you have your child, you can enjoy memorable moments like this."

"Hmm. And speaking of children—when is the Laurie family coming?" Sadaharu asked.

"Oh, I forgot about that. They said they would come next week, and I talked to them about the girl you would like them to adopt."

"Does someone want to give away a child?" Shinjo asked.

"Yes. There are special circumstances."

"Still, that's too bad," Shinjo said, her voice containing an especially heartfelt sigh. "It may seem strange for me to be saying that, but it's how I feel at this moment."

"You are right to feel that way," Sadaharu said.

"Papa, papa," Kaori called. "Is that our car over there? It looks just like it."

"Yes, that's it. Right where we left it. And near where we left Mrs. Kakei's car."

They emerged at last through a tunnel of shade created by the dense leaves of the cherry trees.

"Ah! We made it!"

"Oh, Kaori, wouldn't it be nice if the path were even longer?" Shinjo said.

"Now, then, everyone into the car and we shall pick up Mrs. Kakei's car on the way to the yacht harbor," Sadaharu said.

The harbor offered a kind of floating restaurant serving fried shrimp, bouillabaisse, abalone steak, and so on. Sadaharu took the women there and, feeling that he had not provided enough with only one watermelon, suggested they try something on the menu. Yoko said that she was too full of melon to want anything more, and Shinjo, too, said that she could not eat a thing.

"Still, it's a nice place," Sadaharu said. "And we can look at the boats and keep Kaori company while she eats her ice cream. It's all right if you don't feel like eating."

When they came to the sunny shore lined with vacation condominiums, they saw hundreds of yachts and motor boats set out in their slips like sea creatures on a beach. Yoko asked Shinjo whether she had ever been there before, and she replied that she had not.

"I like to come here to see the boats," Sadaharu said, "but I have no interest in sailing. Having a boat is like taking care of a mistress, but I suppose it is a pleasure for the owner. They say that confronting the sea is a kind of philosophical act, harsh and pure, but the truth is, I don't have time for a hobby that involves any sort of confrontation."

"I rarely come here, but sometimes I meet friends at the yacht harbor," Yoko said.

"And for me this is a special occasion," Shinjo said. "I've often wanted to come here, but none of my friends frequent this kind of place, so I've never had the opportunity."

As he listened to Shinjo, Sadaharu felt strange. Palm trees—but not the real thing—with names like Washington Palm and Canary Palm swayed in the wind, while men and women dressed in resort wear costumes walked about. Sadaharu didn't feel at ease in places like this and never once had longed to be part of it, but he also realized that not being attracted to this type of scene was unusual and in a way perverse. But Sadaharu still could not help feeling that for grown men and women to admire such a place was rather childish.

And so when Shinjo remarked, "Oh, what a big yacht! What a marvelous motorboat! How grand it would be to spend a night on that boat!" Sadaharu felt a bit ill at ease. "You've got to be a child, or the kind of person who believes Santa Claus will bring him presents at Christmas to get excited in a place like that," thought Sadaharu, as he walked along at the head of the group, taking deep breaths as he enjoyed the delicious sea breeze.

Soon it was Thursday of the same week. A letter came from Shinjo addressed to Sadaharu. A thank you note, he thought, but since the envelope was rather thick, Sadaharu took it to his lounge chair and opened it along with his beer before dinner.

"Doctor:

Thank you very much for taking me along on the hike last Sunday. I had no idea that there was a hiking path like that in our area. It has become very precious to me. You said that we should not tell anyone about the path. When you said we should go there only with a sweetheart or a child, I felt my heart leap.

I can tell you this directly, doctor, because of who you are. I want to walk along that path with my lover. If possible, I want to walk on that path together with him and our child. I would like to tell my family what you said about the road, and I feel I should be able to, because we are a real family. If I could have that wish come true for one day only, I think that I would be willing to give up ten years of my life. But I don't suppose that such a day will ever come.

After all, I imagine that someday I will walk that path together with my child and feel the pain of my lost love. Perhaps then I will think that instead of shortening my life by ten years on the contrary I ought to extend it by ten years.

Since the other day, I have been very happy, because you took me to the yacht harbor. My friend, the father of my baby, often talked about that place. Since he is skilled at many sports, when there is a shortage of hands on a friend's boat he often seems to be invited to join the crew. When I walk into a place like that, where you can look up at the boats in the slips (if that's what you call those things), I feel as if I might meet him there by accident.

I'm not particularly religious about gods or Buddha, and even though I feel it would be bad to break my vow and write to him, I wouldn't feel I had done anything wrong if I met him there and told him the truth. But, after we didn't see him at the docks, when we went to the boat restaurant with Kaori I was thinking that he might come through the door, his face all sunburned, and recognize me. To tell you the truth, when Mrs. Kakei urged me to have some cake I had had enough, but I had some lemon pie, anyway, to stretch out the time even a little bit so I would have more of a chance of meeting him. But he didn't appear."

Sadaharu poured the remaining beer into the goblet decorated with the emblem of the brewery. The kind of romance in Shinjo's note was not a grownup story, he thought, but only a tale from a childish world. The letter went on:

"Still, doctor, on that day I thought of something quite amazing. He was not there, and yet I felt his presence everywhere, in every corner—the path on which he strolled, the sun shining on his shoulders, the wind caressing his cheeks. I could see the things he loved and wanted, or what he did not love and rejected. I felt all those things. Everything that I saw became part of what he was seeing and seemed to convey his will.

I suppose all of this is just to say that I've not lost hope that he himself, the live person, will come to me. Until he does, it will involve a long, demanding process, in terms of time and emotional commitment, I suppose, but I intend to wait.

I truly want to thank you, doctor. I thought the distance we traveled was just a short hike, only a walk, really, but the truth is it had so much meaning for me. That path made me understand my true feelings, and for the sake of the child inside me I think that's a necessary thing. I cannot have a baby so casually. Now I know I am having the baby because of a man I love. And that hike last Sunday confirmed my feeling. Now I feel worthy of having this child.

You may think it funny, but I went to that path again on my day off yesterday, Tuesday. It was evening when I suddenly thought of it, and so by the time I started out on the path the sun was low. As I watched the sun set, I walked along the hill path, and in my loneliness I couldn't stop the tears. I've been afraid that if I was too sad it would be bad for the baby, but now I don't think that. Really, I now have to contemplate both loneliness and suffering without fear. I want to see all this through to the end. If that is my fate, then I will have to share that fate with my child.

I've never seen a sunset as splendid as the one last Tuesday. The sun burned with the color of some ripe, red fruit, and it even seemed to be melting. For a while, it looked as though the sun was simply enduring its fate. Without useless struggling, it quietly, almost elegantly, sank below the horizon. For a while, the clouds reflected its light, but finally they took on the deep blue of night. Suddenly, I noticed the planet Venus beginning to shine brightly.

Then I cried again, not only from sadness but also because of my new feeling of resolution.

No matter what happens, I'll always be grateful for everything you gave to me by inviting me out last Sunday.

Kumiko Shinjo."

The telephone rang and Nurse Ono answered, then handed the phone to Sadaharu.

"Sadaharu?"

Yoko Kakei was speaking. Sadaharu guessed that it was something connected with his work since Yoko had a keen sense of propriety and never called about personal matters during his office hours.

"Mr. and Mrs. Laurie are staying at my home tonight and they would like to see the baby."

"Oh? I see. Then should I bring the baby or will they come here?"

"They said that they would come to you."

"Fine. I'll expect them after eight o'clock."

As he hung up the telephone, he thought he had better inform the old lady, Mrs. Komatsu, soon. He did not know whether she would be relieved or saddened, but either way it was humanly impossible for people to raise their own great-grandchildren. Still, Sadaharu did not telephone her that afternoon because he wanted to get to know the Lauries a little better first.

That night, in expectation of the Lauries' visit to see Mrs. Komatsu's great-granddaughter, Miyako, he asked his wife to hurry dinner, and he finished eating early. Even so, the doorbell rang before he had finished his tea, and he could hear Yoko's voice mingling with his wife's voice. Sadaharu called out that he was coming to join them.

He had heard that Mr. Laurie was a lawyer, and so he had imagined a rather stout man with greying hair, someone in his sixties, but in the foyer stood a handsome and elegant male figure, while his wife had the beauty of a sturdier Jacqueline Kennedy. It was hard to judge the age of foreigners, but Sadaharu supposed them to be in their early forties.

"Are these the people?" he asked.

"Yes, Mr. and Mrs. Laurie."

"Please translate for me, Yoko. How do you do? I'm pleased to meet you," Sadaharu said in Japanese.

The guests moved into the living room and seated themselves on the sofa. Sadaharu said frankly, "I am surprised that even though you are so young you are adopting a child. If you like children, why don't you have your own?"

Without a change of expression, Yoko conveyed this to the Lauries. The husband, Edmund Laurie, laughed and replied with something Sadaharu did not get.

"What did he say?" Sadaharu asked Yoko.

"Just that if they happen to be so blessed, they will have their own, but adopting a child has quite another meaning."

"I see. Then please tell them this: The child is a girl. The mother belongs to an old family, but both parents are high school students. Because they wish to keep the child's existence a secret, they say, there has been no public announcement of the birth. The next thing is that I am busy and do not wish to be involved in the red tape, so all of that will be up to the Lauries, but I will assist them in getting in touch with the family."

While Yoko was translating, Sadaharu observed the husband and wife. He had no idea how the husband might look in court, but he had a gentle expression on his face. The wife seemed rather unsociable and by her expression seemed to be listening as though she were being given an explanation in some official's office.

"They say that they understand your position and will take care of all the red tape," Yoko said.

"Then the next thing is the child, and I'll show her to them now. But they should know that she has neither cried out nor even laughed. However, as far as I can determine, there is nothing wrong with her hearing. She turns her eyes toward the direction of a sound."

When Sadaharu finished his explanation, Mrs. Laurie asked him a question. Rather to his surprise, Sadaharu understood in general what she was saying. Nonetheless, lacking confidence in himself, he asked Yoko for confirmation.

"Did she want to know whether they could take the child with them while the red tape is being settled?"

"Ah! Sadaharu—that's right! You do understand English, don't you? Of course, we will have to contact the guardians and obtain their permission in advance, but since the Lauries are already in Japan they want to be with the child as soon as possible, they say."

"I'm perplexed, however," Sadaharu said in an even tone, so as not to give a hint to the American couple. "The wife is young and at an age that suggests she will want to go sight-seeing and shopping and so forth while she is in Japan. Or so I imagine. If the child is with them, they won't be able to enjoy themselves, will they?"

"Yes, that's true, but they really will enjoy having the child with them, and they want to take her as soon as possible. Their hotel can arrange for a baby sitter, so they can go out when they wish."

"That's splendid. Quite natural and wonderful, I would say," Sadaharu replied.

"They only do what they feel like doing," Yoko said.

At that point, Mr. Laurie said something, but Sadaharu had no idea of what he had said, despite Yoko's earlier compliment, and so he had to ask her.

"He just said that his older brother and his wife adopted three children: one white, one black, and one Japanese."

Sadaharu expressed astonishment.

"And he said the Japanese child is the smartest and can write her name even though she is only five, and can do addition, too. The wife's mother, the child's adoptive grandmother, is totally taken with it. The Japanese baby the Lauries are adopting will be the other girl's cousin. They think the two will get along very well. That's what he was saying."

"So, do they want to have a look at the child?"

When Sadaharu spoke, the full-bodied Mrs. Laurie nodded vigorously.

"Fine. The child is in the second-floor nursery. She's gotten quite big, but she is only three months old."

Sadaharu arose, put on his shoes in the foyer, then led the

Lauries outside.

At the nurses' station by the entrance to the nursery, young Nurse Yuasa was on duty. As soon as Sadaharu saw her face, he knew that he'd better not tell her it had already been decided that Miyako would be given to Mr. and Mrs. Laurie.

He couldn't simply imply that the formalities of adoption had not yet been settled; the fact was that if Sadaharu were to tell the nurses that he had found someone to accept Miyako, they would regard him as a mercenary trader in human beings; or if not quite that, then somewhat in the position of a dog owner accused by the Humane Society of mistreating his animals. That was what he was mainly worried about.

"This is the nursery," Sadaharu announced in front of the nurse, acting as though the three visitors were ordinary guests.

"As a general rule, we lock the nursery at night. Rare as it is, even in Japan there have been instances of unattended infants being stolen."

Sadaharu was relieved to see Nurse Yuasa take the hint and slip away.

"This baby is the one," he said.

Sadaharu unlocked the nursery, entered, and stood at the front of the small bed in which Miyako was sleeping. He expected the Lauries would praise the child's good looks, but they said nothing. The husband and wife stood looking at Miyako's upturned face.

Suddenly, Sadaharu wanted to turn away. He had no doubt that the Lauries would provide a good home for Miyako, but for a moment Sadaharu lost sight of his role. He knew very well that no one in this world could guarantee whether Miyako would experience happiness or misery in her life, yet for an instant he felt his heart hesitate. Behind him the three were talking; he could not comprehend a single word. He wondered why there had been no praise, not a word for the beautiful child. But he despised that kind of thinking just as much. The Lauries were not choosing a child because it was beautiful or smart. Indeed, they came together by chance, this child and this couple, simply because they existed on earth. And that was the mystery. There was nothing for human beings to prepare for in this. This was all, and it was done.

Sadaharu half murmured this to himself as he turned toward the three guests. Mrs. Laurie was no ethereal Madonna out of some painting, but rather like a sturdy peasant woman she scooped up Miyako in her arms.

The American couple and Yoko left some thirty minutes later, Sadaharu seeing them off. Immediately, Sadaharu telephoned the elderly Mrs. Komatsu.

"How are you getting along? How has your blood pressure been since the other day?" he asked.

"Oh, it seems to have come down, thank you. But what about Miyako?" Mrs. Komatsu asked.

"She's doing quite well. Gaining weight, just as she should. About the foreigner, the lawyer who said that he would take her, as I mentioned earlier. I met him just now."

"Really?"

Sadaharu conveyed his impression of the Lauries, especially of Mrs. Laurie—her sturdy arms and the good feeling he had had when she held the baby.

"And besides meeting and seeing her, they want to take her as soon as possible, they say. But, of course, I can't allow that until we receive your permission."

"Yes. I spoke with the mother's parents the other day, and they have an acquaintance who is a lawyer and is conveniently nearby in Yokohama, and it seems they wish to get in touch with him. He is a classmate of my daughter's husband and will take care of any technical problems with this, he says."

"Then may I ask that the young mother contact me directly, please? I need to confirm that this is what she wants, or I can't make any move at all."

"Yes, I'll have the Satos call you immediately," Mrs. Komatsu said.

In order not to say any more about his feelings, Sadaharu ended the conversation.

Before five minutes had passed, the telephone rang again.

"Hello," Mr. Sato said, "I'm the son-in-law of the Komatsu family in Zushi." It was the baby's grandfather speaking. "Thank you for all you have done for us. I've been told you've found suitable people to take Miyako."

"Yes. I think they are good people. In America, a lawyer is in the intellectual upper class," Sadaharu said. He was passing on what he had heard from Yoko. "But above all, I wish to make certain that your whole family is in accord with having Miyako adopted. You've no objections to this, I suppose?"

"No, no. There are no objections. The parents are in no position to raise the child."

"And your daughter, the child's mother, how does she feel? Does she feel sad or cry sometimes?"

"Well, the boy involved has changed schools, and our daughter seems to remember it all only as some kind of bad dream. She is quite absorbed in basketball and comes home covered with dirt every day."

Indeed, this is the Age of the Child Parent, Sadaharu thought. Sato's high school daughter, even if capable of being a parent physically, was psychologically still a child. She would have no understanding of motherhood. An individual might seek parenthood, but to think that giving birth was only a "bad dream" shows some lack of self-awareness. And the baby's grandfather, a mature individual, looking on in this disinterested way, formal, irresponsible, unmoved—that gave Sadaharu a strange feeling.

But, in another, unsentimental sense, just as there was someone ready to discard a child, someone else was there to save it, and so as a result each was pleased.

Mr. Sato went on: "I spoke with my mother-in-law the other day, and she thought it ungrateful of me not to have come to see you, considering all the trouble you have been to on our behalf. I intend to introduce the lawyer to you very soon. However, my daughter is still a minor. I want her to forget this incident as soon as possible. Please forgive me for not bringing her to meet you."

Sadaharu thought that if Kaori had gotten pregnant and given birth, he would never give the child up but would make her raise it herself. Or if she could not raise it he would not cover up the matter like this. After all, it wasn't a case of rape, but a result of mutual agreement; it should be accepted as its mother's child. Even if the mother were ten or fifteen years old, some sense of responsibility was called for.

"Please don't take the trouble to come and see me. Couldn't you just have your lawyer friend contact the American lawyer directly at the hotel where he is staying, in order to arrange a meeting? They could discuss matters and decide when they can take the child and then let me know."

Mr. Sato agreed. "I'll do that. The lawyer in Yokohama studied in the United States and is good at languages, so I think he can handle all that himself."

"Well, that relieves me greatly. The matter will be between the two lawyers. I think that will clear up things quite well."

Mr. Sato thanked Sadaharu and promised to arrange the meeting.

Everything was going well for Miyako. Yet there was no satisfaction for Sadaharu. In the beginning, he had felt that he was involved in separating the baby from her natural parents, but that was not quite it either. The case of this child who did not cry, and whose parents and other people around her were so unconcerned, made Sadaharu feel as miserable as he ever had in his life. This kind of treatment struck him as ugly and inhuman, especially since it was directed at a helpless baby.

As it happened, the grandparents of Miyako Sato were cooperative about giving the child to Mr. and Mrs. Laurie, more cooperative than Sadaharu had imagined they would be. They were prompt, direct, and positive. Mr. Sato came immediately to meet with his lawyer friend, his former classmate who had set up practice in Yokohama. Then he met with Mr. and Mrs. Laurie—so Sadaharu learned from the great-grandmother in Zushi and Yoko Kakei. They made all the necessary legal preparations, and the Sato family signed the papers, agreeing that the Lauries could take the child with them at any time. After that, there was a second communication from the elderly Mrs. Komatsu confirming the details, and mentioning that although she had asked her son-in-law to visit Sadaharu first, since he had been instrumental in all this, the lawyer had requested him to come to his office in Yokohama as soon as possible.

"That's perfectly all right," Sadaharu said, "but before handing over the baby to the Lauries, I need authorization from an immediate relative."

"Of course," said Mrs. Komatsu. "My son-in-law said that he would come to visit you tomorrow afternoon. I think I would like to come along too."

"Yes, please do. I'll be here all day," Sadaharu told her.

The following day was Thursday, and Sato appeared alone. He told Sadaharu that just as they were setting out the old lady had felt indisposed. The weather had been terribly hot for a few days, and she was probably feeling the effects of that. Sato had told her to rest and had left her behind.

"That's all right. I hear from Mrs. Komatsu by phone from time to time," Sadaharu said.

Sato had a classic oval face and a dark complexion; there was a look of concern on his face combined with great humility. He was ashamed of his daughter's misconduct, and he was grateful to Sadaharu—but that was all he could say in words, and Sadaharu could not tell by his expression how upset he really was.

"And as far as your family is concerned, the child may be turned over to the Lauries at any time, is that correct?" Sadaharu asked, just to make certain.

"Yes, at any time. In fact, when we met the Lauries we discussed payment to the clinic, and they said that they would pay this month's fee part, but since I couldn't accept that we agreed to prorate the charges up to the time the child leaves the clinic and each pay half."

"I see," Sadaharu said.

The man seemed fearful of not behaving properly at a time like this. Still, Sadaharu recognized a certain prudence in Sato's concern, and, accordingly, had him sign an agreement, a document that stated in effect that he and his family approved of giving Miyako up for adoption. Sadaharu felt that it would be wise to have this record in case proof was needed someday. But what he was most concerned about was the moment when he would actually transfer Miyako to the Lauries.

"Will the Lauries need some special arrangements when they take Miyako?"

That night, when Sadaharu received a telephone call from Yoko, he told her of his concern.

"Oh, I don't think there will be a problem. They've returned from a trip to the Kansai district, and they want to take her as soon as possible. They need your permission, so they asked me to call you."

"I'd like to meet with them on Sunday," Sadaharu said. "How would the evening suit you?"

"That would be fine, I'm sure. If it gets too late, they can stay the night with me."

"Hmm. I'll tell you why later. Anyway, let's settle on Sunday night. I'll have her dressed up in her finest."

"Mrs. Laurie spoke to me about that. They brought everything she will need, so don't worry about a thing."

"Whatever you say. Since she is going to become their daughter, they may do as they see fit."

Sadaharu hung up the phone and went to look for Nurse Okubo.

"May I talk with you for a moment?"

During his break, he went to the now-deserted outpatient section with her.

"It's about little Miyako," he said.

"Yes."

"A very rich American lawyer wants to adopt her. Everyone concerned has discussed the adoption procedures and agreed."

"I see. That's fine, isn't it?"

"Yes, I wouldn't mind being adopted like that myself," Sadaharu said.

The nurse's expression showed her amusement.

"They will take her away soon, and I don't want any melodrama, you understand. I couldn't stand all the nurses crying and carrying on. So, Sunday night, quietly, when there aren't many people about, they will come to take Miyako."

"Yes, I think that's best. Next Sunday I'll be on night duty," Okubo said.

"That's what I'd planned. And the other nurse?"

"Nurse Hanada. I'll speak with her when the time comes."

"Please do. That will be a great help."

"Miyako has become such a lovely little girl. She doesn't make a sound, but I know she is laughing inside. She has a lovely smile."

The next day, Sadaharu, who did not care for melodrama, came upon exactly the kind of scene that he had wished to avoid.

It was just at the midday break. He was returning to his residence for lunch when he saw some of the young nurses holding Miyako for a photograph, with a palm tree in the background. Sadaharu, hearing their cries for him to come over, thought for a moment that his plan had been discovered.

"What are you doing?" he asked, looking innocent.

"Taking Miyako's picture! Don't you want to be in it too?"

"No, no. It wouldn't look right for me to stand there in the middle of all you girls."

"Oh! What an ego!"

"Anyway, come on and join us," another said, but Sadaharu laughed and waved his hand while making his escape.

Now there was no way he could excuse himself later for not having taken the opportunity to inform the nurses about Miyako leaving. Later on, during the afternoon of the next day, Saturday, Sadaharu went with Dr. Hiroshige to look in on a newborn infant in the nursery, one just born by Caesarean section, and encountered another scene he would rather have avoided.

Miyako was asleep in an ordinary baby crib, but toys had been placed on each side of her head, and on the bedframe colored ribbons were tied.

"Eh? What's this?" he asked abruptly.

"It's for Miko. She likes these kinds of things. And when we hold her, she likes to play with a necklace too."

"Hmm. Aren't you all giving this one child an awful lot of attention?"

"But she's growing up. And besides, her parents never come to see her."

Sadaharu left the room without speaking.

Toward evening, a telephone call came from Yoko.

"The Lauries will staying at my house tomorrow night."

"Good. Then there is no need to rush things, is there?"

"And on Monday the baby will be baptized at Father Munechika's church, and after that they will go on to Tokyo. I'm going to be her godmother."

"Why are they in so much of a hurry with everything?" Sadaharu asked.

"Well, really! Maybe they will all be killed in an auto accident tomorrow," Yoko said. "Then they will all find salvation together by the hand of God."

"All right, fine. But you are always thinking about dying, Yoko!"

"Her baptismal name is Margaret, they said. Margaret Miyako Laurie—that's who she will be."

"It's a nice name. Just right for a beauty like her."

Sadaharu felt that his response was quite beside the point.

Chapter Thirteen

Crepe Myrtle

Sadaharu passed Sunday afternoon in what he considered the height of luxury, reclining in his favorite chair, the one he used alternately for reading and dozing. (To a bystander all this might seem less than splendid, the physician sleeping there in his sweaty sports shirt.) It was nearly sunset when he arose and went to take a shower, singing to himself while enjoying the sparkling water.

"At last, at last, I'm selling Miyako at last!"

The sound of his own voice startled Sadaharu. Fortunately, no one, including his wife and daughter, was nearby. It could have been really dangerous had one of the nurses happened to hear him. Young girls are easily excited, and he could imagine how the story would go: "The doctor here is so unscrupulous he uses his position to arrange for a child to be adopted and then he ends up with a huge pile of money." Something like that would be gossipped about and probably even reported to a newspaper. Sadaharu did not mind being considered disreputable in personal matters, an occasional result of his basic shyness. But others might find his attitude difficult to understand.

At about half past five, Sadaharu went to make a preliminary inspection of Miyako, but she had already been bathed by Nurse Hanada.

"Oh my! Doesn't she look pretty," he said to the nurse, who had her back to him. "You know, Nurse Hanada, I couldn't tell you earlier. Could you please apologize for me to the other nurses?

Everyone has made so much of her, it was just too hard to explain."

But in fact his excuse sounded slightly cowardly.

"It's all right," the nurse told him. But her voice clearly held the echo of her own unforgivingness.

The telephone was ringing as Sadaharu returned home, and Kaori came running.

"It's somebody named Komatsu," she declared.

"In a moment," he said casually, but a sudden flash of horror went through Sadaharu's mind. He was sure the elderly Mrs. Komatsu, having gone this far, was about to tell him to stop everything and return Miyako to her.

"Doctor? Is that you?" Mrs. Komatsu said in a weak voice.

"Yes. How are you feeling?" he asked.

"I've heard from my son-in-law. They tell me that Miyako will bc taken away tomorrow or the next day. . . ."

It was Sadaharu's belief that to get along in this world people had to be able to manipulate and deceive one another, yet at this moment he did not wish to deceive Mrs. Komatsu.

"The adoptive parents have arranged to take Miyako with them in a little while."

"Today? Already?"

In her voice was the echo of her grief.

"Yes, immediately. They are not returning to America directly, but they want to begin caring for her starting tonight."

"Then . . . in a little while Miyako will be gone."

"Yes. She has had her bath and is nice and clean."

The old lady spoke in a flurry, "If I come right away, will I be in time? I want to see her one last time," she continued.

"Please, don't do that," Sadaharu said. "You cannot keep seeing her forever."

On the other end of the telephone there was a long silence.

"Now tell me, how are you feeling?" Sadaharu began.

"Oh. Yes. My blood pressure goes up and down. . . . Doctor?"

"Yes. What is it?"

"I've never parted from a blood relative this way. During the war, one of my cousins was killed. My father died of tuberculosis. There was nothing that could be done about either death. And so after they went, even though I was sad, I could accept it. But Miyako . . ."

"Mrs. Komatsu, no matter how much you talk about it, it won't change anything. You will never be able to keep Miyako. Besides, you were the only one interested in raising her. If you think that way, then Miyako is very fortunate to have this opportunity. This is an intellectual family. A lawyer in America has a very high social status. She's becoming the daughter of that family. It's a very desirable situation for her."

For the first time, at that very moment, Sadaharu touched upon a conventional materialistic rationale. He felt particularly comfortable in doing so; it made things easy to explain and they were on common ground.

"So, then, I . . . ," was all Mrs. Komatsu could say.

"Yes, that's right. Please. Let it be. But I'm not saying that you should forget."

"I thought for a moment that I might go to see her off on the day she leaves Japan. But I must give up that idea."

"She will be brought up very well in America. It's a fine thing, you know, that she's being given a chance for a healthy life somewhere. There's nothing more that we can ask for as human beings."

Mrs. Komatsu attempted to respond, but no answer came.

The telephone conversation with Mrs. Komatsu ended with empty formalities. Neither Sadaharu nor Mrs. Komatsu had any real alternative, and for that reason their parting words were all the more empty.

A little while after the Lauries arrived, Sadaharu said to Yoko, "Before you arrived, the baby's grandmother called saying she wanted to come to have a last farewell. I had a bit of trouble stopping her."

"Oh, that's too bad," Yoko said.

"And clothes? Did they bring some?"

"I have them right here."

Yoko seemed to ask Mrs. Laurie if it would be all right to allow Sadaharu to take Miyako's clothes. As usual, Mr. Laurie smiled and nodded, while his wife only nodded, with a serious look on her face. The clothing she handed over was not expensive. It was summer, and Miyako would wear easy-to-wash white cotton linen. Only when the white shoes and socks appeared together was it apparent that these had already been worn and were not new.

"Oh. They're putting shoes on her and she can't even crawl yet?" Sadaharu observed.

Yoko told him, "That's the way it is with Westerners."

"While they get the baby ready let's have a toast to the parents and their new child in my office. I have some special Japanese sake."

Yoko translated for the lawyer, who said that would be fine, and so the four of them went into the small room used by Dr. Hiroshige.

"Please ask them to make Miyako happy," Sadaharu said. "I can't tell them how to do that, but they will do the best they can. And to make her a girl who can help other people, at least a little. Please tell them that."

While Yoko was conveying this, Sadaharu removed the piece of brocade cloth covering the ceramic Aritayaki bottle, pried open the wooden plug, and poured the sake gurgling into cut glass goblets.

"Mr. Laurie says they will be to blame if they can't make Miyako happy. And that they certainly will not fail to do so," Yoko conveyed to Sadaharu.

"Thank heavens. Shall we drink?" Sadaharu said.

The four of them took up their glasses.

"Human life is amazing. In spite of being born totally Japanese, Miyako is going to become an American. I once read something written by a famous person. When he was small, his life was not only not easy, it wasn't even interesting, he wrote. And he thought that he was living some kind of mistake, that he had only been left where he was for a brief time and soon his real parents—nicer ones—would come and get him. A funny character, don't you think? But he remained on this side of his dream until the end, while Miyako is going over to the other side."

Presently, Nurse Okubo came in holding Miyako, and without crying or smiling, even when looking into the face of the Westerner with different colored eyes, the baby was placed in the arms of Mrs. Laurie.

Nurse Okubo spoke: "The nurses have bought or made by themselves a few things for Miyako during her stay, and we wonder if it would bc all right for her to have them. That would make everyone here feel better tomorrow."

Like a spokesperson, she delivered this in a properly cool tone, with Nurse Hanada beside her holding two department store shopping bags containing Miyako's things. Yoko translated.

Mrs. Laurie said, "Of course. Thank you so much. We will carry them with us and take special care of all the things." Yoko interpreted.

"Please do as they request," Sadaharu said, "although it will add to the baggage."

The Lauries said their thanks in English as they shook the hands of both nurses.

"I guess there isn't anything left for me to do," Sadaharu said.

"And about Miyako's hospital expenses," Yoko said, "The Lauries deposited the money into the bank the day before yesterday, and I sent them a receipt in Japanese.

"Well, then, there really is nothing left to do. Shall we go?"

Yoko spoke in Japanese and then repeated her words in English. The Lauries nodded and stood up.

Nurse Okubo said, "I'll carry Miyako as far as the entrance."

As though she understood Japanese, Mrs. Laurie nodded and passed the baby to her. Sadaharu walked ahead with the Lauries and the nurses followed.

"Miko, Miko," Nurse Hanada said in a soft voice. "Be a good girl, won't you, and learn English. When you grow up you won't remember any of us."

"Yes, but she will understand even if she doesn't remember. Her father and mother will tell her. Miyako is very bright," Nurse Okubo replied.

It was a rare summer night, the sky clear with a great scattering of stars.

Sadaharu asked Yoko, "Did you drive?"

"Yes," she answered.

Mrs. Laurie sat in the back seat holding the baby, while her husband carefully put the baby's things on the floor at his feet.

The nurses bade Miko bye-bye and farewell. Sadaharu wished that the car would leave quickly and put a big smile on his face, suddenly noticing the white blossoms of the *hamayu* near him bearing a timely, silent witness.

Next morning at the regular staff meeting, Sadaharu spoke with a solemn expression on his face.

"I'm sure that you have already heard, but Miyako Sato has made a good match and last night was taken into the family of an American lawyer. There was no time to tell all of you before, but I believe the family will make her very happy, so I am glad to make this announcement now. Mr. and Mrs. Laurie, her adoptive parents, wish to express their sincere gratitude to all of you."

Of course, the couple had not actually said that, but Sadaharu felt that this gave him a chance to express his own feelings in their name.

The nurses were all calm, he saw, and he realized that they had known. He really had no idea of their feelings, but Sadaharu was timid enough to be grateful that they did not criticize him directly. Perhaps he only imagined that they were depressed. If he left them alone, they might break into tears, but the older nurses, Okubo and Ono, firmed up the atmosphere with their calm demeanor.

The nurses' attitude occupied Sadaharu's mind all that day. They showed no apparent resentment about the fact that he had given away Miyako, only a kind of disappointment that they had not been able to say goodbye to her. The nurses seemed a bit downcast and gloomy, and he did not hear their usual laughing voices. The girls worked in silence. Only that afternoon, when Sadaharu was about to go into the nursery for newborns, did he catch a bit of their conversation from the room next door.

"I was shocked."

"Well, there was something to be shocked about."

"When Miko wasn't in her bed, it never for a moment crossed my mind that she had been stolen."

"Miko will become such a rich young lady, that even if you visited her she wouldn't give you the time of day."

"Nurse Kurata said that she would like to be adopted into that family instead of Miko."

"And so would I!"

"Oh, you're both disgusting."

It seemed to Sadaharu that they had accepted the change quite well after all.

That afternoon when he returned to the examination room, Sadaharu found Eiko Nakanishi waiting for him.

"When did you come down here?" he asked without thinking.

"Just yesterday. There are so many people here in the summer that for about a month I've been staying in Tokyo."

"Really, it's smart to stay in Tokyo at this time of year. Out here there are no fish, and most of the grocery stores are closed. It's more trouble than New Year's," Sadaharu replied.

"Thanks to you, I've generally been feeling well, but I think that I'd like to have that test you mentioned."

"Test?"

"The test on entering my sixth month, the tapping amniotic fluid and testing the health of the fetus . . ."

"You want to do that? If you wish, one of my classmates, Dr. Yagihara, is still at Meirin University Hospital. I'll ask him to do it. I can only do the extraction, then I have to send the fluid sample to the hospital anyway."

In a hesitant, irresolute way, Sadaharu asked Mrs. Nakanishi whether she really wanted the examination. Sadaharu had of course told her about amniocentesis because he felt it would have been wrong not to, and many hospitals would automatically perform the test in the case of a pregnant woman over thirty-five. Still, Sadaharu did not feel that he should necessarily urge it on her.

"So, I suppose it would be better to have it," she said.

Were it simply a question of treating a problem revealed by the test, Sadaharu would certainly want it performed. But there was always a lingering suspicion in his mind that amniocentesis was often done in many cases in which nothing at all was wrong with the fetus.

"There's nothing particularly dangerous in the test, is there?" Mrs. Nakanishi asked.

"I can't say that it is 100 percent safe, but there is almost no danger. Sometimes the examination doesn't yield a clear result. Even when the test indicates sex distinctions, we aren't completely sure of its accuracy. Before the examination, you'll be asked to sign a consent form. If you wish, I'll call Dr. Yagihara immediately and write a note of introduction for you as well."

Mrs. Nakanishi agreed. "My husband wants me to have the examination. Anyway, it seems miraculous to be able to know in advance if the child is a boy or a girl. Even if I find out, I'll keep it a secret from our relatives."

She spoke lightheartedly, gaily.

There were unusually few patients that day; finally, there was only one chart left on Sadaharu's desk. It was only just past five o'clock, and Sadaharu couldn't believe that it was already the end even of this oddly quiet afternoon. The woman who entered in response to Nurse Ono's call for "Ms. Goda, Ms. Goda," was a small, freckled, long-haired woman with glasses, apparently in her mid-thirties.

"Mrs. Goda. How have you been?" Sadaharu asked.

She moved slowly, without expression, and took a moment to reply.

"I had an abortion here at your clinic nine years ago," she finally blurted out.

Of course, Sadaharu had no memory of her.

"And since then you've had children? I suppose you have."

"Yes. My husband was transferred to Fukuoka, and I had two girls while we were living there."

He saw that she was about to launch into an endless story, but it seemed that at least she had not come to complain about Sadaharu's abortion technique.

"And how old are your children now?"

"Seven and five."

"So then—who has a problem and with what?"

"Oh, there's nothing especially wrong, not in that way." Sadaharu remained silent. "It's just that my husband is now working in Yokohama, and four months ago we began living at his parents' house, and suddenly I began to dream about the child that I had aborted."

Sadaharu thought that was not quite within his specialty, but he asked, "What kind of dream is it?"

"I dream that the aborted child appears. It is a boy about two years old. He looks at me not at all the way a child would, and he says, 'Why only me?' "

"And that's all?"

"That's all. He always asks just that."

Sadaharu stared at her face. She wasn't crying, she didn't even show any color from agitation.

"Mrs. Goda, do you have any guilty feelings about the abortion?"

"No, none at all. I didn't think anything about it at the time. My father-in-law had suffered a stroke and he'd just become like a vegetable. When I mentioned that I seemed to be pregnant, my mother-in-law was displeased and said that Father's illness made having a child just then not such a good idea. I didn't feel like having a child and raising it at that time, so I went along with my mother-in-law and had the abortion. But after that I did in fact have children."

"Before returning, did you ever have such a dream?"

"Never. Since we came back here, though, I've had it often."

Had there been another patient waiting, Sadaharu would have settled matters right there with the excuse of being busy, for plainly the matter of being troubled by dreams of an aborted child was not in the realm of gynecology but rather psychology. But when Sadaharu looked at Goda's chart alone there on his desk, illuminated by the bright western sunlight, he felt that he could not chase her off with the feeble explanation that this sort of thing was not his specialty.

"Why do you think the child speaks as he does in your dream?" he asked.

She seemed to think for a moment, tilting her head blankly, then, without much confidence in her voice, she replied, "Because the other children are still alive, that one says to me, 'Why am I not living?' I'm sure that's what he is saying."

"He seems to be blaming you?" Sadaharu suggested.

"I don't feel that he is blaming me."

"Then isn't it all right? You know, in dreams people think and act totally different from when they are awake."

"Do other people have dreams like this?"

Sadaharu sighed, "Let me see," and pretended to be deep in thought.

"Well, they might. But they probably consider them only dreams."

Goda nodded slightly as though in agreement.

"In fact, I should think that the reason for the dream is simple enough. Remember, you did not have it while you were in Fukuoka, and then when you came back here, you passed by this clinic and remembered the incident."

"Yes, I suppose that is true," Goda said.

"And also, nine years ago, even though you really did want to have a child, you were prevented from doing so by your mother-in-law. Or something like that, anyway. Possibly you are still holding a deep resentment about what happened back then. We might say that it has emerged only now. Are you living in your own place at present?"

"No," she said, "we are together. Since my husband is the eldest son, we promised to live with his parents."

"How about other problems? Are you having trouble with your menstruation?"

"No, nothing like that."

"You know, the fact that other people have abortions does not mean it's all right to do so. Even so, women who have abortions don't have dreams like you."

She assented to that.

"Really?" she said.

"And not only women, either. Doctors are in the same situation. Just think of the fifteen thousand or so gynecologists all over Japan. Based on your story, all of them would be expected to have such a dream every day."

"Do you dream, doctor?" she asked.

"No, I don't. Abortion may not be a good thing, but I do it because it's necessary. I have a drink every night and sleep soundly. I hardly ever dream."

"When I dream I wake up really tired," she said.

"Perhaps you ought to see a psychiatrist. Or if you don't think it's serious enough for that, there is an acquaintance of mine, a Catholic priest at the church in Kurihama, Father Munechika . . . You might go and consult him. You can go even though you are a Buddhist. It wouldn't make any difference to him."

Goda replied that she would think about it.

"Yes, do. And if you think that you might want to meet the priest, just call me and I'll introduce you at any time."

The woman thanked him, and Sadaharu thought that he would like to have a more in-depth talk with her about abortion and her feelings. He wasn't totally serious about sending her to see the priest, even though that struck him as a good idea. He had read somewhere that in Europe and America religion was part of medical practice, and when someone entered a hospital they recorded their religion and the name of a priest to be called in case of need. That part he had heard from Yoko, who had once been in a foreign hospital and experienced this firsthand. She said that many hospitals had a chapel too. He thought his treatment of Goda was appropriate under the circumstances; he had established a psychological link even though his hospital had no chapel.

This patient was hardly an articulate person, but even so she might have observed with some surprise that no matter how many abortions Sadaharu performed he remained unaffected. Though he would have liked to discuss this fact in detail with someone, no one was available and he would have to go on as he was, alone.

But how could he remain so at peace with himself? There were various answers. For one thing, he could not accept that a fetus unable to live outside the womb was a human being. Of that, he was convinced.

He also was convinced that there were many more people like him. A couple of years before, while attending a high school reunion, he had been struck by the words of a classmate named Nakahira, now employed at a run-of-the-mill trading company. Nakahira had boasted, "There isn't anything I wouldn't do."

In their school days, Nakahira had been a rough, burly character they called Guard Dog, but now, over forty and noticeably graying, he appeared quite tame, only his outgoing personality remaining from his youth.

"I'm an international businessman," he went on. "Whatever another country wants to buy, I deliver—no questions asked."

"Even women?" someone asked.

"Sure, women, uranium . . . whatever they ask for."

None of the dozens of people there commented that Nakahira's actions were of questionable morality. It was as though each of them realized that everyone, at one or more times in their careers, had been guilty of some kind of unconscionable behavior.

One person finally remarked that bad publicity might result from smuggling uranium into undeveloped countries. But Guard Dog scoffed at that.

"Look—we don't push the uranium on these countries. But if they say they absolutely have to have it, we provide the means, that's all. And at the time I was referring to, inspection of baggage was much less rigorous, so there was little chance of detection."

"You seem to have done a lot of traveling," someone said.

"I've been to some places where you wondered if they were countries at all—the people were living like animals. I don't mind telling you we Japanese are lucky to be living the way we do today. Probably the only reason we can is that other countries aren't doing as well—if everybody on earth lived as well as we do, we'd probably all start running out of food and oil before long. I hope they never catch up, if that's the case!"

Sadaharu just listened and grinned. He didn't know about the economic validity of what the man was saying, but he was sure one thing at least was true: that everyone lived by taking advantage of those who were weaker.

Guard Dog bragged about not having a conscience, but Sadaharu knew that everyone, doctors included, did both good and bad things. Sadaharu admitted to himself that he both took life and aided it. A doctor does that directly, while most other people do so indirectly, and that was the only real difference between them. If people could only accept that fact, then guilt complexes like Goda might disappear. Although that would mean that everyone would have to accept complicity in harmful actions, at least they would be able to cease denying their involvement. But any statement as general as that would be likely to anger most people, unwilling to admit they have blood on their hands.

In the evening, a cool wind came up, the first of the season. When autumn comes, I can read, Sadaharu thought each summer, and then when autumn came each year, he would use his leisure time for eating and sleeping instead. But this year, around the end of August and the beginning of September, the birth rate was high. Some said that it was because people had gone wild making children over the previous New Year's holiday. Two patients entered the clinic the same day with labor pains. Only at such times, and for brief moments, did Sadaharu truly feel like reading, and that was hardly proof of the strength of his commitment.

According to the head nurse on duty, one patient was probably going to give birth the next day, while the other might give birth late that night. This meant that Sadaharu could return home at his usual time. He glanced at the mail he had not seen during his afternoon break. He ignored the usual stack of direct mail advertising, but next to it was a slender magazine called *Life Plus Alpha.*

Neither the publisher nor the writers were familiar to Sadaharu, but as he thumbed through the pages he noticed an essay titled "Crepe Myrtle." Sadaharu knew little about plants, and here for the first time he learned something about crepe myrtle through the opening lines of the article. "At the height of summer, like my heart's blood the crepe myrtle bloom crimson." The author was a man named Tsujimoto Toru, who seemed to be a television producer.

"I will not identify the location," the author continued, "to protect the person who told me the following story."

The magazine seemed to be neither literary nor a cult publication advocating some particular "-ism." Putting aside the question of category, the magazine projected a feeling of being concerned with human life and spirit. Sadaharu was not particularly attracted to such reading matter, yet he continued, somehow drawn by its low-key style.

"'Mr. Tsujimoto,' the person said to me, 'Long ago this part of the coast was a deserted area where few people were ever seen, primarily because the sea on the north side was extremely rough. Only four buses a day would come through from the nearest town, and you could easily recall the faces of each passenger on those buses. If a pregnant woman or a woman holding a baby got off at the shore and then, on the bus's return trip, got onto the bus empty-handed, anyone might be liable to ask what had happened to the baby.

"'But, Mr. Tsujimoto, we are now in the age of the private car. At any time and any place, one can ride unnoticed. Now when a woman comes she probably holds the infant unnoticed, and no one would be likely to miss the baby when she returned,' he continued.

"'On moonlit nights, you can see a long way along this shore. The sea and the rocks tear at each other. It is a beach where one feels that the moon might be the only witness to human actions.

"'I'm not saying there are many instances of this sort of thing, but if a person really wants to do something to a child . . . that's all I'm saying. In such circumstances, a child's bones would simply look something like seashells, wouldn't they?'

"The person who told me this took me to a cemetary dedicated to infants at a Buddhist temple in the town. A newly decorated stone figure stood beside the grave, and the smell of burning incense nearly choked me."

His cameraman began to photograph, and Tsujimoto stayed with him as usual.

"Two days later, we collected our material and returned to Tokyo. As we were looking at the rushes of the developed film, the cameraman said to me, 'Mr. Tsujimoto. Have a look at this.'

"At first, I thought there was nothing more there than the familiar scene: The communal grave, the stone god, the burning incense. The cameraman was making all the usual straightforward shots, but suddenly, when the camera tilted upward I had to look away. At the time I hadn't noticed, but now the red flowers of the crepe myrtle emerged on film as though the blossoms had sucked up the blood of all the aborted infants who had never seen the light of the sun of this world.

"'Mr. Tsujimoto, this part is too frightening. We'd better have the flowers cut out of this part.'"

When Sadaharu finished reading Tsujimoto's essay, he heard the sound of the front door opening and a man's voice call: "Excuse me." The man did not ring the bell, so Mayumi, in the kitchen, had not heard him. Sadaharu arose and went to meet the visitor.

"I'm from the water service," the man said.

Sadaharu recognized him as the young owner of a business called New Sagami Industrial.

"I received your order to repair the sewer line in back of the house the other day, and I thought that I'd be able to start tomorrow, but my wife's younger brother died today and we have to go some distance for the funeral service. I hope you will excuse the delay."

"Of course," Sadaharu said. What a terrible thing. Had he been ill?"

"No. He was working at a dam. There was an accident with a dump truck and he was run over, I understand. The truck cut off his leg, and he seems to have died of loss of blood."

"How terrible! Did he have any children?"

"Yes, three children. The oldest is five, and his wife is about to have another. It's going to be a problem to care for them now."

"And with small children she can't get a job."

"Yes, I suppose that's true," the man replied. "But you know, doctor, some people are against nuclear energy, and that's all right, but then they have to build other kinds of generating plants, like hydroelectric energy plants or coal or oil plants. People talk about that Three Mile Island nuclear plant in the United States having a big problem, but they don't think of the human sacrifice involved in building other kinds of power plants. I wonder if dying from radiation is so different from my brother-in-law getting run over by a truck in a tunnel. I wonder if it isn't the same thing.

"Where he worked at the dam construction, there have been five deaths so far. If five people had died at Three Mile Island, there would have been a huge uproar and headlines in the newspapers. But dying at the dam—that just gets a few lines in a local paper. It seems the only deaths that count these days are connected with nuclear power, and I think it's a form of discrimination. No one takes it seriously when someone dies at a hydroelectric dam."

Sadaharu agreed. "Even though on that kind of project casualties are bound to happen, no matter what type of power plant is involved."

"That's right! There's no difference, doctor, which is what my dead brother-in-law thought, too. He used to say it was wrong for people to believe that if only they stopped building nuclear plants, nobody would die. Now he's dead anyway—I really feel sorry for him."

"Well, you ought to go as soon as possible. It will take a lot of work to arrange things for the widow and the children."

"It shouldn't take too long. As soon as I get back, I'll get right on to your job. It will just be a few days."

After he had left, Sadaharu thought about what the young man had said, musing as he went back to his easy chair.

No matter what kind of electric power plant was built, human injuries were part of the process, and that included places like Three Mile Island. He thought there was nothing unusual about that. On the other hand, in the early days of dam construction it was common for dozens or even hundreds to die in the process. Such figures gradually decreased, dropping to less than ten victims. Should we think of nuclear energy in the same way? If we do, then such places as Three Mile Island began with an unbelievably small cost in human life compared to hydroelectric power plants. Nuclear energy might be thought of as being accomplished with remarkably small sacrifice of human life.

But the mass media would not see it that way. A loss of ten persons at a nuclear power plant would result in headlines as big as though a president had been assassinated. But the deaths of ten people in the mountains of Japan over a period of years does not even get a column's worth of attention in all. Of course, there is discrimination even in death—that is a bitter reality. Some deaths get ample public sympathy, and some deaths attract no interest at all. To raise quintuplets brings a wealth of happiness, but while countless numbers of midterm fetuses have been aborted who would have been the same size as the living quintuplets, people are interested only in the former and pray for their long life. No one remembers those who, on a wintry beach, say, were transformed into the shells of sea creatures, or became crimson crepe myrtle.

"It's an interesting problem." These words Sadaharu spoke to himself, glad there was no one around to hear him. Unborn infants do neither good nor evil, so in a karmic sense there was no such thing for them as rebirth through living a good life, or death resulting from their evil deeds. There was a saying, too, about the parents' karma being passed on to the child, but Sadaharu did not believe that either. And so, aside from a child's genetic legacy, the fate of an infant was essentially separate from that of its parents.

And yet some children are awaited and desired, while others are not. People who believe that there is some rationale behind all actions and things are quite perplexed by this. When Mrs. Goda's aborted infant asks in a dream, "Why me?" everyone flounders about trying to find an answer.

Again, to himself, Sadaharu said, "Don't flounder around." And then, "There is no rationale. It's just bad luck. Let it pass."

He was speaking to the sad face of the unborn child, a phantom in his mind. And beyond that there was no explanation. The truth was that human beings were all of a kind. If one dies then it's a bad thing; if another person dies, that's a different story. Accepting this, we may even find comfort in our sorrow, yet the majority of people, in response to the question of why some people die, will struggle, only to come up with some kind of illogical response.

The young owner of New Sagami Industrial did not appear until the following week. The timing of his return suggested that he had come directly after completing the first seven days of ritual mourning.

Sadaharu expressed his condolences and then asked, "How did it go? Is the widow holding up?"

"Yes, thank you," the young man replied. "She's trying to pull herself together. And since she is about to have a baby, nothing much about her future can be decided until she gives birth."

"Yes, I guess so. But it's really a tragedy," Sadaharu said. From his pocket he removed an envelope, the kind used in Japan especially for a gift of money as an expression of concern and condolences. "It would have been better if I'd had this ready before you left, but since you will probably be going back again I'll give this to you now."

Sadaharu had kept the envelope in his pants pocket for some time, so its edges were crumpled.

"Thank you, doctor. This really wasn't necessary."

"Not at all. This is just for your sister-in-law. Besides, recently I've had the urge to help people. When I can do something, I do it. So please accept this with an easy mind."

"Thank you. In that case, I will. And I'll tell her that since she has received this from a complete stranger, she should be encouraged to go on living."

Just then the telephone rang. No one else was home to answer the phone, so Sadaharu hurriedly told the man he would expect him tomorrow and went inside.

It was Yoko Kakei. "Sadaharu? I hope I'm not interrupting anything. I'm just calling to tell you that Mr. and Mrs. Laurie are leaving with Miyako tomorrow night. They're returning home by way of Europe since Mr. Laurie has some business there, and they asked me to thank you and to give you their best wishes."

"I see. And did the baptism go as planned?"

"Yes, it did. The very next day. When the priest put water on her forehead, her eyes were open. She didn't cry, just looked at his face and mine. Father Munechika said that she was quite unusual that way."

"That's because she has already been through so much," Sadaharu replied. "Adversity makes us wise, you know. We laugh at that idea today, but it's true. If you want to make a child wise, you have to make demands on it."

"Well, we know that a lot of children are not going to be wise no matter what, so we can't carry that theory too far."

Sadaharu chuckled at her remark. "That's true, Yoko, but it's also funny."

The next night, Sadaharu, receiving a telephone call from Father Munechika, was momentarily confused, thinking that Goda might have gone to see him after all. But after a moment's thought, it seemed unlikely that a non-Christian patient would suddenly be moved by a word from him to go to church.

"I should have called you," Sadaharu said. He had already drunk some beer.

"Are you well?" the priest asked.

The last time they had met, at Yoko's house, they had talked about Providence, he recalled.

"Fine. Getting along," Sadaharu answered.

"Actually, I wanted to consult with you about something . . ." the priest began.

Sadaharu realized this would not be just about the abortion question, and he tried to put his slightly drink-befuddled brain in order.

"What's that?"

"One of my parishioners came in a while ago with a young woman, not a Catholic, the wife of a nearby farmer. She is eight months pregnant and has not once seen a doctor, I was told."

"Really? But she knew that she was eight months pregnant. A novice is not likely to know that."

"Well, she seems to have gone to see a midwife."

"That's all right, of course. Babies are usually born without incident."

"But the midwife—she's over eighty years of age—is apparently not entirely capable anymore. The woman was told that at present, the fetus's position is upside down, feet first. Is there a way to correct that?"

"Yes, there is."

"Well, she seems to have done it once, but somehow the child turned around again. The woman wanted to go to the hospital, but her husband wouldn't let her—so she talked with my parishioner."

"But why . . ." Sadaharu began, and then stopped, thinking of various reasons why the husband had refused to let her visit a hospital.

"The husband is only about thirty-five, but he thinks that the child should be born naturally."

"And so?"

"What he said was that using artificial means to keep a child alive was unacceptable. He thinks that if a child is going to die at birth, then it should be allowed to die. He says he only wants a child that has the strength to live on its own."

"Hmm. Clearly an enlightened mind, that one."

"Having the midwife's help is all right with him, but he won't consider anything like a Caesarean section. It appears that he thinks the child should be sacrificed in such cases."

"I see. And the wife is distressed to be left just to the eighty-year-old midwife."

"So it seems. Yes. In the first place, the midwife herself said that she was afraid her own health would break down before the birth and that the woman should go to a regular obstetrician."

Sadaharu lost control for an instant and laughed.

"Oh, what a terrible thing to be a priest!"

"Exactly. It's like running a general consultation office. And the wife wants to keep it secret from her husband that she wants to see an obstetrician immediately."

"I see."

"Could you please try to persuade him?"

"I doubt I'd be successful. But someone like that is a rare bird nowadays."

"Yes, he's known as an eccentric in the neighborhood. The house does not have a flush toilet, and he has the bath heated only with kindling wood. He has her buy sake in half gallon bottles."

"What's wrong with buying bottled sake?"

"Oh, that's not the point. He sends her with an old-fashioned jug to buy sake from the barrel and gets five-tenths or seven-tenths of a measuring container."

"Oh," Sadaharu said, for an instant forgetting the pregnant woman. "That's the way it used to be done—you went with your jug. I've had some good sake that way, out of the barrel."

"Yes. Well, the husband is thirty-five years old and that's the kind of man he is. So he doesn't want the baby to grow up with a doctor's help. He says that any child of his has to be strong."

"That's fine, in a sense, but children who are born weak gradually grow strong. And sometimes the mind too: even though some children are always ill, their minds grow stronger as they mature. Some are like that. But I once knew a child with heart disease who was a genius. Before surgery, she would run out of breath and looked like a lovely, fragile doll. Then after she had an operation, she suddenly forgot she was ever ill. She turned into a tomboy and now goes around picking fights and swearing. And her parents complain about her new personality. That's the way it goes."

"At any rate," the priest replied, "if she can get to your clinic, will you examine her?"

"Of course. That's my business," Sadaharu said. "I heard the baby the Lauries adopted here was baptized at your church."

"Ah, yes. I met Mrs. Kakei a while ago, and we prayed especially for Miyako. Then Mrs. Kakei went to see the Lauries off at Narita."

The conversation ended, and after Sadaharu finished supper he had a nice feeling inside. The priest had said that he and Yoko had prayed together for the child. Sadaharu thought that God wasn't to be found only at altars, but the image of them praying together there was not at all displeasing to him.

Sadaharu flopped into the chair in front of his personal television set and turned on some idiotic program. He liked to watch the slapstick comedy shows or some action adventure. Both kinds of shows were a long way from real life; he would have nothing to do with any program close to himself. He'd read that a novelist had once remarked that he rarely read novels. Sadaharu understood the feeling. Someone who dealt with literature all day probably would not want to be close to it at other times. People whose occupations brought them close to life and death struggles would not want to watch that on television. Something totally absurd would be fine.

His family always disagreed with his taste in television programs. The year before, he had purchased this TV for his own exclusive use so he could watch silly comedies and murder movies without worrying about what his wife and daughter thought. Today, there was a program he liked, but as he was enjoying the show the screen suddenly became fuzzy. The wavelike pattern was one of the little disappointments endured by people who did not live in Tokyo—the signal in the area being weak and distorted whenever planes flew overhead.

Tonight, oddly, Sadaharu's ear took in a slightly different sound, a kind of popping, and it occurred to him that the plane might be the Lauries', with Miyako on board, heading for Europe. He guessed that scheduled planes flew out in that direction over the Miura

Peninsula. Then some commercials appeared on the screen, so Sadaharu went out to the garden carrying his glass of beer.

Toward the southeast, he saw the slowly receding tail light of a plane sliding among the stars. That was the villain interfering with his television, Sadaharu thought; then, quite without wishing it, he felt the presence of the Laurie family there in that light. Or, rather, he felt the life force of the infant Miyako in that speck in the night sky. Abandoned by her parents, she had made no sound, and now it seemed that Miyako was making her way into life.

Soon, in spite of his effort to follow, both the sound and the light vanished into the distance. There in the sea breeze Sadaharu raised his glass in a toast. He swallowed the beer at one gulp, in honor of Miyako and, no longer able to see the plane, turned to the house. At that moment, the telephone rang; Sadaharu unhurriedly stepped on to the veranda.

"Sadaharu? Is that you?" It was the voice of his widowed mother in Zushi.

"Yes, it is. How are you this evening? What's up?"

In her voice, he could hear that something was amiss, even though he was feeling the effects of his drink.

"Well, I've had a phone call from the Komatsu family, and it seems that the old lady has just passed away."

"Oh?"

"Yes, about half past six this evening. The same fish dealer who delivers to my house was taking her some sashimi, and when no one answered he opened the back door and looked in. Mrs. Komatsu was there on the sofa, dead."

"And there was no theft or signs of violence?"

"No, no indication of that. The police came, but nothing had been disturbed in the house. And her face was calm."

"Yes. She had high blood pressure, you know."

"That's what I'd heard. According to her doctor, her condition was such that this could have happened at any time."

"Yes, she was concerned about her great-granddaughter's situation. I guess worry or fatigue made her blood pressure go up."

"Mrs. Komatsu told me how thankful she was for your concern. She felt so much more at ease because of your help. And the Americans took the child?"

"They did, and they were very pleased too."

For some reason, Sadaharu hesitated to speak to his mother about Miyako leaving Japan that day, that very night.

Instead he said, "It's for the best, I think, that she passed on. Mrs. Komatsu stayed alive for her great-granddaughter, until the matter was settled. At her age, that was quite an effort, too. If she hadn't done what she did, you know, the girl would have had such a difficult life here in Japan."

His mother replied, "Well, I think you helped take care of that. I would say that Mrs. Komatsu was finally at peace and just let herself go."

"Oh, my, then it seems that I killed the old lady!" Sadaharu laughed.

"Oh, hardly that. I mean, she did what she could and then she died. That's an enviable thing. It's just the way it was."

"And you take care of yourself, too, mother. Our Kaori might become an unwed mother and then we would have to ask you to find someone to adopt your great-grandchild."

"I couldn't take such a responsibility! Well, then, thank you for helping her. Good night."

"Good night, mother."

Sadaharu hung up the phone and stretched in relief. Feeling as though there was something to do in the garden, he put on his sandals and went out into the evening breeze.

Until that moment, Sadaharu had been an unemotional sort of man. He did not believe in ghosts. When he received a chain letter in the mail, he would throw it directly into the trash. Mayumi was absorbed in superstitions; her interest very likely was enough for Sadaharu too. But his disposition was not the result of his being a physician and therefore scientific. Even though he was not superstitious, he had no sense of being particularly unfortunate in that respect. Yet he was, in regard to such concepts as sincerity, rather paralyzed by his lack of sensibility. He had never had the experience of being moved to tears by a movie or a play.

Sadaharu went to the end of the dark garden and sat in the swing that he'd had made for Kaori. Now that she was growing up, Kaori rarely used it, and because Sadaharu was not sure how badly rusted it was, she had been warned to stay away from it.

Today, for the first time, Sadaharu felt himself inexorably drawn into a way of thinking that might ordinarily be called superstitious. This evening, he could not help but feel that the death of Mrs. Komatsu had been hardly a matter of chance. The old lady could not have known that today was the Lauries' departure date. It was only yesterday that Yoko had told Sadaharu, and he had told no one. Of course, it was remotely possible that Mrs. Komatsu had been told by the Sato family's lawyer, because neither the real mother nor the grandparents had gone to see the Lauries off, but why would they have bothered to inform the great-grandmother?

Perhaps it was a coincidence. But Sadaharu could not help but believe that Mrs. Komatsu had chosen to die just at the hour of her great-granddaughter's departure. It was not suicide, of course. There was not a sign of human action in her death. And yet in this world there are things that defy even the understanding of poets and artists. And if the soul of Mrs. Komatsu had been called from this world, Sadaharu wondered, might not that correspond with Miyako's departure? Such a reaction was hardly typical of him, and he was uneasy. For that reason, he had told his mother nothing about the matter. Perhaps he was being too melodramatic. He imagined that this kind of mystic feeling was not good for older people, so he had decided not to mention it to his mother.

"Ah, beautifully done," Sadaharu said to himself there in the darkness. He would not want anyone to hear this reaction to someone's death, but in what he said he included inexpressible praise. In the end, there are few people who can die having fulfilled such a responsibility. Like the lives of insects or fish that ended with their laying eggs, he felt that the death of Mrs. Komatsu, who had found a way to extend the life of another human being, possessed a splendor that corresponded to the most fundamental quality of living things.

Chapter Fourteen

Murderous Intent

At first sight, when Sadaharu saw the man arise and enter the examination room, he had an unpleasant association that harkened back to the distant past, to a time before he had opened his present office. The matter had involved a father who doubted his daughter's chastity and had come to ask Sadaharu to determine whether or not she was a virgin.

The man standing before him now had come in with a sour expression, but still he gave no impression of urgency or concern. Behind him followed a woman who appeared to be in her late twenties, her abdomen conspicuously large.

"Chizuko Ushirokawa, is that correct?" Sadaharu said to her for confirmation.

"Yes, that's right."

The man spoke. "My wife has already been to see a midwife in the neighborhood. She said the baby was upside down. Can you have that fixed?"

Sadaharu looked at the woman's mother-and-child record book and saw that she was in her thirtieth week.

The woman then spoke. "My husband will not permit a Caesarean delivery. If the baby is born naturally, that's fine, but if the child cannot be born in the normal way, then he says we should give up on it."

Sadaharu realized this must be the case that Father Munechika had spoken to him about on the telephone, but of course he showed no indication of this to the couple. If he had let on that the woman had gone to consult with a Catholic priest unbeknown to her husband, who knows what kind of reaction this eccentric husband might have had.

"Oh? Why's that? Does your husband hold to some special religious belief?"

Sadaharu knew that many people these days held to one or another extreme way of thinking—like the mother who, believing in the beneficial effects of a special diet, forced her weaning child to eat rich, fatty food, only to have the child develop diabetes by the age of eight. Another woman, certain that glaucoma could be cured without surgery, treated herself by living on one meal a day of brown rice and vegetables. On the fiftieth day, she collapsed in Tokyo Station and was taken away in an ambulance. She was later diagnosed as suffering from malnutrition.

A diet either too rich or too lean will cause illness. Recently, because of the common abuse of overly rich food, some patients had found their conditions improved when they modified their diets, but that did not mean every problem could be resolved that way.

"No, no, that's not the reason," the husband replied. "Kids are all a bunch of weaklings nowadays, and I can't put up with them. The one next door to us has got asthma, right? Can't stand the heat, can't stand the cold, can't take it when it's muggy. I mean, really, how can a human being live like that?

"I couldn't take raising a child like that. I've got no heating and no air conditioner, you know. When it's time for a baby to get born, it's got to do it on its own, and if it can't it's better to stop before it starts off wrong, that's my view."

Already knowing some of the particulars in the case, Sadaharu refrained from inquiring as to the underlying reasons for the man's attitude and went through the formalities of a few tests. The fetus, just as the midwife had said, was indeed completely in a breech position.

"A child like that can't be born, can it?"

"No, that's not the case at all. Most babies have no trouble in such circumstances, but there are exceptions," Sadaharu said.

Sadaharu thought Mr. Ushirokawa would want to ask for examples of the exceptions, but instead he remained silent.

"The nurse will give you a paper with instructions that will teach you a technique. For ten or twenty minutes each night, you lie with your hips raised and your chest lowered, then from that position you lie on your side and go to sleep. If you do that, in most cases the fetus will return to the proper position. Later, we will have to take an X-ray, however."

After he said this, it occurred to Sadaharu that Mr. Ushirokawa might say that doing an X-ray was blasphemy to the gods, but instead the man was silent. The exercise necessary to effect the change of position was called the "knee, chest, side-lying method" and was a technique for turning the fetus naturally to the correct position.

Then, addressing the husband, Sadaharu said, "Let me ask you, what will you do in the event that the child is somehow not born the usual way? I cannot say that there would be no possibility of danger to the mother." When asking such questions, he somehow felt a childish pleasure, as though he were teasing a classmate in middle school. "I would be sorry to hear that you didn't do everything possible to help your wife, that's for sure."

"Could she really be in danger?"

Sadaharu's expression confirmed his statement.

"According to what you said a moment ago, you don't use any heat in the winter, is that right?"

Sadaharu was quizzing the husband in a friendly tone while the wife was dressing.

"Well, we've got a little electric space heater."

"And how about a refrigerator?"

He asked this simply as a matter of curiosity.

"We've got that too."

"Is that completely natural?"

Sadaharu had not intended to be contrary, but it was his honest reaction.

"We raise chickens with leftovers."

"Kitchen scraps?"

"Yeah. Uh huh."

Mrs. Ushirokawa finished dressing and appeared from behind the curtain.

"Leftovers, you say. You mean greens?"

"No. Things we pick out of the cooking pots when washing up the dishes. We go through the garbage, too. We feed it all to them. And if that isn't enough, I buy some store feed," Mrs. Ushirokawa added.

Her husband went on. "The chickens eat just about anything. The other day, a relative's child came and threw out a half-eaten rice cake, so I cut it up and gavc it to the chickens, and they ate it all."

"And I let them into the garden for about an hour every day. They eat earthworms and ants," Chizuko continued.

"Don't the stray cats attack them?" Sadaharu asked.

"I go out with the chickens."

What a strange thing the human mind is. Sadaharu had imagined that she had fled to the priest to complain, but somehow, when he looked at her face, she didn't look or act as though she considered her husband oppressive. Rather, he considered, she felt his objections expressed some of his affection for her. To put it plainly, even if it were necessary for the child to die, Mr. Ushirokawa wanted his wife saved—that seemed to be the bottom line of it all.

In the past, Mr. Ushirokawa's way of thinking was considered quite ordinary. Children died of all the usual ailments—pneumonia, tuberculosis, malnutrition, appendicitis, bacterial infections, wounds—and adults themselves did not live long. Only a sturdy constitution could be passed on, and this worked as a kind of population control.

Now that was no longer the case. Some scientists say that endless technical advancements combined with the ethic of keeping the weak alive will cause humanity to collapse in on itself. For Sadaharu, the future was incomprehensible. If he could be sure of such a thing happening, then he would not be in this kind of human repair work. He cared not a bit that humanity might perish through a shortage of food. After all, both the sun and the earth faced eventual extinction, so it was hardly reasonable to complain if the end were to come a bit earlier than expected. Indeed, Mr. Ushirokawa seemed to think that way; it was probably the basis for his attitude. Still, Sadaharu could not agree with him completely. It might seem simple to say that one should sacrifice the child in order to save the mother, but if that is so the physician's skills are quite superfluous.

One day not long after this Kaori said to Sadaharu, "Papa, the jellyfish are out early this year."

"Oh, you say that every year," he answered.

"No, I don't. This year they really are early."

When Kaori came home from her half day of school on Saturdays and had her lunch, she would go off swimming with her friends. As usual, her mother was never home, so she went accompanied only by the other children. Sadaharu was not unaware of the potential danger, but he was inclined to disregard it. He could not help but believe her when she said that she would sometimes swim out a hundred meters or more before she would dive, but Sadaharu had work to do and could not accompany her, so in the end there was really nothing he could do about it.

As children, we all confront the possibility of drowning, but somehow we escape. Probably Kaori, too, had passed that test. A parent might say things like "You must not swim alone" or "You must not go over your head even with your friends," but when Sadaharu thought of his own attitude he could not claim that even Mr. Ushirokawa was really peculiar or irrational. What is more,

Sadaharu knew that he, too, was making a gamble about the fate of his child similar to the one Mr. Ushirokawa was making about his.

September came and with it many days that smelled of autumn, and then there was a Saturday evening when the wind was dry and cold. Sadaharu ate the dinner prepared by his housekeeper. Mayumi had not returned home by nightfall.

"Did your mother say she was going someplace today?" he asked Kaori.

He would have felt more at ease if he had heard that she had said she was going to stay at a friend's house, even if that were a lie.

"I don't know," Kaori answered.

"Did you see her this afternoon?"

"She was here when I came home, then she went out while I was eating lunch."

Actually, Sadaharu did not notice such things as a rule. If he had spent his time worrying about Mayumi, the household would have collapsed.

It was a little after nine o'clock in the evening when the telephone rang. He often had thought in the past that this was how a message would come from the police saying that Mayumi had smashed up the car somewhere, or that she had been killed, but he also noticed that he thought this not with anxiety but with anticipation, so he forced himself to dismiss such unacceptable thoughts from his mind.

"Doctor Nobeji? This is Chisa Asano's mother," the voice said.

"Oh, yes. Sorry not to have contacted you. How has Chisa been doing?"

Chisa had left the clinic at the end of August, and Sadaharu had not heard from the Asanos since.

"Thank you for your concern. She has been taking a small bowl of rice at every meal."

"That's not too bad, is it? It's best not to constantly urge her to eat."

"I don't know how to tell you this, doctor, but today your wife showed up at our house."

"Oh?" Sadaharu said.

"In fact, she came here to see my husband, but he is away on business. I told her that, but she insisted on staying, saying that the other day he had promised to meet her today and that he was sure to return. She called me a liar when I said he wasn't here and accused me of hiding him." Mrs. Asano tried to control her breathing, but it was a bit irregular. "She can wait as long as she likes, but my husband is not coming home today. I told your wife that when he returns I will have him call her immediately. I asked her to go home, but she keeps saying she'll kill herself if she doesn't see him."

Sadaharu said, "I'm terribly sorry for all this trouble. Could I talk with my wife for a moment?"

He thought this would be the best thing to do—but he knew that he had his hands full.

"I already suggested to her that she talk to you on the phone herself. She said she had nothing to say. But just wait a moment, please."

Mrs. Asano put down the phone. She returned in a few seconds.

"Your wife says that she will not come to the telephone," Mrs. Asano informed Sadaharu, her tone heavy with disgust. "I don't know what to do. She can wait here as long as she likes, but my husband is not coming home, and we can't get any rest, so . . ."

Her words were extremely polite, but Sadaharu clearly heard the contempt in her voice.

"Doctor, I wonder if it would be possible for you to come and get her?"

"I'm sorry, but I don't feel I can bring her home under these circumstances."

"Yes, I understand perfectly. Wait just a moment, please."

Again she left the phone. There was the clicking sound of a switch.

"I'm sorry to make you wait. I've changed telephones to where your wife can't hear me. Now we can speak freely."

Sadaharu said once again that he regretted the incident. "It has upset your family, of course. I fully realize that I'm responsible for my wife and that I should go and get her, but if I do that, then my wife will expect that kind of treatment as a matter of course. My wife has no self-confidence, so she tries to attract the attention of other people by displaying her own weaknesses. She always wants someone to ask about her health, someone to tell her that she is doing fine and looks perfectly fit. If I begin to do that even slightly, then I'll be trapped into doing it twenty-four hours a day—that's impossible for me. I hate to impose on you, but isn't there some way you could get her to leave and send her home?"

"Well, yes, but I've never had occasion to force someone from my home before. I really wonder if she'll get home safely. There may be no problem, but if anything were to happen on the way . . ."

"Don't worry about that. Just send her home," Sadaharu said.

"Are you sure it's all right?"

"Yes. There is nothing else to do."

Sadaharu apologized to Mrs. Asano again and hung up the phone. He did not imagine this was the best decision he could have made, but he was in no mood to agree to go after Mayumi. He went to his study and sat there in his chair for a while, thinking.

Would Mayumi return home after leaving the Asanos? Sadaharu mused about his own reaction. He had often wondered what his life would be like without Mayumi, but as it was, he already went on with his own activities largely without her. The moments when he really had to think about her involved divorce or her death. Both divorce and death, he thought, were often the same kind of thing. If Mayumi had said that she wanted a divorce, he would have readily agreed. If she were to die, he would certainly pity her. For a long time now, Sadaharu had been emotionally separated from Mayumi, but what he could not easily dismiss was Kaori's involvement. He and Mayumi were fundamentally unrelated, but to

Kaori she was mother.

He readily acknowledged the reasons for his feelings. If Mayumi died, Sadaharu thought, wouldn't his life be more stable than at present? Perhaps he was simply a cold-hearted person. If his family life was currently in a shambles, without his wife the situation might be a good deal more pleasant—or so his egotistical nature imagined. But at the same time, he reflected that everyone felt an inherent resistance to wish for the death of another person. No one admits wanting to see another person die, especially under troubling circumstances, because it is obviously wrong to display such a lack of human feeling to others. Sadaharu realized that if Mayumi did not return home safely that night, perhaps he would have to face Kaori and admit that whatever happened to Mayumi would not have occurred if he had gone to pick her up. Children are thoroughly conservative beings, and Kaori would miss her mother even though she often did not know where her mother was.

Sadaharu realized how weary he was with it all. He wanted to escape from all responsibility; he felt that whatever happened to Mayumi would not be his fault. If it were his fault, he would be sincerely sorry.

The relationship between husband and wife, between parent and child, presents the greatest possibility for harm. Unlike kidnapping or homicide, in such relationships the world imagines that people usually love one another. But that is not the case. In the name of what they call love, people in those relationships can act with calm cruelty, one slowly destroying the other by indirect means. Now, at a time when his wife might be contemplating suicide, Sadaharu thought how strange it was that he should recall a case he once had involving a peculiar relationship between a patient and her daughter.

It was before he had opened his practice here, when he was employed at the university hospital, and his patient was a seventy-three-year-old woman with cancer of the uterus. She had come to the hospital when it was already too late, and with her came her forty-year-old daughter.

The attitude of the time was that if a patient was over seventy years old, considering the average life span, he or she ought not to have much complaint about the prospect of dying. But even so, the daughter did not display the slightest sympathy toward her mother. The patient survived longer than might have been expected, and during that time Sadaharu heard from the daughter the story of how she came to feel as she did.

The daughter was an only child. When the patient was still young, sometime before her daughter entered primary school, it was discovered that her husband, a railway employee, had been unfaithful to his wife. For the wife, who had then just turned thirty, this was more than she could bear, and (perhaps not entirely seriously) she made as though to kill her daughter and herself by cutting their wrists and immersing their arms in bath water, so as to induce her husband to leave his lover. She apparently intended that they should bleed to death, but people nearby, hearing the frantic cries of the daughter, broke down the door and rescued them.

In spite of that experience, the daughter remained close to her mother. The husband was shocked by the incident and broke off with the other woman. He managed to control his behavior thereafter. Apparently, the patient had won her battle with the other woman.

Later, though, the patient's husband suddenly died, apparently from drinking methyl alcohol. The daughter graduated from senior high school and became a secretary in a law office. Within a short time, she was dating a civil engineer, an employee of a construction company, whom she had met at a concert, more or less as preliminary to her engagement.

However, her mother, Sadaharu's patient, opposed the marriage. It was not that the young man was inadequate in character or talent; quite simply, the patient opposed her daughter's marriage to a man whose occupation might take the daughter away from her immediate control. And for that reason the marriage of the two young people was delayed for three years, all plans suspended. But when the young man found himself working at the company's home office in Tokyo, the two were finally married, the mother putting on a show of acquiescing in the matter.

Eventually, the son-in-law was assigned to work at the construction site of a dam being built in the mountains of Gifu Prefecture. He thought at last the mother would have to adjust to living apart from her daughter, but in fact she would not consent to her daughter leaving her to go with her husband. The husband was eager to get to his work and so went off alone. The daughter worked at persuading her mother and planned to join her husband, but after more than half a year had passed the mother was still not reconciled to the situation. Instead, one day the patient again tried to kill herself by swallowing sleeping pills. The daughter discovered her and prevented her death.

The fact was that prior to coming to him, Sadaharu's patient had twice attempted suicide with the aim of preventing her only child's separation from her. Of course, the woman herself could not admit this fact. She imagined she was acting for her daughter's happiness because, she thought, if she died the daughter could then join her husband. But no matter how she explained her reasons, the reality was that she could not bear to live alone, a matter that worried her daughter and son-in-law. And in the end, she frustrated the wishes of the two young people and, claiming they would be happy if she were dead, said she wished to commit suicide.

In Sadaharu's view, if that was what she really intended, it would have been better if she had done the job right. He asked the daughter, even though the event was long past, what kind of sleeping pills and how many the mother had swallowed. When he heard from her that his patient had been taken away in an ambulance but that it wasn't necessary for her stomach to be pumped, it seemed to him that the quantity of pills at least had not been great. The patient's real objective seemingly had been to threaten that if she were left alone she would die and to show her daughter that even though she said she wished to live by herself, she in fact could not.

The most terrible thing a person can threaten another with is embodied in the words "die" or "kill." When someone threatens with such words, there is nothing left to do but accede to their request, no matter how demanding they might be.

From that time on, the daughter and her husband lived apart. Since she was unable to take her mother along with them to company housing deep in the mountains, there was nothing for the daughter to do but to remain behind and live with her mother. After that last incident, there was a change in the daughter's mental attitude. Although she did not wish to desert her mother, she came to believe that she was being forced to remain with her. The daughter did not seem to be especially imaginative, but, according to the story she told, bit by bit over a period of months, the morning after her mother attempted suicide for the second time she came to the realization that that was the second time her mother had tried to kill her. The first time was when as a child her mother had tried, in quite a physical sense, to do away with her. Obviously, such an action on the part of the mother was different from that of an ordinary murderer. Her action was most likely prompted by a particularly Japanese kind of emotion, the feeling that she "must not leave the child alone." And precisely because of that, for decades the daughter had lived with someone who had tried to kill her. If it had been someone besides her mother, it would have been unimaginable for her to tolerate the presence of someone who had attempted her murder.

The night she took her mother to the hospital after the second suicide attempt, the patient remained in a deep sleep. Out of regard for the six other patients in the hospital room, the daughter remained by her mother's bed throughout the night, without a moment's sleep. The bed was the one nearest to the door of the room, and from there she could see a single star outside.

Toward dawn, the patch of sky visible to her began to whiten, and gradually the star paled. She was extremely tired, but she felt that a light was dawning in her own mind and feelings, a realization that for a second time her mother, the woman who was sleeping so deeply and peacefully in front of her, had tried to kill her. This second time was a kind of murder of the spirit. If her mother were actually to die now, the daughter thought, she would by that act be forever telling her daughter "You are the one who drove me to die. You killed me." By her own death, she would try to inflict on her daughter and son-in-law a psychologically fatal wound—that would be her revenge.

"Your mother has won," was what the husband had said. And after that the husband and wife had separated. The daughter had already lost her natural love for her mother, but the mother had won and the daughter had lost, and that was that.

Now on top of it all was the mother's illness.

For long while, the daughter carried on, even after having lost respect for her mother, and she believed that her own feeling that her mother's death would be a kind of liberation for her was all the more confirmation of her own lack of compassion. As though in atonement, she came to the hospital each day without fail.

As he recalled those matters between the mother who was his patient and her daughter, Sadaharu realized how much suicide was an act of psychological violence toward the living. With Mayumi, too, suicide would be a device for revenge. In spite of the degree of freedom in which she lived, she felt malice toward various people: Sadaharu, Mr. Asano, Mrs. Asano. Beyond this, she held a grudge against the world, toward people who had not become her allies and supporters. No, Mr. Asano was a bit different; she would hope that he at least retained some tender feelings for her.

In any case, the story involved adultery. Human beings are required to live by stricter rules. Sick people cannot live normally, no matter how they protest, and Mayumi was playing games with her life through her repeated threats of dying.

Sadaharu himself opposed even surrendering to hijackers, believing that going along with their demands would be compounding the crime. He would never sympathize with a child who threatens suicide because no one will buy him the game he wants. Sadaharu felt they all might as well drop dead. In his present position, he had his hands full with people who wanted to live.

And if Mayumi did not return, he would not blame himself for that at all. Of course, he thought of what Kaori would think, but he knew that life was a desperate struggle. Even in daily life, when there was no war, human beings killed and thereby destroyed their own souls. He would have to keep in mind the inevitability of this fact.

He remained sitting and thinking for some thirty minutes. He thought it likely that most people would find it strange that a physician could not cure an illness in his own family. But that is the way life is.

Another thirty minutes, Sadaharu thought, and he would lock the front door and go to sleep. Staying up waiting for her was simply giving in to psychological violence.

For this attitude, Sadaharu felt he would surely be showered with criticism by most people. So be it. Just as he thought the husband of Chizuko Ushirokawa had been too hard on his pregnant wife, others would think him cold for turning his back on a woman, his wife, who had expressed her wish to die. Nothing could be done about that. He might be thought of as being gentle or heartless, but either way it was a matter of making his own choice about how he would live.

He thought it would be better for his and Mayumi's marriage to end. If the present situation were to continue, they could never crawl out of this quagmire. And the older Mayumi grew, the more clever she became at manipulating Sadaharu for her own purposes. Like the woman who was dying of cancer of the uterus, the one who seemed so weak, she had within her a hidden ability to force those close to her to follow her wishes.

At that moment, Sadaharu heard the engine of a car approaching from a distance, then stop before the house. He did not immediately respond. The doorbell rang, and, since Kaori seemed to be in the living room watching television, Sadaharu went to unlock the door. Standing outside was Chisa Asano, supporting the half-conscious Mayumi.

"I've brought your wife home."

"I really appreciate your help. Won't you come in? Mayumi, come in."

At that moment, it seemed to Sadaharu that Mayumi was more of a child—and more of a problem—than the college student Chisa.

As though speaking to himself, Sadaharu murmured, "Has she taken any drugs?"

"She said she wanted some tranquilizers, but mother and I insisted that would be dangerous. Still, she managed to swallow two capsules, no more than that."

"Thank you so much. If that's all, she'll be all right."

Without a word to Chisa, Mayumi made her way upstairs to the bedroom.

Sadaharu thanked Chisa again. "How about the taxi?"

"Oh, I drove her here myself," the girl replied.

He sat facing her in the sitting room, aware suddenly of her air of health and vigor.

"Well, sit down for a moment. You look great!"

"Yes. I've been eating more lately," Chisa said as she sat on the sofa. "Like most men these days, my father spends a lot of time at work, and my mother has her own problems—besides the one with your wife. I don't think she's living a normal life. Some days, she doesn't get dinner ready, and I have to fix my parents' meal myself."

"Really? When I spoke with her on the telephone a while ago, she didn't seem to be very upset."

"Mother was brought up not to show her feelings. The more agitated she is, the more restrained she appears. I feel sorry for her," Chisa said.

"And it's the reverse with you. You're healthy now and eating properly, aren't you?" Sadaharu spoke his mind rather directly.

"Yes, if I prepare a meal and don't eat, then mother won't eat either."

"Now that you've become a normal, healthy girl, you should realize your obligations to your parents," Sadaharu told her.

"Yes, I know."

"Well, we've really put your family to a lot of trouble over my wife."

"Will she be all right?"

"I can't tell."

"Can't she be watched?"

"Yes, and I will try to watch over her. But there's a limit to what can be done. And I don't really think I'll be able to improve the situation that much."

"At first, when I heard Mother and Father quarrel about your wife, I thought she must be a terrible person, but today, when I met her, I realized she was gentle and sincere."

"Yes," Sadaharu said, "gentleness and sincerity have always been considered good qualities, but they are good only when one has some talent and self-control—and can tell white lies if necessary. It's foolish to call yourself honest and upright unless you have the personality to back it up. Someone may seem gentle, but in today's world that can be a dangerous quality. Of course we all have a right to live our own lives. I take that as my basic principle and try to extend that to my wife. But she is not me. I cannot go around straightening out all the consequences of her actions."

After a silence, Chisa replied, "Doctor, still you are really a kind person."

"No. Actually I'm not. If I were, I would have just gone over to your house and picked up Mayumi."

"Oh, no. What I meant was that being kind makes you spoil people."

"Ah. A cruel person can act kindly. And even though we scorn others, we can be kind to them. You know, criticizing someone is a sign of caring. I lost that ability to care a long time ago."

When Chisa left a few minutes later, Sadaharu saw her off and returned to the house; the television set was still on and he could hear the sound of Kaori's carefree laughter.

"Kaori."

"Hmm? What?"

"It's about time to be off to bed."

"Mother?"

"She's home, upstairs."

There was once a time when Sadaharu thought of trying to explain to Kaori about her mother, but right now that was just too much trouble for him. What Kaori did not know about, there was no need for him to clarify.

"Just five more minutes and this show will be over," she said.

"All right, if that's all," Sadaharu allowed.

He went to lock the front door. Peeping outside, he saw the trembling leaves of the barren banana plant.

Why do we do such things as lock doors? Sadaharu thought, suddenly feeling strange. He had never once worried about thieves entering the house. Perhaps it was because they had no valuable possessions. The house contained nothing small that a thief could carry off. All he could conclude was that he locked the door so that no harm would befall Kaori.

He went straight to his study, his personal sanctuary. Then, thinking for a moment, he went out to the kitchen to get ice for his whiskey. He kept his whiskey bottles next to his books. For some time, he had become used to spending nights sleeping in this study. At first, when he bought his expensive reclining chair, he had intended to use it just for reading during the day. The first time he fell asleep there and awoke in the morning, he thought it was just a fluke, a consequence of too much drink. Then when it went from a single occasion to a frequent occurrence, he thought he was becoming slovenly. Tonight was the first time he had deliberately come to his study to sleep. He felt that he was giving up his right to his second-floor castle, but he thought of this as a comedy rather than a tragedy.

Sadaharu poured whiskey over the ice that filled his glass and thought of what a strange thing it was for one to have hopes for one's children, without holding any hope for the world. At this point, this was the only course available to him.

The following week, Sadaharu arranged to take Mayumi for psychiatric treatment at Nobi National Hospital, where a doctor of his acquaintance practiced. He thought Mayumi would violently object to this, and he was relieved when that turned out not to be the case.

"Go there and take a rest for a while. It's near the sea and quiet, and the surroundings are really perfect. It's a place where I'd like to go for a rest myself."

This he said to his wife, as, when little Miyako had been taken to her new home, he had also exclaimed, "It sounds so good I'd like to go myself!" The wish was meant only half seriously, but Sadaharu was always yearning for some other place.

While Mayumi was being examined at Nobi Hospital, Sadaharu went out of the reception building and walked outside. He inhaled the smell of the sea. If she were not my own wife, he reflected, I could probably think she was just some woman burdened by a miserable life. How did Mayumi expect to grow old spending her life being pitied and comforted?

She was not truly ill, but probably her doctors would prescribe several weeks of hospitalization. Not that a stay in the hospital would cure her, but since she took innate pleasure in talking about herself, she would rather enjoy receiving psychiatric treatment.

For Sadaharu, the whole thing had more of the feeling of taking a child to nursery school. He was not permanently disposing of her but rather acting out a charade of the real thing; it would earn him a bit of extra time for living. Of course, it was hardly fitting to call such a thing a "charade," but this kind of acting was not unique to Sadaharu. Every family gets along by such means.

The sea air penetrated the quiet of the pine forest. From time to time, a car would come to the hospital, but it was mostly a place where one could hear the sound of the wind like the breathing of the earth. Even the passionate color of the canna plant seemed emboldened by this air.

After a while, Sadaharu returned to the reception area of the psychiatric department. He knocked and opened the door; a nurse appeared.

"My name is Sadaharu Nobeji," he said. "I'll wait outside. . . ."

But from an office came the voice of Dr. Hirashima.

"That's all right, please come in."

"Have you finished?" Sadaharu asked.

"Yes, I had a good talk with your wife."

"That's good," Sadaharu said, entering the strangely bare examination room, so unlike that of a gynecologist, and seating himself in a chair next to Dr. Hirashima, as he was invited to do. Dr. Hirashima seemed to be a bit older than Sadaharu.

"Well. Your wife has agreed to a stay in the hospital."

Sadaharu said he was glad to hear that. He was also relieved. Today, unlike a few days earlier when she was having a fit and crying that she was going to kill herself, Mayumi had her hair prettily arranged and was wearing a tastefully stylish blouse. After all, she was the daughter of an artist, and good taste in clothes was more or less her birthright. Anyone looking at her would imagine she was an unbelievably happy woman. No matter what foolish things she might do, her husband would not throw Mayumi out. He would try to continue living with her, or so people would say, adding that she should understand how fortunate she was. Sadaharu himself did not think that way. The Mayumi who stood in front of him knew herself to be a failure as a human being.

"Someone like me is just excess baggage to you. Kaori told me she felt like she was growing up without a mother."

"That's the way life is. Everyone knows it," Sadaharu had told her. "Children do grow up, even without their parents. The proof is that she would survive even if I died too."

"Maybe, but that's just because of the land you own and the money you've earned. I haven't done anything. I can't tell whether I've lived or not."

Sadaharu looked at this woman, attractive and well-groomed, who had realized in her thirties that her life was a total failure. At least she made herself look presentable. He thought about that and pitied her.

Chapter Fifteen

Dark Seedlings

Because he felt something dark and inexplicable about the pregnant woman, Sadaharu thought he had better confirm her address.

He asked casually, "Mrs. Furukawa, are you still living at the municipal apartments?"

She replied that she was. Yasuko Furukawa, a little over thirty years of age, already had a four-year-old boy. Sadaharu had not examined her at the beginning of her pregnancy; she had come to him in about her fifth month. Until then, she had been living in an apartment in Yokosuka, where she had been consulting a gynecologist. Now, as he recalled, she was living in a municipal apartment near town.

"I suppose the scenery is better, being right by the sea."

"Yes, but it's quite humid, and the laundry doesn't dry very well."

The place where she lived was built on reclaimed land, so the ocean was right there as soon as you stepped outside, and it looked as if the wind and light were dancing together. Seeing it, someone from Tokyo would have thought it an area of vacation homes, but of course living there presented certain inconveniences. Even so, Sadaharu thought her response was rather strange, and he felt somewhat uneasy at it.

"About the baby's delivery, doctor. How much will it cost at your clinic?"

"Normally, you would remain a week after the birth. I suppose that would be about two hundred thousand yen."

"I see."

He took that to mean she felt it was expensive. Sadaharu had not intended to give her a high figure; in most cases, the cost was partially covered by the husband's company health insurance.

"At home you have your husband and child, three of you?"

"And my husband's mother. She is seventy-seven. For some time, she's been confined to bed, in diapers."

So that's it, Sadaharu thought. Living that close to the ocean, it's hard to dry diapers.

"But about a week ago, mother stopped eating, so we had to take her to a private hospital in Kurihama. And what with the cost of the semiprivate room and the price of diapers, and the need for someone to stay with her . . . well, I stay during the day, and we have someone from the Housewives' Association with her during the night. All of that is costing us about three hundred thousand yen a month."

"And you are expecting about November 20th?" Sadaharu murmured and then asked, "Is your mother-in-law on intravenous feeding at the hospital?"

"Yes. She is being nourished by injections and through a nasal tube."

"I see. How long has she been like this, in diapers?"

"About a year now, but she's been senile for a long time." Furukawa answered Sadaharu's questions in something of a daze. "She would do things like wander off and not return, or put her food in the closet. Often she would soil herself and hide it. Then the house would smell, and it seemed almost impossible to get the smell out."

"Yes, still, she is in her seventies," Sadaharu observed, but he also knew that at that age many people are still youthful, completely undiminished intellectually. "She's rather old to be your husband's mother," he added.

"My husband is thirty-nine. He was the baby of the family. His mother was nearly forty when he was born."

"So he has older brothers and sisters, doesn't he?"

"Yes. An older sister in Yokosuka and one in Hiratsuka."

"Can you call on them for some help, with the hospital or with money?"

"While I'm here for the birth, we'll have help from my sister-in-law in Hiratsuka, but both of my husband's sisters are married and have left home, my husband being the only son, you see. They say it's up to us to take care of mother."

That was the usual excuse given to pass on the responsibility of taking care of troublesome parents. But even though they avoided caring for aging parents, under postwar laws girls marrying into another family seldom gave up their rights to inherit property.

"But even if you leave the clinic one or two days early, you won't be able to watch your mother-in-law at night."

"Yes, but my sister-in-law says she'll do that for one week, and if I can't go after that I'll have to ask someone to go during the daytime also. We have a little money—what we've saved to buy a house—and my husband says we can use that. But if we use more than three hundred thousand yen a month . . . well, the truth is, we have no idea how long this will go on."

"Yes, that's a problem everywhere these days. Well, this is your second child and it will probably not require that long a stay in the clinic. At least we can be hopeful about that estimate."

And so the matter remained unresolved.

As he saw his patient off, Sadaharu considered Furukawa's situation; in contrast, his own household seemed quite peaceful. Since Mayumi had entered the hospital, both he and Kaori hardly concealed their feelings of relief. Sadaharu was grateful that he did not have to worry about where Mayumi had gone and what she might be doing. If he could have arranged it, he would have had her stay in the hospital for the rest of her life. Of course, some people would whisper that Kaori's mother was a mental case, and a few might even say that she was a nymphomaniac. But Sadaharu valued his peace more than he feared gossip. When it came time for Kaori to marry, there might be some problem, but he could accept that as a matter of course. Such things should not matter to whichever young man might ask Kaori to share his life, and he would be the only person with a possible concern.

That Saturday afternoon, Sadaharu, assisted by Dr. Hiroshige, performed operations on two patients with possible endometriosis. One woman was thirty-five; until four months ago, she had been on the pill, but then she had abnormal bleeding and her menstrual cramps had become more and more painful. The other patient, thirty-two years old, already had two children, but she was experiencing considerable dyspareunia—pain during intercourse.

The first patient believed that this ruined planet was no place to raise children and said that she wouldn't mind if her uterus were removed, since then she could have intercourse without contraception. But the younger patient and her husband both liked children, and it was painful for Sadaharu to have to tell her beforehand that she might lose her uterus. He would like to have said, as he usually did, "Really! The uterus is barely three inches long—you'll never miss it!" But for either of the patients today, that kind of reassurance would hardly do, and so he remained silent.

Opening up the abdomen of the woman who had no hope for this world, he found the uterus and the adnexae adhering to the pelvic cavity, in what is called a frozen pelvis. The uterus had deteriorated so that it had lost mobility; Sadaharu took a tissue sample and sent it for a biopsy.

The second patient, the one who wanted children, displayed what is called a chocolate cyst, which occurs when an ovary adhering to the pelvis is separated, and a chocolate-colored fluid flows from the torn cyst. Such a condition usually occurs in connection with a rather wide adhesion, but this patient's ovaries seemed functional, and since the oviduct looked healthy Sadaharu was relieved to conclude that she probably could still conceive.

He used to lecture a lot about the technique of the operation to

Dr. Hiroshige. One first had to keep in mind the entire process of the operation. It wasn't sufficient to approach the matter without preparation. Only after one had considered the entire structure, adapting to circumstances and maintaining as much as possible the balance of the whole, only then should one proceed, bringing everything together aesthetically. By "aesthetically," Sadaharu meant without doing anything contrary to nature and yet without underestimating nature's power. Humbly yet firmly, one carried through to one's objective, which had to be in concert with the body's original function. In the matter of suturing, Sadaharu required of Dr. Hiroshige that he move the needle with a two-stroke rhythm of the sewing wrist for strength and elegance. Sadaharu himself, in suturing the abdominal wall, secured the scissors with his ring and little fingers of the hand that held the needle; he could thus perform the trick of cutting the ligature with the scissors as soon as he pulled out the needle. This kind of quick-draw gunslinging, so to speak, was not usually needed, but in extreme situations when he might not have an assistant it could turn out to be useful.

As Sadaharu came out of the operating room, one of his nurses informed him that Mrs. Kakei had called and that she wished to speak with him when the operation was finished.

Sadaharu acknowledged the message. He anticipated something disagreeable and went to his desk in the empty outpatient examination room, where he dialed Yoko's house.

"Sadaharu here. I had my hands full. Sorry. Do the Lauries want to return Miyako?"

"Now, what kind of a thing is that to say! They said Miyako is a wonderful baby and sent a letter saying how enchanted they were and that they would take photographs when they arrived home and send copies to you."

"Ah, that's great. My nurse told me that you had called, and I was almost sure that was what it was about. Or perhaps that Miyako was deaf, at least."

"If Miyako were really deaf, I think that the Lauries would hold onto her all the more. Making a deaf child happy is very worthwhile, and even if she were deaf and mute there are lots of things that the Lauries could do to help."

"Yes, of course."

"I called you today about a troubling matter," Yoko said.

"What about?"

"Have you heard from Eiko Nakanishi?"

"No, nothing."

"I see. Well, she called me the day before yesterday. You had arranged for her to get an examination at the university hospital. It seems the results were unfavorable."

"Oh? I haven't heard a thing."

"Eiko said she felt devastated. She didn't have the strength to talk to anyone, but she said she called because she thought she ought to let me know, at least. According to what she said the day before yesterday, that was the situation. And just now I had a call from her husband saying that since they're coming to Miura tomorrow, they wished to stop by here in the evening. Also, Eiko wanted to pay a call on you Monday morning, he said, and I said I would ask you to come over when they're at my home. Is tomorrow night all right?"

"The truth is," Sadaharu replied, "Mayumi is in the hospital. Saturday and Sunday nights I try to stay home, for Kaori's sake, but it might be all right if I drop by for a short visit."

"Mayumi? When did she go to the hospital? I didn't know a thing about it. What's the matter?"

"There is nothing the matter with her physically. She has always been kind of psychologically depressed, but the other day she created a disturbance at someone else's house, so I'm having her looked after by a psychiatrist for a while."

"Oh, really."

"So about Mrs. Nakanishi—I was having her examined at Meirin University Hospital. A friend of mine there will know what the difficulty is."

It was Saturday afternoon, and Dr. Yagihara had already left Meirin, but he had not yet returned home. When Sadaharu called, a child answered and said in an immature-sounding voice, "Papa went to play tennis."

"Well, when he returns tell him to please call Dr. Nobeji, all right?"

He hung up, but since the child was, he imagined, a girl in an early grade of elementary school, he was not convinced she would really convey the message. Nonetheless, a little after six o'clock in the evening a call came from Dr. Yagihara.

"You called earlier?" he asked.

"Right," Sadaharu replied. "Your daughter passed on the message, I see. How old is she?"

"She's our youngest, in the second grade," Dr. Yagihara told him.

"She's really very smart, passing on a message like that. Most college students would forget, or get the name wrong, you know," Sadaharu said, praising the girl and then explaining that he had called about Mrs. Nakanishi.

"Yes, she's the first case I've actually had like that. But I know that in a practice with hundreds of births the statistics are that there will be some abnormality."

"What's the problem?" Sadaharu asked.

"It's Down's syndrome."

"I see. So that's that. At the mother's age, about one in a hundred come up with that."

"I heard that you tried hard on this case," Dr. Yagihara said.

"It wasn't all that much work, just luck. I haven't seen the patient yet, but it seems to have been quite a shock to her."

"She asked me if the baby would be able to grow up, and I told her that if it did not have an abnormal heart it might live into adolescence. And with good treatment, there is a possibility that it would live longer, but I told her it was a question of what was meant by living. Probably it couldn't be called living in the normally accepted sense. And even if the child lives to the age of twenty, the parents aren't so young now, so they would be sixty-five or so."

"Or sixty-six or seven."

"And if they don't consider their age, they'll end up dying and leaving the child in the care of an institution."

"That's the point. They can't just die when it's convenient."

"So I advised them to think it over. But if they decide to terminate the pregnancy, they shouldn't wait much longer. I told them to see you immediately, since they went to you about having a child in the first place. But, they say they don't want to get you involved if they decide to terminate, so they want to come to the hospital here. But that would be like stealing one of your patients."

"That's fine with me. Please take her. I don't like these midterm abortions."

"Well, neither do I. I thought I'd push it onto you."

"All right, then. I'll meet with them tomorrow and have a talk."

"Sorry to have delayed so long in telling you all this," Dr. Yagihara said.

"No, not at all," Sadaharu replied.

He hung up the phone and wished this was a case he could be spared from dealing with. If examination of the amniotic fluid was done properly, one could tell beforehand whether there was a chromosome or metabolic abnormality in the fetus. And if the shoot was bad, it could be plucked early. In the old days, out of natural selection, people were born indiscriminately, mysteriously, but now parents and doctor could participate in the child's right to life. Strangely enough, even pacifists who agonized over the deaths of common people and prime ministers who spoke of the sacredness of human life whenever there was a hijacking—all these humanistic voices were silent regarding this kind of situation. It came down to a conspiracy of silence, a kind of passive participation in the idea that somehow there exists a mechanism of selection that ought to eliminate persons who are not well made.

Sadaharu himself was one of those people. But more precisely, in his mind he found himself saying to people in the same position as his: Can't we at least admit it to ourselves when we kill someone?

On Sunday, the temperature dropped a little. The lingering heat of summer this year had not seemed especially bad.

"Papa," said Kaori, "there are mosquito wrigglers floating on the pond. I think we should put in some goldfish."

Since Kaori's mother was not at home, Sadaharu got up early on weekends, at about half past seven, the same time as his daughter. There was a small pond in the garden that had held three goldfish. But the day after the gardener put fertilizer on the grass in the spring, there was a lot of rain; some of the fertilizer was washed into the pond, and the fish had all died.

"Then shall we go and buy some a little later?" Sadaharu suggested.

"Let's go! Let's go! And can we buy some sparklers, too?" Kaori asked.

Sadaharu conceded that would be all right.

Soon after ten o'clock, father and daughter went out in the car. Sparklers were available in a nearby candy shop, but for goldfish they had to go down to the waterfront.

"Let's buy a really interesting one with big eyes, or maybe a black one," Sadaharu suggested.

"Oh, Papa, daddy, that's dumb. That kind is weak and no good. The best ones are the ordinary fish," Kaori told him.

"Then let's get about ten, shall we?"

"Oh, no. If you get a lot, they die. Last time, we got three and they did just fine. So this time no more than five. Honestly, Papa, your arithmetic isn't so good."

"You know, you're right," Sadaharu acknowledged.

Some parents care little about their children and the children misbehave, and some parents bother little about their children and the children are quite attentive to the parents. Sadaharu was thinking how odd this was when from somewhere a voice called his name. Noticing it was behind him, Sadaharu turned.

"Oh, it's you!" he exclaimed.

It was Mayuko Serizawa, looking a bit dazed as she stared at Sadaharu. She was a little heavier than when she had first appeared at Sadaharu's clinic about the middle of April. However one looked at Serizawa, though, she did not seem the kind of girl sometimes described as butch.

"You haven't been back to the clinic," he said. "I've wondered how you were getting along."

Sadaharu was smiling, having left Kaori at the goldfish tank.

"I had a hernia operation in the middle of summer," Serizawa said. "Dr. Abe at the hospital is known for his skill in hernia operations, so Dr. Yagihara urged me to have it done there."

"That's fine," Sadaharu said. "And how do you feel now?"

"Oh, fine, after that stiffness in my abdomen went away."

"And did you have the vaginal operation?"

"Dr. Yagihara said that Dr. Abe was the best surgeon for that in Japan, if I wanted it, but I decided not to. Either way, I couldn't have children, and I doubt I'll ever get married."

Her voice was quiet, now, and Sadaharu thought the business at the motel with her boyfriend might have given her the resolve to accept her situation. But above all, despite not having the operation, Serizawa undoubtedly now considered herself to be a woman, and that was a relief to Sadaharu.

"Yes, that's so. Marriage—it's all right if you want it, but, really, the worlds of men and women are forever separate. And when one of a pair dies, it all falls apart anyway. I think it's best to follow your instincts about what's best for you."

"Do you really think so?" Mayuko asked.

"Yes, I do. You know, I don't talk about my work at all to my wife. I've never thought of getting a divorce, but we live almost completely separate lives. We don't feel like husband and wife."

About 10 percent of Sadaharu's description was exaggeration for

Serizawa's benefit, but basically he was telling her the truth as he saw it.

"While I was in the hospital, and afterward, I thought about a lot of things," she said.

Sadaharu allowed himself a thin smile. "Oh? Well, I think that's all right. When people are ill, they have deep thoughts. But that doesn't mean it's better to be ill."

"I thought about my situation. As a woman, I'm deformed. And I can't think of myself as a man. So I've decided simply to live as a human being, not to think of myself as either a man or a woman."

"But that's really marvelous," Sadaharu continued.

"In a way, there are too many males and females in the world. The magazines have nothing but articles on sex. And when young women go to work, even there they trade on being female, calling it feminism.

"There are a lot of people I know who I wish would be more like human beings than what are considered to be women."

"Of course, if I don't marry I'll have to consider my future," Serizawa said in a more serious tone.

"Yes, but even so, you are working now and living your own life. You haven't any real worries, have you?"

"No, I don't. But I can't stay an office worker for very long. Everyone else gets married, and when a woman reaches thirty or thirty-five it's difficult to stay with a company."

"Is that the way it is?" Sadaharu answered.

"Also, when I'm at work people are always asking about when I'm going to get married. And there are always lots of opportunities to go out with men. Anyway, I've decided to learn Japanese sewing."

"Really. That's an excellent idea," Sadaharu said.

"I'm rather good with my hands, and I think I can become pretty good at making kimono. If I do that, then I can stop . . . working and stay at home. And since to make a kimono you don't have to be either a man or a woman, I can live my own life."

Sadaharu agreed. "If it were a sushi shop . . . well, somehow it just doesn't taste right when a woman makes sushi. But as far as sewing a kimono, it doesn't matter whether a man or a woman does it."

"Doctor, what do you think of my plan?" Serizawa asked.

"I think it's great, really wonderful. Without getting married you can stay at home, and you can have both men and women friends. You can earn money and travel with friends and go out to dinner with them. That will be just great."

"That's true, isn't it, but I haven't even thought that far ahead."

"You know, it's really something, because you're not sick at all. You can do whatever you want. And, ordinarily, people don't spend that much time being either male or female, they're usually just being human," Sadaharu said laughing.

"I agree. The fundamental point is to be human."

"I suppose so. Then no matter how old we get, we can remain happy," Sadaharu said.

"I'm so glad I met you today, doctor," Serizawa said.

"I was wondering how you were doing."

"Only a few people know about my physical condition. I haven't spoken about my future to anyone who doesn't know."

"If you have any future difficulties, come to see me at the clinic," Sadaharu said. "And if it is something I can't deal with, I'll refer you to Dr. Yagihara."

Serizawa thanked him.

"Before I ran into you," Sadaharu said, "I was about to help my daughter pick out some goldfish. She's been examining them all this while and still seems to be having trouble choosing five fish. Instead of my doing it, would you help her? The long thin ones like you are the kind of healthy Japanese goldfish she wants."

Hearing this, Mayuko laughed brightly for the first time.

Sadaharu arrived at Yoko's house somewhat earlier than expected that evening and, without mentioning Serizawa's name, told

Yoko about his meeting with her.

"Living neither as a man nor a woman is like living a lie, but it's not totally unthinkable. Actually, when a man doesn't care for a woman, it disgusts him when she tries to act "female" around him—I'm sure that's true for women too. A woman can't even stand washing out the coffee cup of a man she doesn't like; she won't even carry it to the sink. I met an office worker like that once."

Sadaharu had conceived a dangerous plan for meeting the Nakanishi couple: to get drunk just short of the point of rudeness. He kept talking while he quickly downed a glass of whiskey.

"I was opposed to surgery that would construct a vagina for her. But she really is a woman, and it would be another matter if she said she wanted to marry, even though she can't have children."

Sadaharu was grateful that Yoko was listening in silence, so he continued his monologue.

"Anyway, I don't think it would feel very pleasant to have a sex change operation. You know, once when I was drinking in Shinjuku, I was consulted by a transsexual."

"What!" Yoko exclaimed."

"He said he had been operated on at a famous place in Morocco, but afterward the wound didn't heal properly. It's an area of the body where there are a lot of bacteria. The interior of the artificial vagina gradually became inflamed, since there was no way for the wound to drain."

"Excuse me, Sadaharu."

Yoko spoke his name rather formally. For a moment, Sadaharu imagined she was about to scold him for bringing up this indiscreet topic of a sex change operation.

"Hmm? Yes?"

"The wound, as you say, didn't heal?"

"That's right."

"Then, if it didn't heal, that is . . . that would be quite unnatural, wouldn't it?"

"Yes, and so he'd had a kind of metallic, basket-shaped mold fitted at the hospital, someplace like Meirin where Dr. Abe works. But he often forgot to insert it. And then he had a problem."

"What did the poor fellow do?"

"Well, I sent him to see Dr. Abe at Meirin. He was really pathetic. He had been experiencing a great deal of discomfort for some time. That made me think that if my own patient does not want to have a sex change, it's for the best that she remain just as she is."

"Yes, that must be true. It's not just her, you know. Every one of us lives without understanding ourselves."

"And in most cases," Sadaharu added, "what we don't understand is a blessing."

"Yes, and Eiko must really be pitied for that reason."

In his growing alcoholic haze, Sadaharu thought for a moment that Yoko was criticizing him.

The Nakanishis arrived somewhat later than anticipated, but, at least outwardly, they did not seem upset.

"Ah, young people. How strange they are today," Mr. Nakanishi observed. "On the way out here, we met a crowd of about five youngsters, seated in a circle in the middle of the road, drinking Coca-Cola out of cans."

"Well, there are only country roads out here, but even so cars do pass over them from time to time," Yoko said.

"Of course! If it were us and we didn't want to be run over or have to move every time a car came along, we would stop by the side of the road, but it didn't seem to occur to that bunch to think of moving until a car came along."

"If they wanted to drink Coca-Cola, they could go to the beach," Yoko said.

"I wonder why they were on a country road?"

"Why? There's no telling."

Sadaharu sat there taking in this aimless conversation as though he were listening to music. Too many conversations, he felt, were purely practical, concerned with conveying information, or developing an intellectual argument. What was going on now was pointless but oddly comforting. Coca-Cola? It had nothing to do with anything, but talking about it came as a kind of merciful balm. At Sadaharu's age, he probably didn't even think of drinking more than a can a year. Just that difference in taste was probably an indication of what had captivated those young people.

"Eiko, what would you like to drink?" Yoko asked.

"If you wish to have a drink, Eiko, please do so," Mr. Nakanishi said. "There is no need to worry about the child."

Sadaharu listened to their talk as though to a night wind. He halfway thought the matter was probably already decided, and he concluded that very likely the priest would not appear tonight.

"I'm afraid we have some bad news to tell you," Mr. Nakanishi said to him. "I suppose you may have already heard, but the result of the examination was not at all good, and my wife and I were extremely saddened. When Dr. Yagihara explained to us about what continuing the pregnancy would mean . . . either way seemed equally bad to us. Just a while ago, in fact, we contacted Dr. Yagihara and made an appointment to enter the hospital next Tuesday in order to have the pregnancy terminated. We should have gone to you, I suppose, but . . ."

"Not, not at all. I'm not the one for that operation," Sadaharu answered, waving the hand not holding the whiskey glass.

Yoko asked, "If I may—in what way was the result of the examination bad?"

"There's no secret about it," Mrs. Nakanishi said. "But I think we should ask Dr. Nobeji to explain."

"I've only heard from Dr. Yagihara by telephone," Sadaharu said, "and I'm not a specialist in chromosomal disorders, so I'm not completely clear about this, but he said it was a trisomy."

"Yes, that's what he told us, too."

"It means 'three,' the 'tri-' part. Chromosomes usually come in pairs, but they can divide into three. Chromosomes are given numbers to distinguish them. What we call Down's syndrome is a condition in which chromosome No. 21 divides into three."

"So that's it," Yoko sighed.

"Yes, and it's strange. It's not inherited or anything like that; but it does occur often."

"And does this always happen when there are three chromosomes?"

"Well, having three chromosomes is rather abnormal."

Sadaharu was feeling somewhat drunk.

"When we asked, Dr. Yagihara said that the child would probably have Down's syndrome, and when I asked him whether he meant 'probably' or 'definitely,' he said that it would certainly be the case," Mr. Nakanishi said.

Sadaharu answered the husband, saying, "Yes, that's the way he would put it."

"I asked him whether there might be some error in the test."

"And what did he say to that?"

"He said the test wasn't 100 percent reliable, but close."

"Yes, that's right. There was nothing else he could say."

"At first, Eiko said that she wanted the child, even if it had Down's syndrome, even if it was retarded, even if it did not live very long. If it died at age twenty, that might be better for both of us, because then we would die only after our child had gone before us. And it wouldn't matter to us even if it could never say a word. If only we could hold our own child in our arms. At the time, Eiko was holding the cat, and the cat was warm, she said. But if this were our own child . . . that's what has always been on her mind. We would gladly live just to raise a happy child to the age of twenty years. . . ."

No one spoke. Mr. Nakanishi continued.

"But Dr. Yagihara explained some of the realities to us. The child could reach the age of twenty, perhaps even live longer. But its heart would be damaged, and it would have malformations of the digestive organs. And if there were additional complications accompanying this, then the child would require many difficult and painful operations, and we would have to endure the treatments along with the child. He told us that some parents, who couldn't bear to see their child suffer, begged for the treatment to be discontinued."

According to what Mr. Nakanishi said, the night before he and his wife had stood by the shore, trying to come to terms with the situation. Their only real legacy was the child inside Mrs. Nakanishi. If the child were born with one eye, or three arms, the couple would still accept it as their own. If it could not speak, or see, or even if it were of subnormal intelligence, he said, if only his wife could hold it and feel its warmth on her skin, then she would also be able to feel that her own life had been worthwhile.

But this kind of child could neither live a meaningful life on its own as an adult, nor in future could it marry. Even if she gave birth to this one child, it still could not be their heir. Mr. Nakanishi had reasoned patiently with his wife. Mrs. Nakanishi had said only, "But even so, it's our child."

The night before, Mr. Nakanishi had been awakened by his wife crying out in the dark. His wife's voice seemed to be laughing, although he was sure that she had cried herself to sleep.

"Eiko! Wake up!" he said, shaking her.

"Oh, oh," she muttered. "What a terrible dream I just had. The doctor told me our child was malformed, and I was so sad I didn't want to live. And I woke up . . . and I was so relieved it was just a dream, and I was so happy."

Mr. Nakanishi said that for a moment he thought his wife had lost her mind. He had grasped her hand and stayed silent. For some seconds Eiko's face had been in turmoil, then once again she had broken into tears.

" 'Oh! But the dream was true,' Eiko sobbed, and I replied, 'No, no. You're wrong, you can't say that. The dream was a dream, that's all.' I didn't sleep at all after that, lying awake all night until dawn."

Sadaharu said, "Yes. I've had dreams like that, too. I've had them asleep and also when I was awake."

"Now, aren't you strange," Yoko said, "dreaming while you are awake."

"Oh, yes, absolutely. Usually I'm in jail, or in a hospital."

"Eh?"

"Right at this moment, I'm having a dream. I'm really under a life sentence, or I'm an invalid, and I've been in prison or a hospital for decades. In reality, my present life is a long, long dream. Then all of sudden I'll wake up, and when I do I'll be in a hospital, or a jail. My real self is over there, and my present self is only a passing dream."

"And is the here-and-now self happy, Sadaharu?" asked Yoko.

"Ah, the here-and-now self is so happy he can only think it's all a dream," he laughed.

Looking into his wife's face, Mr. Nakanishi said, "I think my wife has been in a continuous dream. Most of all, the dream was to have a child. Then the dream turned into a nightmare. If it were only a nightmare, it would be all right, but this is really happening, and we can't wake up."

Yoko said, "Eiko, hasn't your drink gotten a bit weak?"

"Oh, yes, would you freshen it a bit?" Mrs. Nakanishi said as Yoko poured her whiskey. "I'm happy today. Or to put it precisely, until tomorrow."

"Why is that?" Yoko asked.

"It's just that until tomorrow the three of us will be together. What we have now will never be the same afterward."

Everyone was silent.

Then Mr. Nakanishi spoke. "Dr. Nobeji. May I ask, if we had the Down's syndrome child, what would it be like? I know it's terrible to ask someone about one's own future. But for us it is unimaginable. If we try to imagine that future, we only see the bright side. Dr. Yagihara told us that if the child had some congenital deformity, then having an operation would only cause it suffering, but when we heard that we thought it would still be better if the child lived, even in pain."

"I'd think of myself in such circumstances," Sadaharu began, "rather than the newborn retarded child. I've observed some parents' psychological reactions. I have a sense of how they will feel about such a child. At first, you know, in the hospital, everything about the child is cute. The parents think only about keeping the child alive. Then sometime later on, one day, suddenly they think: How nice it would be if this child were to die. It takes physical strength and economic resources to care for such a child, and no matter who they are, one day the parents tire of the burden.

"Of course, there are some people who have never once thought that their child ought to be dead, that it should die. And I don't say such people are just lying for the sake of appearances. I have my doubts, but I suppose there are people who can think that way.

"But most people are different. Eventually, the parents come to hate the abnormal child. They know the child is pitiful, yet they lose their love for it. The reason is simply that at a certain point, the child becomes their attacker. And human beings hate those who assault them, whether parent or child.

"In fact, isn't that really the problem? That if they don't want the child to assault them, then the parents themselves must become the assailants, rather than the child? Then for the sake of the child's existence and its soul, the parents become the attackers and the child the victim. Rather than hating and losing the child, it is better to remove the child and let it die. Just disregard the question whether this way of thinking is good or bad. The fact is that it exists."

Mrs. Nakanishi said, "The truth is, I've given the child a name."

"Oh, now, that was premature, wasn't it?" Sadaharu said lightly.

"No, I gave it a name when I knew it wouldn't be born and live. I call it Mio, meaning 'unborn'—it's neither a boy's nor a girl's name."

The moment was hardly one in which to speak, but Yoko saved the occasion.

"Well, I think that was a very good thing for you to do. It's good to have a name, and from now on, when we think about the child or talk about it, that will certainly be convenient."

As usual, Mrs. Nakanishi smiled with her eyebrows tilting, then quickly turned away to wipe her eyes.

"Instead of praying for a nameless child, I think it is really better that you pray for someone specific and clearly say the name Mio," Yoko added.

"Do you really think so?"

"Yes, I do. The two of you are not a childless couple, you see. You had a child, but you lost it. You are really quite splendid, you know, very unusual people. Mio made you parents, and from now on you can speak of Mio and make Mio a part of your life."

"Oh, Yoko, you always find a way to keep our spirits up," Sadaharu said, watching Mrs. Nakanishi out of the corner of his eye. He grinned and continued, "Usually the way to console someone in these circumstances is to urge them to try to forget the problem. All things must pass, and we should let them go. You are Japanese, aren't you?"

"You are a pantheist, but I'm not. I'm a monotheist, and I don't like to lead people on," Yoko said to Sadaharu.

"Of course, of course," he responded. "The world is as kind as it is cruel—that's the pantheist idea. The problem gets covered up along the way."

"We have to keep our eyes opened to every possibility," Yoko said. "The Nakanishis are people who can do that. It is surely no waste that Mio had half a year of life. Even a retarded child. And isn't Mio's existence a marvelous thing philosophically? The Nakanishis have been driven to the limit of human endurance, and they have been shown what extremes life can hold. They've seen the glorious sunset of life and the dark waves of night, and all because of Mio. What kind of child can this be who not yet even born can give its parents a vision of such extremes of life and death?"

"Mrs. Kakei, you put it like that. . . ." Mr. Nakanishi said, unable to say more.

"Of course, we can't deny how sad it is. I've never felt such sorrow before," Mr. Nakanishi added.

Mrs. Nakanishi buried her face in her hands.

"After what Mrs. Kakei has said, your loss seems all the greater," Sadaharu said to Mr. Nakanishi. "If a human being loses something, the best thing is for him to hold on to the idea of what it represents all the more tightly. And if it's a wound, then the deeper the wound the better. Because holding on to the idea or living with the pain of a wound are proof of being alive."

"But the child—Mio—I had no idea it fulfilled us so, or that it could fulfill us," Mr. Nakanishi said, then spoke his wife's name. Mrs. Nakanishi tried to lift her head while wiping her tears. "I think that Mrs. Kakei's words are very meaningful. If you're all right, let's go home now and think this over."

"Yes," Mrs. Nakanishi replied.

"So, you're leaving now?" Sadaharu said, barely managing to stand, his body dulled by alcohol.

"Yes," Mr. Nakanishi said. "I can't put it very well, but I keep feeling as though all of this is a bad dream."

"Like a bad dream, indeed," Sadaharu said.

"As Eiko said, we only have tonight and tomorrow for the three of us, parents and child, so I think we ought to spend that time undisturbed."

Mrs. Nakanishi wiped her tears and tried to smile.

"Thank you so much, really. That I've become a mother . . ."

Again, she could not speak.

"I suppose you don't have your car," Sadaharu said.

"No, we came in the car. That's why I didn't have anything to drink," Mr. Nakanishi replied.

"Mrs. Kakei, Dr. Nobeji, thank you so much."

Saying this, Mrs. Nakanishi followed her husband to the door and was about to leave when she stopped, turning to Yoko. As though no one else in the world existed, Yoko wrapped her arms around Mrs. Nakanishi, who buried her face in Yoko's shoulder.

Mr. Nakanishi went out into the windy night to bring the car and after a time drove up to the entrance, headlights shining like the eyes of an animal.

"Thank you so much, really."

"Good night."

"Take care."

Sadaharu drew himself up to his full height on the top step of the entrance. Without speaking, he raised his hand with his whiskey glass still in it, remaining there with Yoko until the car's red taillights disappeared.

Yoko did not move, and Sadaharu asked, "Are you all right?"

"Yes, I'm all right. Let's go inside." She turned on her heel, a bit unsteady.

Sadaharu came down the steps and held Yoko by her elbow, supporting her.

"Something wrong?"

"No. It's just that there is nothing we can do for them. The thought of that makes me a feel ill. I'm . . . disappointed with myself."

"Tell the truth now, Yoko. You're disappointed with me, aren't you?" He laughed. "I don't take myself seriously, and I'm not too sensitive, so anything you have to say is all right with me."

"There's nothing I can say. I simply could not tell them that there are parents who keep Down's syndrome children and treasure them, that they should keep their child and raise it. What good is my religion, I wonder."

Sadaharu put his other hand on Yoko's shoulder to support her.

"Now, that's the devil whispering in your ear, Yoko. I've never supposed you were merely doctrinaire in your faith. You're not so grand as all that, my dear."

"That's the truth," she murmured.

"And shall I tell you something else? Parents who have a Down's syndrome child are prepared to care for it three hundred and sixty-four days of the year. But one day, one year, I imagine, they won't want to bother about it. Or let's say it's not one day but ten, maybe a hundred, or even one day in two. Some people may conclude that the child is a burden to them. And it's not that I think those parents are evil. If they want their child to live, even for just one day, then I would recognize them as parents. And I have no religious faith. I think that people are all more or less the same—the Nakanishis are no different. They only seem different because they know about their child beforehand. If other couples knew beforehand that they were going to have a Down's syndrome child, they would have an abortion. Most of them."

Yoko was silent, her mind elsewhere.

"Your hands are cold," Sadaharu said, "Let's go inside. I thought you might ask the priest to come this evening."

"No," Yoko said.

It was barely a reply. Sadaharu took her to a chair in the living room and brought a small glass of sherry.

"Have some of this," he said, handing her the glass. He went to fill his own glass with whiskey, returning to Yoko's side.

"I felt it would be best not to invite the priest," Yoko said in a low voice.

"I agree with you. It would have been cruel if you'd asked him, no matter how things went. Or maybe it would have been better just to put all the responsibility on him, do you think?" Sadaharu said.

Sadaharu removed his slippers and sat cross-legged on the rug in front of Yoko's chair, so that he could see the expression on her face.

Chapter Sixteen

Repose of the Soul

Perhaps this year the jellyfish had appeared early, signalling the beginning of autumn, but it did seem that the lingering heat of summer was less fierce than usual.

When Sadaharu paid his weekly visit to Mayumi at the Nobi Hospital, he saw clusters of pink cosmos fluttering in the breeze on the slope near the hospital entrance, which faced the always tranquil sea. Cosmos were autumn flowers, he thought, yet they were blooming at a time he preferred to call the end of summer.

Since entering the hospital, Mayumi had seemed to be in a good mood. Sadaharu thought she might have complained about his "putting her in a place like this," but not once had she assumed that tone.

"They told me that nowadays there are only a few people who are really crazy," she said to him. "Mrs. Tsuda even has a job, but with her insomnia she said that she couldn't keep her strength up. Mrs. Koshikawa has a phobia about germs and refuses to take her meals. And little Etsuko was hearing things, but now she is happy and going back and forth to high school every day. They're just a little neurotic, that's all."

Mayumi chatted about her acquaintances among the patients, people Sadaharu did not even know.

"Really? Then this place is more like a kind of boarding house than a hospital, isn't it?"

"That's right. Dr. Hirashima says that people with strong sensibilities are susceptible to neurosis. Insensitive people don't get this kind of illness. He said that if I had found a creative outlet and become an artist, like my father, then I probably would not be ill."

Mayumi's father was a painter. Sadaharu did not believe that Dr. Hirashima, the doctor in charge of her case, had actually said this. Mayumi's way of dealing with her life was always half real and half fantasy. He suspected that now Mayumi would believe that Dr. Hirashima understood her genius more than anyone else. She thought he valued her highly, and consequently she felt he had become a supporter. Psychiatric patients, it is said, all go through a period of being in love with their doctor, so Sadaharu remained silent.

Mayumi had begun to be absorbed in decorating her room at the hospital like some kind of fantasy land. This was a national hospital that had rough ferroconcrete walls. Mayumi had accumulated a mountain of things—flowers, slippers, gowns, tissue box covers, and more—and had covered her nightstand with lace.

"Yesterday, Yoko brought me this orchid and a hand mirror," Mayumi told him.

"Really, that was nice."

Yoko knew that Sadaharu had neither the time nor inclination to look after such tedious things, so, without saying anything to Sadaharu, she brought the things that Mayumi wanted.

The other night he had left Yoko's house soon after the Nakanishis had left, feeling almost driven away.

"Sadaharu, I need to be alone, please," Yoko had said. "At a time like this, I have to be alone, to think. That's the way it is."

Sadaharu perfectly understood Yoko's feelings at that moment. No one could help her. Invariably she felt she had to bear the world's burdens alone. Yoko understood the frightening significance of things that Mayumi did not even know existed.

At that moment, Sadaharu thought that Yoko had lost her grip on whatever held her together and gave her strength. Because he himself was a certain type of person, he was not surprised when other people showed signs of weakness. Indeed, he even imagined it might be beneficial for Yoko to let herself go—but Yoko had sent Sadaharu away. In spite of her living alone, Yoko said if she had "a companion who would weep with her," it would spoil her. Sadaharu supposed the phrase came from a line in the Bible.

That night, perhaps because he'd had enough to drink, Sadaharu had felt it might be possible to pass through some kind of barrier that existed between himself and Yoko. To put it as politely as possible, Sadaharu was flexible; in less complimentary terms, he had no moral standards. He had never thought about her seriously as a woman. If his relationship with Yoko had changed then, Sadaharu would have felt they had taken an opportunity created by another's misfortune, but he also felt that was only natural. If Yoko was searching for something, then as a matter of course he would provide it. That was his basic attitude toward her, but he did not know whether it was because he was attracted to her as a woman or because he was expecting her someday to take the place of his dead sister. He didn't dare think about it too carefully. But psychologically, Yoko had not brought him even a step closer to her. This may have been due to her lack of feeling for him or simply to her personality.

Either way, Sadaharu felt that the result was refreshingly interesting. He'd had his fill of seeing men and women resolve themselves into simply male and female stereotypes. If they had nothing to say to one another, perhaps there was nothing else for them to do but resort to basic body language. But when he and Yoko spoke, they could create a kind of elegant world between them. Such a pair had no need to become ordinarily male and female.

"Mrs. Kakei is the one person who knows what I like," Mayumi had said, which was exactly what Sadaharu himself would have liked to say. "That hand mirror, for instance. I couldn't stand to have one near me that was in poor taste. No matter whom else I could explain that to, they would never get it right. Only Yoko buys me just what I like."

"That's wonderful," Sadaharu said. "She has such good taste."

After spending a short time in Mayumi's room, he would have nothing to say. He would mention a birth, or perhaps a patient who needed care after an operation, and then he would leave. But today his excuse was quite natural, since in fact Kumiko Shinjo, the beauty shop owner, had begun labor pains and had entered the clinic.

It was at about noon that day that Shinjo had come in, complaining that her abdomen felt a bit stretched. This was two or three days after her scheduled delivery date. Sadaharu had told her on her previous visit to come back in a week even if there were no labor pains the night before that visit. But although she had felt nothing like pains, she had felt uneasy and awakened many times.

"And then this morning, I fell into a deep sleep." That was just like Shinjo.

"I want you to be calm instead of coming to the clinic all flustered, so come in any time," Sadaharu had told her.

He had said this because Shinjo had already told him of seeing signs of the beginning of labor in the form of vaginal discharge. That afternoon, she had come to the clinic with her mother, bringing her personal effects, Sadaharu had learned before leaving to visit Mayumi.

He returned a little before five o'clock, and then stopped by Dr. Hiroshige's room to explain his intrusion, since this was Hiroshige's duty day.

"How is Shinjo doing?" he asked.

"Ah, still a little irregular," was the reply. "Sometimes she seems to have pains about twenty minutes apart, and at other times they come at fifteen-minute intervals. The cervix is already one finger wide, which is large for this stage."

"To tell you the truth, I gave this patient an abortion that didn't work," Sadaharu said, massaging his neck.

"Oh? How did that happen?" Dr. Hiroshige asked.

"Uterus bicornis, probably. I thought I did the procedure properly, but if I have any excuse it may be that it was performed too early."

"If it was uterus bicornis, I heard of three cases last year. Personally, I haven't yet encountered one. Did she decide to give birth? It's a good thing her husband agreed."

"It seems there isn't any husband. The child will be hers alone," Sadaharu said.

"I see."

"That's why I'd like to be on the scene today, at least if it doesn't bother you. I think the patient might like that too."

"No, in fact it would be a help if you attend," Dr. Hiroshige said.

"Since you've already examined her, I should leave her care to you, but I'll just look in once in a while."

"Yes, please do."

Sadaharu went first to the ward record room that was also the night duty room. There he found both Nurse Ono and the strong Nurse Iwanami, so he called out to them: "I've come to see how Ms. Shinjo is doing. Won't you come with me?"

He then entered Shinjo's room, and finding her and her mother together, asked "How do you feel?" without particularly directing his words to either.

"Thank you. We appreciate your concern," said the dependable-looking mother.

"So, in a little while you will have a grandchild," Sadaharu said, feeling a bit strange; these people probably thought his words rather brash, after he had failed in the abortion.

"If the father were here, it would be a happy occasion indeed."

"Even so, it's an auspicious event that a grandchild is being born, isn't it?" Sadaharu said to the mother.

"And, mother," Shinjo added lightly, "everyone in the neighborhood believes the story I told them."

"Yes. That's because they aren't involved in the matter," her mother replied.

"And the pain?" Sadaharu asked. "Have you had any severe pain yet?"

"Yes, a little while ago. It's coming at about ten-minute intervals."

"I'll just look you over a bit. Mrs. Shinjo, would you mind stepping outside?"

With that, Sadaharu sent Shinjo's mother out of the room.

"Last night you didn't sleep well, but since you slept this morning I don't suppose you feel tired?" Sadaharu questioned her while putting on his gloves.

"But I'm not relaxed, and I really don't remember sleeping well," Shinjo answered.

"You will probably have another sleepless night tonight, too. It's a job, but keep at it one more night."

"Will it take that long?"

"Oh, the baby will never be born if you keep acting so unconcerned."

"Don't joke, doctor. I'm afraid."

"Ms. Shinjo, do you know how many people there are on earth?"

"I don't know."

"Well, since there are a lot of countries where they can't produce anything as eloquent as a census, we can't know for certain, but we think there are already over four billion. And they all produce children."

"I see. Then I suppose I'll give birth like everyone else," Shinjo said, shutting her eyes and smiling a little tensely.

"Hmm. There seems to have been no change since Dr. Hiroshige examined you," Sadaharu said as he took his gloves off. "So just relax."

"I can't. I'm really afraid."

"Dr. Hiroshige will look at you, and I'll get his report. I'll be waiting in the house, ready to come over at any time."

"Thank you, doctor," Kumiko said. "I suppose today is your day off."

"Yes, it is, but I have no special plans. Don't worry about that."

Returning home, he found that his housekeeper was gone, but on the table was a plate of sliced beef she had prepared; he would grill the marinated meat together with vegetables and eat it for dinner. Both he and Kaori liked food prepared this way, but when Mayumi was at home she rarely permitted it, claiming the odor of smoke and grease polluted the house. His housekeeper understood the situation, and whenever Mayumi was away she prepared a grilled meat dish for them.

"Papa, let's eat," Kaori said. "Do you want a beer?"

When her mother was away from home, Kaori seemed quite inclined to take her place.

"No. Tonight I have some work to do so I won't drink any beer."

"Oh, that's somcthing new," Kaori observed.

Sadaharu lit the gas grill and wondered whether he was really drinking that much.

"Kaori, you should visit your mother sometime," Sadaharu told her.

"Yes-s-s, I guess so, but I don't think she's exactly dying to see me," was Kaori's reply.

"Well, I think she is, in her heart, though she doesn't show it on her face, even when I visit her," Sadaharu said.

"I think I wouldn't cry even if Mother died now."

"Oh? Really? And I suppose you wouldn't cry even if I died," Sadaharu replied.

"Hmm, no. If you died, I think I would cry."

"Now that's quite nice of you, Kaori. After all, your father is your sole support, so you should take care of me."

"No, that's not why. It's because, you know, we're always together. It's like the chest of drawers. The house is so lonely without it."

"My! What a funny expression. Imagine. A chest of drawers."

Sadaharu laughed, putting his face into the smoke from the sizzling meat.

When they finished the meal, the two put the dishes into an American dishwasher, added soap, and pushed the button. For about fifty minutes, the machine made its churning noise while doing its work. The machine was much too big to be used for washing dishes just for the two of them; but since neither Sadaharu nor Kaori wanted to wash their own, they entrusted the work to this extravagant device.

Sadaharu returned to his study and put on a record of Mozart's *Requiem*, the mass for repose of the soul.

Usually, Sadaharu had no particular need for music, but once in a while, like the hunger for a sweet pastry that overtook him now and then, he wished to hear music. It was said that this D-minor work, K. 626, was Mozart's last, and he died before completing it. At the passage "that day of flowing tears," Mozart collapsed and the work was completed by his disciple, according to a book Sadaharu had read. Thinking of this as he listened, Sadaharu felt that Mozart must have died of tuberculosis or pneumonia. He was not able to guess further, in spite of a passage in which one can imagine some difficulty in breathing, since he did not know which part of the piece was composed last, and because of not having read the composer's biography. There were too many ardent Mozart scholars and fans in the world for Sadaharu to advance some irresponsible thesis of his own.

At a little after seven o'clock, a phone call came from Dr. Hiroshige, but it was only to say that there was no particular change in Shinjo's condition. The cervix was about two fingers wide and pains were about fifteen seconds in duration.

"That's fine," Sadaharu told him. "I'll leave it in your hands. I'll be at home."

As Sadaharu responded to the call, he could hear the music of the *Requiem* mass in the background. He made a rough mental calculation of the progress of Shinjo's delivery. At a little after seven o'clock, she was still at an early stage with an enlargement of two fingers' width, and so he felt that the birth would not take place until the middle of the night. If the process had been a little more advanced in the afternoon, they might have used a stimulant and induced labor, but it would be unreasonable at this point to step up the tempo just so that the birth would be completed that evening in time for everyone to get some sleep.

The record finished; it occurred to Sadaharu to telephone Yoko.

"Ah, you're at home?"

Having made the call himself, he realized this was a peculiar greeting, but could do nothing to correct it.

"I'm always here," Yoko answered.

"Have you heard anything from the Nakanishis?"

"Yes, Mr. Nakanishi called to tell me it had all ended safely. He said that his wife would be staying in the hospital for two or three days. I asked whether I could go and see her, but he said it would be better for me to wait until she composed herself, so I haven't been yet."

"Time will take care of everything," Sadaharu said in his typically irresponsible way.

"Oh. Mr. Nakanishi seems to have received the remains, and they've prepared a cemetery plot for the child where the three of them will be together in the future. They are quite pleased."

Sadaharu grunted at that.

"Whenever one dies, whether at six months or at the age of eighty, a child is a child, Mr. Nakanishi said. You know, when humans suffer they say the most original and fine things," Yoko said.

After finishing his conversation with Yoko on the telephone, Sadaharu thought that perhaps the reason he did not say "original and fine things" was that he had not suffered enough. Exactly. He had never once thought that he had the motivation to become such a "fine" person. For Yoko, there was a kind of religiosity in the idea. Sadaharu was fond of that quality, but he did not possess it himself. It seems that all human beings have a role to play, and for Yoko it was some pursuit of the sublime. But Sadaharu differed in that his wish was to devote himself to the ordinary. He felt there was an infinite variety to what was ordinary, and understanding that was his job.

The next telephone call from Dr. Hiroshige came at about half past ten.

"If you can, Doctor, would you come around for a look. I've just examined her and she is about three fingers wide."

"Right. I'll be there presently."

Kaori seemed to be already sound asleep. Sadaharu locked the door as he left the house with Kaori inside.

When he entered Room 210, Dr. Hiroshige and Nurse Iwanami were already there, apparently waiting for him.

"She seems to be in considerable pain," Dr. Hiroshige said.

"What are the frequency and length of the contractions?" Sadaharu asked.

"Every five minutes for about thirty seconds."

"Blood pressure?"

Many people with normal blood pressure showed a sudden rise in pressure during labor.

"One-thirty-six over ninety," Iwanami reported.

"Ms. Shinjo, how are you doing? Do you feel much pain?" Sadaharu asked Shinjo.

"I didn't think it would be this bad. For some reason, I'm not handling it very well. I'm sorry," she said.

"And your mother?"

"She got terribly tired, and I sent her home," Shinjo said. "When she left, the pain wasn't this bad. If I had known how bad the pain would be, I would have asked her to stay."

Sadaharu laughed, "Your mother can't help you with this. Shall we use something to relieve the pain? Dr. Hiroshige is attending today, and he is very good with caudal anesthesia. We could have him administer some."

"Yes, please. I've never felt such pain. Can I get it right away?"

"Please try to hold on a little while longer. When you are nearly completely open he will do it. When the pain is most severe, you'll get some relief."

Instead of replying, Shinjo grimaced. The pain seemed to have returned, but she made no sound. Shinjo's face became blotched, her strength concentrated in the lines around her jaw until, finally, the tension eased.

"Good. Now please try to bear it," Sadaharu said again to encourage her, then left the room and returned to his home.

He went to his sleeping chair in his study and began to look at a magazine, not concerned about falling asleep. Not knowing when he would be called, he did not feel like reading anything of much length. He had no idea how much time had passed, but when the telephone rang, he was fast asleep in his chair.

Before he began reading his magazine, he'd prepared well by switching on the electric insect trap, which had saved him from being bitten by mosquitoes. He felt quite rested. As he went to the phone, he reflexively looked at his watch and saw that it was quarter past two in the morning. He thought he had fallen asleep some time before half past eleven.

"Doctor, Ms. Shinjo is nearly completely open and wants you to come," Nurse Iwanami said.

"All right. I'll be right there."

He yawned widely and went out by the front door. Nurses Ono and Iwanami would have to be up all night. When a birthing was unscheduled, it was especially hard work for them, but for no special reason Sadaharu did not wish to induce labor.

Shinjo was already in the delivery room. Her labor pains were coming every two or three minutes and continued for about fifty seconds. Naturally, she had no time to rest or be free from pain.

"Ms. Shinjo," he said as he checked on her condition himself, "for a first birth it's coming along very well."

"Really? It feels like an awfully long time."

"Now we can get Dr. Hiroshige to give you anesthesia. Until then, you will only have to bear one or two pains."

"Now you won't have any more pain, Ms. Shinjo," Sadaharu said a little later. Sadaharu was watching Dr. Hiroshige's practiced hand, but thought that today Dr. Hiroshige had run out of luck. The injection needle seemed to have punctured a blood vessel, and he noticed a slight amount of blood. Dr. Hiroshige had to stop the injection, and only a small amount of anesthetic was injected. The pain would not completely stop, and very likely the birth would not automatically proceed while the patient simply chatted and hummed a merry tune. Sadaharu did not inform Shinjo of this, yet to the degree that the anesthetic took hold, the pain became much lighter and the birth canal expanded considerably. Looking on the bright side of things, the small quantity of anesthetic would preserve the necessary strength of her contractions. There was, after all, a peculiar kind of relationship here. If the anesthetic really helps, then the birth canal expands, but the contractions are weaker; and if the anesthetic does not have much effect, then the canal's resistance remains, but so does the strength of the contractions to expel the child. Weighing these contrary elements to determine which is better reveals that no unequivocal good exists anywhere in this world.

The clinic staff was quite busy when the telephone rang in the records room and Nurse Iwanami went to answer, returning with the news that a pregnant woman who was not due for another ten days had suddenly begun to have labor pains at about eight o'clock that evening and wanted to come in immediately—so her husband was saying on the phone.

"It's Toshiko Tanaka."

"Mrs. Tanaka is having her third child," Dr. Hiroshige said. "I examined her last week."

"If it's her third, she'll be in a hurry. Tell her to come in immediately," Sadaharu directed.

Nurse Iwanami went back to the phone. Sadaharu spoke to Dr.

Hiroshige, who was fastening the tokodynamometer to Shinjo "Mrs. Umemura in Room 304 will probably deliver in the morning. This has turned into quite a rush."

Dr. Hiroshige replied, "Deliveries always seem to be on weekends. They're all like that lately. When people try to enjoy Saturday, the births all seem to come on Sunday."

"Not so," Sadaharu replied. "Since people play on Sunday, too, there are a lot of births on Monday. As soon as you leave, I get terribly busy."

Shinjo said nothing, her eyes tightly closed. After Dr. Hiroshige had administered the anesthetic, he had placed her in a stable position and then artificially ruptured the membrane. The baby's head directly forced through the opening and began to descend. It was a small matter, but when Dr. Hiroshige assisted on Saturday and Sunday, Sadaharu observed his amniotomy technique and from that alone felt he could rely on him. Using the tip of the Kocher one can accomplish this easily, but Dr. Hiroshige kept the tip of the sharp instrument shorter than his finger and manipulated it while scrutinizing the point of contact. If one did not do that when the membranes were broken, the hair of the baby's head might be scraped off.

Ten minutes later, Sadaharu heard the bell ring at the entrance of the clinic and looked at his watch. It was ten past three in the morning. Nurse Ono went to answer and returned presently.

"Doctor, Mrs. Tanaka says her water has broken."

"All right, I'll have a look," Dr. Hiroshige said. "Dr. Nobeji, would you look after this patient?"

Sadaharu did as he was asked. Today, Dr. Hiroshige was the one in charge, and in the circumstances as he knew them he thought it best to turn Shinjo over to Sadaharu.

Sadaharu had Nurse Iwanami bring a standing screen and then prepare the delivery table beside it. In his practice thus far, Sadaharu had not dealt with three patients giving birth at once, but he had often dealt with about two and a half.

"Now, Ms. Shinjo, next time really bear down. It's pretty busy here tonight, but it's a good scene, having all these babies born."

Shinjo nodded in the brief interval between contractions, but she had no voice, and her lips were dry.

Presently, Mrs. Tanaka was brought in, and according to Dr. Hiroshige she was already three fingers open.

Sadaharu called to her through the curtain, "Mrs. Tanaka, it's a good thing you didn't come much later."

She was quite calm, since this was her third child.

"Sorry for the trouble, but I thought I would be able to hold off until morning," Tanaka said.

"Don't expect the impossible. You can't stop delivering a baby halfway."

Sadaharu glanced at the needle moving over the graph paper recording Shinjo's rate of contractions and the state of her labor pains.

"Ah, Ms. Shinjo. You're a super student, that's for sure. Pushing with each contraction. The baby is coming on fine, just work at it."

From the other side of the curtain, Dr. Hiroshige said, "Ms. Shinjo, you don't feel much pain, do you, even when you are stretched?"

Just then a contraction came. Shinjo was holding on to the grips at either side of the table. She seemed to smile through dry lips and her bared teeth.

"It's all right, but it still hurts there," she said in gasps after the pain subsided.

"Where?"

"At the top of my right thigh."

Because the anesthetic had leaked and Dr. Hiroshige had stopped the injection part way, there was still feeling in the region.

Sadaharu said, "Now . . . five or six more times. I want you to try hard. And that will be the end of it."

Shinjo was silent.

Sadaharu could already feel the baby's hair and head. Without relinquishing all self-consciousness and modesty, a person cannot get through this final period. This was very hard on the mother, but Sadaharu thought that it was hardly a pleasure for the baby trying to be born either.

Whether created by God or not, the extremely well-made mechanism of the human body provides the lungs of the newborn infant with -70 centimeters of water pressure at birth. Sudden entry into the atmosphere creates the conditions necessary for the lungs to function. What makes this high vacuum possible is the normal birth process. (And so one might well argue that performing the once-popular Caesarean section is counter-productive. Still, a physician can hardly go along with the husband like Mr. Ushirokawa who says that only children born in the normal fashion have a right to live.) If a baby could speak at that moment, it would say that it was rushing toward life, conscious of a great pressure and an inability to breathe at the dividing point between existence and nonexistence.

Finally, the baby's black hair appeared, enough to see, amid the mother's tautly stretched skin; under the bright shadowless glow of the surgery light, the surface of Shinjo's body shone with a silvery glow. Dr. Hiroshige went to Shinjo's head, confirmed that she was bearing down easily, and then placed his hand to the uterine fundus, helping the baby slide out.

He inserted a rubber tube like a catheter into the baby's windpipe, produced suction, and the baby cried.

"Ms. Shinjo," Sadaharu said. "It's a fine girl, and looking strong as a boy."

"Thank you," Shinjo said.

"No defects, a high nose. A real beauty."

Shinjo was silent, but Sadaharu felt that she was smiling. Nurse Iwanami weighed the child.

"How much?" Sadaharu asked.

"Seven pounds, three ounces," she replied.

"Ah, that's fine," Sadaharu said, then washed and left the delivery room.

Sadaharu thought it was all right to leave, because Dr. Hiroshige was there with two nurses trained to check for hemorrhaging. He was not neglecting Mrs. Tanaka, but because it was so hectic Sadaharu decided to leave her to Dr. Hiroshige, in the absence of an emergency, intending to get a couple of hours' sleep. If necessary, Sadaharu could then relieve Dr. Hiroshige, who had been up all night.

Sadaharu went outside through the passage between the clinic and his house, scratched his head vigorously, yawned, and thought how much Shinjo's life would be changed in the future. He had expected Shinjo's child to be a boy. His was a very businesslike profession, involved with the birth and death of human beings. Thirty or forty years from now, a boy might say to him, "Thanks to you, I am alive," but a girl would not. At that future time, a girl, clinging to a life with limited possibilities, might well challenge him. Sadaharu felt that a boy would be more likely than a girl to acknowledge the comic irony of having been saved from extermination. Many men acknowledge the slender margin in those critical moments that decide life and death, but women think more seriously of their own existence than men do and cannot accept such risks.

The time was just before dawn. The sky was completely dark, yet the darkness was full of life. As he entered the door of his house, Sadaharu felt how strange it was that he had been listening to the Mozart *Requiem* while waiting for a baby to be born.

Before going upstairs to his bedroom, Sadaharu drank a straight whiskey to put himself to sleep. As he tasted the liquor, he wondered if the birth of a human being was a good thing or not. It might be just an excuse, he thought, but although from the point of view of Yoko and the priest he was a destroyer of human life, he knew also that he lent his skills to bringing human life into the world. The birth of a child was a happy thing for everyone, and giving life was a respected occupation—everyone said so. Certainly it might be true, but in his heart Sadaharu could hardly deny that living in this world required many years of endurance far greater than that involved in being born.

Soon he was asleep. He awakened at eight o'clock as though by an internal alarm clock and immediately telephoned the clinic. Everything was in order, he learned: At 4:45 A.M., Toshiko Tanaka had given birth to an eight-pound, six-ounce boy; Dr. Hiroshige, too, was taking a nap.

"The patient on the third floor, uh . . ."

Lately, he had taken to forgetting the names of people. He could only conclude that it was the effect of age.

"Mrs. Baba?"

"Yes. How are her contractions?"

"Still at two fingers."

"Then it will be all right to leave her with Dr. Hiroshige."

"Yes. I think that will be all right," the nurse replied.

Sadaharu hung up the phone and then, the day being Sunday and his housekeeper's day off, he remembered that he would have to do the servant's tasks. He filled the electric pot with water, turned on the switch, put the toaster and bread on the table. He brought the coffee cup and spoon, but then noticed there was no instant coffee or butter. From the refrigerator, he brought the butter, saw that it was enough, sat in a chair, then noticed there was no butter knife. In such matters, Sadaharu truly lacked skill. Finally, when he put the bread in the toaster, the telephone rang.

"Sadaharu, this is Yoko. Were you up?"

"Oh. Good morning. Yes, I'm up and cooking. Sunday is the housekeeper's day off."

"I called about Ms. Shinjo. I've been thinking about her."

"She had her baby, a girl. The weight is perfect, a perfect baby."

"Oh, that's fine! She'll be happy to be a mother."

"Yes, and now the work begins. But I suppose it's just as well it is a girl. With a boy, she would have to be part father, too."

"Please congratulate her for me. I'll visit her while she's at the clinic."

"Yes, please do. I'll tell her. Last night, there were two babies born here, and this morning we're expecting the third. My goodness, but there are a lot of babies born in September."

"I was born in September too," Yoko said.

"Really? Well, I didn't mean anything in particular by that. I just can't remember other people's birthdays. I can't even recall my own."

"And at our age, it's just as well to forget birthdays," Yoko remarked.

"Right. What are you doing today?"

"It's Sunday, so I'm going to mass at the church in Kurihama. After that, this evening, I've got an invitation from the cultural attache at the American Embassy, so I'm finally going to Tokyo. It's been a long while."

"Tokyo? Ah, the city is nice. A bit wild, but enjoyable after all. I haven't been to Tokyo in the longest time."

Chapter Seventeen

In the Evening Sea

Sadaharu had noticed that this year the summer heat had not lingered as long as usual, and perhaps that was why the last ten days of September brought an unusual rush of new babies. Between the Sunday when Shinjo's daughter was born and the following Saturday, there were nine births. The small nursery was full, and beyond the glass window, as though in an aquarium, a swarm of parents' faces seemed to leap over each other to catch a glimpse of their own children.

After finishing lunch one day, Sadaharu returned to the clinic to find Shinjo asking to leave that day. "It's for the convenience of the people who are coming to pick me up, about five o'clock today, if that's all right."

"Yes, anytime will be fine," Sadaharu said.

He went to look in on the babies in the nursery. There were twelve infants before him, one with jaundice but getting better, not anything to worry about, and one with elevated brain pressure, producing the "sundown" phenomenon. Just as the sun went down completely, the eyeballs, in reaction, turned downward. Previously, this symptom was said to have appeared in one in ten newborn babies, but Sadaharu thought that recently the rate had become somewhat higher. If left alone, the condition cured itself in about a month; after that the condition persisted in barely 1 percent of those affected.

Most of the children were healthy. (In the strict sense of the word, of course, there was hardly a person who was completely without defect.) When he looked at the children, Sadaharu often felt that he was looking at beans. There were differences in the size and shape, but generally they were perfect beans.

He went over to Shinjo baby and said to the nurse, "Does Ms. Shinjo's baby have a name yet?"

The usual practice, until a name was given, was just to write "Baby Tanaka," "Baby Sato," or the like.

"Yes, she decided on a name about three days ago and brought it in," Nurse Yuasa replied.

Sadaharu read the card. "Hmm, Yoko Shinjo."

"She said she knew a wonderful lady named Yoko and that she hoped her baby would turn out like her," the nurse told him.

Yoko Shinjo suddenly opened her eyes, pursed her lips, and stared at Sadaharu. She had a high nose and a regular face. Sadaharu looked next at the boy beside her. This was the tiny baby born on July 10 to Takako Ogura, wife of the rice shop owner in Miura City. The infant had now grown to almost eight pounds, and with the samurai-like name of Morimitsu Ogura had become, after the departure of Miyako, master of the nursery.

"Nurse Yuasa, lend me your flashlight, please," Sadaharu said, having searched for and not found his own pencil light. Bringing the light close to the baby's eyes, he moved it back and forth; the baby, following the light with his eyes, seemed to be dazzled.

"Thank you. There doesn't seem to be any problem," he announced more or less into thin air.

"Little Mo's eyes are fine," the nurse said.

"Little Mo?" Sadaharu asked.

"Yes. Morimitsu is a bit long for a name. People just started calling him Mo. At first we thought Mitsu would be good, but that sounded like a girl's name. Then again, someone else said that Little Mo sounds like a cow."

"How about Mogyu, like 'Fierce Bull.' Would that be acceptable?" Sadaharu said.

"Oh, somehow Little Mo fits this child just right. That's what we decided," she said.

"I was worried about his eyes."

"I don't think there's anything to worry about. When we open and close the curtains, Mo is the first to notice, and he looks toward the window and makes a face at the bright light."

"Yes, that's normal. Well, everything seems to be in order. We can send him home today."

Very likely, he could have been sent home earlier, but since the child's mother had had hepatitis he was left for a while at the clinic.

Sadaharu went to Shinjo's room. Even though it was "her room," because of the rush of babies she was sharing it with an expectant mother. This woman was still not ready to deliver, and, saying that she hoped to speed things along, she had gone walking on thc rooftop sun deck, leaving Shinjo alone in the room.

"It looks like you're all ready to leave," Sadaharu said, looking around her bed.

"Yes, and I'm so happy. This morning I got ready right away. I'm a working woman, and when there is something to do I get it done fast."

"And you picked a name for your baby," Sadaharu said.

"Yes. I'd like her to grow up like Yoko Kakei, whom I met on our picnic. Mrs. Kakei came to visit me, and I asked her permission. She said, 'Yes, please do.' Still, the name is written a little differently from hers. Using identical characters would be too much."

"I think that writing it with the '*yo*' meaning 'sun' is fine. The evening sun is beautiful here. Still, I thought you might use part of the father's name. Wasn't it Yoichi or Yotaro?" Sadaharu asked.

"No, it wasn't," Shinjo said, a stern expression on her face. "I've put him out of my mind completely."

"Oh, of course," Sadaharu conceded.

"Until that day we all went on the picnic, I was still dreaming that we could live together, and I was just waiting for his phone call. I probably told you, didn't I?"

"Ah, is that so?" Sadaharu made only a vague reply.

"Then I gradually came to think of him as not worth concerning myself about. Irresponsible. Selfish. Especially when I was in labor, I absolutely felt I'd never forgive him."

"Pretty awful, eh?" Sadaharu laughed.

"A woman giving birth alone goes through a bitter and terrible experience," Shinjo said. "He didn't care enough to spare a kind word. Whatever the reason, while he put me through an ordeal like that, he kept silent and invisible, like a blank wall. Men are just irresponsible. Well, so much for that. Only now I think I won't bother to acknowledge him as the baby's father at all. Now I feel like I produced my child alone."

"Yes, well, in fact you are really the person who gave birth to the child," Sadaharu said.

"While I was in love with him, I was miserable. And yet now that I'm starting to hate him I feel better."

"Quite so. Love is no good; it's unstable too. Compared to love, hating lasts much longer. Nowadays, I've come to the conclusion that there is no difference between loving and hating. Hating isn't so bad, you know, and there are plenty of stable human relationships based on hatred."

"You know, doctor," Shinjo said, "you're always thinking about life from an unusual angle."

"No, not really," Sadaharu said. "But it's my basic philosophy not to be serious. Actually, I'm rather proud of that. Recently, I've begun to think loving and hating are different expressions of the same concern. It's still nice to hear about love, and I've come to think that hatred is better than indifference. At any rate, it's a human thing. Being indifferent seems cold, something inorganic, metallic."

There was a knock on the door, which opened immediately.

Nurse Okubo was there, holding Shinjo's baby. The infant was crying softly.

"Ms. Shinjo, will you nurse her? She began crying, so I've brought her to you. The other room is full of mothers nursing."

"Oh, of course! Please bring her in. It hasn't been three hours, but it's all right, isn't it?"

"Of course. She hardly drank at all last time. There's no need to be that much on schedule. When she gets hungry early, just feed her early."

"Oh, I see," Shinjo said.

"And her diapers are changed too."

Slightly embarrassed, Shinjo opened her gown and gave the infant her breast. Her face became calm.

"Are you producing milk?" Sadaharu asked.

"Oh, yes, but not a lot, and when she cries right after feeding bccause there isn't enough I've learned to give her prepared baby formula."

For a few seconds, Sadaharu stared at the infant's small cheek, barely visible, then he said, "Fine. Drop by the examination room for outpatients about four o'clock, before you go," and he left the room.

He remembered how he had thought at the moment the baby was born that he had hoped it would be a boy—a cowardly psychological reaction, almost laughable. It was a girl, and Sadaharu feared the moment—more likely with a girl than a boy—when she might come to rebuke him, as an adult, with such bitterly sarcastic words as, "It seems I owe my existence today to your incompetence."

He did not feel especially moved by the plump little ears or soft cheeks of Shinjo's baby. In Sadaharu's business, it was not likely that he would be moved by such things under ordinary circumstances. But this was the result of an accident, the failed abortion of which this child was the unmistakable result. The course of these events had been without voice, sound, or weight, something fundamentally undramatic, leaving a feeling of softness and warmth. And if Sadaharu were to speak of it in an unconsidered way, without looking back at his own mistake, the birth was a kind of ironic, even comical statement. Sadaharu was profoundly aware of its force, feeling something like a defeated dog with its tail between its legs. It was as though something had been shoved in his face. It wasn't quite the feeling of being mugged with a knife on some dark road, but more like being burdened with the weight of a large warm stone, round and heavy, that he had to bear upon his back.

Sadaharu was about to return to the examination room with his invisible burden when at the entrance he saw the old woman from the Ogura rice shop (wearing white bobby socks), her son, and his wife.

"Oh, doctor, thanks to you he is going home today," said the grandmother, showing her gold teeth in a face beaming with happiness.

Sadaharu spoke to the young mother. "Is your liver better?"

"Yes, thank you. My blood test was finally all right."

"That's fine, just fine. I checked the baby just a while ago. His eyes are perfect. Have a look when you get home. He follows the light and squints just fine at the brightness. Take him home any time."

"Thanks so much for taking such care when he was born. I was worried about his being so small. Now, thanks to you, we have a son and heir."

Sadaharu left the Ogura family and went to the outpatient examination room. It was too early for afternoon consultations; none of the nurses had yet arrived.

Every corner of the room was flooded with the indirect light of the western sun. It could feel hot in summer, but it made patients feel that the world was indeed a bright place. As far as Sadaharu was concerned, one could not have too much of that attitude. Perhaps that was because Sadaharu himself was lacking in character. When too much of the world's reality was thrust upon him, he found he recoiled. If possible, he wished to be misled, even when he knew the truth. He wished to believe a thing was true even when he clearly saw otherwise, even if he suspected a different reality.

He sat at his desk, tilting his chair back, stretching his back and thinking still of the Ogura family and the baby. A premature infant, born weighing only three pounds, six ounces or so, but now at almost eight pounds strong and ready to go home. He wondered how it would get by in its life. Like most children, perhaps, he would struggle to get through school, drive his own autobike, want to buy a guitar.

In spite of having a daughter of his own, Sadaharu understood little of women's lives. Kaori didn't want dresses, but she often asked him to buy goldfish or comic books. And from time to time, when he was seated, she would lock her arms around his neck. Shinjo's daughter, too, would be like that, surely. No, Shinjo is a disciplined person, he thought, and will probably turn into a typical education-minded Japanese mother, excessively protective of her daughter, bringing her up as an academic prodigy.

Sadaharu had happened to be around at a moment when the lives of those two babies, now ready to leave the clinic for home, might have been abruptly ended. And he knew that at the time he had felt nothing extraordinary in the atmosphere. Anyone, not only a gynecologist, might casually and unintentionally cut off a human life. Or, to put it another way, a person might easily find himself acting as a life support through the chance use of power. Sadaharu tried to believe that all of this was fine just as it was. After all, human beings are not divine; inconsistency must be accepted.

His thoughts were interrupted by the sound of excited voices coming from the direction of the foyer. In this bright town with its strong sea breeze, people sometimes raised a noisy commotion about nothing at all. That did not seem to be the case just now, however.

He heard the nurses rushing about and, just as he was starting to think he would have to see what the matter was, the receptionist opened the door without knocking.

"Doctor, there is a woman in labor. She's three weeks early. Someone in the neighborhood brought her in."

"Nurse Okubo?"

"She's already upstairs. Some people are helping carry the woman."

"What's her name?"

"Yasuko Furukawa. She was expecting October 20, and she was going to come for an examination last week, but her mother-in-law had to go to the hospital for something and she went along to help her, so it seems she couldn't come in."

Sadaharu remembered the story. The mother-in-law was in the hospital and that was costing money. Since she would have to act as nurse, Furukawa had wanted to know when she could leave the clinic, how much the fee would be, and so forth. She had been very concerned about such matters.

He immediately went upstairs to the delivery room. The Ogura family was there looking through the window into the nursery at Mo getting his checkup before leaving the clinic. They greeted Sadaharu, and he returned some meaningless salutation and slipped past them into the delivery room.

"Mrs. Furukawa, you're pretty early, aren't you," he said to her while washing up and as she was being prepared by the nurses.

"I thought I still had three weeks," she said.

"Right. But giving birth isn't like regular annual festivals. Sometimes it doesn't happen on schedule. When did the contractions begin?"

"This morning. I felt a little funny, but I went to the hospital to take care of my mother-in-law, and then the pains got gradually worse, so I went home in the afternoon. Should I have waited a little longer, doctor? Because this was so sudden, my husband's sister—who I was counting on—can't get here right away, and if there is no one at the hospital then my mother-in-law's diapers won't get changed properly."

"Now, now, try to be reasonable," Sadaharu told her.

When pregnant women approach the scheduled time of delivery, they invariably hope the baby will come early, to lighten their burden. But Furukawa wanted to stretch the time out. Sadaharu was not surprised to encounter this kind of thinking, given her unfortunate situation, but still he felt like telling the story to Yoko.

"Mrs. Furukawa, it's impossible for you to hold out any longer. Your cervix is almost completely open already," he said.

Sadaharu made a cut so that the baby could descend easily.

"And don't worry about your old mother-in-law. No matter how few helpers there are at the hospital, it is a hospital, after all, and there is no way that her diapers won't be changed."

He performed the minimal examination for an emergency delivery and started an intravenous drip to secure a vein. Also, as he did for more than half of his patients, he prepared to administer nitrous oxide gas to Furukawa. A birth is not in itself an enjoyable event, nor, as those without experience may think, is it characterized by total happiness. It involves a kind of struggle, a fight to bear life. It may seem unnatural to have a needle in the arm of a healthy woman giving birth, but loss of blood in some cases is enough to kill the woman, so establishing an intravenous line for possible transfusion is a necessary precaution. Should loss of blood become severe, finding the vein becomes difficult or impossible; therefore, advance preparation is necessary.

When he looked at this woman reluctantly giving birth, Sadaharu felt compassion for her. Not that the second child was unwanted in Furukawa's case, but there was no indication either that they were particularly waiting for it. The child was a fact, and so it was born, that was the sense of it all. In that kind of situation, it was best not to get especially involved. Half of the children born had parents with that attitude. The life of a human being, whose birth process was begun so unconsciously, can even so take on great significance—that fact itself was for Sadaharu both delicious and fascinating.

Each time a contraction came, Furukawa groaned slightly for a while, but when the gas took effect she became quiet. Just as Nurse Okubo directed, when she felt the contractions come Furukawa strained, and under the mask her face reddened. Finally the child's black hair became visible, and the baby, making a normal turn, came sliding with its head turned to one side into Sadaharu's receiving hands. As always, Sadaharu had a breathing catheter ready. He turned the baby's head toward him, but at that moment he heard Nurse Hasebe, the young nurse standing beside him, catch her breath in a sudden gasp. Sadaharu felt her hand pull away, and he felt something change in the room's atmosphere, but Nurse Okubo, without a flicker of expression, moved to support Sadaharu's hands.

Automatically, Sadaharu prepared to clear the infant's airway through nose and throat, just as he was accustomed to doing, but he was perplexed as to where to insert the end of the catheter he held between his thumb and index finger.

There before him was certainly a human baby boy, but the mouth and nose area did not seem human, but rather like it belonged to some other kind of living thing. The nose looked smashed down and spread out, and in the area of the groove below the nose two thick lumps of flesh showed, with the upper lip split between them. The catheter could enter neither the nose nor the mouth; the center was a large, continuous cleft. Somehow, Sadaharu induced breathing with the catheter, and the infant cried in a weak voice.

Nurse Okubo and Sadaharu silently continued their work. After they cut the umbilical cord, the afterbirth emerged. To weigh the placenta and check its size Nurse Hasebe went to the sink with the basin, as though fleeing.

"What is the child's weight?" Sadaharu asked Nurse Okubo.

"Five pounds, eleven and a half ounces."

For Sadaharu, it was a blessing that the new mother was asleep. In addition to a severe harelip and cleft palate, the child had no eyes at all! There was no bridge at the nose, the sockets of both eyes seeming to run horizontally across the head, and around the sunken region were wrinkles like those of an elderly man.

"Move the mother first," Sadaharu said, directing the three nurses to prepare her. No one else said a word. The anesthetic was now wearing off, and if her name were called Furukawa would awaken, but since she still appeared unconscious, there was no need to show her the child.

Nurse Okubo said to Sadaharu, "This is the first one like this since I've been working here," as he examined the baby. "Is this the first for you, doctor?"

"No, just before you came there was a child born without a brain. I was more shocked then. I thought it looked like a frog."

Sadaharu continued his examination, murmuring, "It feels like the lower jaw is bent backwards. The legs don't move well, either."

The infant's hip joints did not open widely enough. Very likely it had malformed internal organs, too, but at this point only the visible deformities could be confirmed.

"It's remarkable there are five fingers on each hand. Most cases like this have an extra finger."

"Doctor, these two fingers are joined together," Nurse Okubo said, inspecting the opposite hand.

"They can be separated easily enough," Sadaharu said. "Well, he seems to be breathing well enough, so I'll tell her later. If she asks, tell her the child's weight is a little under and that it is in the incubator. Let me know when the father comes."

"Yes, doctor."

Sadaharu went downstairs to the examination room. He'd kept a patient waiting thirty minutes past her appointment.

To Nurse Ono he said, "A distressed child has been born. Severe malformation. Please have a look later."

The nurse said she would.

Suddenly, Sadaharu realized that he had counted the aborted child of Eiko Nakanishi as one of the children "born" there. He considered Mrs. Nakanishi's case an abnormal birth, and he'd thought that for the present, statistically speaking, another such child was unlikely. In such a way, he sometimes made use of other people's misfortune.

Next morning at the staff meeting, Sadaharu asked the night duty nurse how Furukawa was doing.

"She's normal in everything, no bleeding or other problems. The baby also has no distress," she said.

"Did the husband come to see the baby yesterday?"

"No. No one appeared. Unfortunately, it seems the husband is away on business, and I was told that the older child had been left in the care of a neighbor."

Nurse Okubo gave her usual disciplined response.

"And the mother asked about the baby, I suppose?" Sadaharu queried.

"Yes, she did. I told her the baby was a bit under weight and had been put in the incubator, and she was generally satisfied with that. But she wanted to see the baby. She's allowed to go to the toilet today, and I think we might expect her to take a look in the nursery."

"Yes, that's true," Sadaharu said. "The problem can't be avoided much longer. I'll talk with her now."

Among physicians in this situation, there are those who first broach the matter to the next of kin, letting the relatives tell the woman, but Sadaharu thought it best not to take that course. If the mother's physical or psychological condition was very bad, that would be another matter, but this was something that should be first heard by the mother and father.

The meeting ended, and Sadaharu immediately set out for Furukawa's room. He was intent on getting this over quickly.

Furukawa was wearing a pink negligee and was resting, her face relaxed as though she had slept well.

"Mrs. Furukawa. How do you feel?" he asked.

"Fine, thanks," she said.

"I came to see you yesterday afternoon, but you were sound asleep, so I left without speaking."

"Oh, I'm sorry. I've been a little tired, going back and forth to the hospital so much lately."

"That's all right. Nothing at all wrong with sleeping. But the baby's condition—that's not good at all."

She did not show any surprise but asked, "Is the baby that small?"

"Hmm, five pounds, eleven and a half ounces, so it's not so small, but five and a half pounds is premature. So . . . well . . . it's on the edge. Also, after being born all children have a loss in body weight. I suppose he's less than that today."

Furukawa was silent.

"However, that's not all. The baby has a rather severe harelip. And, also, the eyes are bad." She remained silent as before. "I know you are a strong woman and because you can deal with this, I think I can tell you plainly," Sadaharu said to her. "Shall I bring the child for you to see?"

Furukawa nodded. At that moment, Nurse Okubo came into the room and Sadaharu directed her to go and bring in Furukawa's baby.

In the nursery, Nurse Okubo put the baby in a padded wrap, in part so that it would not be seen by other people. Meanwhile, Sadaharu stood gazing out the window. In his heart, he was asking himself why God gave greater burdens to already wretched people. He intended to say as much to Yoko next time they met. For that was just what this was for Furukawa and her baby, and the Nakanishi couple who had been granted only one child. Wasn't it unfair that a couple that already had two or three children should have a fourth or fifth healthy child?

Hearing the sound of the nurse about to enter the room, Sadaharu turned around. Still not having seen the child's face, Furukawa smiled faintly, as though to dispel her anxiety, and asked, "Is it all right to take him out of the incubator?"

"For a short while," Sadaharu replied.

The mother was sitting up in bed, and Nurse Okubo placed the baby on her lap.

For a few moments, the mother stared at the infant's face. Sadaharu thought that perhaps out of shock, her mind could not register what was before her eyes. Furukawa did not start crying, but after a moment, in a high, tense voice, she asked Sadaharu: "If he's treated, can he be cured?"

To come closer to Furukawa's face, Sadaharu sat down in a chair next to the bed.

"I think it would be extremely risky. If we can keep him alive, the fingers can be fixed. You can have that done by a plastic surgeon."

He spoke while showing her the fist made by holding the index and middle fingers down with the thumb and the last two fingers.

"I would guess that his heart is bad, too, but we can't be sure yet. Nothing can be done about the eyes because he doesn't have eyeballs. I would like to explain that part to your husband, so would you call him as soon as you have the chance?"

Slowly, Furukawa seemed to be thinking. Finally, in a small voice, she said, "May I nurse him?"

"Yes, you may."

Sadaharu gave his place to Nurse Okubo, but Furukawa's attempt to nurse the baby soon ended.

"His mouth is bad, and it's very difficult," Nurse Okubo said. "He doesn't have the strength to suck. But don't worry. Later on, we can express your milk. We can put a tube through his nose so he can drink."

Then Sadaharu spoke. "Take him back to the nursery, now. It's best for him not to be out of the incubator too long."

Held in Nurse Okubo's arms, the baby left the room.

Then, for the first time, as though a barrier had given way, Furukawa began to sob.

Chapter Eighteen

Who Am I?

Saturday morning of the following week, Yoko telephoned to invite Sadaharu to come to her house that evening.

"Thanks, I really appreciate it. I've been wanting to visit you lately. This week has done nothing but depress me," he replied happily.

"Remember, this is Saturday," Yoko said. "Didn't you say you wouldn't go out on account of Kaori?"

"No, it's all right. Mayumi has come home from the hospital."

"Oh? When was that?"

"Last Wednesday."

"Then shouldn't you stay home with her?"

"No, she's invited three friends over and they will all have a better time if I'm not here."

"And how is Mayumi feeling?"

"It's a novelty for her to be at home, and she's keeping busy. She appreciated how nice they were to her at the hospital, and I suppose that she will go back eventually."

"Sadaharu, you should be nice to her yourself."

"Yes, of course." Sadaharu's tone clearly expressed his indifference to that responsibility.

"In fact, today is Father Munechika's birthday. I just found out about it, so I'm having a party for him, just on the spur of the moment."

"How old is he?"

"Thirty-seven, I believe."

"Ah, a great age, the prime of manhood."

"And what about you?"

"I'm already over the hill. I was a precocious child, and I suppose I'll age early."

Sadaharu told Mayumi that he was invited to the priest's birthday party and would not need dinner, and Mayumi happily sent him off. Sadaharu, too, was pleased. He really needed no special reason to be. If his wife, daughter, and the people around him were not unhappy just for one day, Sadaharu considered it an unqualified blessing.

Sadaharu decided to go on foot to Yoko's house by a shortcut through the fields, about a thirty-minute walk. When he returned home, he would be drunk, and he would have someone call a taxi; he thought it best not to take his car under the circumstances.

The mood of autumn was spreading, and the afterglow of evening light on the sea had a sharp clarity. The path through the fields of young radishes wound upward; and at a high point Sadaharu stopped for a moment in the middle of the seldom-trod path, standing with legs apart, surrendering himself to the flood of light shimmering on the sea and in the western sky. Invariably at such moments, Sadaharu thought it like a dream that he could live amid the almost poetic splendor of this all but unbelievably perfect world. Even to imagine that this was only one bright corner of what was ordinarily a long, bad dream didn't trouble him; he felt the dream was worth seeing. At such times, and only briefly, Sadaharu thought he would be willing to die at any moment, and yet, reflecting on this, he was able to contemplate his own foolish sentimentality.

He entered Yoko's house through the gate dyed crimson in the evening glow from the sea and went on through the unlocked door of the foyer. Inside, he found only the sound of the stereo playing, the lady of the house nowhere to be found.

Wondering where Yoko had gone, Sadaharu went over to the

stereo. He found himself charmed by the song and the voice of the male singer and examined the record jacket on the sofa.

"Hmm, Elvis Presley," he murmured to himself. "Not bad at all, this song." He read the title: "Who Am I?"

Then the back door slammed, and he heard the sound of Yoko's approaching footsteps.

"I came in by myself. Where did you go?"

He spoke first to let Yoko know he was here, so as not to startle his friend.

"I went to pick some fresh parsley for the potato salad," she told him.

"This is a nice song," he said.

"Oh, do you like it?"

Sadaharu grunted assent.

"It's an album of Presley's hymns. He sings this sort of thing very well. Oh! The next song is my favorite."

"What's it called?"

"'Evening Prayer.' Every day at sundown, people from grandmothers to children pray the kind of prayer this song is about."

"Then I'll listen to it in the setting sun."

Sadaharu went out to the garden, noticing that behind him Yoko turned up the volume.

"My translation is not so good," Yoko said. She held the paper sheet with the lyrics and, standing next to Sadaharu, softly spoke the words in Japanese:

> "If I have wounded any soul today,
> If I have caused one's feet to go astray,
> If I have walked in my own willful way,
> Dear Lord, forgive.
> Forgive the sins I have confessed to thee,
> Forgive the secret sins I do not see . . ."

Without moving, Sadaharu stood facing the ocean, listening as the serene melody took hold of him.

"What a fine song, Yoko. It almost brought me to tears. 'Forgive the sins I have confessed to thee,' "—he quoted. The song had ended. "You must have put this on especially for me to hear, didn't you?"

"Certainly not! I often listen to this in the evening. Besides, don't be self-centered. You're not the only one who is moved by this music."

"Sorry. I had no idea who Elvis Presley was, but when I heard that one brief song, I was really envious."

"Why is that?"

"He doesn't ever have to do anything more in his life. This short 'Evening Prayer' is enough. It may be that he was born just to sing this song."

"Well, that's the highest praise, really. Even though he made a mess of his life at the end, evidently," Yoko replied.

They could hear the priest's little car come through the driveway, and the two stopped talking. Yoko went to the foyer to receive him.

"So . . . I heard it was your birthday. Congratulations!" Sadaharu said as the priest entered.

"Thanks very much. I've made it half way."

"Oh, not yet, not yet," Sadaharu said.

"Sadaharu fell in love with Elvis's 'Evening Prayer.' Isn't that something?" Yoko said.

"I wonder, can I still buy that record?" Sadaharu asked.

"No need to do that, Sadaharu. I'll lend it to you for a while to take home." Yoko said. She spoke as though to a child and turned off the stereo.

"Sadaharu seems to have been waiting for an occasion to meet with us. He didn't know it was your birthday, Father. Or maybe he did know by telepathy."

Sadaharu laughed. "You see, I'm a bit self-centered and only want salvation for myself."

They had entered the guest room, as usual, and drank a toast of whiskey. Yoko asked if she should open some champagne she had chilled, but both Sadaharu and the priest claimed that was too good for their tastes and declined.

"Has something come up?" Father Munechika asked Sadaharu.

"Yes, the fact is, a deformed child, a kind rarely seen around here, was born at the clinic. To tell the truth, it doesn't even have a human face. It's more like a baby pig—severe harelip, no eyeballs."

"Are there many abnormal babies these days? Mrs. Nakanishi had one too. It's getting frightening," the priest said.

"Well, you shouldn't think of it in such simple terms," Sadaharu said. "I don't know the statistics, but I guess the number may be generally increasing. In the old days, there were a lot of spontaneous abortions, and deformed babies who died immediately at birth might not have always been registered by parents, so the statistics themselves are not completely reliable. Also, the frequency of this kind of abnormality is rather exaggerated. I've been in practice ten years, you know, and in that time I've had only two cases of births of deformed children. The hundreds of others were all more or less healthy infants."

"More or less."

"Well, I suppose a lot of them were not too well put together. Some were stupid, or not good looking, or had a mean disposition. . . ." Sadaharu laughed. "And I'm not including the Nakanishis since their child was not born at my clinic. Anyway, in ten years, two examples."

"Really."

"Yes. This recent child was terrible, a chromosome defect, I would say, but to know that we would have to make a careful examination. What we do know is that such a child was born and is nonetheless living, at least so far. Excuse me for bringing this up before a priest, but, to be frank, we're doing all we can with tube feeding and the incubator to keep alive a child I would kill if it were mine. It's someone else's child, you see."

The whiskey had taken hold and Sadaharu, in a somewhat complaining tone, gossiped about the home situation of the woman who had given birth to the child.

"I mean, even though she was ready to go into labor, because she had no one to attend her mother-in-law in the hospital she wanted to postpone the delivery. The usual attitude is to look forward to giving birth and lightening your load as soon as possible. She's really got problems."

"How did she react when she saw the baby?"

"Dumbfounded. She even tried to nurse the child, but its lip is split up to the nose—pathetic, really terrible. After that, she broke into tears. Just to look at that baby—I feel like telling parents with healthy children not to complain if their kids are a little slow at school, not to nag them."

Yoko said, "But it's not a question of how much the parents want it that determines if they'll have a healthy baby. Look at the Nakanishis. They tried so hard and still didn't have a normal child."

Sadaharu smiled. "Well, I have no religion, but in cases like that, there's nothing I can say, Yoko. I just lend a hand to the parents in childbearing. It seems to me that sexual intercourse is the incentive God provides for producing babies. And only God knows what kind of baby will be the result."

"That's exactly the point of another of Presley's songs, the one called 'Known Only to Him,'" the priest said.

Father Munechika quoted the title in English, and Yoko translated it for Sadaharu.

"That's it, exactly," he said.

"Here are the words," the priest said. Sadaharu closed his eyes disinterestedly, as though he couldn't be bothered to try to read it if it was in English. "This part is especially good," the priest added, looking over the lyrics.

"I know not what the future holds,
But I know who holds the future,

It's a secret known only to him.
In this world of fear and doubt
On my knees I ask the question
Why the lonely, heavy cross I must bear.
Then he tells me in my prayer . . ."

At that point, the priest ceased his rather ponderous emoting, not really suited to his age, and Sadaharu asked, "What does he say—God, that is?"

"Well, essentially, that because you are a good person, I will give you more strength than your allotted share. That's about it," Father Munechika replied.

"Hmm, allotment," Sadaharu chuckled. "Well, it's an old expression, really. *Omake shiteokimasho*: I'll give you something extra."

"That's right," the priest said.

"A nice god, indeed. Does God give the strength to endure as well?"

Since Sadaharu wished to hear the song itself, Yoko went to look for it among the records on the shelf.

Sadaharu mused as he listened, "It's as though simple country men and women had walked out of a plain log cabin on some newly plowed land and joined their voices in song as the evening sun went down, in some vacant lot beside a ditch—it all seems so filled with innocence and good will."

"Sadaharu. What did the mother of the abnormal child do?" Yoko asked.

"She left the clinic, child in arms, four days later. The birth itself was quite normal."

"And will the child live?"

"I'm not a pediatrician, so I can't be definite, but probably two months, maybe six. I wrote a letter of introduction for her to a children's specialist for the time being."

Sadaharu suddenly became aware that his words were becoming tangled strangely.

"The best thing might be to put it in an incubator, don't you think?" Yoko asked.

"Yes, that's what's called for, of course. But meanwhile, as I said, in terms of work and finances the family faces bankruptcy. It was costing them while the child was in my own incubator, so I couldn't say much about that."

"Won't health insurance apply?"

"Yes, it will. But because the child is not the principal of the insurance, the parents will have to pay the balance. And if they do that . . . let's see, that would come to . . . I'm a little weak on the calculation, but the oxygen and the rest is expensive, so for one day it will cost about six or seven thousand yen, won't it? To leave the child in my clinic for a month, they will have to lay out about two hundred thousand yen. So when they say that they really want to take the child home, I can't say a word against it, not a word. Whatever they do, surviving is the main important thing."

"Still, what a sad story!"

Sadaharu said to her, "If you treat every single person as an object of pity, you can't be in this business."

Forgetting his manners, Sadaharu rested his stockinged feet on the low table.

"Religion is such a powerful thing," he went on. "And I'm not saying that to flatter you two, but that song, it's for the best, really, that only God knows. Others don't need to understand at all."

"They understand as best they can, and for the believing Christian I think there are two value systems. At least there are for me," Yoko said in a low voice.

"What are they?"

"It's just that someone considered guilty by the usual standards of society and criminal law, even when under a death sentence or an indeterminate life sentence, may still be innocent as a Christian—granted that this is rare. And on the contrary, even though he has done nothing considered in the least wrong by society, someone may have sinned terribly as a Christian," Yoko said.

"I myself would like to commit a really big sin. If I did, I would insist on Father Munechika getting involved. He would have to know all about the bad thing I was up to, so he would be my accomplice. He would have to be. Actually, it would be interesting to see what a priest would do under circumstances like that. You see, at my age I've pretty much run out of interesting things to do, so seeing how a priest would react to such a situation would be the most interesting thing I could imagine."

"That's a very flattering invitation," Father Munechika said, "but I'm sure that you would be disappointed, Dr. Nobeji."

"Why's that?"

"Because you know that I have no power. You know that I could do nothing but pray."

Sadaharu laughed and said, "But when you pray, God would say that because you are such a good person he will give you extra power."

In the drawer of Sadaharu's desk in his outpatient examination room was a very cheerful photograph. It was something he'd brought back that evening from Yoko's house along with the Elvis Presley album.

Miyako Sato—no, Margaret Miyako Laurie—had arrived at the Lauries' house in Colorado, and the photograph was taken two days later. Miyako sat on the floor on a thick carpet, and she was laughing. She had on a cream-colored dress, full of frills, cute and fancy. But what caught Sadaharu's attention most was the line in English on the back of the photograph: "Miyako is laughing out loud!"

It was a sentence deserving of the exclamation mark.

At the morning staff meeting, Sadaharu showed the picture to all the nurses, who scrambled around, trying to get a good look. For a while, Sadaharu just watched, enjoying the unusual sight of nurses jumping about like a bunch of ping-pong balls.

The conversation at Yoko's house that evening had brought

Sadaharu a great deal of pleasure. And he had also had a satisfactory amount of alcohol. He had told some lies and also some truths. The truth was, it seems, that he had wished the priest to be present at the scene of a sin he might have committed, and he had made the request in somewhat bad taste. But the priest, though seeing through his scheme, took it as an expression of Sadaharu's confidence, a confidence that, even considering his relationship with Yoko, he could not share with her. But the priest was different. By permitting the priest to witness his imaginary sin, Sadaharu felt he had honored him.

But there was one part that Sadaharu did not reveal to either of them, and it stayed in his mind that in not doing so he put a lie to the whole matter. At present, the matter was not yet completely settled, and because of that he could not discuss the matter, since it concerned the mother of the deformed child.

The thing was that the child had little chance of living very long, but in order to prolong its life the child had to be taken to a pediatrician as soon as possible, and proper measures had to be followed. Sadaharu thought he should explain this to Furukawa's husband, and he had asked Furukawa any number of times to have her husband come to the clinic.

According to the attending nurse's account, on the evening of the day following delivery, the husband had come and looked at the child's face for a minute or two. When the nurse was about to call in Sadaharu, the husband suddenly left. When Sadaharu spoke to Furukawa, she said that he would certainly return on the next day. But on that day, he suddenly had to go away on business, or he had some special duty or the like, which was not at all to the point. Then, on the fourth day, Furukawa announced that she would take the child and return home.

"But the baby has a tube in his nose," Sadaharu said, "and without that he can't take any milk. The tube must be sterilized daily because any milk left inside will spoil. Now, I don't think you're up to that, so the fact is you have to take the child to a pediatrician immediately."

"All right, I'll leave the clinic now and take him to the pediatrician immediately," Furukawa said compliantly.

Sadaharu asked, "Where do you go for child care? Where do you take your older child?"

"We've gone to the Nobi National Hospital, and sometimes to the Kondo Clinic."

"You know Dr. Kondo?"

"Yes."

"Ah, then I'll write a note to Dr. Kondo. There's no reason why you shouldn't go home, but please take the child to Dr. Kondo right away."

"My mother-in-law is in the Tanahashi Hospital, where they also have a pediatric clinic. Is that all right, too?"

"Yes, of course." Sadaharu said. "Anywhere is all right. Give them the case history I'll prepare for you. Take this and go tomorrow without fail. If you don't change the tube, even though this one is clean, food will spoil inside. If you go to Dr. Kondo he will understand quite well, and I'll give you this letter of introduction besides."

Sadaharu wondered whether he should telephone Dr. Kondo, too, since he usually did that. But there was a strong possibility that she would not go there and go to Tanahashi instead, thinking that she could combine that with her trips to attend to the old woman. If he called and the patient did not go to Dr. Kondo, then the doctor might think that Sadaharu was something of a nuisance.

The child, born at a little over five pounds eleven ounces in body weight, remained at barely five and a half pounds. This change was not good, but when Sadaharu considered the extent of its handicap he could not really complain. Quite literally, there was nothing Sadaharu could say, so he released Furukawa from the clinic. He thought several times that he would give Dr. Kondo a call to ask about the child, but each time it seemed more likely that Furukawa had gone to the Tanahashi clinic at the same time that she went to her mother-in-law, or perhaps even to the Nobi National Hospital, and so he put off calling.

After all, when she said that she wanted to return home, he could hardly lock her in the clinic. Before she left the clinic he wished to make contact with her husband, somehow, but he could not force him to come to the clinic either. And when he went to Yoko's house, where he intended to discuss some delicate psychological aspects of the Furukawa case, Sadaharu got drunk and became maudlin, returning home without saying a thing about it. He came to the conclusion that what he had planned to say was perhaps not really important.

Sadaharu listened time and again to the Elvis Presley album he'd borrowed:

> "When I think of how he came so far from glory,
> Came to dwell among the lowly such as I,
> To suffer shame and such disgrace,
> On Mt. Calvary take my place,
> That I ask myself this question:
> 'Who am I?' "

Surely, he prayed also for that pigfaced, eyeless baby. Because our caring God loves him, but . . . With that, Sadaharu arose shakily from his chair and went for some more whiskey.

Early the following morning, the telephone rang. Sadaharu was sound asleep. He thought at first he was hearing the ringing in a dream, then finally the ringing stabbed into him, the unhappy shock of reality, and Sadaharu got up. Mayumi remained asleep, facing the other way.

"Doctor!" came the voice of Nurse Kurata, on night duty. "The woman who was here the other day, Mrs. Furukawa, and her husband are here together, and they say there is something wrong with the baby, so they've brought it here."

"I'm on my way," Sadaharu said, quickly changing his clothes and glancing at his watch as he put his arm through the sleeve of his white gown. It was just past half past four in the morning; already, the clear dawn air was flowing, bringing its own ancient mood. On the way to the other building, he took a deep breath, then ducked inside the building filled with the scents of things and people. In the outpatient room, the light shone brightly. Nurse Ono was there along with Nurse Kurata.

Husband and wife, hair all disheveled, held the child in an old baby blanket.

"Mrs. Furukawa, what's the matter?" Sadaharu asked.

"Until last night there was nothing especially the matter, but a while ago, when I got up to give him milk, somehow he didn't seem to be breathing regularly."

It had been a week since Sadaharu had seen the child's face. Now, almost at first glance, he sensed that the child was dead, but when he felt the skin it seemed to be warm enough, and so he tried to believe that the baby was alive.

With the child held in its mother's arms, Sadaharu listened through his stethoscope, but he could detect no heartbeat. He took out his pocket flashlight to perform the regular procedure in such cases by trying to detect any eye pupil reaction, but he realized that since there were no eyeballs, that was impossible, and he replaced the light.

"He doesn't seem to be breathing now," Sadaharu said.

"When we left home he was breathing occasionally, with effort."

"Yes. But now I can't hear any heartbeat. I'm going to try a heart massage."

Sadaharu pushed time after time on the child's chest. The bones of such babies were fragile, and he could not use full force, for fear of breaking the ribs.

This was only acting. No, a formality, Sadaharu thought. He himself did not believe the child would revive. What was more, all the people here might well be praying that the child would not return to life.

Of course, the heartbeat did not return.

"Mrs. Furukawa, after you left the clinic here, did you take the child to a pediatrician?"

"I had intended to do that, but I was still shaky and I was still suffering somewhat from anemia and dizziness, so I thought I'd wait just a little bit longer."

"I wanted to meet with your husband earlier," Sadaharu said, looking at Mr. Furukawa. "In any case, I wanted you to take the child to a specialist earlier."

"I'm sorry," the husband replied. "I understood that the child was unusual, but my company is not doing very well, so for my family it's not . . ."

"When did you remove the nose tube?"

"The day after I got home it came off," Mrs. Furukawa said.

Sadaharu was silent.

"I turned him face up, and when I fed him a little at a time it seemed to go into his mouth somehow. After a week, I'd be able to go to take care of my mother-in-law, and I intended to take the child along to Dr. Tanahashi and have him examined at the same time."

"And there was nothing wrong until last night?" Sadaharu asked her.

"That's right, nothing."

"Did you notice any trouble at that time?"

The husband answered. "His breathing somehow started coming at long intervals. Then we became concerned and brought him here. He seemed to be breathing even when we arrived."

"It would really have been best if you had taken him to the pediatrician, Dr. Kondo, instead of bringing him here," Sadaharu said.

"Yes, but we haven't gone there since leaving here. Both my wife and I could only think of coming here, since Dr. Kondo didn't know the child's history."

Sadaharu paused, then asked, "Yesterday or the day before, did you notice anything wrong with the child? A fever, difficulty in breathing?"

"No, nothing in particular. Since yesterday, he hardly cried at all, just slept. I noticed that his breathing was a little fast, but . . ."

"Hmm. The diaper is wet. We'll change it." Sadaharu spoke to the nurse and for a while applied his stethoscope to the baby.

All was quiet. He could not hear a heartbeat. Instead, the sound of the ocean's morning tide seemed to come through the baby's chest. The infant had gone into eternity, Sadaharu felt, and he stroked its head. There was no need to close the eyes, which had never been open.

"What was his name?" he asked.

"We hadn't yet given him a name."

"It's been a week since he was born, and we have to send in a birth report, properly speaking. So please give him a name, now. If you don't, I won't be able to write out a death certificate."

"Give him a name . . . but . . ." Mrs. Furukawa began.

"Had you thought of a name beforehand?"

"We . . . we've been so busy since he was born. We thought we would do it, but . . . Doctor, I wonder, would you do it for us?"

"Yes. Fine. we'll say 'Megumu.' Megumu Furukawa, the 'blessed' child."

It did not take the nurses long to wash the baby.

"The baby is still warm. Please hold him, and I'll do the paper work immediately," Sadaharu said. He took the death certificate form from his desk drawer.

Sadaharu had to fill in the item labeled "Day, Month, Year of the onset of illness," and he asked for details. It transpired that since yesterday the baby's breathing had become a little rough, and then it had gone into a coma. As for the immediate cause of death, Sadaharu knew that in many instances that was unknown. Megumu was not unusual in that regard. For many people, the cause of death depended upon complicated elements.

Now, however, Sadaharu had no doubt. In the entry "Immediate Cause of Death," he wrote "acute pneumonia." It would be assumed that because the mother's milk had trickled in from above, it had entered the bronchial tubes and led to pneumonia. There was even a strong possibility that the child's rough breathing was a result of that.

In the space labeled "Other Bodily Conditions," Sadaharu wrote "cleft palate, harelip, lack of eyeballs, abnormal chromosome; from the onset of the sickness to time of death: two days." Then he studied his watch, not to determine when the baby was brought to the clinic but the time when the nurses began to wash the infant. That was 4:44 A.M.

"Well, this is all I can do for you," Sadaharu said to the couple.

"Thank you very much."

The two nurses remained silent but stood by to see the couple off. Sadaharu did not move from his desk. Remembering, he took out from his desk drawer the photograph of Miyako Sato to look at again.

"Miyako is laughing out loud!"

Almost every baby born, even with some degree of damage, cries out and laughs eventually. More than that, an ordinary baby, even if left alone without anyone doing anything to it, will laugh out loud. But Megumu Furukawa had neither laughed nor properly drunk milk, and in the end he died without crying.

In ancient times, it is said, the Hebrews thought these things were the workings of fate. People who did evil would suffer sickness and die young. But when applied to infants, that idea was an obvious mistake. Sadaharu returned Miyako's photograph to the drawer, took off his white coat and hung it over the chair. Then he put on his sandals and went outside and, instead of returning to his house, set out walking toward the sea.

This was not a time to take a nap. It was rare to be up, accidentally, in the hour of such a splendid dawn, so Sadaharu thought he would take a walk; then he would return home.

He went on, and then headed in the direction of Yoko's house. He had no intention of dropping in. Yoko was an early riser and probably by this time was up, watering her potted flowers. Later, on the terrace facing the ocean, she would eat one slice of buttered toast and drink a cup of hot, black tea. That was her routine, she had said.

Now, Sadaharu was not thinking of taking part in such a pleasant and peaceful breakfast. He thought of the hill next to Yoko's house, shaped like a horse's back, and he planned to climb it while it reverberated with the waves and sea wind.

This was the place where Sadaharu's mind always became bare. No one was there, and "God" always sent a strong wind blowing.

He shambled along, thinking he understood the whole matter.

He realized that he had known what would happen when he had sent Yasuko Furukawa home with her child. As long as she insisted on going home with the baby, he had no power to restrain them; that was his excuse. Telling her she had to go to the Kondo Clinic, even writing a note for her to take to the National Hospital, or to another doctor, that was his escape clause. He knew almost for a certainty that she and her husband would not be inclined to go anywhere.

Just moments before, Sadaharu had held Megumu, had given him a name. There were no signs of strangulation, no bruises. The baby seemed undernourished, but it was probably true that milk had somehow flowed to that mouth torn like the top of a pomegranate. For each day that it lived, this child had strangled its parents' livelihood and made them wish for its death, while at the same time they tried to keep it alive. Or rather, while thinking how miserable they were in keeping the child alive, they reacted by feeding it milk in overflowing quantities. The Furukawas, both husband and wife, wanted the child both to live and yet not to live. Whether or not they had thought about it, analyzed it all, they behaved that way.

And Sadaharu was no different. He thought it was his duty to act so as to keep the child alive, and at the same time he wished he could stop its breath. And this, he thought, was a kind of love. If Megumu had been his own child, then perhaps he would have struggled more to save it. He could do that because he had both money and means. And with the background of medical science that told him Megumu might, just might, live for six months, Sadaharu would be satisfied with having kept the child alive, barely.

But the Furukawas were different. Every day the child lived was a drain on them, and they still had to spend their money keeping the old mother alive.

And Megumu, with his wrinkled face, pomegranate-torn mouth, and piglike nose: if he had any consciousness, surely he would have asked, "Who am I?" And seated beside him was a God who had even died for his sake. If he knew of such a God, then, for once, perhaps he would understand that he was in no way an abnormal human being. Then, for once, he would experience a humanity completely free of all externals and know that the only problem was one of the soul.

When it progresses that far, perhaps humanity will assent and be able to accept death. Sadaharu thought that perhaps Megumu would say these words in a clear voice, from his torn upper lip that was unable even to suck milk, and with his nonexistent eyes wide open: "That's enough. I will die."

In Sadaharu's imagination, Megumu said: "By my dying, people are saved. It is a wonderful thing. Thank you for giving me that task."

In the morning sun, the short green grass rolled in waves on Horseback Hill. From eons past and into the infinite future, the sea, sun, wind, the warmth and calm, without permission and without denial, all simply existed.

He had thought to help bring the matter of the child to a tacit conclusion, whatever others might say. Sadaharu felt it wouldn't have been honest toward God for him to have done more than he had in such a situation. Yoko, the priest, other physicians might not agree with what he had done. But Sadaharu wanted the child to die quickly. And now, by its death, the child had liberated its parents. It may be a difficult thing to say, but wasn't that child like a martyr? Wasn't it the same as giving up one's life to save the lives of others?

Sadaharu did not consider asking any forgiveness for his intent. Since it was an unforgivable thing, Sadaharu simply thought of himself as trying to be of assistance.

At the end of the world—and he had no idea if that would ever come, outside the realm of the Bible—would there not again be something like continuous rain bringing about the great flood of Noah? Then an ark vastly larger than the ancient ark would be built, and people would struggle with one another to get aboard. That was the scene Sadaharu pictured in his imagination.

Sadaharu knew without being told that aboard the ark only people who had done good things would be permitted. He would see those people pouring onto the boat, and from a distance he himself would watch the ship depart. As for himself, without the desire or conviction to believe, he did not even imagine that he wanted his life to be saved. That was his first reason, but then also he thought he lacked the qualifications to ride on that boat, or to judge himself.

Yet on that boat would ride people he loved: Yoko, the priest, and Megumu Furukawa, who had just died. And very likely, too, there would be the retarded mother Yoko had written about from Brazil, the Nakanishis, and Kumiko Shinjo. It seemed to him that he waved to Mayumi and to Kaori. He could hear Yoko's voice calling, "Sadaharu!" Ah, someone was there to call his name. How marvelous, he thought. He'd like to set their minds at ease by informing them that as long as he had a bottle of whiskey he would be all right, despite everything.

Call it a regret, but he had not told the priest all that had transpired. To have done that would indeed have been a mark of his sincerity. Perhaps he had underrated the priest after all. Even when he sent the mother and child home, and afterward when he deliberately neglected confirming that she had made contact with a pediatrician, even when he filled out the death certificate with feigned innocence—if he had really respected Father Munechika, it would have been better to have told him all that he had done.

Sadaharu walked in the green grass that reached up to his chest to stand on the cliff at the top of the hill. He could hear sounds coming from the open window of Yoko's house. Here was a world apart from everyone, a world where Sadaharu was commanded to stand alone in the buffeting wind.